# THE LAST DON

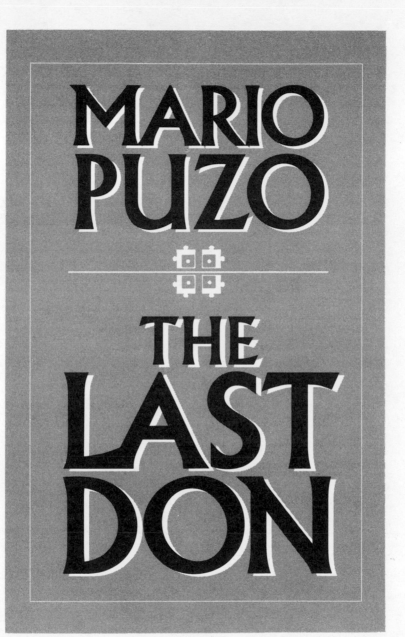

# MARIO PUZO

# THE LAST DON

HEINEMANN : LONDON

First published in Great Britain 1996
by William Heinemann
an imprint of Reed International Books Ltd
Michelin House, 81 Fulham Road, London SW3 6RB
and Auckland, Melbourne, Singapore and Toronto

A CIP catalogue record for this title
is available from the British Library

ISBN 0 434 60498 4

Printed and bound in Great Britain
by Clays Ltd, St Ives plc

*For*

*Virginia Altman*
*Domenick Cleri*

# PROLOGUE

## Quogue
## 1965

ON PALM SUNDAY, one year after the Great War against the Santadio, Don Domenico Clericuzio celebrated the christening of two infants of his own blood and made the most important decision of his life. He invited the greatest Family chiefs in America, as well as Alfred Gronevelt, the owner of the Xanadu Hotel in Vegas, and David Redfellow, who had built up a vast drug empire in the United States. All his partners to some degree.

Now the most powerful Mafia Family head in America, Don Clericuzio planned to relinquish that power, on the surface. It was time to play a different hand; obvious power was too dangerous. But the relinquishing of power was dangerous in itself. He had to do it with the most skillful benignity and with personal goodwill. And he had to do it on his own base.

The Clericuzio estate in Quogue comprised twenty acres surrounded by a ten-foot-high redbrick wall armed by barbed wire and electronic sensors. It held, besides the mansion, the homes for his three sons as well as twenty small homes for trusted Family retainers.

Before the arrival of the guests, the Don and his sons sat around the white wrought-iron table in the trellised garden at the back of the mansion. The oldest, Giorgio, was tall, with a small, fierce mustache and the lanky frame of an English gentleman, which he adorned with tailored clothes. He was twenty-seven, saturnine, with savage wit and closed face. The Don informed Giorgio that he, Giorgio, would be applying to the Wharton School of Business. There he would learn all the intricacies of stealing money while staying within the law.

Giorgio did not question his father; this was a royal edict, not an invitation to discussion. He nodded obedience.

The Don addressed his nephew, Joseph "Pippi" De Lena, next. The Don loved Pippi as much as he did his sons, for in addition to blood—Pippi being his dead sister's son—Pippi was the great general who had conquered the savage Santadio.

"You will go and live permanently in Vegas," he said. "You will look after our interest in the Xanadu Hotel. Now that our Family is retiring from operations, there will not be much work here to do. However you will remain the Family Hammer."

He saw Pippi was not happy, that he must give reasons. "Your wife, Nalene, cannot live in the atmosphere of the Family, she cannot live in the Bronx Enclave. She is too different. She cannot be accepted by them. You must build your life away from us." Which was all true, but the Don had another reason. Pippi was the great hero general of the Clericuzio Family, and if he continued to be "Mayor" of the Bronx Enclave, he would be too powerful for the sons of the Don when the Don no longer lived.

"You will be my *Bruglione* in the West," he told Pippi. "You will become rich. But there is important work to do."

He handed Pippi the deed to a house in Las Vegas. The Don then turned to his youngest son, Vincent, a man of twenty-five. He was the shortest of the children, but built like a stone door. He was spare in speech, and he had a soft heart. He had learned all the classic peasant Italian dishes at his mother's knee, and it was he who had wept so bitterly at his mother's dying young.

The Don smiled at him. "I am about to decide your destiny," he said, "and set you on your true path. You will open the finest restaurant in New York. Spare no expense. I want you to show the French what real food is all about." Pippi and the other sons laughed, even Vincent smiled. The Don smiled at him. "You will go to the best cooking school in Europe for a year."

Vincent, though pleased, growled, "What can they teach me?"

The Don gave him a stern look. "Your pastries could be better," he said. "But the main purpose is to learn the finances of running such an enterprise. Who knows, someday you may own a chain of restaurants. Giorgio will give you the money."

The Don turned finally to Petie. Petie was the second and the most cheerful of his sons. He was affable, at twenty-six no more than a boy, but the Don knew he was a throwback to the Sicilian Clericuzio.

"Petie," the Don said, "Now that Pippi is in the West, you will be Mayor of the Bronx Enclave. You will supply all the soldiers for the Family. But also, I have bought you a construction company business, a large one. You will repair the skyscrapers of New York, you will build state police barracks, you will pave the city streets. That business is assured but I expect you to make it a great company. Your soldiers can have legitimate employment and you will make a great deal of money. First you will serve an apprenticeship under the man who now owns it. But remember, your primary duty is to supply and command soldiers of the Family." He turned to Giorgio.

"Giorgio," the Don said, "You will be my successor. You and Vinnie will no longer take part in that necessary part of the Family which invites danger, except when it is absolutely necessary. We must look ahead. Your children, my children, and little Dante and Croccifixio must never grow up in this world. We are rich, we no longer have to risk our lives to earn our daily bread. Our Family will now serve only as financial advisors to all the other Families. We will serve as their political support, mediate their quarrels. But to do this we must have cards to play. We must have an army. And we must protect everyone's money, for which they will let us wet our beaks."

He paused. "Twenty, thirty years from now, we will all disappear into the lawful world and enjoy our wealth without fear. Those two infants we are baptizing today will never have to commit our sins and take our risks."

"Then why keep the Bronx Enclave?" Giorgio asked.

"We hope someday to be saints," the Don said, "But not martyrs."

An hour later Don Clericuzio stood on the balcony of his mansion and watched the festivities below.

The huge lawn, carpeted with picnic tables crowned with wing-like green umbrellas, was filled with the two hundred guests, many of them soldiers from the Bronx Enclave. Christenings were usually joyful affairs, but this one was subdued.

The victory over the Santadio had cost the Clericuzio dearly. The Don had lost his most dearly beloved son, Silvio. His daughter Rose Marie had lost her husband.

Now he watched the crowds of people mulling around the several long tables filled with crystal urns of deep red wine, bright white tureens of soups, pastas of every kind, platters laden with a variety of sliced meats and cheese, and crispy fresh breads of all sizes and shapes. He allowed himself to be soothed by the soft music of the small band playing in the background.

Directly in the center of the circle of picnic tables, the Don saw the two baby carriages with their blue blankets. How brave the two babies were, they had not flinched when struck with Holy Water. Beside them were the two mothers, Rose Marie and Nalene De Lena, Pippi's wife. He could see the babies' faces, so unmarked by life, Dante Clericuzio and Croccifixio De Lena. He was responsible for ensuring that these two children would never have to suffer to earn a living. If he succeeded, they would enter the regular society of the world. It was curious, he thought, that there was no man in the crowd paying homage to the infants.

He saw Vincent, usually dour with a face like granite, feeding some small children from the hot dog cart he had built for the feast. It resembled the New York street hot dog carts, except that it was bigger, it had a brighter umbrella, and Vincent gave out better food. He wore a clean white apron, and he made his hot dogs with sauerkraut and mustard, with red onions and hot sauce. Each small child had to give him a kiss on the cheek for a hot dog. Vincent was the most tenderhearted of his sons, despite his rough exterior.

On the boccie court, he saw Petie, playing with Pippi De Lena, Virginio Ballazzo, and Alfred Gronevelt. Petie was a practical joker, which the Don disapproved of; it always seemed a dangerous business to him. Even now Petie was disrupting the game with his tricks as one of the boccie balls flew into pieces after the first hit.

Virginio Ballazzo was the Don's underboss, an executive officer in the Clericuzio Family. He was a high-spirited man and was pretending to chase Petie, who was pretending to run. This struck the Don as ironic. He knew his son Petie was a natural-born assassin, and that the playful Ballazzo had a certain reputation in his own right.

But neither of them was a match for Pippi.

The Don could see the women in the crowd glancing at Pippi. Except for the two mothers, Rose Marie and Nalene. He was such a fine-looking man. As tall as the Don himself, a rugged strong body, a brutally handsome face. Many of the men were observing him also, some of them his soldiers from the Bronx Enclave. Observing his air of command, the litheness of his body in action, knowing his legend, *The Hammer,* the best of the "Qualified Men."

David Redfellow, young, rosy-cheeked, the most powerful drug dealer in America, was pinching the cheeks of the two infants in their carriages. Finally, Alfred Gronevelt, still clad in his jacket and tie, was obviously ill at ease at playing a strange game. Gronevelt was the same age as the Don himself, near sixty.

Today Don Clericuzio would change all their lives, he hoped for the better.

Giorgio came to the balcony to summon him to the first meeting of the day. The ten Mafia chiefs were assembling in the den of the house for the meeting. Giorgio had already briefed them as to Don Clericuzio's proposal. The christening was an excellent cover for the meeting, but they had no real social ties with the Clericuzio and wanted to be on their way as soon as possible.

The den of the Clericuzio was a windowless room with heavy furniture and a wet bar. All ten men looked somber as they sat around the large dark marble conference table. They each in turn greeted Don Clericuzio and then waited expectantly to hear what he had to say.

Don Clericuzio summoned his sons, Vincent and Petie, his executive officer, Ballazzo, and Pippi De Lena to join the meeting. When they arrived, Giorgio, cold and sardonic, made a brief introductory remark.

Don Clericuzio surveyed the faces of the men before him, the most powerful men in the illegal society that functioned to supply the solutions to the true needs of the people.

"My son Giorgio has briefed you on how everything will work," he said. "My proposal is this. I retire from all my interests with the exception of gambling. My New York activities I give to my old friend Virginio Ballazzo. He will form his own Family and be independent of the Clericuzio. In the rest of the country I yield all of my interests in the unions, transportation, alcohol, tobacco, and drugs to your Families. All my access to the law will be available. What I ask in return is that you let me handle your earnings. They will be safely held and available to you. You will not have to worry about the Government tracking down the money. For it I ask only a five percent commission."

This was a dream deal for the ten men. They were thankful that the Clericuzio were retreating when the Family could just as well have gone forward to control or destroy their empires.

Vincent walked around the table and poured each of them some wine. The men held their glasses up and toasted the Don's retirement.

After the Mafia dons made their ceremonious farewells, David Redfellow was escorted into the den by Petie. He sat in the leather armchair opposite the Don, and Vincent served him a glass of wine. Redfellow stood out from the other men not only because of his long hair but because he wore a diamond earring and a denim jacket with his clean, pressed jeans. He had Scandinavian blood. He was blond with clear blue eyes and always had a cheerful expression and a casual wit.

The Don owed a great debt of gratitude to David Redfellow. It was he who proved that lawful authorities could be bribed on drugs.

"David," Don Clericuzio said, "You are retiring from the drug business. I have something better for you."

Redfellow did not object. "Why now?" he asked the Don.

"Number one," the Don said, "the government is devoting too much time and trouble to the business. You would have to live with anxiety the rest of your life. More importantly, it has become too dangerous. My son Petie and his soldiers have served as your bodyguards. I can no longer permit that. The Colombians are too wild, too foolhardy, too violent. Let them have the drug business. You will retire to Europe. I will arrange for your protection there. You can keep yourself busy by buying a bank in Italy and you will live in Rome. We will do a lot of business there."

"Great," Redfellow said. "I don't speak Italian and I know nothing of banking."

"You will learn both," Don Clericuzio said. "And you will live a happy life in Rome. Or you can stay here if you wish, but then you will no longer have my support, Petie will no longer guard your life. Choose as you like."

"Who will take over my business?" Redfellow asked. "Do I get a buyout?"

"The Colombians will take over your business," the Don said. "That cannot be prevented, that is the tide of history. But the government will make their life misery. Now, yes or no?"

Redfellow thought it over and then laughed. "Tell me how to get started."

"Giorgio will take you to Rome and introduce you to my people there," the Don said. "And through the years he will advise you."

The Don embraced him. "Thank you for listening to my advice. We will still be partners in Europe and believe me, it will be a good life for you."


When David Redfellow left, the Don sent Giorgio to summon Alfred Gronevelt to the den. As the owner of the Xanadu Hotel in Vegas, Gronevelt had been under the protection of the now defunct Santadio Family.

"Mr. Gronevelt," the Don said. "You will continue to run the Hotel under my protection. You need have no fear for yourself or your property. You will keep your fifty-one percent of the Hotel. I will own the forty-nine percent formerly owned by the Santadio and be represented by the same legal identity. Are you agreeable?"

Gronevelt was a man of great dignity and great physical presence, despite his age. He said carefully, "If I stay, I must run the Hotel with the same authority. Otherwise I will sell you my percentage."

"Sell a gold mine?" the Don said incredulously. "No, no. Don't fear me. I'm a businessman above all. If the Santadio had been more temperate, all those terrible things would never have happened. Now they no longer exist. But you and I are reasonable men. My delegates get the Santadio points. And Joseph De Lena, Pippi, gets all the consideration due him. He will be my *Bruglione* in the West at a salary of one hundred thousand a year paid by your hotel in any manner you see fit. And if you have trouble of any kind with anyone, you go to him. And in your business, you always have trouble."

Gronevelt, a tall, spare man, seemed calm enough. "Why do you favor me? You have other and more profitable options."

Don Domenico said gravely, "Because you are a genius in what you do. Everyone in Las Vegas says so. And to prove my esteem I give you something in return."

Gronevelt smiled at this. "You've given me quite enough. My hotel. What else can be as important?"

The Don beamed at him benevolently, for though he was always a serious man, he delighted in surprising people with his power. "You can name the next appointment to the Nevada Gaming Commission," the Don said. "There is a vacancy."

Gronevelt for one of the few times in his life was surprised, and also impressed. Most of all he was elated, as he saw a future for his hotel that he had not even dreamed of. "If you can do that," Gronevelt said, "we will all be very rich in the coming years."

"It is done," the Don said. "Now you can go out and enjoy yourself."

Gronevelt said, "I'll be getting back to Vegas. I don't think it's wise to let everyone know I'm a guest here."

The Don nodded. "Petie, have someone drive Mr. Gronevelt to New York."

Now, besides the Don, only his sons, Pippi De Lena, and Virginio Ballazzo were left in the room. They looked slightly stunned. Only Giorgio had been his confidant. The others had not known the Don's plans.

Ballazzo was young for a *Bruglione,* only a few years older than Pippi. He had control over unions, garment center transportation, and some drugs. Don Domenico informed him that from now on he was to operate independently of the Clericuzio. He had only to pay a tribute of 10 percent. Otherwise, he had complete control over his operations.

Virginio Ballazzo was overcome by this largesse. He was usually an ebullient man who expressed his thanks or complaints with brio, but now he was too overcome with gratitude to do anything but embrace the Don.

"Of that ten percent, five will be reserved by me for your old age or misfortune," the Don told Ballazzo. "Now forgive me, but people change, they have faulty memories, gratitude for past generosities fades. Let me remind you to be accurate in your accountings." He paused for a moment. "After all, I am not the tax people, I cannot charge you those terrible interests and penalties."

Ballazzo understood. With Don Domenico, punishment was always swift and sure. There was not even a warning. And the punishment was always death. After all, how else could one deal with an enemy?

Don Clericuzio dismissed Ballazzo, but when the Don escorted Pippi to the door, he paused for a moment, then pulled Pippi close to him and whispered in his ear, "Remember, you and I have a secret. You must keep it a secret forever. I never gave you the order."


On the lawn outside the mansion, Rose Marie Clericuzio waited to speak to Pippi De Lena. She was a very young and very pretty widow, but black did not suit her. Mourning for her husband and brother suppressed the natural vivacity so necessary to her particular kind of looks. Her large brown eyes were too dark, her olive skin too sallow. Only her newly baptized blue-ribboned son, Dante, resting in her arms, gave her a splash of color. All through this day she had maintained a curious distance from her father, Don Clericuzio, and her three brothers, Giorgio, Vincent, and Petie. But now she was waiting to confront Pippi De Lena.

They were cousins, Pippi ten years older, and when she was a teenager, she had been madly in love with him. But Pippi was always paternal, always off-putting. Though a man famous for his weakness of the flesh, he had been too prudent to indulge that weakness with the daughter of his Don.

"Hello Pippi," she said. "Congratulations."

Pippi smiled with a charm that made his brutal looks attractive. He bent down to kiss the infant's forehead, noticing with surprise that the hair, which still held the faint smell of incense from the church, was thick for a child so young.

"Dante Clericuzio, a beautiful name," he said.

It was not so innocent a compliment. Rose Marie had taken back her maiden name for herself and her fatherless child. The Don had convinced her to do this with an impeccable logic, but still she felt a certain guilt.

Out of this guilt, Rose Marie said, "How did you convince your Protestant wife to have a Catholic ceremony and such a religious name?"

Pippi smiled at her. "My wife loves me and wants to please me."

And it was true, Rose Marie thought. Pippi's wife loved him because she did not know him. Not as she herself had known him and once loved him. "You named your son Croccifixio," Rose Marie said. "You could have pleased her at least with an American name."

"I named him after your grandfather, to please your father," Pippi said.

"As we all must," Rose Marie said. But her bitterness was masked by her smile, her bones structured in such a way that a smile appeared naturally on her face and gave her an air of sweetness that took the sting out of anything she said. She paused now, faltering. "Thank you for saving my life."

Pippi stared at her blankly for a moment, surprised, slightly apprehensive. Then he said softly, "You were never in any danger," and he put his arm around her shoulder. "Believe me," he said. "Don't think about these things. Forget everything. We have happy lives ahead of us. Just forget the past."

Rose Marie dipped her head to kiss her infant but really to hide her face from Pippi. "I understand everything," she said, knowing that he would repeat the conversation to her father and her brothers. "I have made peace with it." She wanted her family to know that she loved them still and that she was content her infant had been received into the Family, sanctified now by Holy Water, and saved from everlasting Hell.

At that moment Virginio Ballazzo gathered Rose Marie and Pippi up and swept them to the center of the lawn. Don Domenico Clericuzio emerged from the mansion, followed by his three sons.

Men in formal dress, women in gowns, infants in satin, the Clericuzio Family formed a half circle for the photographer. The crowd of guests clapped and shouted congratulations, and the moment was frozen: the moment of peace, of victory, and of love.

Later the picture was enlarged and framed and hung in the Don's study room, next to the last portrait of his son Silvio, killed in the war against the Santadio.

The Don watched the rest of the party festivities from the balcony of his bedroom.

Rose Marie wheeled her baby carriage past the bowlers, and Pippi's wife, Nalene, slim, tall, and elegant, came along the lawn carrying her infant, Croccifixio, in her arms. She put the child in the same carriage with Dante, and the two women gazed down lovingly.

The Don felt a surge of joy that these two infants would grow up sheltered and safe and would never know the price that had been paid for their happy destiny.

Then the Don saw Petie slip a baby bottle of milk into the carriage and everyone laughed as the two babies fought for it. Rose Marie raised her son Dante from the carriage, and the Don remembered her as she was just a few short years before. The Don sighed. There is nothing so beautiful as a woman in love, nor so heartbreaking as when she is made a widow, he thought with regret.

Rose Marie was the child he had most loved, she had been so radiant, so full of cheer. But Rose Marie had changed. The loss of her brother and her husband was too great. Yet, in the Don's experience, true lovers would always love again and widows grew tired of black weeds. And now she had an infant to cherish.

The Don looked back on his life and marveled it had come to such glorious fruition. Certainly he had made monstrous decisions to achieve power and wealth, but he felt little regret. And it all had been necessary and proved correct. Let other men groan over their sins,

Don Clericuzio accepted them and placed his faith in the God he knew would forgive him.

Now Pippi was playing boccie with three soldiers from the Bronx Enclave, men older than him, who had solid business shops in the Enclave, but who were in awe of Pippi. Pippi with his usual high spirits and skill was still the center of attention. He was a legend, he had played boccie against the Santadio.

Pippi was exuberant, shouting with joy when his ball jostled the opposing ball away from the target bowl. What a man Pippi was, the Don thought. A faithful soldier, a warm companion. Strong and quick, cunning and withholding.

His dear friend Virginio Ballazzo had appeared on the boccie court, the only man who could rival Pippi's skill. Ballazzo gave a great flourish as he let his ball go, and there was a loud cheer as he made the successful hit. He raised his hand to the balcony in triumph, and the Don clapped. He felt a sense of pride that such men flowered and prospered under his rule, as had all the people who had gathered together on this Palm Sunday in Quogue. And that his foresight would protect them in the difficult years to come.

What the Don could not foresee were the seeds of evil in as yet unformed human minds.

# BOOK I

# Hollywood
# Las Vegas
# 1990

# CHAPTER 1

BOZ SKANNET'S RED CAP of hair was sprayed by the lemon-colored sunlight of California spring. His taut, muscular body throbbed to enter a great battle. His whole being was elated that his deed would be seen by more than a billion people all over the world.

In the elastic waistband of Skannet's tennis slacks was a small pistol, concealed by the zippered jacket pulled down to his crotch. That white jacket blazed with vertical red lightning bolts. A blue-dotted scarlet bandana bound his hair.

In his right hand he held a huge, silvery Evian bottle. Boz Skannet presented himself perfectly to the showbiz world he was about to enter.

That world was a huge crowd in front of the Dorothy Chandler Pavilion in Los Angeles, a crowd awaiting the arrival of movie stars to the Academy Awards ceremony. Specially erected grandstands held the spectators, the street itself was filled with TV cameras and reporters who would send iconic images all over the world. Tonight people would see their great movie stars in the flesh, shed of their manufactured mythic skins, subject to real-life losing and winning.

Uniformed security guards with shiny brown batons tucked neatly in holsters formed a perimeter to keep the spectators in check.

Boz Skannet didn't worry about them. He was bigger, faster, and tougher than those men, and he had the element of surprise. He was wary of the TV reporters and cameramen who fearlessly staked out territory to intercept the celebrities. But they would be more eager to record than prevent.

A white limousine pulled up to the entrance of the Pavilion, and Skannet saw Athena Aquitane, "the most beautiful woman in the world," according to various magazines. As she emerged, the crowd pressed against the barriers shouting her name. Cameras surrounded her and charged her beauty to the far corners of the earth. She waved.

Skannet vaulted over the grandstand fence. He zigzagged through the traffic barriers, saw the brown shirts of the security guards start to converge, the pattern familiar. They didn't have the right angle. He slipped past them as easily as he had the tacklers on the football field years before. And he arrived at exactly the right second. There was Athena talking into the microphone, head tilted to show her best side to the cameras. Three men were standing beside her. Skannet made sure that the camera had him, and then he threw the liquid from the bottle into Athena Aquitane's face.

He shouted, "Here's some acid, you bitch." Then he looked directly into the camera, his face composed, serious, and dignified. "She deserved it," he said. He was covered by a wave of brown-shirted men with their batons at the ready. He knelt on the ground.

At the last moment Athena Aquitane had seen his face. She heard his shout and turned her head so that the liquid struck her cheek and ear.

A billion TV people saw it all. The lovely face of Athena, the silvery liquid on her cheek, the shock and the horror, the recognition when she saw her attacker; a look of true fear that for a second destroyed all her imperious beauty.

The one billion people around the world watched as the police dragged Skannet off. He looked like a movie star himself as he raised his shackled hands in a victory salute, only to collapse as an enraged police officer, finding the gun in his waistband, gave him a short, terrible blow to the kidney.

Athena Aquitane, still reeling from shock, automatically brushed the liquid from her cheek. She felt no burning. The liquid drops on her hand began to dissolve. People were crashing all around her, to protect her, to carry her away.

She pulled loose and said to them calmly, "It's only water." She licked the drops off her hand to be sure. Then she tried to smile. "Typical of my husband," she said.

Athena, showing the great courage that helped make her a legend, walked quickly into the Pavilion of the Academy Awards. When she won the Oscar for best actress, the audience rose and clapped for what seemed like forever.

In the chilled penthouse suite of the Xanadu Casino Hotel of Las Vegas, the eighty-five-year-old owner lay dying. But on this spring day, he thought he could hear, from sixteen floors below, an ivory ball clacking through red and black slots of roulette wheels, the distant surf of crapshooters hoarsely imploring tumbling dice, the whirring of thousands of slot machines devouring silver coins.

Alfred Gronevelt was as happy as any man could be while dying. He had spent nearly ninety years as a hustler, dilettante pimp, gambler, accessory to murder, political fixer, and finally as the strict but kindly lord of the Xanadu Casino Hotel. For fear of betrayal, he had never fully loved any human being, but he had been kind to many. He felt no regrets. Now, he looked forward to the tiny little treats left in his life. Like his afternoon journey through the Casino.

Croccifixio "Cross" De Lena, his right-hand man for the last five years, came into the bedroom and said, "Ready Alfred?" And Gronevelt smiled at him and nodded.

Cross picked him up and put him in the wheelchair, the nurse tucked the old man in blankets, the male attendant took his post to wheel. The nurse handed Cross a pillbox and opened the door of the penthouse. She would remain behind. Gronevelt could not abide her on these afternoon jaunts.

The wheelchair rolled easily over the false green turf of the penthouse garden and entered the special express elevator that descended the sixteen floors to the Casino.

Gronevelt sat straight in his chair, looking right and left. This was his pleasure, to see men and women who battled against him with the odds forever on his side. The wheelchair made a leisurely tour through the blackjack and roulette area, the baccarat pit, the jungle of crap tables. The gamblers barely noticed the old man in the wheelchair, his alert eyes, the bemused smile on his skeletal face.

Wheelchair gamblers were common in Vegas. They thought fate owed them some debt of luck for their misfortune.

Finally the chair rolled into the coffee shop/dining room. The attendant deposited him at their reserved booth and then retired to another table to await their signal to leave.

Gronevelt could see through the glass wall to the huge swimming pool, the water burning a hot blue in the Nevada sun, young women with small children studding its surface like colored toys. He felt a tiny rush of pleasure that all this was his creation.

"Alfred, eat a little something," Cross De Lena said.

Gronevelt smiled at him. He loved the way Cross looked, the man was so handsome in a way that appealed to both men and women, and he was one of the few people that Gronevelt had almost trusted during his lifetime.

"I love this business," Gronevelt said. "Cross, you'll inherit my points in the Hotel and I know you'll have to deal with our partners in New York. But never leave Xanadu."

Cross patted the old man's hand, all gristle beneath the skin. "I won't," he said.

Gronevelt felt the glass wall baking the sunlight into his blood. "Cross," he said, "I've taught you everything. We've done some hard things, really hard to do. Never look back. You know percentages work in different ways. Do as many good deeds as you can. That pays off too. I'm not talking about falling in love or indulging in hatred. Those are very bad percentage moves."

They sipped coffee together. Gronevelt ate only a flaky strudel pastry. Cross had orange juice with his coffee.

"One thing," Gronevelt said, "Don't ever give a Villa to anyone who doesn't make a million drop. Never forget that. The Villas are legendary. They are very important."

Cross patted Gronevelt's hand, let his hand rest on the old man's. His affection was genuine. In some ways he loved Gronevelt more than his father.

"Don't worry," Cross said. "The Villas are sacred. Anything else?"

Gronevelt's eyes were opaque, cataracts dimming their old fire. "Be careful," he said, "Always be very careful."

"I will," Cross said. And then, to distract the old man from his coming death, he said, "When are you going to tell me about the great Santadio War? You worked with them then. Nobody ever talks about it."

Gronevelt gave an old man's sigh, barely a whisper, almost emotionless. "I know time's getting short," he said. "But I can't talk to you yet. Ask your father."

"I've asked Pippi," Cross said, "But he won't talk."

"What's past is past," Gronevelt said. "Never go back. Not for excuses. Not for justification, not for happiness. You are what you are, the world is what it is."

Back in the penthouse suite, the nurse gave Gronevelt his afternoon bath and took his vital signs. She frowned and Gronevelt said, "It's only the percentages."

That night he slept fitfully, and as dawn broke he told the nurse to help him to the balcony. She settled him in the huge chair and wrapped him in blankets. Then she sat beside him and took his hand to check his pulse. When she tried to take her hand back, Gronevelt continued to hold it. She permitted it and they both watched the sun rise above the desert.

The sun was a red ball that turned the air from blue-black to dark orange. Gronevelt could see the tennis courts, the golf course, the swimming pool, the seven Villas gleaming like Versailles and all flying the Xanadu Hotel flag: forest green field with white doves. And beyond, the desert of endless sand.

I created all this, Gronevelt thought. I built pleasure domes in a wasteland. And I made myself a happy life. Out of nothing. I tried to be as good a man as possible in this world. Should I be judged? His mind wandered back to his childhood, he and his chums, fourteen-year-old philosophers, discussing God and moral values as boys did then.

"If you could have a million dollars by pushing a button and killing a million Chinamen," his chum said triumphantly, as if posing some great, impossible moral riddle, "would you do it?" And after a long discussion they all agreed they would not. Except Gronevelt.

And now he thought, he had been right. Not because of his successful life but because that great riddle could not even be posed anymore. It was no longer a dilemma. You could pose it only one way.

"Would you push the button to kill ten million Chinamen"—why Chinamen?—"for a thousand dollars?" That was now the question.

The world was turning crimson with light, and Gronevelt squeezed his nurse's hand to keep his balance. He could look directly into the sun, his cataracts a shield. He drowsily thought of certain women he had known and loved and certain actions he had taken. And of men he had to defeat pitilessly, and the mercies he had shown. He thought of Cross as a son and pitied him and all of the Santadio and the Clericuzio. And he was happy he was leaving it all behind. After all, was it better to live a happy life or a moral life? And did you have to be a Chinaman to decide?

That last confusion destroyed his mind utterly. The nurse, holding his hand, felt it grow cold, the muscles tense. She leaned over and checked his vital signs. There was no doubt he was no more.

Cross De Lena, heir and successor, arranged the state funeral of Gronevelt. All the luminaries of Las Vegas, all the top gamblers, all of Gronevelt's women friends, all the staff of the Hotel, had to be invited and notified. For Alfred Gronevelt had been the acknowledged genius of gambling in Las Vegas.

He had spurred and contributed funds to build the churches of all denominations, for as he often said, "People who believe in religion and gamble deserve some reward for their faith." He had forbidden the building of slums, he had built first-rate hospitals and top-notch schools. Always, he claimed, as a matter of self-interest. He despised Atlantic City, where under the guidance of the state they pocketed all the money and did nothing for the social infrastructure.

Gronevelt had led the way in convincing the public that gambling was not a sordid vice but a middle-class source of entertainment, as normal as golf or baseball. He had made gambling a respectable industry in America. All of Las Vegas wanted to honor him.

Cross put aside his own personal emotions. He felt a deep sense of loss; there had been a genuine bond of affection between them throughout his whole life. And now Cross owned fifty-one percent of the Hotel Xanadu. Worth at least $500 million.

He knew his life must change. Being so much more powerful and rich, there would have to be more danger. His relationship with Don Clericuzio and his Family would become more delicate, in that he was now their partner in an enormous enterprise.

The first call Cross made was to Quogue, where he spoke to Giorgio, who gave him certain instructions. Giorgio told him that none of the Family would attend the funeral except Pippi. Also, Dante would be on the next flight out to complete the mission already discussed, but he was not to attend the funeral. The fact that Cross now owned half the Hotel was not mentioned.

There was a message from his sister, Claudia, but when he called, he got her answering service. There was another message from Ernest Vail. He liked Vail and was carrying fifty grand of his markers, but Vail would have to wait until after the funeral.

There was also a message from his father, Pippi, who was a life-long friend of Gronevelt. And whose advice he needed on how to conduct his future life. How would his father react to his new status, his new wealth? That would be as ticklish a problem as dealing with the Clericuzio, who would have to adjust to the fact that their *Bruglione* in the West was so powerful and wealthy in his own right.

That the Don himself would be fair, Cross had no doubt; that his own father would support him was almost a given. But the Don's children, Giorgio, Vincent, and Petie, how would they react, and the grandson, Dante? He and Dante had been enemies since they were baptized together in the Don's private chapel. It was a running joke in the Family.

And now Dante would be arriving in Vegas to do the "job" on Big Tim the Rustler. That bothered Cross because he had a perverse fondness for Big Tim. But his fate had been decided by the Don himself, and Cross worried about how Dante would do the job.

The funeral for Alfred Gronevelt was the grandest ever seen in Las Vegas, a tribute to genius. His body lay in state in the Protestant church his money had built, which combined the grandness of

European cathedrals with brown slanting walls from Native American culture. And with famed Vegas practicality, a huge parking lot, decorated with Native American motifs rather than European religious.

The choir that sang the praises of the Lord and recommended Gronevelt to Heaven was from the university where he had endowed three chairs in the humanities.

Hundreds of mourners who had graduated from college because of scholarships Gronevelt had funded looked truly grieved. Some of the crowd were high rollers who had lost fortunes to the Hotel and seemed mildly cheered that at last they had triumphed over Gronevelt. Women, on their own, some middle-aged, wept silently. There were representatives from the Jewish synagogues and Catholic churches he had helped to build.

It would have been against everything Gronevelt believed in to shut down his casino, but there were those managers and croupiers who were not on the day shift. Even some recipients of the Villas made their appearance and were accorded special respect by Cross and Pippi.

The governor of the state of Nevada, Walter Wavven, attended the funeral, escorted by the mayor. The Strip itself was cordoned off so that the long procession of silver hearses, black limos, and mourners on foot could follow the body to the cemetery and Alfred Gronevelt could pass through, for the last time, the world he had created.

That night the citizen visitors of Vegas gave Gronevelt the final tribute he would have most loved. They gambled with a frenzy that set a new record for the "Drop," except of course for New Year's Eve. They buried their money with his body to show their respect.

At the end of that day, Cross De Lena prepared to begin his new life.


That night, sitting alone in her beach house in the Malibu Colony, Athena Aquitane tried to decide what to do. The breeze from the ocean coming through the open doors made her shiver as she sat on the couch thinking.

It is hard to imagine a world-famous movie star as she was when she was a child. Hard to imagine her going through the process of becoming a woman. A movie star's charisma is so powerful that it seems as if their adult images as heroes, as beauties, had sprung full grown out of the head of Zeus. They never had a history of bed-wetting, never had acne, never had an ugly face to grow out of, never had the shrinking shyness and nerdiness of adolescence, never masturbated, never begged for love, never were at the mercy of fate. It was very hard, now, for Athena even to remember such a person.

Athena thought that she had been born as one of the luckiest people on earth. Everything came to her naturally. She had a wonderful father and mother, who recognized her gifts and nurtured them. They adored her physical beauty but did everything in their power to educate her mind. Her father tutored her in sports, her mother in literature and the arts. She could never remember a time in her childhood that she had been unhappy. Until she was seventeen years old.

She fell in love with Boz Skannet, who was four years older, a regional football star at his college. His family owned the biggest bank in Houston. Boz was almost as handsome as Athena was beautiful, plus he was funny, he was charming, he adored her. Their two perfect bodies came together like magnets, nerve endings high voltage, flesh all silk and milk. They entered a special heaven and to ensure that this would last forever, they married.

Within a few short months Athena became pregnant, yet with her usual bodily perfection, she gained very little weight; she never felt sick and enjoyed the idea of having a baby. So she continued going to college, studying drama, and playing golf and tennis. Boz could overpower her in tennis, but she beat him easily in golf.

Boz went to work in his father's bank. Once she had the baby, a little girl that she'd named Bethany, Athena continued going to school, since Boz had enough money to hire a nanny and a maid. Marriage made Athena even more hungry for knowledge. She read voraciously, especially plays. She was delighted by Pirandello, dismayed by Strindberg; she wept over Tennessee Williams. She grew more vibrant, her intelligence framed her physical beauty by giving it dignity that beauty sometimes does not have. It was not surprising that many men, young and old, fell in love with her. Boz Skannet's friends envied him having such a wife. Athena prided herself in her perfection, until in later years she found that this very perfection irritated many people, including friends and lovers.

Boz joked that it was like a Rolls that he had to park in the street every night. He was intelligent enough to know that his wife was destined for greater things, to know that she was extraordinary. And he could see very clearly that he was fated to lose her, as he had lost his own dreams. There had been no war to prove his courage, though he knew himself to be fearless. He knew he had charm and good looks but no particular talent. He was not interested in amassing a huge fortune.

He was jealous of Athena's gifts, her certainty of her place in her world.

So Boz Skannet went forward to meet his fate. He drank to excess, he seduced his colleague's wives, and at his father's bank, he initiated shady transactions. He became proud of his cunning, as any man does of a newly acquired skill, and used it to hide his growing hatred of his wife. For was it not heroic to hate one so beautiful and perfect as Athena?

Boz's health was extraordinary despite debauch. He clung to it. He worked out in the gym, took boxing lessons. He loved the physicality of the ring, where he could smash his fist into a human face; the cunning of switching from jab to hook; the stoicism of receiving punishment. He loved hunting, the killing of game. He loved the seduction of naïve women, the schematism of romance.

Then with his newfound cunning he thought of a way out. He and Athena would have more children. Four, five, six. That would bring them together again. That would stop her from leaping up and away from him. But by that time Athena could see this for what it was and said no. She said more. "If you want children, have them with the other women you're screwing."

It was the first time that she had spoken coarsely to him. He was not surprised that she knew of his unfaithfulness, he had not attempted to hide it. In fact, that was his cunning. Then it would be he who had driven her away, not she who had left.

Athena observed what was happening to Boz, but she was too young and too intent on her own life to give it the necessary attention. It was only when Boz turned cruel that Athena, at twenty years of age, found the steel in her character, an impatience with stupidity.

Boz started playing those clever games of men who hate women. And it seemed to Athena that he was actually going insane.

He always picked up their dry cleaning on his way home from work, because as he often said, "Honey, your time is more valuable than mine. You have all your special classes in music and drama besides your degree work." He thought she would not detect his spiteful reproach because of the offhand tone of his voice.

One day Boz came home carrying an armload of her dresses while she was taking a bath. He looked down at her, all gold hair and white skin, rounded breasts and buttocks decorated with foamy soap. His voice thick, he said, "How would you like it if I threw this shit right into the tub with you?" But instead, he hung the clothes in the closet, helped her out of the water, and rubbed her dry with rosy pink towels. Then he made love to her. A few weeks later the scene was repeated. But this time he threw the clothes in the water.

One night he threatened to break all the dishes at dinner but did not. A week later, he smashed everything in the kitchen. He always apologized after these instances. Always tried to make love afterward. But now Athena refused him and they slept in separate bedrooms.

Another night at dinner Boz held up his fist and said, "Your face is too perfect. Maybe if I broke your nose, it would have more character, like Marlon Brando."

She ran into the kitchen, and he followed her. She was terribly frightened and picked up a knife. Boz laughed and said, "That's the one thing you can't do." And he was right. He easily took the knife away from her. "I was only kidding," he said. "You're only fault is you have no sense of humor."

Athena, at twenty, could have turned to her parents for help, but she did not, nor did she confide in friends. Instead she carefully thought things out, she trusted her intelligence. She saw that she would never finish college, the situation was too dangerous. She knew the authorities could not protect her. She considered briefly a campaign to make Boz truly love her again so that he would be the old Boz, but now she had such a physical aversion to him that she couldn't stand even the thought of him touching her, and she knew that she would never be able to give a convincing performance of love, though that option appealed to her dramatic sense.

What Boz did that finally forced her hand and made her certain she had to leave didn't have to do with her, it concerned Bethany.

He often tossed their one-year-old daughter into the air playfully and then pretended he was not going to catch her, only doing so with a last-minute lunge. But once he let the infant bounce, accidentally it seemed, on the sofa. And then finally one day he quite deliberately let the little girl fall to the floor. Athena gasped with horror and rushed to pick the baby up, to hold her, to comfort her. She stayed awake all night sitting beside the crib of the infant to be certain she was all right. Bethany had a fearful lump on her head. Boz tearfully apologized and promised he would no longer tease in such a fashion. But Athena had come to a decision.

The next day she cleared out her checking account and her savings account. She made intricate travel arrangements so that her movements could not be followed. Two days later, when Boz came home from work, she and the baby had disappeared.

Six months later Athena surfaced in Los Angeles, without a baby, and started her career. She easily got a mid-level agent and worked in small theater groups. She starred in a play at the Mark Taper Forum that led to small parts in small movies, and then was cast in a supporting role in an A movie. In her next picture she became a Bankable Star, and Boz Skannet reentered her life.

She bought him off for the next three years, but she wasn't surprised by what he did at the Academy. An old trick. This time just a little joke . . . but the next time, that bottle would be full of acid.


"There's a big flap at the Studio," Molly Flanders told Claudia De Lena that morning. "A problem with Athena Aquitane. Because of the attack at the Academy Awards, they're worried she won't go back to work on her picture. And Bantz wants you at the Studio. They want you to talk to Athena."

Claudia had come to Molly's office with Ernest Vail. "I'll call her as soon as we finish here," Claudia said. "She can't be serious."

Molly Flanders was an entertainment lawyer, and in a town of fearsome people she was the most feared litigator in the motion picture business. She absolutely loved fighting in the courtroom, and she nearly always won because she was a great actress and had a superb grasp of the law.

Before getting into entertainment law, she had been the premier defense attorney in the state of California. She had saved twenty murderers from the gas chamber. The worst any of these clients had to suffer was a few years for different degrees of manslaughter. But then her nerves had given way and she had switched to entertainment law. She often said it was less bloody and it had greater and more witty villains.

Now she represented A-picture directors, Bankable Stars, top-notch screenwriters. And on the morning after the Academy Awards, one of her favorite clients, Claudia De Lena, was in her office. With her was her screenwriting partner of the moment, a once famous novelist, Ernest Vail.

Claudia De Lena was an old friend, and though one of the least important of Flanders's clients, the most intimate. So when Claudia asked her to take on Vail, she agreed. Now she regretted it. Vail had come with a problem that even she couldn't solve. Also, he was a man she could feel no affection for, though she usually learned to like even her murder clients. Which made her feel a little guilty about giving him bad news.

"Ernest," she said, "I went over all the contracts, all the legal papers. And there is no point in your continuing to sue LoddStone Studios. The only way you can get the rights back is to croak before your copyright expires. Which means sometime in the next five years."

A decade before, Ernest Vail had been the most famous novelist in America, praised by critics, read by a vast public. One novel had a franchise character LoddStone had exploited. They bought the rights, made the picture, and achieved an enormous success. Two sequels also made a fortune in profit. The Studio had on its drawing board four more sequels. Unfortunately for Vail his first contract had given all the rights to the characters and title to the Studio, on all planets in the universe, in all forms of entertainment, discovered and undiscovered. The standard contract for novelists who had not yet amassed clout in movies.

Ernest Vail was a man who always had a grim, sour expression on his face. For which he had good reason. The critics still acclaimed his books, but the public no longer read them. Also, despite his talent, he had made a mess of his life. During the last twenty years his wife had left, taking their three children with her. On the one book that had become a successful movie, he had made a one-time score, but the Studio would make hundreds of millions over the years.

"Explain that to me," Vail said.

"The contracts are foolproof," Molly said. "The Studio owns your characters. There's only one loophole. Copyright law states that when you die all rights to your works revert to your heirs."

For the first time Vail smiled. "Redemption," he said.

Claudia asked, "What kind of money are we talking about?"

"On a fair deal," Molly said, "five percent of gross. Figure they get five more pictures out of it and they are not disasters, total rentals, a billion worldwide, so we're talking around thirty or forty million." She paused for a moment and smiled sardonically. "If you were dead, I could get your heirs a much better deal. We'd really have a gun to their heads."

Vail said, "Call the people at LoddStone. I want a meeting. I'll convince them that if they don't cut me in, I'll kill myself."

"They won't believe you," Molly said.

"Then I'll do it," Vail said.

"Talk sense," Claudia said amiably. "Ernest, you're only fifty-six years old. That's too young to die for money. For principle, for the good of your country, for love, sure. But not for money."

"I have to provide for my wife and kids," Vail said.

"Your ex-wife," Molly said. "And for Christ's sake, you've been married twice since."

"I'm talking about my real wife," Vail said. "The one who had my kids."

Molly understood why everybody in Hollywood disliked him. She said, "The Studio won't give you what you want. They know you won't kill yourself, and they won't be bluffed by a writer. If you were a Bankable Star, maybe. An A director, maybe. But never a writer. You're just shit in this business. Sorry, Claudia."

Claudia said, "Ernest knows that and I know that. If everybody in this town wasn't scared to death of a blank piece of paper, they'd get rid of us entirely. But can't you do something?"

Molly sighed and put in a call to Eli Marrion. She had enough clout to get through to Bobby Bantz, the president of LoddStone.


Claudia and Vail had a drink together afterward in the Polo Lounge. Vail said reflectively, "Big woman, Molly. Big women are easier to seduce. And they're much nicer in bed than small women. Ever notice?"

Not for the first time Claudia wondered why she was so fond of Vail. Not many people were. But she had loved Vail's novels, still did. "You're full of shit," she said.

Vail said, "I meant big women are sweeter. They bring you breakfast in bed, they do little things for you. Feminine things."

Claudia shrugged.

Vail said, "Big women are good-hearted. One brought me home from a party one night and really didn't know what to do with me. She looked around the bedroom exactly like my mother used to look around her kitchen when there was nothing in the house to eat and she was figuring out how to throw a meal together. She was wondering, how the hell we were going to have a good time with the materials at hand."

They sipped their drinks. As always, Claudia warmed to him when he was so disarming. "You know how Molly and I became friends?" Claudia said. "She was defending some guy who had murdered his girlfriend and she needed some good dialogue for him to use in the courtroom. I wrote the scene just as if it were a movie, and her client got manslaughter. I think I wrote the dialogue and the plot-line for three other cases before we stopped."

"I hate Hollywood," Vail said.

"You just hate Hollywood because LoddStone Studios screwed you on your book," Claudia said.

"Not just that," Vail said. "I'm like one of those old civilizations like the Aztecs, the Chinese empires, the Native American Indians, who were destroyed by a people with more sophisticated technology. I'm a real writer, I write novels to appeal to the mind. That kind of writing is a very backward technology. It can't stand up against movies. Movies have cameras, they have sets, they have music and they have these great faces. How can a writer conjure that up with just words? And movies have narrowed the field of battle. They don't have to conquer the brain, only the heart."

"Fuck you, I'm not a writer," Claudia said. "A screenwriter is not a writer? You just say that because you're not good at it."

Vail patted her on the shoulder. "I'm not putting you down," he said. "I'm not even putting down film as an art. I'm just defining."

"It's a lucky thing I love your books," Claudia said. "It's no wonder nobody out here likes you."

Vail smiled amiably. "No, no," he said. "They don't dislike me. They just have contempt for me. But when my estate gets the rights to my characters back on my death, they'll have respect."

"You're not serious," Claudia said.

"I think I am," Vail said. "It's a very tempting prospect. Suicide. Is it politically incorrect these days?"

"Oh shit," Claudia said. She wrapped her arm around Vail's neck. "The fight is just beginning," she said. "I'm sure they'll listen when I ask for your points. Okay?"

Vail smiled at her. "No hurry," he said. "It will take me at least six months just to figure out how to do myself in. I hate violence."

Claudia realized suddenly that Vail was serious. She was surprised at the panic she felt at the thought of his death. It was not that she loved him, though they had been lovers briefly. It was not even that she was fond of him. It was the thought that the beautiful books he had written were to him less powerful than money. That his art could be defeated by such a contemptible foe as money. Out of that panic she said, "If worse comes to worst, we'll go to Vegas and see my brother, Cross. He likes you. He'll do something."

Vail laughed. "He doesn't like me that much."

Claudia said, "He has a good heart. I know my brother."

"No, you don't," Vail said.

Athena had come home from the Dorothy Chandler Pavilion the night of the Academy Awards without celebrating and had gone right to bed. She tossed and turned for hours, but she couldn't sleep. Every muscle in her body felt taut. I won't let him do this again, she thought. Not again. I won't live in terror again.

She made herself a cup of tea and tried to drink it, but when she saw the small tremor in her hand, she became impatient, walked outside, and stood on the balcony looking into the dark night sky. She stood for hours, but her heart still raced in terror.

She dressed. In white shorts and tennis shoes. And as the red sun began to show itself over the horizon, she ran. She ran faster and faster along the beach, trying to stay on the hard wet sand, trying to follow the coastline as the cold water washed over her feet. She had to clear her head. She couldn't let Boz beat her. She had worked too hard and too long. And he would kill her, she never doubted that. But first he would play with her, torment her, finally he would disfigure her, he would make her ugly, thinking it would make her his again. She felt her own fury beating in her throat, and then the cool wind spraying ocean water in her face. No, no!

She thought about the Studio, they'd be frantic, they'd threaten her. But it was money, not her, they were concerned about. She thought about her friend Claudia, how this could have been her big break, and she felt sad. She thought about all the others, but she knew she couldn't afford the luxury of compassion. Boz was crazy, and people who weren't crazy would try to reason with him. He was smart enough to make them think they could win, but she knew better. She couldn't take the chance. She couldn't allow herself to take that chance. . . .

By the time she reached the large black boulders that meant the north beach ended, she was completely out of breath. She sat, trying to slow her heart down. She looked up when she heard the caw of seagulls as they swept down and seemed to glide along the water. Her eyes filled, but she pulled herself back with determination. She swallowed past the lump in her throat. And for the first time in a long time she wished her parents weren't so far away. Some part of her felt like a small child and wished desperately to run home to safety, to someone who could put their arms around her and just make everything better. She smiled at herself then, a crooked, wry smile, remembering when she really believed that was possible. Now, she was so loved by everyone, so admired, so adored . . . and so what? She felt more empty than she thought any human was capable of feeling, more lonely. Sometimes when she found herself passing an ordinary woman with her husband and children, a woman living an ordinary life, she felt such longing. Stop! she told herself. Think. It's up to you. Come up with a plan and carry it through. It's not only your life that depends on you. . . .

It was midmorning before she walked back home. And she walked with her head held high and her eyes staring straight ahead: She knew what she had to do.


Boz Skannet was kept in custody overnight. His lawyer organized a press conference when he was released. Skannet told reporters that he was married to Athena Aquitane, though he had not seen her for ten years, and that what he had done was just a practical joke. The liquid was only water. He predicted that Athena would not press charges, intimating he possessed a terrible secret about her. In this he proved correct. No charges were filed.


That day Athena Aquitane informed LoddStone Studios, the studio making one of the most costly pictures in movie history, that she would not return to work on that film. Because of the attack made on her, she feared for her life.

Without her, the film, a historical epic called *Messalina,* could not be completed. The fifty million dollars invested would be a total loss. It also meant that because of this no major studio would ever dare cast Athena Aquitane in a movie again.

LoddStone Studios released a statement that their star had suffered extreme exhaustion but that in a month she would be recovered enough to resume shooting.

# CHAPTER 2

L ODDSTONE STUDIOS WAS the most powerful movie-making entity in Hollywood, but Athena Aquitane's refusal to go back to work was a costly treachery. It was rare that mere "Talent" could deal such a damaging blow, but *Messalina* was the Studio "Locomotive" for the Christmas season, the big picture that would power all the Studio's releases through the long, hard winter.

It happened that the next Sunday was the date of the annual Festival of Brotherhood charity party, held at the Beverly Hills estate of Eli Marrion, major shareholder and chairman of LoddStone Studios.

Far back in the canyons above Beverly Hills, Eli Marrion's huge mansion was a showplace of twenty rooms, but the oddity of it was that it had only one bedchamber. Eli Marrion never liked anyone sleeping in his house. There were guest bungalows, of course, along with two tennis courts and a large swimming pool. Six of the rooms were devoted to his large collection of paintings.

Five hundred of the most eminent people in Hollywood were invited to this charity festival with an admission fee of one thousand dollars per person. There were bars and buffet tents and dancing tents spread over the grounds, and there was a band. But the house itself was off-limits. Toilet facilities were provided by portable units in gaily decorated, wittily designed tents.

The mansion, the guest bungalows, the tennis courts, and the swimming pool were roped off and barred by security men. None of the guests were offended by this, Eli Marrion was too lofty a personage for offense to be taken.

But as guests frolicked on the lawns, gossiping and dancing for an obligatory three hours, Marrion was in the huge conference room of the mansion with a group of people most concerned with the completion of the film *Messalina.*

Eli Marrion dominated this gathering. His body was eighty years old but so cleverly disguised you took it for no more than sixty. His gray hair was perfectly cut and tinted to silver, his dark suit broadened his shoulders, added flesh to his bones, insulated his pipe-thin shanks. Mahogany shoes anchored him to earth. A white shirt was vertically cut with a rose-colored tie that pinked his grayish pallor. But his rule over LoddStone Studios was absolute only when he wanted it to be. There were times when it was more prudent to let mere mortals exercise their free will.

Athena Aquitane's refusal to complete a film in progress was a problem serious enough to command even Marrion's attention. *Messalina,* a hundred-million-dollar production, the studio Locomotive, with video, TV, cable and foreign rights presold to cover the cost, was a golden treasure that was about to sink like an old Spanish galleon, never to be retrieved.

And there was Athena herself. At the age of thirty, a great star, already signed to do another blockbuster for LoddStone. A true Talent, of which there was nothing more valuable. Marrion adored Talent.

But Talent was like dynamite, it could be dangerous and you had to control it. You did that with love, with cajolery in its most abject form, you showered it with worldly goods. You became a father, a mother, a brother, a sister, even a lover. No sacrifice was too great. But there came a time when you could not be weak, when indeed you must be merciless.

So now in this room with Marrion were the people to enforce his will. Bobby Bantz, Skippy Deere, Melo Stuart, and Dita Tommey.

Eli Marrion, facing them in this familiar conference room, twenty million dollars worth of paintings, tables, chairs, and rugs, the crystal goblets and jugs totaling at least a half million more, could feel his bones crumbling within. Each day he was astonished how difficult it was to present himself to the world as the all-powerful figure he was presumed to be.

Mornings were no longer refreshing, it was fatiguing to shave, to knot his tie, to button the buttons on his shirt. More dangerous was the mental weakness. This took the form of pity for people less powerful than himself. Now he was using Bobby Bantz more, giving him more power. After all, the man was thirty years younger and was his closest friend, loyal to him for so long.

Bantz was president and chief executive officer of the Studio. For over thirty years, Bantz had been Marrion's hatchet man, and through the years they had become very close, like father and son, as it is said. They suited each other. After the age of seventy, Marrion had become too tenderhearted to do the things that absolutely had to be done.

It was Bantz who took over from movie directors after their artistic cut and made their films acceptable to audiences. It was Bantz who disputed percentages of directors, stars, and writers and made them either go to court to collect or settle for somewhat less. It was Bantz who negotiated very tough contracts with Talent. Especially writers.

Bantz refused to give even the standard lip service to writers. It was true you needed a script to start, but Bantz believed that you lived and died by casting. Star power. Directors were important because they could steal you blind. Producers, no slouches when it came to thievery, were necessary for the manic energy that started a movie.

But writers? All they had to do was make that initial tracing on blank white paper. You hired another dozen to work it over. Then the producer shaped the plot. The director invented Business (sometimes a whole new picture), and then the stars came up with inspired bits of dialogue. Then there was the Creative Staff of the Studio who, in long, carefully thought out memos, gave writers insights, plot ideas, and wish lists. Bantz had seen many a million-dollar script from a big-shot screenwriter paid a million dollars, only to find when the picture was finished it contained not a single plot incident or word of dialogue of the writer's. Sure, Eli had a soft spot for writers, but that was because they were so easy to screw on their contracts.

Marrion and Bantz had traveled the world together selling movies to film festivals and market centers, to London and Paris and Cannes, to Tokyo and Singapore. They had decided the fate of young artists. They had ruled an empire together, as Emperor and chief vassal.

Eli Marrion and Bobby Bantz agreed that Talent, those who wrote, acted in, and directed movies, were the most ungrateful people in the world. Oh, those hopeful pure artists could be so engaging, so grateful for their chance, so accommodating when they were fighting their way up, but how they could change after achieving fame. Honey-making bees turned into angry hornets. It was only natural that Marrion and Bantz kept a staff of twenty lawyers to throw a net over them.

Why were they always so much trouble? So unhappy? There was no doubt about it, people who pursued money rather than art had longer careers, got more pleasure in life, were much better and more socially valuable people than those artists who tried to show the divine spark in human beings. Too bad you couldn't make a movie about that. That money was more healing than art and love. But the public would never buy it.

Bobby Bantz had gathered them all up from the festival going on outside the mansion. The only Talent there was the director of *Messalina,* a woman named Dita Tommey, in the "A" class and known as the best with female stars, which in Hollywood today meant not homosexual but feminist. The fact that she was also a lesbian was irrelevant to all these men in the conference room. Dita Tommey brought in her pictures under budget, her pictures made money, and her liaisons with females caused far less trouble on a picture than a male director screwing his actresses did. Lesbian lovers of the famous were docile.

Eli Marrion sat at the head of the conference table and let Bantz lead the discussion.

Bantz said, "Dita, tell us exactly how we stand on the picture and what your thoughts are on solving the situation. Hell, I don't even understand the problem."

Tommey was short and very compact and always spoke to the point. She said, "Athena is scared to death. She is not coming back to work unless you geniuses come up with something that can erase that fear. If she doesn't come back, you guys are out fifty million bucks. The picture cannot be finished without her." She paused for a moment. "I've shot around her in the past week, so I've saved you money there."

"This fucking picture," Bantz said. "I never wanted to make it."

This provoked other men in the room; the producer, Skippy Deere, said, "Fuck you, Bobby," and Melo Stuart, Athena Aquitane's agent, said, "Bullshit."

In truth, *Messalina* had been enthusiastically supported by everyone. It had received one of the easiest "green lights" in history.

*Messalina* told the story of the Roman Empire under the Emperor Claudius from a feminist point of view. History, written by males, painted the Empress Messalina as a corrupt and murderous harlot, who one night took on the whole population of Rome in sexual debauch. But in the movie creating her life almost two thousand years later, she was revealed as a tragic heroine, an Antigone, another Medea. A woman who, using the only weapons available to her, tried to change a world in which men were so dominant that they treated the female sex, half the human race, as if they were slaves.

It was a great concept—rampant sex acts in full color and a highly relevant and popular theme—but it needed a perfect package to make the whole thing credible. First Claudia De Lena wrote a script that was witty and had a strong story line. Dita Tommey as director was a pragmatic and politically correct choice. She had a dry intelligence and was a proven director. Athena Aquitane was perfect as *Messalina* and had completely dominated the picture so far. She had the beauty of face and body, and the genius of her acting made everything plausible. More important, she was one of the three female Bankable Stars in the world. Claudia, with her own offbeat genius, had even given her a scene in which Messalina, seduced by the growing Christian legends, saved martyrs from the sure death of the amphitheater. When Tommey read the scene she said to Claudia, "Hey, there's a limit."

Claudia grinned at her and said, "Not in the movies."

Skippy Deere said, "We have to shut down the picture until we get Athena back to work. That will cost a hundred fifty grand a day. The situation is this. We've spent fifty million. We're halfway through, we can't write Athena out and we can't double her. So if she doesn't come back, we scrap the picture."

"We can't scrap it," Bantz said. "Insurance doesn't cover a star refusing to work. Drop her out of a plane, then insurance pays. Melo, it's your job to get her back. You're responsible."

Melo Stuart said, "I'm her agent but I can only have so much influence on a woman like her. Let me tell you this. She is genuinely frightened. This is not one of your temperamental things. She's scared, but she's an intelligent woman, so she must have a reason. This is a very dangerous, a very delicate, situation."

Bantz said, "If she torpedoes a hundred-million-dollar movie, she can never work again, did you tell her that?"

"She knows," Stuart said.

Bantz asked, "Who's the best person to talk sense into her? Skippy, you tried and failed. Melo, you did. Dita, I know you did your best. I even tried."

Tommey said to Bantz, "You don't count, Bobby. She detests you."

Bantz said sharply, "Sure, some people don't like my style but they listen to me."

Tommey said kindly, "Bobby, none of the Talent likes you, but Athena doesn't like you personally."

"I gave her the role that made her a star," Bantz said.

Melo Stuart said calmly, "She was born a star. You were lucky to get her."

Bantz said, "Dita, you're her friend. It's your job to get her back to work."

"Athena is not my friend," Tommey said. "She is a colleague who respects me because after I tried to make her, I desisted gracefully when I failed. Not like you, Bobby. You kept trying for years."

Bantz said amiably, "Dita, who the hell is she not to fuck us? Eli, you have to lay down the law."

All attention was fixed on the old man, who seemed bored. Eli Marrion was so thin that one male star had joked he should wear an eraser on his skull, but this was more malicious than apt. Marrion had a comparatively huge head and the broad gorilla face of a much heavier man, a broad nose, thick mouth, yet his face was curiously benign, somewhat gentle, some even said handsome. But his eyes gave him away, they were cold gray and radiated intelligence and an absolute concentration that daunted most people. It was perhaps for this reason that he insisted that everyone call him by his first name.

Marrion spoke in an emotionless voice. "If Athena won't listen to you people, she won't listen to me. My position of authority won't impress her. Which makes it all the more puzzling that she is so frightened over such a senseless attack by such a foolish man. Can't we buy our way out of this?"

"We will try," Bantz said. "But it makes no difference to Athena. She doesn't trust him."

Skippy Deere, the producer, said, "And we tried muscle. I got some friends in the police department to lean on him, but he's tough. His family has money and political connections and he's crazy in the bargain."

Stuart said, "Exactly how much does the Studio lose if it closes down the picture? I'll do my best to let you recoup on future packages."

There was a problem about letting Melo Stuart know the extent of the damages; as Athena's agent, it would give him too much leverage. Marrion did not answer but nodded to Bobby Bantz.

Bantz was reluctant, but spoke. "Actual money spent, fifty million. Okay, we can eat fifty million. But we have to give back the foreign sales money, the video money, and there's no Locomotive for Christmas. That can cost us another . . ." He paused, not willing to give that figure, "and then if we add the profits that we lose . . . shit, two hundred million dollars. You'd have to give us a break on a lot of packages, Melo."

Stuart smiled, thinking he would have to jack up his price for Athena. "But actually, in real cash put out, you only lose fifty," he said.

When Marrion spoke his voice had lost its gentleness. "Melo," he said, "How much will it cost us to get your client back to work?" They knew what had happened. Marrion had decided to act as if this was just a scam.

Stuart read the message. How much are you going to stick us up for on this little scheme? This was an attack on his integrity but he had no intention of getting on his high horse. Not with Marrion. If it had been Bantz, he would have been wrathfully indignant.

Stuart was a very powerful man in the movie world. He didn't have to kiss even Marrion's ass. He controlled a stable of five A directors, not strictly Bankable but very powerful indeed; two male Bankable Stars; and one female Bankable Star, Athena. Which meant he had three people who could assure a green light for any movie. But still it was not wise to anger Marrion. Stuart had become powerful by avoiding such dangers. Certainly this was a great situation for a stickup but not really. This was a rare time when straightforwardness could pay off.

Melo Stuart's greatest asset was his sincerity, he truly believed in what he sold, and he had believed in Athena's talent even ten years before, when she was an unknown. He believed in her now. But what if he could change her mind and bring her back before the cameras? Surely that was worth something, surely that option should not be closed off.

"This is not about money," Stuart said with passion. He felt a rapture for his own sincerity. "You could offer Athena an extra million and she would not go back. You must solve the problem of this so-called long-absent husband."

There was an ominous silence. Everybody paid attention. A sum of money had been mentioned. Was it an opening wedge?

Skippy Deere said, "She won't take money."

Dita Tommey shrugged. She didn't believe Stuart for a moment. But it wouldn't be her money. Bantz simply glared at Stuart, who coolly kept looking at Marrion.

Marrion analyzed Stuart's remark correctly. Athena would not come back for money. Talent was never so cunning. He decided to wrap up the meeting.

He said, "Melo, explain very carefully to your client, if she does not come back in one month's time the Studio abandons the picture and takes the loss. Then we sue her for everything she owns. She must know she can't work again for a major American studio afterwards." He smiled around the table. "What the hell, it's only fifty million."

They all knew he was serious, that he had lost his patience. Dita Tommey panicked, the picture meant more to her than anyone. It was her baby. If it succeeded she would be among those directors who would be Bankable. Her OK could get a green light. Out of her panic, she said, "Get Claudia De Lena to talk to her. She's one of Athena's closest friends."

Bobby Bantz said contemptuously, "I don't know what's worse, a star fucking somebody below the line or being friends with a writer."

At this Marrion again lost his patience. "Bobby, don't bring irrelevancies into a business discussion. Have Claudia talk to her. But let's wrap this thing up one way or another. We have other pictures to make."

But the next day a check for five million dollars arrived at Lodd-Stone Studios. It was from Athena Aquitane. She had returned the advance money she had been paid to do *Messalina*.

Now it was in the hands of the lawyers.

In just fifteen years Andrew Pollard had built the Pacific Ocean Security Company into the most prestigious protection organization on the West Coast. Starting in a suite of hotel rooms, he now owned a four-story building in Santa Monica with over fifty permanent HQ staff, five hundred investigators and guards under freelance contracts, plus a floating reserve group who worked for him a good part of the year.

Pacific Ocean Security provided services for the very rich and very famous. It protected the homes of movie magnates with armed personnel and electronic devices. It provided bodyguards for stars and producers. It supplied uniformed men to control the crowds at great media events such as the Academy Awards. It did investigative work in delicate matters such as providing counterintelligence to ward off would-be blackmailers.

Andrew Pollard became successful because he was a stickler for details. He planted ARMED RESPONSE signs on the grounds of his rich clients' houses that flashed in the night with an explosion of red light, plus he had patrols in the neighborhoods of the walled-in mansions. Careful in picking his personnel, he paid high enough wages so that they worried about being fired. He could afford to be generous. His clients were the richest people in the country and paid accordingly. He was also clever enough to work closely with the Los Angeles Police Department, top and bottom. He was a business friend of Jim Losey, the legendary detective, who was a hero to the rank and file. But most important, he had the backing of the Clericuzio Family.

Fifteen years before, while still a young police officer, still a little careless, he had been entrapped by the Internal Affairs Unit of the New York City Police Department. It was small graft, almost impossible to avoid. But he had stood fast and refused to inform on his superiors who were involved. The Clericuzio Family underlings observed this and set in motion a series of judicial moves so that Andrew Pollard was given a deal: Resign from the New York Police Department and escape punishment.

Pollard migrated to Los Angeles with his wife and child, and the Family gave him the money to set up his Pacific Ocean Security Company. Then the Family sent out word that Pollard's clients were not to be molested, their houses could not be burglarized, their persons were not to be mugged, their jewelry was not to be stolen and if stolen in error must be returned. It was for this reason that the flaming ARMED RESPONSE signs also flashed the name of the protection agency.

Andrew Pollard's success was almost magical, the mansions under his protection were never touched. His bodyguards were as nearly well trained as FBI men, so the company was never sued for inside jobs, sexual harassment of their employers, or child molesting, all of which happened in the world of security. There were a few cases of attempted blackmail, and there were some guards who sold intimate secrets to the scandal sheets, but that was unavoidable. All in all, Pollard ran a clean, efficient operation.

His company had computer access to confidential information about people in all walks of life. And it was only natural that when the Clericuzio Family needed data, it would be supplied. Pollard earned a good living and he was grateful to the Family. Plus the fact that every once in a while there was a job he could not ask his guards to do, and he would then make application to the western *Bruglione* for some help in the way of strong-arm.

There were slyer predators for whom Los Angeles and Hollywood were like some Edenesque jungle, teeming with victims. There were the movie executives lured into blackmailers' honey traps, the closeted movie stars, sadomasochistic directors, pedophile producers, all frightened their secrets would get out. Pollard was noted for dealing with these cases with finesse and discretion. He could negotiate the lowest possible payment and ensure that there would be no second dip.

Bobby Bantz summoned Andrew Pollard to his office the day after the Academy Awards. "I want all the info you can get on this Boz Skannet character," he told Pollard. "I want all the background on Athena Aquitane. For a major star, we know very little about her. I also want you to make a deal with Skannet. We need Athena for another three to six months on the picture, so structure a deal with Skannet so that he goes far away. Offer him twenty grand a month but you can go as high as a hundred."

Pollard said quietly, "And after he can do what he wants?"

"Then it's a job for the authorities," Bantz said. "You have to be very careful, Andrew. This guy has a powerful family. The movie industry cannot be accused of any off-color tactics, it might ruin the picture and hurt the Studio. So just make the deal. Plus we are using your firm for her personal security."

"And if he doesn't go for the deal?" Pollard asked.

"Then you have to guard her day and night," Bantz said. "Until the picture is done."

"I could lean on him just a little," Pollard said. "In a legal way of course. I'm not suggesting anything."

"He's too well connected," Bantz said. "The police authorities are leery of him. Even Jim Losey, who's such a good buddy of Skippy

Deere, won't use any muscle. Aside from public relations, the Studio could be sued for enormous amounts of money. I'm not saying you should treat him like a delicate flower but . . ."

Pollard got the message. A little rough stuff to scare the guy but pay him what he wanted. "I'll need contracts," he said.

Bantz took an envelope from his desk drawer. "He signs three copies and there's a check in there for fifty thousand dollars as a down payment. The figures in the contract are open, you can fill it in when you make the deal."

As he went out Bantz said after him, "Your people didn't help at the Academy Awards. They were sleeping on their fucking feet."

Pollard did not take offense. This was vintage Bantz.

"Those were just crowd-control guards," he said. "Don't worry, I'll put my top crew around Miss Aquitane."

In twenty-four hours Pacific Ocean Security computers had everything on Boz Skannet. He was thirty-four years old, a graduate of Texas A&M, where he had been Conference All-Star running back and then gone on to one season of professional football. His father owned a bank in Houston, but more important, his uncle ran the Republican political machine in Texas and was a close personal friend of the president. Mixed into all of this was a lot of money.

Boz Skannet was a piece of work in and of himself. As a vice president in his father's bank, he had narrowly escaped indictment in an oil lease scam. He had been arrested for assault six times. In one case he had beaten two police officers so severely they had to be hospitalized. Skannet was never prosecuted because he paid damages to the officers. There was a sexual harassment charge settled out of court. Before all this he had been married at twenty-one to Athena and had become the father of a baby girl the next year. The child was named Bethany. At age twenty, his wife disappeared with their daughter.

All this gave Andrew Pollard a picture. This was a bad guy. A guy who carried a grudge against his wife for ten years, a guy who fought armed police officers and was tough enough to send them to the hospital. The chances of scaring such a guy were nil. Pay him the money, get the contract signed, and stay the hell out of it.

Pollard called Jim Losey, who was handling the Skannet case for the Los Angeles PD. Pollard was in awe of Losey, who was the cop he would have liked to become. They had a working relationship. Losey received a handsome gift every Christmas from Pacific Ocean Security. Now Pollard wanted the police dope, wanted to know everything Losey had on the case.

"Jim," Pollard said, "Can you send me an info sheet on Boz Skannet? I need his address in L.A. and I'd like to know more about him."

"Sure," Losey said. "But the charges against him have been dropped. What are you in this for?"

"Protection job," Pollard said. "How dangerous is this guy?"

"He's fucking crazy," Losey said. "Tell your bodyguard team that if he gets close they should start shooting."

"You'd arrest me," Pollard said, laughing. "It's against the law."

"Yeah," Losey said, "I'd have to. What a fucking joke."

Boz Skannet was staying in a modest hotel on Ocean Avenue in Santa Monica, which worried Andrew Pollard because it was only a fifteen-minute drive to Athena's house in Malibu Colony. He ordered a four-man team to guard Athena's house and put a two-man team into Skannet's hotel. Then he arranged to meet with Skannet that afternoon.

Pollard took three of his biggest and toughest men with him. With a guy like Skannet you never knew what might happen.

Skannet let them into his hotel suite. He was affable, greeted them with a smile, but did not offer any refreshment. Curiously enough, he was wearing a tie, shirt, and jacket, perhaps to show that after all he was still a banker. Pollard introduced himself and his three bodyguards, all three showing their Pacific Ocean Security IDs. Skannet grinned at them and said, "You guys are sure big. I'll bet a hundred bucks I can kick the shit out of any one of you in a fair fight."

The three bodyguards, well-trained men, gave him small acknowledging smiles, but Pollard deliberately took offense. A calculated umbrage. "We're here to do business, Mr. Skannet," he said. "Not to endure threats. LoddStone Studios is prepared to pay you fifty thousand down right now and twenty thousand a month for eight months. All you have to do is leave Los Angeles." Pollard took the contracts and the big green-and-white check out of his briefcase.

Skannet studied them. "Very simple contract," he said. "I don't even need a lawyer. But it's also very simple money. I was thinking a hundred grand in front and fifty thousand a month."

"Too much," Pollard said. "We have a judge's restraining order against you. You get within a block of Athena and you go to jail. We have security around Athena twenty-four hours a day. And I've set up surveillance teams to keep track of your movements. So for you this is found money."

"I should have come to California sooner," Skannet said. "The streets are paved with gold. Why pay me anything?"

"The studio wants to reassure Miss Aquitane," Pollard said.

"She really is that big a star," Skannet said musingly. "Well, she was always special. And to think I used to fuck her five times a day." He grinned at the three men. "And brainy in the bargain."

Pollard looked at the man with curiosity. The guy was handsome as the rugged Marlboro man in the cigarette ads, except that his skin was red with sun and booze and his body build was bulkier. He had that charming drawl of the South, which was both humorous and dangerous. A lot of women fell in love with such men. In New York there had been some cops with the same kind of looks, and they had scored like bandits. You sent them out on murder cases and in a week they were consoling the widows. Jim Losey was a cop like that, come to think of it. Pollard had never been so lucky.

"Let's just talk business," Pollard said. He wanted Skannet to sign the contract and take the check in front of the witnesses, then maybe later if they had to, the Studio could make a case for extortion.

Skannet sat down at the table. "Have you got a pen?" he asked.

Pollard took his pen out of the briefcase and filled out the figures of twenty thousand a month. Skannet noted him doing so and said cheerfully, "So, I could have gotten more." Then he signed the three copies. "When do I have to leave L.A.?"

"This very night," Pollard said. "I'll take you to your plane."

"No thanks," Skannet said. "I think I'll drive to Las Vegas and gamble with this check."

"I'll be watching," Pollard said. Now was the time he felt he should show some muscle. "Let me warn you, if you show up in Los Angeles again, I'll have you arrested for extortion."

Skannet's red face brimmed with glee. "I'd love that," he said. "I'll be as famous as Athena."

That night the surveillance team reported that Boz Skannet had left but only to move into the Beverly Hills Hotel, and that he had deposited the fifty-thousand-dollar check in an account he had at the Bank of America. This indicated a number of things to Pollard. That Skannet had influence, because he had gotten into the Beverly Hills Hotel, and that he didn't give a shit about the deal he had made. Pollard reported this to Bobby Bantz and asked for instructions. Bantz told him to keep his mouth shut. The contract had been shown to Athena to reassure her and persuade her to go back to work. He did not tell Pollard she had laughed in their faces.

"You can stop the check," Pollard said.

"No," Bantz said, "he cashes it and we got him in court on fraud, extortion, whatever. I just don't want Athena to know he's still in town."

"I'll double the security on her," Pollard said. "But if he's crazy, if he really wants to harm her, that won't help."

"He's a bluffer," Bantz said. "He didn't do it the first time, why would he do anything now?"

"I'll tell you why," Pollard said. "We burglarized his room. Guess what we found? A container of real acid."

"Oh shit," Bantz said. "Can you tell the cops? Jim Losey maybe."

Pollard said, "Having acid is not a crime. Burglary is. Skannet can put me in jail."

"You never told me anything," Bantz said. "We never had this conversation. And forget what you know."

"Sure Mr. Bantz," Pollard said. "I won't even bill you for the information."

"Thanks a lot," Bantz said sarcastically. "Keep in touch."

. . .

Claudia was briefed by Skippy Deere. And instructed as was proper to their roles as producer and writer on a picture.

"You have to absolutely kiss Athena's ass," Deere said. "You have to grovel, you have to cry, you have to have a nervous breakdown. You have to remind her of everything you've ever done for her as an intimate and true friend and as a fellow professional. You must get Athena back on the picture."

Claudia was used to Skippy. "Why me?" she said coolly. "You're the producer, Dita is the director, Bantz is president of LoddStone. You guys go kiss her ass. You've had more practice than me."

"Because it was your project all the way," Deere said. "You wrote the original screenplay on spec, you got me and you got Athena. If the project fails, your name will always be associated with that failure."

When Deere left and she was alone in her office, Claudia knew Deere was right. In her desperation she thought of her brother, Cross. He was the only one who could help her, help make the problem of Boz disappear. She hated the thought of trading on her friendship with Athena, and knew Athena might refuse her but Cross never would. He never had.

She put in a call to the Xanadu Hotel in Vegas, but she was told that Cross would be in Quogue and would not be back until the next day. This brought back all the childhood memories she always tried to forget. She would never call her brother in Quogue. She never would voluntarily have anything to do with the Clericuzio again. She never wanted to remember her childhood again, never to think of her father or any of the Clericuzio.

# BOOK II

# The Clericuzio
# and
# Pippi De Lena

# CHAPTER 3

T HE CLERICUZIO FAMILY legend of ferocity had been established more than a hundred years ago in Sicily. There the
Clericuzio had waged a twenty-year war with a rival family over the
ownership of a piece of forest. The patriarch of the opposing clan,
Don Pietro Forlenza, was on his deathbed, having survived eighty-
five years of strife only to suffer a stroke, which his doctor predicted
would end his life within a week. A member of the Clericuzio penetrated the sick man's bedchamber and stabbed him to death, shouting that the old man did not deserve a peaceful death.

Don Domenico Clericuzio often told this old story of murder to
show how foolish were the old-fashioned ways, to point out that ferocity without selection was mere braggadocio. Ferocity was too precious a weapon to waste, it must always have an important purpose.

And indeed he had the proof, for it was ferocity that led the Clericuzio Family in Sicily to destruction. When Mussolini and his Fas-
cists came to absolute power in Italy, they understood that the Mafia
had to be destroyed. They did it by suspending due process of law
and by using irresistible armed force. The Mafia was broken at the
cost of thousands of innocent people going to jail or exile with them.

Only the Clericuzio clan had the courage to oppose Fascist de-
crees with force. They murdered the local Fascist prefect, they attacked Fascist garrisons. Most infuriating of all, when Mussolini
gave a speech in Palermo they stole his prized bowler hat and umbrella imported from England. It was this peasant humor and contempt, which made a laughingstock of Mussolini in Sicily, that
finally led to their ruin. There was a massive concentration of armed

forces in their province. Five hundred members of the Clericuzio clan were killed outright. Another five hundred were exiled to the arid islands in the Mediterranean that served as penal colonies. Only the very heart of the Clericuzio survived, and the family shipped young Domenico Clericuzio to America. Where, proving that blood will tell, Don Domenico built his own empire, with far more cunning and foresight than his ancestors had shown in Sicily. But he always remembered that a lawless state was the great enemy. And so he loved America.

Early on he had been told the famous maxim of American justice, that it was better that a hundred guilty men go free than that one innocent man be punished. Struck almost dumb by the beauty of the concept, he became an ardent patriot. America was his country. He would never leave America.

Inspired by this, Don Domenico built the Clericuzio empire in America more solidly than the clan had in Sicily. He ensured his friendship to all political and judicial institutions with great gifts of cash. He did not rely on one or two streams of income but diversified in the finest tradition of American business enterprise. There was the construction industry, the garbage disposal industry, the different modes of transportation. But the great river of cash came from gambling, which was his love, in contrast to the income from drugs which, though most profitable, he distrusted. So in later years it was only in gambling that he allowed the Clericuzio Family to be involved operationally. The rest wetted the Clericuzio beak with a tithe of 5 percent.

After twenty-five years the Don's plan and the dream was coming true. Gambling was now respectable and, more important, increasingly legal. There were the ever-burgeoning state lotteries, those swindles perpetrated by the government on its citizens. The prizes stretched over twenty years, which, in effect, amounted to the state never paying the money at all, just the interest on the money withheld. And then that was taxed in the bargain. What a joke. Don Domenico knew the details, because his Family owned one of the management companies that ran the lottery for several states at a very good fee.

But the Don was banking on the day when gambling on sports would become legal in all the United States as it was now legal only in Nevada. He knew this from the tithe he collected on illegal gambling. Profits on the Super Bowl football game alone, if gambling became legal, would come to a billion dollars, in just one day. The World Series with its seven games would yield equal profit. College football, hockey, basketball, all rich streams. Then there would be intricate, tantalizing lotteries on sports events, legal gold mines. The Don knew he would not live to see that glorious day, but what a world it would be for his children. The Clericuzio would be the equal of the Renaissance princes. They would become the patrons of art, advisors and leaders of government, respectable in history books. A trailing cloak of gold would brush out its origins. All his descendants, his followers, his true friends, would be secure forever. Certainly the Don had the vision of a civilized society, the world, as this great tree shedding the fruit that must feed and shelter humanity. But in the roots of this great tree would be the immortal python of the Clericuzio, sucking nourishment from a source that could never fail.

If the Clericuzio Family was the Holy Church for the many Mafia empires scattered over the United States, then the head of the Family, Don Domenico Clericuzio, was the Pope, admired not only for his intelligence but for his strength.

Don Clericuzio was also revered for the strict moral code he enforced in his Family. Every man, woman, and child was completely responsible for his actions, no matter the stress, the remorse, or the hard circumstances. Actions defined a man; words were a fart in the wind. He disdained all social sciences, all psychology. He was a devout Catholic: payment for sins in this world, forgiveness in the next. Every debt had to be paid, and he was strict in his judgment in this world.

As in his loyalty. The creatures of his blood first; his God second (did he not have his own chapel in the house?); and third, his obligation to all the subjects in the domain of the Clericuzio Family.

As for the society, the government—patriot though he was—never entered the equation. Don Clericuzio had been born in Sicily, where society and the government were the enemy. His concept of free will was very clear. You could will yourself as a slave to earn your daily bread without dignity or hope, or you earned your bread as a man who commanded respect. Your Family was your society, your God was your punisher, and your followers protected you. To those on earth you owed a duty: that they would have bread to put in their mouths, respect from the world, and a shield from the punishment of other men.

The Don had not built his empire so that his children and his grandchildren would someday recede into a mass of helpless humanity. He built and kept building power so that the Family name and fortune would survive as long as the Church itself. What greater purpose could a man have in this world than to earn his daily bread, then in the next world to present himself to a forgiving deity? As for his fellow man and their faulty structures of society, they could all swim to the bottom of the ocean.

Don Domenico led his Family to the very heights of power. He did so with a Borgia-like cruelty and a Machiavellian subtleness, plus solid American business know-how. But above all with a patriarchal love for his followers. Virtue was rewarded. Injuries avenged. A livelihood guaranteed.

Finally, as the Don had planned, the Clericuzio reached such a height that it no longer took part in the usual operations of criminal activity except in the most dire circumstance. The other Mafia Families served chiefly as executive Barons, or *Brugliones,* who when in trouble went to the Clericuzio hat in hand. In Italian the words *"Bruglione"* and "baron" rhyme, however in the Italian dialect *"Bruglione"* means someone who fumbles the smallest tasks. It was Don Domenico's wit, sparked by the Barons' constant pleas for help, that changed the word "baron" to *Bruglione.* The Clericuzio made peace between them, sprang them from jail, hid their illegal gains in Europe, arranged foolproof ways for them to smuggle their drugs into America, used its influence with judges and different government regulators, both federal and state. Help with municipalities was usually not required. If a local *Bruglione* could not influence the city he lived in, he was not worth his salt.

The economic genius of Don Clericuzio's oldest son, Giorgio, cemented the Family power. Like some divine laundress he washed the great spouts of black money that a modern civilization spews from its guts. It was Giorgio who always tried to moderate his father's ferocity. Above all, Giorgio strove to keep the Clericuzio Family out of the glare of public notice. So the Family existed, even to the authorities, like some sort of UFO. There were random sightings, rumors, tales of horror and benignity. There were mentions in FBI and police department files, but there were no newspaper stories, not even in those publications that gloried in depicting the exploits of various other Mafia Families who, through carelessness and ego, came to misfortune.

Not that the Clericuzio Family was a toothless tiger. Giorgio's two younger brothers, Vincent and Petie, though not as clever as Giorgio, had almost the Don's ferocity. And they had a pool of enforcers who lived in an enclave of the Bronx that had always been Italian. This enclave of forty square blocks could have been used in a film of Old Italy. There were no bearded Hasidic Jews, blacks, Asians, or bohemian elements in the population, nor did any of these own a business establishment there. There was not one Chinese restaurant. The Clericuzio owned or controlled all real estate in the area. Of course some of the Italian families' progeny sprouted long hair and were guitar-playing rebels, but these teenagers were shipped to relatives in California. Every year, new, carefully screened immigrants from Sicily arrived to repopulate. The Bronx Enclave, surrounded by areas with the highest crime rate in the world, was singularly free of evildoing.

Pippi De Lena had risen from Mayor of the Bronx Enclave to *Bruglione* of the Las Vegas area for the Clericuzio Family. But he remained directly under the rule of the Clericuzio, who still needed his special talent.

Pippi was the very essence of what was called *Qualificato,* that is, a Qualified Man. He had started early, making his "bones" at the age of seventeen, and what had made the deed even more impressive was he had done so with the garrote. For in America, young men in their callow pride disdained the rope. Also, he was very strong physically, of good height and with intimidating bulk. He was, of course, expert with firearms and explosives. All this aside, he was a charming man because of his zest for life; he had a geniality that put men at ease, and women appreciated his gallantry, which was half rustic Sicilian and half movie American. Though he took his work very seriously, he believed that life was to be enjoyed.

He did have his little weaknesses. He drank heartily, he gambled always, he was excessively fond of women. He was not as merciless as could be wished by the Don, perhaps because Pippi enjoyed too much the social company of other people. But all these weaknesses somehow made him more potent as a weapon. He was a man who used his vices to drain poison out of his body rather than to saturate it.

It helped his career, of course, that he was the nephew of the Don. He was of the blood, and that was important when Pippi broke the family tradition.

No man can live his life without making mistakes. Pippi De Lena, at the age of twenty-eight, married for love, and to compound that error he chose as a wife a completely inappropriate woman for a Qualified Man.

Her name was Nalene Jessup, and she danced in the show at the Las Vegas Xanadu Hotel. Pippi always proudly pointed out that she was not a showgirl who presented herself in the front line with her tits and ass showing, she was a *dancer.* Nalene was also an intellectual, by Vegas standards. She was bookish, took an interest in politics, and since her roots were in the particularly WASP culture of Sacramento, California, had old-fashioned values.

They were complete opposites. Pippi had no intellectual interests, he rarely read, listened to music, or attended movies or theater. Pippi had the face of a bull, Nalene the face of a flower. Pippi was extroverted, full of charm, yet he exuded danger. Nalene was so gentle in nature that not one of her fellow showgirls and dancers had ever been able to pick a fight with her, as they often did with each other to pass the time.

The only thing Pippi and Nalene had in common was dancing. For Pippi De Lena, the feared Clericuzio Hammer, was a veritable idiot savant when he stepped onto the ballroom floor. This was the poetry he could not read, the medieval gallantry of Holy Knights, the tenderness, the exquisite refinement of sex, the only time he reached out to something he could not understand.

For Nalene Jessup, it was a glimpse into his innermost soul. When they danced together for hours before making love, it made their sex ethereal, a true communication between kindred souls. He talked to her when they danced, alone in her apartment, or on the dance floors of the Vegas hotels.

He was a good storyteller with good stories to tell. He expressed his adoration of her in a flattering and witty way. He had an overwhelming masculine presence, which he laid at her feet as a slave, and he listened. He was proud and interested when she talked of books, the theater, the duties of democracy to lift up the downtrodden, the rights of blacks, the liberation of South Africa, the duty to feed the unfortunate poor of the Third World. Pippi was thrilled by these sentiments. They were exotic to him.

It helped that they suited each other sexually, that their opposites attracted each other. It was helpful to their love that Pippi saw the true Nalene but that Nalene did not see the real Pippi. What she saw was a man who adored her, who showered gifts upon her, who listened to her dreams.

They married a week after they met. Nalene was only eighteen, she knew no better. Pippi was twenty-eight and truly in love. He, too, was brought up with old-fashioned values, certainly from different poles, and they both wanted a family. Nalene was already an orphan, and Pippi was reluctant to include the Clericuzio in his newfound rapture. Also, he knew they would not approve. Better to face them with the deed and work things out gradually. They were wed in a Vegas chapel.

But here was another lapse in judgment. Don Clericuzio approved that Pippi married. As he often said, "A man's primary duty in life is to earn his own living," but to what purpose if he did not have a wife and children? The Don took umbrage that he had not been consulted, that the wedding had not been celebrated as part of the Clericuzio Family. After all, Pippi had Clericuzio blood.

The Don peevishly commented, "They can dance to the bottom of the ocean together," but nevertheless he sent lavish wedding presents. A huge Buick, the ownership of a collection agency that yielded the princely income for that time of one hundred thousand dollars a year; a promotion. Pippi De Lena would continue to serve the Clericuzio Family as one of its closely affiliated *Brugliones* in the West, but he was banished from the Bronx Enclave, for how could this alien wife live in harmony with the faithful. She was as foreign to them as the Muslims, the blacks, the Hasidim, and the Asians who were banned. So in essence, though Pippi remained the Clericuzio Hammer, though he was a local Baron, he lost some influence in the palace in Quogue.

The best man at the little civil ceremony of marriage was Alfred Gronevelt, owner of the Xanadu Hotel. He gave a small dinner party afterward, where bride and groom danced the night away. In the years following, Gronevelt and Pippi De Lena developed a close and loyal friendship.

The marriage lasted long enough to produce two children: a son and a daughter. The eldest, christened Croccifixio but always called Cross, at age ten was the physical image of his mother, with a graceful body and an almost effeminately handsome face. Yet he had the physical strength and superb coordination of his father. The younger, Claudia, at the age of nine, was the image of her father, blunt features only saved from ugliness by the freshness and innocence of childhood, yet without her father's gifts. But she had her mother's love of books, music, and theater, and her mother's gentleness of spirit. It was only natural that Cross and Pippi were close to each other, and that Claudia was closer to her mother, Nalene.

In the eleven years before the De Lena family broke apart, things went very well. Pippi established himself in Vegas as the *Bruglione,* the Collector for the Xanadu Hotel, and he still served as Hammer to the Clericuzio. He became rich, he lived a good life, though by the

Don's edict not an ostentatious one. He drank, he gambled, he danced with his wife, he played with his children and tried to prepare them for their entry into adulthood.

Pippi had learned in his own dangerous life to look far ahead. It was one of the reasons for his success. Early on he saw past Cross as a child to Cross as a man. He wanted that future man to be his ally. Or perhaps he wanted at least one human being close he could fully trust.

And so he trained Cross, taught him all the tricks of gambling, took him to dinner with Gronevelt so that he could hear stories of all the different ways a casino could be scammed. Gronevelt always opened up by saying, "Every night, millions of men lie awake figuring out how to cheat my casino."

Pippi took Cross hunting, taught him how to skin and gut animals, made him know the smell of blood, see his hands red with it. He made Cross take boxing lessons so that he could feel pain, taught him the use and care of guns but drew the line at teaching him the garrote; that was after all an indulgence of his own and not really useful in these modern days. Plus there could be no way of explaining such a rope to the boy's mother.

The Clericuzio Family owned a huge hunting lodge in the mountains of Nevada, and Pippi used it for his family's vacations. He took the children hunting while Nalene studied her books in the warmth of the lodge. On the hunt Cross easily shot wolves and deer and even some mountain lions and bears, which revealed that Cross was capable, that he had a good aptitude for guns, was always careful with them, always calm in danger, never flinched when he reached into the bloody guts, the slimy intestines. Dissecting limbs and heads, dressing the kill, he was never squeamish.

Claudia displayed no such virtues. She flinched at the sound of a gun and threw up while skinning a deer. After a few trips she refused to leave the lodge and spent time with her mother reading or walking along a nearby brook. Claudia refused even to fish, she could not bear to put the hard steel hook into the soft center of a worm.

Pippi concentrated on his son. He briefed the boy on basic behavior. Never show anger at a slight, tell nothing of yourself. Earn respect from everyone by deeds, not words. Respect the members of your blood family. Gambling was recreation, not a way to earn a living. Love your father, your mother, your sister, but beware of loving any other woman than your wife. And a wife was a woman who bore your children. And once that happened to you, your life was forfeit to give them their daily bread.

Cross was such a good pupil that his father doted on him. And he loved that Cross looked so much like Nalene, that he had her grace, that he was a replica of her without the intellectual gifts that were now destroying the marriage.

Pippi had never believed in the Don's dream that all of the younger children would disappear into legitimate society; he did not even believe it to be the best course of action. He acknowledged the old man's genius, but this was the romantic side of the great Don. After all, fathers wanted their sons to work with them, to be like them; blood was blood, that never changed.

And in this Pippi proved himself to be right. Despite all of Don Clericuzio's planning, even his own grandson, Dante, proved to be resistant to the grand design. Dante had grown to be a throwback to the Sicilian blood, thirsting for power, strongwilled. He never feared breaking the laws of society and of God.

When Cross was seven and Claudia six, Cross, aggressive by nature, fell into the habit of punching Claudia in the stomach, even in front of their father. Claudia cried for help. Pippi, as the parent, could resolve the problem in different ways. He could order Cross to stop, and if Cross did not, he could pick him up by the scruff of the neck and dangle him in midair, which he often did. Or he could order Claudia to fight back. Or he could cuff Cross against the wall, which he had done once or twice. But one time, perhaps because he had just had dinner and was feeling lazy, or more likely because Nalene always argued when he used force on the children, he lit up his cigar calmly and said to Cross, "Every time you hit your sister, I give her a dollar." As Cross continued punching his sister, Pippi rained dollar bills on the gleeful Claudia. Cross finally stopped in frustration.

Pippi swamped his wife with gifts, but they were gifts a master gives to his slave. They were bribes to disguise her servitude. Expensive gifts: diamond rings, fur coats, trips to Europe. He bought her a vacation house in Sacramento because she hated Vegas. When he gave her a Bentley, he wore a chauffeur's uniform to deliver it to her. Just before the end of their marriage, he gave her an antique ring certified as part of the Borgia collection. The only thing he restricted was her use of credit cards, she had to pay them out of her household allowance. Pippi never used them.

He was liberal in other ways. Nalene had complete physical freedom, Pippi was not a jealous Italian husband. Though he would not travel abroad except on business, he allowed Nalene to go to Europe with her women friends, because she so desperately wanted to see the museums in London, the ballet in Paris, the opera in Italy.

There were times that Nalene wondered about his lack of jealousy, but over the years she came to realize that no man in their circle would dare pay court to her.

On this marriage Don Clericuzio had commented sarcastically, "Do they think they can dance all their lives?"

The answer proved to be no. Nalene was not a good enough dancer to rise to the top, her legs paradoxically too long. She was of too serious a temperament to be a party girl. All this had made her settle for marriage. And she was happy for the first four years. She took care of the children, she attended classes at the University of Nevada and read voraciously.

But Pippi no longer was interested in the state of the environment, had no concern about the problems of whining blacks who couldn't even learn to steal without getting caught, and as far as the Native Americans, whoever they were, they could drown them at the bottom of the ocean. Discussions of books or music were completely beyond his horizon. And Nalene's demand that he never strike their children left him bewildered. Young children were animals; how could you make them behave in a civilized way without flinging them against a wall? He was always careful never to hurt them.

So in the fourth year of their marriage, Pippi took on mistresses. One in Las Vegas, one in Los Angeles, and one in New York. Nalene retaliated by getting her teaching degree.

They tried hard. They loved their children and made their lives pleasant. Nalene spent long hours with them reading and singing and dancing. The marriage was held together by Pippi's good humor. His vitality and animal exuberance somehow smoothed over the troubles of man and wife. The two children loved their mother and looked up to their father: the mother because she was so sweet and gentle, beautiful and full of natural affection; the father because he was strong.

Both parents were excellent teachers. From their mother, the children learned the social graces, good manners, dancing, how to dress, grooming. Their father taught the ways of the world, how to protect themselves from physical harm, how to gamble and train their bodies in athletics. They never resented their father for being physically rough with them, mainly because he did so only as discipline, never got angry when he did so, and then never held a grudge.

Cross was fearless but could bend. Claudia did not have her brother's physical courage but had a certain stubbornness. It helped that there was never any lack of money.

As the years went on, Nalene observed certain things. At first very small. When Pippi taught the children how to play cards—poker, blackjack, gin—he would stack the deck and clean them out of their allowance money, then at the end he would give them a glorious streak of luck so that they could fall asleep flushed with victory. What was curious was that Claudia as a child loved gambling far more than Cross. Later Pippi would demonstrate how he had cheated them. Nalene was angry, she felt he was playing with their lives as he played with hers. Pippi explained it was part of their education. She said it was not education but corruption. He said he wanted to prepare them for the reality of life, she wanted to prepare them for the beauty of life.

Pippi always had too much cash in his wallet, as suspicious a circumstance in the eyes of a wife as in the eyes of the tax collector. It was true that Pippi owned a thriving business, the Collection Agency, but they lived on too rich a scale for such a small operation.

When the family took vacations in the East and moved in the social circles of the Clericuzio Family, Nalene could not miss the respect with which Pippi was treated. She observed how careful men were with him, the deference, the long meetings the men held in private.

There were other little things. Pippi had to travel on business at least once a month. She never knew any of the details of his travel, and he never talked about his trips. He was legally licensed to carry a firearm, which was logical for a man whose business it was to collect large sums of money. He was very careful. Nalene and the children never had access to the weapon, he kept the bullets locked in separate cases.

As the years went by, Pippi took more trips, Nalene spent more time in her home with the children. Pippi and Nalene grew more apart sexually, and since Pippi was more tender and understanding in lust, they grew further and further apart.

It is impossible for a man to hide his true nature over a period of years from someone close to him. Nalene saw that Pippi was a man completely devoted to his own appetites, that he was violent in nature though never violent to her. That he was secretive, though he pretended openness. That though he was amiable, he was dangerous.

He had small personal follies that sometimes were endearing. For instance, other people had to enjoy what he enjoyed. Once they had taken a couple to dinner to an Italian restaurant. The couple did not particularly care for Italian food and ate sparingly. When Pippi observed this he could not finish his meal.

Sometimes he talked about his work at the Collection Agency. Nearly all the major hotels in Vegas were his clients, he collected delinquent gambling markers from customers who refused to pay up. He insisted to Nalene that force was never used, only a special kind of persuasion. It was a matter of honor that people pay their debts, everybody was responsible for their actions, and it offended him that men of substance did not always meet their obligations. Doctors, lawyers, heads of corporations, accepted the complimentary services of the hotel and then reneged on their side of the bargain. But they were easy to collect from. You went to their offices and made a loud fuss so that their clients and colleagues could hear. You made a scene, never a threat, called them deadbeats, degenerate gamblers who neglected their professions to wallow in vice.

Small business men were tougher, nickel-and-dime guys who tried to settle for a penny on a dollar. Then there were the clever ones who wrote checks that bounced and then claimed there had been a mistake. A favorite trick. They gave you a check for ten thousand when they only had eight thousand in their account. But Pippi had access to bank information, so he would merely deposit the extra two thousand to the man's account and then draw out the whole ten thousand. Pippi would laugh delightedly when he explained such coups to Nalene.

But the most important part of his job, Pippi explained to Nalene, was convincing a gambler not only to pay his debt but to keep gambling. Even a busted gambler had value. He worked. He earned money. So you simply had to postpone his debt, urge him to gamble in your casino without credit, and pay off his debt whenever he won.

One night Pippi told Nalene a story he thought enormously funny. That day he had been working in his Collection Agency office, which was in a small shopping mall near the Xanadu Hotel, when he heard gunfire in the street outside. He ran out just in time to see two masked armed men escaping from a neighboring jewelry shop. Without thinking Pippi drew his gun and fired at the men. They jumped into a waiting car and escaped. A few minutes later the police arrived, and after interrogating everyone, they arrested Pippi. Certainly they knew his gun was licensed, but by firing it he had committed a crime of "reckless endangerment." Alfred Gronevelt had gone down to the police station to bail him out.

"Why the hell did I do that?" Pippi asked. "Alfred said it was just the hunter in me. But I'll never understand. Me, shooting at robbers? Me, protecting society? And then they lock me up. They lock *me* up."

But these little revelations into his character were to some extent a clever ruse on Pippi's part, so that Nalene could glimpse part of his character without penetrating to the true secret. What made her finally decide on divorce was Pippi De Lena's arrest for murder. . . .

Danny Fuberta owned a New York travel agency that he had bought with his earnings as a loan shark under the protection of the now extinct Santadio Family. But he earned most of his livelihood as a Vegas junket master.

A junket master signed an exclusive contract with a Vegas hotel to transport vacationing gamblers into their clutches. Danny Fuberta chartered a 747 jet every month and recruited approximately two hundred customers to fly on it to the Xanadu Hotel. For a flat rate of a thousand dollars, the customer got a free round-trip flight from New York to Vegas, free booze and food in the air, free hotel rooms, free food and drink in the hotel. Fuberta always had a long waiting list for these junkets, and he picked his customers carefully. They had to be people with well-paying jobs, though not necessarily legal ones, and they had to gamble in the casino at least four hours every day. And, of course, where possible they had to establish credit at the Cashier's cage in the Hotel Xanadu.

One of Fuberta's greatest assets was his friendship with scam artists, bank robbers, drug dealers, cigarette smugglers, garment center hustlers, and other lowlifes who made handsome livings in the cesspools of New York. These men were prime customers. After all, they lived lives of great stress, they needed a relaxing vacation. They earned huge sums of black money, in cash, and they loved to gamble.

For every junket plane filled with two hundred customers that Danny Fuberta delivered to the Xanadu, he received a flat fee of twenty thousand dollars. Sometimes he received a bonus when the Xanadu customers lost heavily. All this in addition to the initial package charge provided him with a handsome monthly income. Unfortunately, Fuberta also had a weakness for gambling. And there came a time when his bills outpaced his income.

A resourceful man, Fuberta soon thought of a way to make himself solvent again. One of his duties as junket master was to certify the casino credit to be advanced to the junket customer.

Fuberta recruited a band of extremely competent armed robbers. With them Fuberta hatched a plan to steal $800,000 from the Xanadu Hotel.

Fuberta supplied the four men with false credentials identifying them as garment center owners with huge credit ratings, the particulars culled from his agency files. On the basis of these credentials, he certified them for the two-hundred-grand credit limit. Then he put them on the junket.

"Oh, they all had a picnic," Gronevelt said later.

During the two-day stay, Fuberta and his gang ran up huge room service bills, treated the beautiful chorus girls to dinner, signed for presents at the gift shop, but that was the least of it. They drew black chips from the casino, signed their markers.

They split into two teams. One team bet against the dice, the other team bet with the dice. In that way all they could lose was the percentage or break out even. So they drew a million dollars' worth of chips from the casino signing markers, which Fuberta later turned into cash. They looked like they were gambling furiously but were really treading water. In all this they created a great flurry of action. They fancied themselves actors, they implored the dice, they scowled when they lost, cheered when they won. At the end of the day they gave their chips to Fuberta to cash and signed markers to draw fresh chips from the cage. When the comedy ended two days later, the syndicate was $800,000 richer, they had been happy consumers of another twenty thousand in goodies, but they had a million dollars in markers in the cage.

Danny Fuberta, as the mastermind, got four hundred grand, and the four armed robbers were well satisfied with their share, especially when Fuberta promised them another shot. What could be better, a long weekend in the grand hotel, free food and booze, beautiful girls. And a hundred grand to boot. It was certainly better than robbing a bank where you risked your life.

Gronevelt uncovered the scam the very next day. The daily reports showed the markers high even for Fuberta's junket. The Drop at the table, the record of money kept after the night's play, was a figure too low for the amount of money wagered. Gronevelt called for the videotape from the "Eye in the Sky" surveillance camera. He didn't have to watch more than ten minutes before he understood the whole operation and know that the million dollars of markers was so much cigarette paper, the identities false.

His reaction was one of impatience. He had suffered countless scams over the years, but this one was so stupid. And he liked Danny Fuberta; the man had earned many dollars for the Xanadu. He knew what Fuberta would claim: that he, too, had been deceived by the false IDs, that he, too, was an innocent victim.

Gronevelt was annoyed by the incompetence of his Casino personnel. The Stick at the crap table should have caught on, and certainly the Box man should have picked up the cross-betting. It was not that clever a trick. But people went soft with good times, and Vegas was no exception. He thought regretfully that he would have to fire the Stick and the Box man, at least send them back to spinning a roulette wheel. But one thing he could not duck. He would have to turn the whole matter of Danny Fuberta over to the Clericuzio.

First he summoned Pippi De Lena to the hotel and showed him the documents and the film of the Eye in the Sky. Pippi knew Fuberta but not the other four men, so Gronevelt had snapshots made from isolated video stills and gave them to Pippi.

Pippi shook his head. "How the hell did Danny think he could get away with this? I thought he was a smart hustler."

"He's a gambler," Gronevelt said. "They believe their cards are always winning cards." He paused for a moment. "Danny will convince you he's not in on this. But remember, he had to certify that they were good for the money. He'll say he did it on the basis of their ID. A junket master has to certify that they are who they are. He had to know."

Pippi smiled and patted him on the back. "Don't worry, he won't convince me." They both laughed. It didn't matter if Danny Fuberta was guilty. He was responsible for his mistakes.

Pippi flew to New York the next day. To present the case to the Clericuzio Family in Quogue.

After passing through the guarded gates, he drove up the long paved road that cut through a long plateau of grass, its wall armed with barbed wire and electronics. There was a guard at the door of the mansion. And this was in a time of peace.

Giorgio greeted him, and he was led through the mansion into the garden at the rear. In the garden were tomato and cucumber plants, lettuce, and even melons, all framed by large-leafed fig trees. The Don had no use for flowers.

The Family was seated at the round wooden table eating an early lunch. There was the Don, glowing with health despite his near seventy years, visibly drinking in the fig-perfumed air of his garden. He was feeding his ten-year-old grandson, Dante, who was handsome but imperious for a boy the same age as Cross. Pippi always had the urge to give him a smack. The Don was putty in the hands of his grandson; he wiped his mouth, crooned endearments. Vincent and Pctic looked sour. The meeting could not start until the kid finished eating and was led away by his mother, Rose Marie. Don Domenico beamed at him as the boy walked away. Then he turned to Pippi.

"Ah, my *Martèllo*," he said. "What do you think of Fuberta, that rascal? We gave him a living and he grows greedy at our expense."

Giorgio said placatingly, "If he repays, he could still be a money-maker for us." The only valid plea for mercy.

"It's not a small sum of money," the Don said. "We must have it back. Pippi, what do you think?"

Pippi shrugged. "I can try. But these are people who don't save for a rainy day."

Vincent, who hated small talk, said, "Let's see the photos." Pippi produced the pictures and Vincent and Petie studied the four armed robbers. Then Vincent said, "Me and Petie know them."

"Good," Pippi said. "Then you can straighten out those four guys. What do you want me to do with Fuberta?"

The Don said, "They have shown contempt for us. Who do they think we are? Some helpless fools who have to go to the police? Vincent, Petie, you help Pippi. I want the money back and these *mascalzoni* punished." They understood. Pippi was to be in charge. The sentence on the five men was death.

The Don left them for his walk in the garden.

Giorgio sighed. "The old man is too tough for the times we live in. This is more risk than the whole thing is worth."

"Not if Vinnie and Pete handle the four hoods," Pippi said. "That OK with you, Vince?"

Vincent said, "Giorgio, you'll have to talk to the old man. Those four won't have the money. We have to make a deal. They go out and earn and pay us back and they're home free. If we bury them, no money."

Vincent was a realistic enforcer who never let the lust for blood overcome more practical solutions.

"OK, I can sell Pop that," Giorgio said. "They were just helpers. But he won't let Fuberta off."

"The junket masters have to get the message," Pippi said.

"Cousin Pippi," Giorgio said smiling, "what bonus do you expect on this?"

Pippi hated when Giorgio called him cousin. Vincent and Petie called him cousin out of affection, but Giorgio only did so when in negotiation.

"For Fuberta it's my duty," Pippi said. "You gave me the Collection Agency and I get wages from the Xanadu. But getting the money back is hard so I should get a percentage. Just as Vince and Petie if they get some from the hoods."

"That's fair," Giorgio said. "But this is not like collecting markers. You can't expect fifty percent."

"No, no," Pippi said, "just let me wet my beak."

They all laughed at the old Sicilian idiom. Petie said, "Giorgio, don't be cheap. You don't want to chisel me and Vincent." Petie now ran the Bronx Enclave, chief of the Enforcers, and he was always promoting the idea that the button men should get more money. He would split his share with his men.

"You guys are greedy," Giorgio said with a smile. "But I'll recommend twenty percent to the old man." Pippi knew that meant it would be fifteen or ten. It was an old story with Giorgio.

"How about we pool it?" Vince said to Pippi. Meaning the three of them would share whatever money was recovered no matter from whom. It was meant as a friendly gesture. There was a far better chance of recovering money from people who were to live than people who were to die. Vincent understood Pippi's value.

"Sure, Vince," Pippi said. "I'd appreciate that."

He saw Dante walking hand and hand with the Don far off at the edge of the garden. He heard Giorgio say, "Isn't it amazing how Dante and my father get along? My father was never that friendly to me. They whisper to each other all the time. Well, the old man is so smart, the kid will learn."

Pippi saw that the boy had his face turned up to the Don. The two looked as if they shared a terrible secret that would give them dominion over Heaven and Earth. Later Pippi would believe that this vision put on him the evil eye, and triggered his misfortune.

Pippi De Lena had gained his reputation over the years by his careful planning. He was not just some rampaging gorilla but a skilled technician. As such he relied on psychological strategy to help in the physical execution of a job. With Danny Fuberta there were three problems. First of all he had to get the money back. Second, he had to coordinate carefully with Vincent and Petie Clericuzio. (That part was easy. Vincent and Petie were extremely efficient in their work. In two days they tracked down the hoods, forced a confession, and arranged for compensation.) Then third, he had to kill Danny Fuberta.

It was easy for Pippi to run into Fuberta accidentally, to turn on his charm and insist the man be his guest for lunch at a Chinese restaurant on the East Side. Fuberta knew Pippi was a collector for the Xanadu, they had necessarily done business over the years, but Pippi seemed so delighted to run into him in New York that Fuberta could not refuse.

Pippi played it in a very low key. He waited until they had ordered and then he said, "Gronevelt told me about the scam. You know you have a responsibility for those guys being certified for credit."

Fuberta swore his innocence, and Pippi gave him a big grin and slapped him on the shoulder in a comradely way. "Come on Danny," he said, "Gronevelt has the tapes, and your four buddies already fessed up. You're in big trouble but I can square things if you give back the money. Maybe I can even keep you in the junket business."

To back up his statement, he took out the four photos of the hoods. "These are your boys," he said, "and right now they are spilling out their guts. Laying all the shit on you. They told us about the split. So if you come up with your four hundred grand, you're clear."

Fuberta said, "Sure, I know these boys, but they're tough guys, they wouldn't talk."

"It's the Clericuzio who are asking," Pippi said.

"Oh shit," Danny said. "I didn't know they had the Hotel."

"Now you know," Pippi said. "If they don't get the money back, you're in big trouble."

"I should just walk out of here," Fuberta said.

"No, no," Pippi said. "Stick around, the Peking duck is great. Look, this can be straightened out, it's no big deal. Everybody tries to scam once in awhile, right? Just get the money back."

"I don't have a dime," Fuberta said.

For the first time Pippi showed some irritation. "You have to show a little respect," Pippi said. "Give a hundred thousand back and we'll take your marker for the other three hundred."

Fuberta thought it over as he munched a fried dumpling. "I can give you fifty," he said.

"That's good, that's very good," Pippi said. "You can pay off the rest by not taking your fee for running junkets to the Hotel. Is that fair?"

"I guess," Fuberta said.

"Don't worry any more, enjoy the food," Pippi said. He rolled some duck into a pancake, anointed it with black sweet sauce, and handed it to Fuberta. "This is terrific, Danny," he said. "Eat. Then we do business."

They ate chocolate ice cream for dessert and made arrangements for Pippi to pick up the fifty grand at Fuberta's travel agency after working hours. Pippi grabbed the lunch check, paying cash. "Danny," he said, "you notice how chocolate ice cream in a Chinese restaurant has so much cocoa? The best. You know what I think? The first Chinese restaurant in America got the recipe wrong and the ones that came after just copied that first wrong recipe. Great. Great chocolate ice cream."

But Danny Fuberta had not hustled for the forty-eight years of his life without being able to read the signs. After leaving Pippi he dived underground, sending a message that he was traveling to collect the money he owed the Xanadu Hotel. Pippi was not surprised. Fuberta was only using tactics common in such cases. He had disappeared so that he could negotiate in safety. Which meant he had no money and there would be no bonus unless Vincent and Petie collected on their end.

Pippi drew some men from the Bronx Enclave to scour the city. The word was put out that Danny Fuberta was wanted by the Clericuzio. A week went by, and Pippi became more and more irritated. He should have known that Fuberta would only be alerted by the demand for repayment. That Fuberta had figured out that fifty grand would not be enough, if he even had fifty grand.

After another week, Pippi became impatient, so that when the break came he moved more daringly than was prudent.

Danny Fuberta surfaced in a small restaurant on the Upper West Side. The owner, a Clericuzio soldier, made a quick call. Pippi arrived just as Fuberta was leaving the restaurant and, to Pippi's surprise, drew a gun. Fuberta was a hustler, had no experience in strong-arm. So when he fired, the shot was wide. Pippi put five bullets in him.

There were a few unfortunate things about this scene. One, there were eyewitnesses. Two, a patrol car arrived before Pippi could make his getaway. Three, Pippi had made no preparation for a shooting, he had meant to talk Fuberta into a secure location. Four, though a case could be made for self-defense, some witnesses said that Pippi shot first. It came down to the old truism that you were more in danger with the law when you were innocent than when you were guilty. Also, Pippi had a silencer on his gun, in preparation for his final friendly chat with Fuberta.

It helped matters that Pippi reacted perfectly to the disastrous arrival of the patrol car. He did not try to shoot his way out but followed the guidelines. The Clericuzio had a strict injunction: Never fire at an officer of the law. Pippi did not. He dropped his gun to the pavement, then kicked it away. He submitted peacefully to arrest and denied completely any connection with the dead man lying just a few feet away.

Such contingencies were foreseen and planned against. After all, no matter how much care was taken, there was always the malignancy of fate. Pippi now seemed to be drowning in a typhoon of ill fortune, but he knew he had only to let himself relax, that he could count on the Clericuzio Family to tow him to shore.

First there were the high-priced defense lawyers who would get him out on bail. Then there were the judges and prosecutors who could be persuaded to become stalwart in the defense of fair play, the witnesses whose memory could be made to fail, the staunchly independent American jurors who if given the slightest encouragement would refuse to convict in order to foil authority. A soldier of the Clericuzio Family did not have to shoot his way out of trouble like some mad dog.

But for the first time in his long service to the Family, Pippi De Lena had to stand trial in a court of law. And the usual legal strategy was that his wife and children must attend the trial. The jurors must know that on their decision rested the happiness of this innocent family. Twelve men and women tried and true had to harden their hearts. "Reasonable doubt" was a godsend to a juror wrung by pity.

During the trial, the police officers testified they had not seen Pippi with the gun or kicking it. Three of the eyewitnesses could not identify the defendant, the other two were so adamant in their identification of Pippi that they alienated jury and judge. The Clericuzio soldier who owned the restaurant testified that he had followed Danny Fuberta out of the restaurant because the man had not paid his check, that he had witnessed the shooting, and that the shooter definitely was not Pippi De Lena, the defendant.

Pippi had worn gloves at the time of the shooting, which was why there were no prints on the gun. Medical evidence was given for the defense that Pippi De Lena suffered from intermittent skin rashes, mysterious and incurable, and that the wearing of gloves had been recommended.

As maximum insurance a juror had been bribed. After all, Pippi was a high executive in the Family. But this final precaution had not been needed. Pippi was acquitted and deemed forever innocent in the eyes of the law.

But not by his wife, Nalene De Lena. Six months after the trial, Nalene told Pippi they must divorce.

There is a cost for those who live on a high level of tension. Physical parts of the body wear down. Excessive eating and drinking tax the liver and heart. Sleep is criminally evasive, the mind does not respond to beauty and will not invest in trust. Pippi and Nalene both suffered from this. She could not bear him in her bed, and he could not enjoy a partner who did not share his enjoyment. She could not hide the horror of knowing he was a murderer. He felt an enormous amount of relief that he did not any longer have to hide his true self from her.

"OK, we'll divorce," Pippi said to Nalene. "But I'm not losing my kids."

"I know who you are now," Nalene said. "I won't see you again and I will not have my children living with you."

This surprised Pippi. Nalene had never been forceful or outspoken. And it surprised him that she dared to speak to him, Pippi De Lena, in such a fashion. But women were always reckless. He then considered his own position. He was not equipped to bring up children. Cross was eleven and Claudia was ten, and he recognized the fact that, despite his closeness with Cross, both children loved their mother more than they did him.

He wanted to be fair to his wife. After all, he had received from her what he wanted, a family, children, a bedrock to his life, which every man needed. Who knew what he would have become if it had not been for her?

"Let's reason this out," he said. "Let's split without any bad feelings." He turned on the charm. "What the hell, we've had a good twelve years. We've had some happy times. And we have two wonderful kids, thanks to you." He paused, surprised again by her stern face. "Come on Nalene, I've been a good father, my kids like me. And I'll help you in whatever you want to do. Naturally you can keep the house here in Vegas. And I can get you one of the shops in the Xanadu. Dresses, jewelry, antiques. You'll earn your two hundred grand a year. And we can sort of share the kids."

Nalene said, "I hate Las Vegas. I always did. I have my teaching degree and a job in Sacramento. I've already enrolled the children in school up there."

It was at that moment that Pippi, with a sense of astonishment, realized that she was an opponent, she was dangerous. It was a concept completely foreign to him. Women, in his frame of reference, were never dangerous. Not a wife, not a mistress, not an aunt, not the wife of a friend, not even the daughter of the Don, Rose Marie. Pippi had always lived in a world where women could not be an enemy. Suddenly he felt that rage, that flow of energy, that he could feel toward men.

Out of that he said, "I'm not going to Sacramento to see my kids." He always became angry when someone rejected his charm, refused his friendship. Anyone who refused to be reasonable with Pippi De Lena was courting disaster. Once he decided on confrontation, Pippi took it to the limit. Also, he was astonished that his wife had already made plans.

"You said you know who I am," Pippi said. "So be very careful. You can move to Sacramento, you can move to the bottom of the ocean for all I care. But you take only one of my children with you. The other stays with me."

Nalene looked at him coolly. "The court will decide that," she said. "I think you should get a lawyer to talk to my lawyer." She almost laughed in his face when she saw his astonishment.

"You have a lawyer?" Pippi said. "You're taking me to the law?" Then he began to laugh. His laughter seemed to carry him away. He was almost hysterical.

It was strange to see a man who for twelve years had been a supplicating lover, a beggar for her flesh, her protection from the cruelties of the world, turn into a dangerous and threatening beast. At that moment she finally understood why other men had treated him with such respect, why they feared him. Now his ugly charm had none of that geniality that was so disarming. Oddly, she was not so much frightened as she was hurt that his love for her could so easily vanish. After all, for twelve years they had cradled each other's flesh, laughed together, danced together, and nurtured their children together, and now his gratitude for the gifts she had given him counted for nothing.

Pippi said to her coldly, "I don't care what you decide. I don't care what a judge decides. Be reasonable and I'll be reasonable. Be tough and you won't have anything."

For the first time she was terrified of all the things she loved; his powerful body, his large, heavy-boned hands, the irregular, blunt features she had always thought manly, that other people called ugly. All through their marriage, he had been more courtier than husband, had never raised his voice to her, had never even made a mild joke at her expense, had never scolded when she ran up bills. And it was true he had been a good father, only rough with the kids when they did not show respect for their mother.

She felt faint, but Pippi's face became more distinct, as though framed in some shadow. Extra flesh padded his cheeks, the very slight cleft in his chin seemed to be filled in with a tiny dot of black putty. His thick eyebrows had spears of white in them, but the hair on his massive skull was black, each strand as thick as horsehair. His eyes, usually so merry, were now a merciless flat tan.

"I thought you loved me," Nalene said. "How can you frighten me so?" She began to weep.

This disarmed Pippi. "Listen to me," he said. "Don't listen to your lawyer. You go to court, let's say I lose all the way down the line. You're still not going to get both kids. Nalene, don't make me be tough, I don't want to be. I understand you don't want to live with me anymore. I always thought I was so lucky to have you as long as I did. I want you to be happy. You'll get far more from me than you'll get from any court judge. But I'm getting old, I don't want to live without a family."

For one of the few times in her life Nalene could not resist malice. "You have the Clericuzio," she said.

"So I have," Pippi said. "You should remember that. But the important thing is, I don't want to be alone in my old age."

"Millions of men are," Nalene said. "And women too."

"Because they're helpless," Pippi said. "Strangers decide their lives. Other people veto their existence. I don't let anyone do that."

Nalene said scornfully, "You veto them?"

"That's right," Pippi said. He smiled down at her. "That's exactly right."

"You can visit them all you want," Nalene said. "But they both have to live with me."

At that he turned his back and said quietly, "Do what you want."

Nalene said, "Wait." Pippi turned to her. She saw on his face something so terrible in its soulless ferocity that she murmured, "If one of them wants to go with you, then OK."

Pippi suddenly became exuberant, as if the problem were resolved. "That's great," he said. "Your kid can visit me in Vegas and my kid can visit you in Sacramento. That's perfect. Let's settle it tonight."

Nalene made a last effort. "Forty is not old," she said. "You can start another family."

Pippi shook his head. "Never," he said. "You're the only woman who ever had the Indian sign on me. I married late and I know I'll never marry again. You're lucky I'm smart enough to know I can't keep you, and I'm smart enough to know I can't start over again."

"That's true," Nalene said. "You can't make me love you again."

"But I could kill you," Pippi said. He was smiling at her. As if it were a joke.

She looked into his eyes and believed him. She realized this was the source of his power, that when he made a threat people believed him. She summoned her last reserve of courage.

"Remember," she said, "if they both want to stay with me, you have to let them go."

"They love their father," Pippi said. "One of them will stay here with their old man."


That evening after dinner, the house iced with air conditioning, the desert heat outside too strong, the situation was explained to Cross, eleven years old, and Claudia, ten. Neither seemed surprised. Cross, as handsome as his mother was beautiful, already had the inner steeliness of his father, and his wariness. He was also completely without fear. He spoke up instantly. "I'm staying with Mom," he said.

Claudia was frightened by the choice. With a small child's cunning, she said, "I'm staying with Cross."

Pippi was surprised. Cross was closer to him than to Nalene. Cross was the one who came hunting with him, Cross liked to play cards with him, to golf and box. Cross had no interest in his mother's obsession with books and music. It was Cross who came down to the Collection Agency to keep him company when he had to catch up on paperwork on Saturday. In fact he had been sure that Cross would be the one he would get to keep. It was Cross he was hoping for.

He was tickled by Claudia's cunning answer. The kid was smart. But Claudia looked too much like himself, he didn't want to look at an ugly mug so much like his every day. And it was logical that Claudia go with her mother. Claudia loved the same things Nalene did. What the hell would he do with Claudia?

Pippi studied his two children. He was proud of them. They knew their mother was the weaker of the two parents, and they were sticking up for her. And he noticed that Nalene, with her theatrical instinct, had prepared cleverly for the occasion. She was dressed severely in black trousers and a black pullover, her golden hair was bound severely with a thin black headband, her face framed into a narrow, heartbreaking white oval. He was conscious of his own brutal appearance as it must appear to small children.

He turned on his charm. "All I'm asking is for one of you to keep me company," he said. "You can see each other as much as you want. Right Nalene? You kids don't want me living here in Vegas all alone."

The two children looked at him sternly. He turned to Nalene. "You have to help," he said. "You have to choose." And then he thought angrily, Why do I give a shit?

Nalene said, "You promised that if they both wanted to go with me, they could."

"Let's talk this out," Pippi said. His feelings were not hurt—he knew his children loved him, but they loved their mother more. He found that natural. It did not mean they had made the right choice.

Nalene said scornfully, "There's nothing to talk about. You promised."

Pippi did not know how terrible he looked to the other three. Did not know how cold his eyes became. He thought he had controlled his voice when he spoke, he thought he spoke reasonably.

"You've got to make a choice. I promise that if it doesn't work out, you can have your own way. But I have to have a chance."

Nalene shook her head. "You're ridiculous," she said. "We'll go to court."

At that moment Pippi made up his mind what he had to do. "It doesn't matter. You can have your way. But think about this. Think about our life together. Think about who you are and who I am. I beg of you to be reasonable. To think about all our futures. Cross is like me, Claudia is like you. Cross would be better off with me, Claudia would be better off with you. That's the way it is." He paused for a moment. "Isn't it enough for you to know they both love you better than me? That they would miss you more than they would me?" The last phrase hung in the air. He did not want the children to understand what he was saying.

But Nalene understood. Out of terror, she reached out and pulled Claudia close to her. At that moment Claudia looked at her brother beseechingly and said, "Cross . . ."

Cross had an impassive beauty of face. His body moved gracefully. Suddenly he was standing beside his father. "I'll go with you, Dad," he said. And Pippi took his hand gratefully.

Nalene was weeping now. "Cross, you'll visit me often, as much as you want. You'll have a special bedroom in Sacramento. Nobody else will use it." It was, finally, a betrayal.

Pippi almost bounded into the air with exuberance. It was such a weight lifted from his soul that he would not have to do what he had for one instant decided to do. "We have to celebrate," he said. "Even when we divorce, we'll be two happy families instead of one happy family. And live happily forever after." The others stared at him stony faced. "Well, what the hell, we'll try," he said.


Claudia never visited her brother and father in Vegas after the first two years. Cross went every year to Sacramento to visit Nalene and Claudia, but by his fifteenth year the visits dwindled to the Christmas holidays.

The two different parents were two different poles in life. Claudia and her mother became more and more alike. Claudia loved school; she loved books, the theater, films; she reveled in her mother's love. And Nalene found in Claudia her father's high spiritedness, his charm. She loved her plainness, which had none of the brutality of her father. They were happy together.

Claudia finished college and went to live in Los Angeles to try her hand in the film business. Nalene was sorry to see her go, but she had built up a satisfactory life with friends in Sacramento and had become an assistant principal at one of the public high schools.

Cross and Pippi had also become a happy family, but in a far different way. Pippi weighed the facts. Cross was an exceptional athlete in high school but an indifferent student. He had no interest in college. And although he had extraordinarily good looks, he was not excessively interested in women.

Cross enjoyed life with his father. Indeed, no matter how ugly the decision that had been made, it seemed to have turned out to be the right one. Indeed two happy families, but not together. Pippi proved to be as good a parent to Cross as Nalene was to Claudia, that is, he made Cross in his image.

Cross loved the workings of the Xanadu Hotel, the manipulation of customers, the fight against scam artists. And Cross did have a normal appetite for the showgirls; after all, Pippi must not judge his son by himself. Pippi decided that Cross would have to join the Family. Pippi believed the Don's oft-repeated words, "The most important thing in life is to earn your bread."

Pippi took Cross in as a partner in the Collection Agency. He brought him to the Xanadu Hotel for dinner with Gronevelt and maneuvered so that Gronevelt would take an interest in his son's welfare. He made Cross one of the foursome in his golf games with high-rolling gamblers at the Xanadu, always pairing Cross against himself. Cross, at the age of seventeen, had that particular virtue of the golf hustler, he played much better on a particular hole where the bets were high. Cross and his partner usually won. Pippi accepted these defeats with good grace; though they cost him money, they earned his son an enormous amount of goodwill.

He took Cross to New York for the social occasions of the Clericuzio Family: all holidays—particularly the Fourth of July, which the Clericuzio Family celebrated with great patriotic fervor; all the Clericuzio weddings, and funerals. After all, Cross was their first cousin, he had the blood of Don Clericuzio running in his veins.

When Pippi made his once-a-week foray at the tables of the Xanadu to win his eight-thousand-dollar weekly retainer with his special dealer, Cross sat watching. Pippi instructed him in the percentages of all forms of gambling. He taught him the management of the gambling bankroll, never to play when he felt unwell, never to play for more than two hours a day, never to play more than three days a week, never to bet heavily when he was on a losing streak, and always to ride a winning streak with a cautious intensity.

It did not seem unnatural to Pippi that a father should let his son see the ugliness of the real world. As the junior partner in the Collection Agency, it was very necessary for Cross to have such knowledge. For the collections were sometimes not as benign as Pippi had described to Nalene.

On a few of the more difficult collections, Cross showed no signs of abhorrence. He was yet too young and too pretty to inspire fear, but his body looked strong enough to enforce any orders Pippi might give.

Finally Pippi, to test his son, sent him out on a particularly tough case, where only persuasion, not force, could be used. The sending of Cross was in itself a signal that the collection would not be pressed, a sign of goodwill to the debtor. The debtor, a very small Mafia *Bruglione* in the northern corner of California, owed a hundred grand to the Xanadu. It was not a big enough matter to involve the Clericuzio name, things had to be handled on a lower level, the velvet glove rather than the iron fist.

Cross caught the Mafia Baron at a bad time. The man, Falco, listened to the reasoned approach made by Cross, then took out a gun and held it to the young man's throat. "Another word out of you and I'll shoot out your fucking tonsils," Falco said.

Cross, to his own surprise, felt no fear. "Settle for fifty grand," he said, "You wouldn't want to kill me for a lousy fifty grand? My father wouldn't like it."

"Who's your father?" Falco asked, his gun still steady.

Cross said, "Pippi De Lena, and he's going to shoot me anyway for settling for fifty grand."

Falco laughed and put his gun away. "OK, tell them I'll pay the next time I come to Vegas."

Cross said, "Just call me when you come in. I'll give you your usual comp RFB."

Falco had recognized Pippi's name, but there had also been something in Cross's face that had stopped him. The lack of fear, the coolness of his response, the little joke. All of this smacked of someone whose friends would avenge him. But the incident persuaded Cross to carry a weapon and a bodyguard on his future collections.

Pippi celebrated his courage with a vacation for both of them at the Xanadu. Gronevelt gave them two good suites and a purse of black chips for Cross.

At this time Gronevelt was eighty years old, white-haired, but his tall body was vigorous and still supple. He also had a pedagogical streak. He delighted in instructing Cross. When he handed him the purse of black chips, he said, "You can't win so I'll get these back. Now listen to me, you have one chance. My hotel has other diversions. A great golf course, gamblers from Japan come here to play on it. We have gourmet restaurants and wonderful girlie shows in our theater with the greatest stars from film and music. We have tennis courts and swimming pools. We have a special tour plane that can fly you over the Grand Canyon. All free. So there's no excuse that the five grand you have in that purse should be lost. Don't gamble."

On that three-day vacation, Cross followed Gronevelt's advice. Every morning he golfed with Gronevelt, his father, and a high roller staying at the Hotel. The betting was always substantial but never outrageous. Gronevelt noted with approval that Cross was at his best when the stakes were highest. "Nerves of steel, nerves of steel," Gronevelt said admiringly to Pippi.

But what Gronevelt approved of most was the kid's good judgment, his intelligence, his knowing the proper thing to do without being told. On the last morning, the high roller playing with them was in a sullen mood and with good reason. A skillful and ardent gambler, tremendously wealthy from a lucrative string of porn houses, he had lost nearly $500,000 the night before. It was not so much the money itself that bothered him as the fact that he had lost control in the middle of a streak of bad luck and had tried to press himself out of it; the mistake of a callow gambler.

That morning when Gronevelt proposed the moderate stake of fifty dollars a hole, he sneered and said, "Alfred, with what you took off me last night, you could afford a grand a hole."

Gronevelt was offended by this. His early-morning golf was a social occasion; linking it to the business of the Hotel was bad manners. But with his usual courtesy he said, "Of course. I'll even give you Pippi as your partner. I'll play with Cross."

They played. The porn house magnate shot well. So did Pippi. So did Gronevelt. Only Cross failed. He played the worst game of golf the others had ever seen. He hooked his drives, he dived into the bunkers, his ball sailed into the little pond (built on the Nevada desert at enormous expense), his nerve broke completely when he putted. The porn-house magnate, five thousand dollars richer, his ego restored, insisted on them sharing breakfast.

Cross said, "Sorry I let you down, Mr. Gronevelt."

Gronevelt looked at him gravely and said, "Someday, with your father's permission, you'll have to come work for me."

Cross, over the years, had observed closely the relationship between his father and Gronevelt. They were good friends, had dinner together once a week, and Pippi always deferred to Gronevelt in a very obvious way, which he did not do even with the Clericuzio. Gronevelt in his turn didn't seem to fear Pippi yet gave him every courtesy of the Xanadu, except a Villa. Plus Cross had caught on to Pippi's winning eight thousand dollars every week at the Hotel. Cross then made the connection. The Clericuzio and Alfred Gronevelt were partners in the Xanadu Hotel.

And Cross was aware that Gronevelt had some special interest in him, showed him extra consideration. As witness the gift of black chips on this vacation. And there had been many other kindnesses. Cross had total comp at the Xanadu for himself and his friends. When Cross graduated from high school, Gronevelt's present had been a convertible. From the time he was seventeen, Gronevelt had introduced him to the showgirls of the Hotel with obvious affection, to give him some weight. And Cross, over the years, came to know that Gronevelt himself, old as he was, often had women to his penthouse suite for dinner, and from the gossip of the girls, Gronevelt was a catch. He never had a serious love affair, but he was so extraordinarily generous with his gifts that the women were in awe of him. Any woman who stayed in his favor for a month became rich.

Once in one of their teacher and pupil talks, as Gronevelt instructed him in the lore of running a great casino hotel like the Xanadu, Cross dared to ask him about women in the context of employee relations.

Gronevelt smiled at him. "I leave the women in the shows to the entertainment director. The other women I treat exactly as if they were men. But if you're asking advice about your love life, I must tell you this. An intelligent, reasonable man in most cases has nothing to fear from women. You must beware of two things. Number one and most dangerous: the damsel in distress. Two: a woman who has more ambition than you do. Now don't think I'm heartless, I can make the same case for women, but that's not to our purpose. I was lucky, I loved the Xanadu more than anything else in the world. But I must tell you I regret not having any children."

"You seem to live the perfect life," Cross said.

"You think so?" Gronevelt said. "Well, I pay the price."


At the mansion in Quogue, a great fuss was made over Cross by the females of the Clericuzio Family. At the age of twenty he was in the full flower of youthful maleness—handsome, graceful, strong, and for his age, surprisingly courtly. The Family made jokes, not entirely free from Sicilian peasant malice, that thank God he looked like his mother and not his father.

On Easter Sunday, while more than a hundred relatives were celebrating Christ's resurrection, the final piece of the puzzle about his father was made clear to Cross by his cousin Dante.

In the vast walled garden of the Family mansion, Cross saw a beautiful young girl holding court with a group of young men. He watched his father go over to the buffet table for a platter of grilled sausage and make a friendly remark to the girl's group. He saw the girl visibly shrinking away from Pippi. Women usually liked his father; his ugliness, his good humor and high spirits disarmed them.

Dante had also observed this. "Beautiful girl," he said, smiling. "Let's go over and say hello."

He made the introductions. "Lila," he said, "this is our cousin Cross."

Lila was their age but not yet fully developed as a woman; she had the slightly imperfect beauty of adolescence. Her hair was the color of honey, her skin glowed as if refreshed from some inner stream, but her mouth was too vulnerable, as if not fully formed. She wore a white angora sweater that turned her skin to gold. Cross fell in love with her for that moment.

But when he tried to speak to her, Lila ignored him and walked to the sanctuary of matrons at another table.

Cross said a little sheepishly to Dante, "I guess she doesn't like my looks." Dante smiled at him wickedly.

Dante had turned into a curious young man with enormous vitality and a sharp, cunning face. He had the coarse black hair of the Clericuzio, which he kept confined underneath a curious Renaissance-style cap. He was very short, no more than five feet and a few inches, but he had an enormous confidence, perhaps because he was the favorite of the old Don. He carried with him always the air of malice. Now he said to Cross, "Her last name is Anacosta."

Cross remembered the name. A year before the Anacosta Family had suffered a tragedy. The head of the family and his oldest son had been shot to death in a Miami hotel room. But Dante was looking at Cross, waiting for some sort of answer. Cross made his face impassive. "So?" he said.

Dante said, "You work for your father, right?"

"Sure," Cross said.

"And you try to date Lila?" Dante said. "You're sick." He laughed.

Cross knew this was danger of some kind. He remained silent. Dante went on, "Don't you know what your father does?"

"He collects money," Cross said.

Dante shook his head. "You have to know. Your Dad takes people out for the Family. He's their number one Hammer."

It seemed to Cross that all the mysteries of his life were blown away on a sorcerer's wind. Everything was very clear. His mother's disgust of his father, the respect shown Pippi by his friends and the Clericuzio Family, his father's mysterious disappearances for weeks at a time, the weapon he always carried, sly little jokes he had not understood. He remembered his father's trial for murder, dismissed from his childhood memories in some curious way the night his father had taken his hand. Then, a sudden warmth for his father, a feeling that he must protect him in some way now that he was so naked.

But over all this Cross felt a terrible anger that Dante had dared to tell him this truth.

He said to Dante, "No, I don't know that. And you don't know that. Nobody knows that." He almost said, And you can go fuck yourself you little creep, but instead he smiled at Dante and said, "Where the hell did you get that fuckin' hat?"


Virginio Ballazzo was organizing the children's Easter egg hunt with the panache of a born clown. He gathered the children around him, beautiful flowers in Easter garb, their tiny faces like petals, skin like eggshells, hats beribboned with pink, and their faces rosy with excitement. Ballazo gave each of them a straw basket and a fond kiss and then shouted to them, "Go!" The children scattered.

Virginio Ballazzo himself was a treat to look at, his suits made in London, his shoes in Italy, shirts in France, his hair cut by a Michelangelo of Manhattan. Life had been good to Virginio and had blessed him with a daughter almost as beautiful as the children.

Lucille, called Ceil, was eighteen years old and on this day served as her father's assistant. As she handed out baskets, the men on the lawn whistled to themselves over her beauty. She was in shorts and an open white blouse. Her skin was dark with an undertone of rich cream. Her black hair was twisted around her head like a crown, and so she stood a youthful queen created by superb health, youth, and the genuine happiness that high spirits can give.

Now out of the corner of her eye she could see Cross and Dante quarreling, and she saw that for a moment Cross had suffered a crushing blow, his mouth crumpling.

She had one basket left on her arm, and she walked over to where Dante and Cross were standing. "Which one of you wants to hunt for eggs?" she asked, her smile flashing with good humor. She held out the basket.

The two of them looked at her with dazed admiration. The late-morning light turned her skin to gold, her eyes danced in delight. The white blouse swelled invitingly and yet so virginally, her round thighs milky white.

At that moment, one of the little girls began to scream. They all looked toward her. The child had found a huge egg, as big as a bowling ball and painted with vivid reds and blues. The child had been struggling to put it in her basket, her beautiful white straw hat askew, her face wide-eyed with astonishment and resolution. But the egg broke and a small bird flew out, which is what made the child scream.

Petie ran across the lawn and scooped up the young child to comfort her. It was one of his practical jokes, and the crowd laughed.

The little girl carefully straightened her hat, then shouted in a treble voice, "You tricked me," and slapped Petie in the face. The crowd roared with laughter as she ran away from Petie, who was still pleading for forgiveness. He caught her up in his arms and gave her a jeweled Easter Egg dangling from a gold chain. The little girl took it and gave him a kiss.

Ceil took Cross by the hand and led him to the tennis court, which was a hundred yards from the mansion. They sat in the three-walled tennis hut, its exposed side away from the festivities, so they could have privacy.

Dante watched them go with a sense of humiliation. He was very conscious that Cross was more attractive, and he felt snubbed. Yet he felt proud to have such a handsome cousin. To his surprise he found himself holding the basket, so he shrugged and joined the Easter egg hunt.

Hidden in the tennis shack, Ceil took Cross's face in her hands and kissed him on the lips. They were tender, brushing kisses. But when he put his hands under her blouse, she pushed him away. She had a brilliant smile on her face. "I wanted to kiss you since I was ten years old," she said. "And today was such a perfect day."

Cross was aroused by her kisses but only said, "Why?"

"Because you're so beautiful and so perfect," Ceil said. "Nothing is wrong on a day like today." She slipped her hand into his. "Don't we have wonderful families?" she said. Then abruptly she asked, "Why did you stay with your father?"

"It was just the way it worked out," Cross said.

"And did you just have a fight with Dante?" Ceil asked. "He's such a creep."

"Dante is OK," Cross said. "We were just kidding around. He's just a practical joker like my Uncle Petie."

"Dante is too rough," Ceil said, then kissed Cross again. She held his hands tight. "My father is making so much money, he's buying a house in Kentucky and a 1920 Rolls-Royce. He has three antique cars now and he's going to buy horses in Kentucky. Why don't you come over tomorrow and see the cars? You always loved my mother's cooking."

"I have to go back to Vegas tomorrow," Cross said. "I work in the Xanadu now."

Ceil gave his hand a tug. "I hate Vegas," she said. "I think it's a disgusting city."

"I think it's great," Cross said, smiling. "Why do you hate it if you've never been there?"

"Because people throw away hard-earned money," Ceil said with youthful indignation. "Thank God my father doesn't gamble. And all those sleazy showgirls."

Cross laughed. "I wouldn't know," he said. "I just run the golf course. I've never seen the inside of the casino."

She knew he was making fun of her, but she said, "If I invite you to visit me at college when I go away, will you come?"

"Sure," Cross said. In this game he was far more experienced than she was. And he felt a tenderness about her innocence, her holding of his hands, her ignorance of her father and the Family's true purpose. He understood that she was just staking out a tentative claim, the lovely weather, the explosion of celebration in her body of womanhood, and he was touched by the sweet, unsexy kisses.

"We better go back to the party," he said, and they strolled hand in hand to the picnic area. Her father, Virginio, was the first to notice them and rubbed one finger against another and said, "Shame, shame," gleefully. Then he embraced them both. It was a day Cross always remembered for its innocence, the young children chastely clad in white to announce the resurrection, and because he finally understood who his father was.

When Pippi and Cross went back to Vegas, things were different between them. Pippi obviously knew that the secret was out, and he paid Cross some attentions of extra affection. Cross was surprised that his feeling toward his father had not changed, that he still loved him. He could not imagine a life without his father, without the Clericuzio Family, without Gronevelt and the Xanadu Hotel. This was the life he had to lead, and he was not unhappy to lead it. But there began to build up in him an impatience. Another step had to be taken.

# BOOK III

## Claudia De Lena
## Athena Aquitane

# CHAPTER 4

CLAUDIA DE LENA drove from her apartment on the Pacific Palisades toward Athena's Malibu house and pondered what she would say to persuade Athena to come back to work on *Messalina*.

It was as important to her as it was to the Studio. *Messalina* was her first truly original script; her other work had been adaptations of novels, rewrites or doctoring of other scripts, or collaborations.

Also, she was a coproducer of *Messalina,* which gave her a power she had never previously enjoyed. Plus an adjusted gross of the profits. She would see some really big money. And she could then take the next step, to producer-writer. She was perhaps the only person west of the Mississippi who did not want to direct; that required a cruelty in human relationships that she could not tolerate.

Claudia's relationship with Athena was a true intimacy, not the professional friendship of fellow workers in the movie industry. Athena would know how much the picture meant to her career. Athena was intelligent. What really puzzled Claudia was Athena's fear of Boz Skannet. Athena had never been afraid of anything or anyone.

Well, one thing she would accomplish. She would find out exactly why Athena was so fearful, and then she could help. And certainly, she had to save Athena from ruining her own career. After all, who knew more about the intricacies and traps of the movie business than she did?

Claudia De Lena dreamed of a life as a writer in New York. She was not discouraged when, at the age of twenty-one, her first novel was turned down by twenty publishers. Instead, she decided to move to Los Angeles and try her hand at movie scripts.

Because she was witty and vivacious and talented, she soon made many friends in Los Angeles. She enrolled in a movie-script writing course at UCLA and met a young man whose father was a famous plastic surgeon. She and the young man became lovers, and he was bewitched by her body and intelligence. He revised her status from comradely bed partner to "serious relationship." He brought her home to his family for dinner. His father, the plastic surgeon, was enchanted by her. After dinner the surgeon put his hands around her face.

"It's unfair that a girl like you is not as pretty as you should be," he said. "Don't take offense, it's a perfectly natural misfortune. And it's my business. I can fix it if you let me."

Claudia was not offended, but she was indignant. "Why the hell should I be pretty? What good does that do me?" she said with a smile. "I'm pretty enough for your son."

"All the good in the world," the surgeon said. "And when I get through with you, you'll be too good for my son. You are a sweet and intelligent girl, but looks are power. Do you really want to spend the rest of your life standing around while men flock to good-looking women who have not one tenth of your intelligence? And you have to sit around like a dummy because your nose is too thick and you have a chin like a Mafia hood." As he said this he patted her cheek and said gently, "It won't take much doing. You have beautiful eyes and a beautiful mouth. And your figure is good enough for a movie star."

Claudia flinched away from him. She knew she resembled her father; the Mafia hood remark had touched a nerve.

"It doesn't matter," she said. "I can't pay your fee."

"Another thing," the surgeon said. "I know the movie business. I have prolonged the careers of stars male and female. Now when the day comes for you to pitch a movie at a studio, your looks will play an important part. That may seem unfair to you, I know you're talented. But that's the movie world. Just think of it as a professional move, not some male-female thing. Though of course it is." He saw that she still hesitated. "I'll do it without a fee," he said. "I'll do it for you and for my son. Even though I fear that once you're as pretty as I think you will be, he will lose a girlfriend."

Claudia had always known she was not pretty, now the memory of her father preferring Cross came back to her. If she had been pretty, would her destiny have been changed? For the first time she took a good look at the surgeon. He was a handsome man, his eyes were gentle as if he understood everything she was feeling. She laughed. "Okay," she said. "Turn me into Cinderella."

The surgeon didn't have to do that much. He thinned her nose, rounded her chin, and scaled her skin. When Claudia reentered the world, she was a handsome, proud-looking woman with a perfect nose, a commanding presence, perhaps not quite pretty but somehow even more attractive.

The professional results were magical. Claudia, despite her youth, obtained a personal interview with Melo Stuart, who became her agent. He got her minor rewrites on scripts and invited her to parties where she met producers, directors, and stars. They were enchanted by her. In the next five years, despite her youth, she was ranked as a Class A writer on A films. In her personal life the effect was equally magical. The surgeon had been right. His son could not meet the competition. Claudia had a string of sexual conquests— some really submissions—that would have made a film star proud.

Claudia loved the movie business. She loved working with other writers, she loved arguing with producers, cajoling directors: the first with how to save money doing the script a certain way, the other with how a script could be done on the highest artistic level. She was in awe of actresses and actors, how they were attuned to her words, making them sound better and more touching. She loved the magic of the set, which most people found boring, she enjoyed the camaraderie of the crew and had no compunction about screwing "below the line." She was thrilled with the whole process of opening a movie and watching its success or failure. She believed in movies as a great art form, and when called in to do a rewrite, she fancied herself a healer and did not look to make changes solely to get screen credit. At the age of twenty-five she had an enormous reputation and friendships with many stars, the closest one being with Athena Aquitane.

What was more of a surprise to her was her ebullient sexuality. Going to bed with a man she liked was as natural to her as any act of friendship. She never did it for advantage, she was too talented; she sometimes joked that stars slept with her to get her next script.

Her first adventure had been with the surgeon himself, who proved to be much more charming and adept than his son. Perhaps enchanted by his own handiwork, he offered to set her up in an apartment with a weekly allowance, not only for the sex but for the enjoyment of her company. Claudia refused good-humoredly and said, "I thought there was no fee."

"You've already paid the fee," he said. "But I hope we can see each other now and then."

"Of course," Claudia said.

What she found extraordinary in herself was that she could make love to so many different kinds of men, of varying ages, types, and looks. And enjoy all of it. She was like an aspiring gourmet, who explored all sorts of strange delicacies. She played mentor with budding actors and screenwriters, but that was not the role she liked. She wanted to learn. And she found older men far more interesting.

On a memorable day, she had a one-night stand with the great Eli Marrion himself. She enjoyed it, but it was not truly successful.

They met at a LoddStone Studio party, and Marrion was intrigued with her because she was not afraid of him and made some penetrating and disparaging remarks on the Studio's latest blockbuster production. Also, Marrion had heard her repel Bobby Bantz's amorous advances with a witty remark that left no ill feelings.

Eli Marrion had given up sex the last few years. It was more work than fun, since he was nearly impotent. When he invited Claudia to come with him to the Beverly Hills bungalow owned by LoddStone, he assumed that she accepted because of his power. He had no idea that it was her sexual curiosity. What would it be like to go to bed with so powerful a man who was so old? That would not have been enough, but in addition she found Marrion attractive despite his age. His gorilla-like face could actually turn handsome when he smiled, which he did when he told her that everyone called him Eli, including his grandchildren. His intelligence and his natural charm intrigued her because she had heard about his ruthlessness. It would be interesting.

In the bedroom of the downstairs apartment of the Beverly Hills Hotel bungalow, she observed with amusement that he was shy. Claudia rejected any coyness, she helped him undress, and while he folded his clothes over a stuffed chair, she got herself naked, gave him a hug, and followed him beneath the bedcovers. Marrion tried to joke, "When King Solomon was dying, they sent virgins to his bed to keep him warm."

"Well, then, I'm not going to help you much," Claudia said. She kissed him and fondled him. His lips were pleasantly warm. His skin had a dryness and waxiness that was not distasteful. She had been surprised by his tinyness when he shed his clothing and shoes, and she considered for a moment what a three-thousand-dollar suit could do for a man in power. But his smallness with the huge head was also endearing. She was not at all put off. After ten minutes of fondling and kissing (the great Marrion kissed with the innocence of a child), they both realized that he was now fully impotent. Marrion thought, This is the last time I will ever be in bed with a woman. He sighed and relaxed as she cradled him in her arms.

"Okay, Eli," Claudia said. "Now I'll tell you in detail why your movie is lousy from a money standpoint and an artistic one." Still gently fondling him, she delivered a penetrating analysis of the script, the director, and the actors. "It's not that it's just a bad movie," Claudia said. "It's an unwatchable movie. Because it has no story sense and so all you have is some fucking director giving you a slide show of what he thinks is a story. And the actors just go through the motions because they know it's bullshit."

Marrion listened to her with a benign smile. He felt very comfortable. He realized that an essential part of his life was over, finished by an approaching death. That he would never again make love to a woman, or even try, was not humiliating. He knew Claudia would not talk about this night, and if she did, what would it matter? He still retained his worldly power. He could still change the destinies of thousands, as long as he remained alive. And now he was interested in her analysis of the film.

"You don't understand," he said. "I can bring a picture into existence but I can't execute the picture. You're quite right, I will never hire that director again. The Talent doesn't lose money, I do. But Talent has to take the blame. My question is, Will a movie make money? If it becomes a work of art, that's just a happy accident."

As they spoke, Marrion got out of bed and began to dress. Claudia hated it when men put on their clothes, they were so much more difficult to talk to. Marrion, to her, was infinitely more lovable naked, strange as that seemed; his spindly legs, his meager body, his huge head, all made her feel an affectionate pity. Oddly enough, his penis, flaccid, was bigger than that of most men in a similar state. She made a mental note to ask her surgeon about that. Did a penis grow larger as it grew more useless?

Now she saw how fatiguing it was for Marrion to button his shirt and put in his cuff links. She jumped out of bed to help him.

Marrion studied her nakedness. Her body was better than many of the stars he had gone to bed with, but he felt no mental flicker and the cells of his body did not react to her beauty. And he did not really feel regret or sadness.

Claudia helped put on his trousers, button his shirt, put in the cuff links. She straightened his maroon tie and brushed back his gray hair with her fingers. He slipped on his suit jacket and there he stood, all his visible power restored. She kissed him and said, "I had a good time."

Marrion was studying her as though she were some sort of opponent. Then he smiled his famous smile that erased the ugliness of his features. He accepted the fact that she was truly innocent, that she had a good heart, and he believed that it was because of her youth. It was just too bad that the world she lived in would change her.

"Well, at least I can feed you," Marrion said. He picked up the phone to call room service.

Claudia was hungry. She polished off a soup, duck with vegetables, and then a huge bowl of strawberry ice cream. Marrion ate very little but did his share in polishing off the bottle of wine. They talked about movies and books, and Claudia learned to her astonishment that Marrion was a far better reader than she was.

"I would have loved to be a writer," Marrion said. "I love writing, books give me so much pleasure. But you know I've rarely met a writer I could like personally, even when I adore their books. Ernest Vail for instance. He writes beautiful books but he's such a pain in the ass in real life. How can that be?"

"Because writers are not their books," Claudia said. "Their books are the distillation of the very best that is in them. They're like a ton of rocks that you have to crush to get a little diamond, if that's what you do to get a diamond."

"You know Ernest Vail?" Marrion asked. Claudia appreciated that he said this without a trace of salaciousness. He must have known about her love affair with Vail. "Now, I love his writing but I can't stand him personally. And he has a grudge against the Studio that is insane."

Claudia patted his hand, a familiarity that was permissible since she had seen him naked. "All the Talent has a grudge against the Studio," she said. "It's not personal. And besides, you're not exactly a sweetheart in business relationships. I may be the only writer in town who really likes you." They both laughed.

Before they parted, Marrion said to Claudia, "Any time you have a problem, please call." It was a message that he would not wish to pursue their personal relationship.

Claudia understood. "I'll never take advantage of that offer," she said. "And if you have trouble with a script, you can call me. Free advice but you have to pay my deal price if I have to write." Telling him that professionally he would need her more than she would need him. Which of course was not true but told him that she had her own faith in her talent. They parted friends.

On the Pacific Coast Highway, traffic was slow. Claudia looked to her left to see the sparkling ocean and marveled at how few people were on the beach. How different from Long Island, where she had visited when she was younger. Above her head she could see the hang gliders sailing just over the power lines and onto the beach. On her right side she saw a crowd around a sound truck and huge cameras. Somebody was shooting a movie. How she loved the Pacific Coast Highway. And how Ernest Vail had hated it. He said driving on that highway was like catching a ferry to Hell. . . .

Claudia De Lena first met Vail when she was hired to work on the movie script of his bestselling novel. She had always loved his books, his sentences were so graceful, they flowed into each other like musical notes. He understood life and the tragedies of character. He had a novelty of invention that always delighted her as fairy stories had enchanted her in her childhood. So she had been thrilled to meet him. But the reality of Ernest Vail was another thing entirely.

Vail was then in his early fifties. His physical presence had none of the grace of his prose. He was short and heavy and had a bald spot that he didn't bother to hide. He may have understood and loved the characters in his books, but he was totally ignorant of the niceties of everyday life. This was perhaps one of his charms, his childlike innocence. It was only when she got to know him better that Claudia discovered that beneath this innocence was an offbeat intelligence that could be enjoyed. He could be witty as a child is unconsciously witty, and he had a child's fragile egotism.

Ernest Vail seemed to be the happiest man in the world at that breakfast at the Polo Lounge. His novels had earned him a solid critical reputation and good but unimportant money. Then this latest book had broken through and become an enormous bestseller and was now being made into a movie by LoddStone Studios. Vail had written the script, and now Bobby Bantz and Skippy Deere were telling him how wonderful it was. And to Claudia's astonishment, Vail was swallowing their praise like some starlet headed for the casting couch. What the hell did Vail think Claudia was doing at this meeting? What dismayed her was that this was the same Bantz and Deere who had the day before told her that the script was a "piece of shit." Not being cruel or even pejorative. A Piece of Shit was simply something that didn't quite work.

Claudia was not put off by Vail's homeliness, after all she herself had been homely until she blossomed into handsomeness under the surgeon's knife. She was even somewhat charmed by his credulity and his enthusiasm.

Bantz said, "Ernest, we're bringing in Claudia to help you. She's a great technician, the best in the business, and she'll make it a real movie. I smell a big hit. And remember—you have ten percent of the net."

Claudia could see Vail swallow the hook. The poor bastard didn't even know that 10 percent of the net was 10 percent of nothing.

Vail seemed to be genuinely grateful for help. He said, "Sure, I can learn from her. Writing scripts is a lot more fun than writing books but it's new to me."

Skippy Deere said reassuringly, "Ernest, you have a natural flair. You can get a lot of work out here. And you can get rich on this picture, especially if it's a hit and especially if it wins the Academy."

Claudia studied the men. Two pricks and a dope, not an unusual trio in Hollywood. But then she had not been any smarter. Hadn't Skippy Deere screwed her, literally and figuratively? Yet she couldn't help admiring Skippy. He seemed so absolutely sincere.

Claudia knew the project was already in serious trouble and that the incomparable Benny Sly was working behind her and that Sly was turning Vail's intellectual hero into a franchise by writing him into a James Bond–Sherlock Holmes–Casanova. There would be nothing left of Vail's book but the bare bones.

It was out of this pity that Claudia agreed to have dinner with Vail that night to plan how they would work on the screenplay together. One of the tricks in collaboration was to stave off any romantic involvement, and she did this by presenting herself as unattractively as possible in work sessions. Romance was always distracting to her when writing.

To her astonishment the two months they spent working led to an enduring friendship. When they were both fired from the project on the same day, they went to Vegas together. Claudia had always loved gambling, and Vail had the same vice. In Vegas she introduced him to her brother Cross and was surprised that the two men hit it off. There was absolutely no basis for their friendship that she could see.

Ernest was an intellectual who had no interest in sports or golf. Cross hadn't read a book for years. She asked Ernest about this.

"He's a listener and I'm a talker," he said. Which struck Claudia as being not a real explanation.

She asked Cross; though he was her brother, he was the greater mystery. Cross pondered the question. Finally he said, "You don't have to keep an eye on him, he doesn't want anything." And as soon as Cross said it, she knew it was true. To her it was an astonishing revelation. Ernest Vail, to his misfortune, was a man who had no hidden agendas.

Her affair with Ernest Vail was different. Though he was a world-renowned novelist, he had no power in Hollywood. Also, he had no social gifts; indeed, he inspired antagonism. His articles in magazines addressed sensitive national issues and were always politically incorrect, but ironically this angered both sides. He jeered at the American democratic process; writing about feminism, he declared that women would always be subjugated by men until they became physically equal, and advised feminists to set up paramilitary training groups. On racial problems, he wrote an essay on language in which he insisted the blacks should call themselves "coloreds" because "black" was used in so many pejorative ways—black thoughts, black as hell, black countenance—and that the word always had a negative connotation except when used in the phrase "simple black dress."

But then he enraged both sides when he maintained that all Mediterranean races be designated as "colored." Including Italians, Spaniards, Greeks, et cetera.

When he wrote about class, he claimed that people with a great deal of money had to be cruel and defensive, and that the poor ought to become criminals since they had to fight laws written by the rich to protect their money. He wrote that all welfare was simply a necessary bribe to keep the poor from starting a revolution. About religion, he wrote that it should be prescribed like medication.

Unfortunately nobody could ever figure out whether he was joking or serious. None of these eccentricities ever appeared in his novels, so a reading of his works gave no insights.

But when Claudia worked with him on the screenplay of his best-selling novel, they established a close relationship. He was a devoted pupil, he gave her all the deference, and she on her part appreciated his somewhat sour jokes, his seriousness about social conditions. She was struck by his carelessness about money in practice and his concern about money in the abstract; his pure dumbness about how the world worked in terms of power, especially Hollywood. They got along so well that she asked him to read her novel. She was flattered when he came to the studio the next day with notes on his reading.

The novel had finally been published on the strength of her success as a screenwriter and the arm twisting of her agent, Melo Stuart. It had received a few reviews of faint praise and some derisive ones merely because she was a screenwriter. But Claudia still loved her book. It did not sell, nor did anyone purchase the movie rights. But it was in print. She inscribed one to Vail: "To America's greatest living novelist." It didn't help.

"You're a very lucky girl," Vail said. "You're not a novelist, you're a screenwriter. You will never be a novelist." Then without malice or derision he spent the next thirty minutes trying to strip her novel bare and showing her that it was a piece of nonsense, that it had no structure, no depth, no resonance in characterization, and that even her dialogue, her strong point, was terrible, witty without point. It was a brutal assassination but carried out with such logic that Claudia had to recognize its truth.

He ended up with what he thought was a kindness. "It's a very good book for an eighteen-year-old woman," Vail said. "All the faults I've mentioned can be repaired by experience, simply by getting older. But there's one thing you can never repair. You have no language."

At this Claudia, though crushed, took offense. Some of the reviewers had praised the lyrical quality of the writing. "You're wrong on that," she said. "I tried to write perfect sentences. And the thing I admire most in your books is the poetry of your language."

For the first time Vail smiled. "Thank you," he said. "I wasn't trying to be poetic. My language sprang out of the emotion of the characters. Your language, your poetry in this book is imposed. It's completely false."

Claudia burst into tears. "Who the fuck are *you*?" she said. "How can you say something so terribly destructive. How can you be so fucking positive?"

Vail seemed amused. "Hey, you can write publishable books and starve to death. But why, when you're a genius screenwriter? As for my being so positive, this is the only thing I know, but I know it absolutely. Or I'm wrong."

Claudia said, "You're not wrong but you are a sadistic prick."

Vail eyed her warily. "You're gifted," he said. "You have a great ear for movie dialogue, you're expert in story line. You really understand movies. Why would you want to be a blacksmith instead of an automobile mechanic? You are a movie person, you are not a novelist."

Claudia looked at him with wide-eyed wonder. "You don't even know how insulting you are."

"Sure I do," Vail said. "But it's for your own good."

"I can't believe you're the same person who wrote your books," she said venomously. "Nobody could believe you wrote them."

At this Vail broke into a delighted cackle. "That's true," he said. "Isn't that wonderful?"

All through the next week he was formal with her while they worked on the script. He assumed their friendship was over. Finally Claudia said to him, "Ernest, don't be so stiff. I forgive you. I even believe you're right. But why did you have to be so brutal? I even thought you were making one of those male power moves. You know, humiliate me then push me into bed. But I know you're too dumb for that. For Christ's sake, give a little sugar with your medicine."

Vail shrugged. "I have only one thing going for me," he said. "If I'm not honest about those things then I'm nothing. Also, I was brutal because I'm really very fond of you. You don't know how rare you are."

Claudia said smilingly, "Because of my talent, my wit, or my beauty?"

Vail waved his hand dismissively. "No, no," he said. "Because you are blessed, a very happy person. No tragedy will ever bring you down. That is very rare."

Claudia thought about it. "You know," she said, "there's something vaguely insulting about that. Does that mean I'm basically stupid?" She paused for a moment. "It's considered more sensitive to be melancholy."

"Right," Vail said. "I'm melancholy and so I'm more sensitive than you?" They both laughed and then she was hugging him.

"Thank you for being honest," she said.

"Don't get too cocky," Vail said. "Like my mother always said, 'Life is like a box of hand grenades, you never know what will blow you to kingdom come.' "

Claudia was laughing when she said, "Christ, do you always have to sound the note of doom? You'll never be a movie writer and that line shows it."

"But it's more truthful," Vail said.

Before they finished their collaboration on the script, Claudia dragged him into bed. She was fond enough of him that she wanted to see him with his clothes off so they could really talk, really exchange confidences.

As a lover Vail was far more enthusiastic than he was expert. He was also more grateful than most men. Best of all, he loved to talk after sex, his nakedness did not inhibit his lecturing, his intemperate judgments. And Claudia loved his nakedness. With his clothes off he seemed to have a monkey's agility and impetuousness, and he was very hairy: a matted chest, patches of furry hair on his back. Also, he was as greedy as a monkey, clutching her naked body as if she were a fruit hanging from a tree. His appetite amused Claudia. She relished the inherent comedy of sex. And she loved that he was famous all over the world, that she had seen him on TV and thought him a little pompous on literature, the grievous moral state of the world, so dignified clutching the pipe he rarely smoked and looking very professorial in his tweed jacket with sewn-leather elbow patches. But he was far more amusing in bed than on TV; he did not have an actor's projection.

There was never any talk of true love, of a "relationship." Claudia had no need for it and Vail had only a literary sense of the term. They both accepted that he was thirty years the elder and, aside from that, no bargain really except for his fame. They had nothing in common except literature, perhaps the worst basis for establishing a marriage, they agreed.

But she loved arguing with him about movies. Vail insisted that moving pictures were not art, that they were a regression to the primitive paintings found in lost caves. That film had no language, and since the progression of the human species depended on language, it was merely a regressive, minor art.

Claudia said, "So painting is not an art, Bach and Beethoven are not art, Michelangelo is not art. You're talking bullshit." And then she realized he was teasing her, that he enjoyed provoking her, though prudently only after sex.

By the time they were both fired from the script, they were really close friends. And before Vail went back to New York, he gave Claudia a tiny, lopsided ring with four different colored jewels. It didn't look expensive but it was a valuable antique that he spent a lot of time looking for. She always wore it thereafter. It became in her mind a lucky talisman.

But when he left, their sexual relationship was over. When and if he ever returned to L.A. she would be in the middle of another affair. And he recognized that their sex had been more friendship than passion.

Her farewell gift to him was a thorough education in the ways of Hollywood. She explained to him that their script was being rewritten by the great Benny Sly, the legendary rewriter of scripts, who had even been mentioned for a special Academy Award for rewrites. And that Benny Sly specialized in turning uncommercial stories into one-hundred-million-dollar blockbusters. Undoubtedly he would turn Vail's book into a movie that Vail would hate but that would surely make a lot of money.

Vail shrugged. "That's okay," he said. "I have ten percent of the net profits. I'll be rich."

Claudia looked at him with exasperation. "Net?" she cried out. "Do you buy Confederate money too? You'll never see a penny no matter how much the movie makes. LoddStone has a genius for making money disappear. Listen, I had net on five pictures that made a ton of money and I never saw a penny. You won't either."

Vail shrugged again. He did not seem to care, which made his actions in the years to follow even more puzzling.

Claudia's next affair made her remember Ernest saying life was like a box of hand grenades. For the first time, despite her intelligence, she fell guardedly in love with a completely unsuitable man. He was a young "genius" director. After that she fell deeply and unguardedly in love with a man who most women in the world would have fallen in love with. Equally unsuitable.

The initial flush of ego that she could attract such primary alpha males was quickly dampened by how they treated her.

The director, an unlikable ferret of a man only a few years older than she, had made three offbeat movies that not only were critical successes but had made a goodly sum of money. Every studio wanted a relationship with him. LoddStone Studios gave him a three-picture deal and also gave him Claudia to rewrite the script he was planning to shoot.

One of the elements of the director's genius was that he had a clear vision of what he wanted. At first he condescended to Claudia because she was a woman and a writer, both inferior in the power structure of Hollywood. They quarreled immediately.

He asked her to write a scene she felt did not belong to the structure of the plot. On its own Claudia recognized that the scene would be a flashy bit that would be just a show-off scene for the director.

"I can't write that scene," Claudia said. "It does nothing for the story. It's just action and camera."

The director said curtly. "That's why they're movies. Just do it the way we discussed it."

"I don't want to waste your time and mine," Claudia said. "Just go write with your fucking camera."

The director didn't waste time even getting angry. "You're fired," he said. "Off the picture." He clapped his hands.

But Skippy Deere and Bobby Bantz made them reconcile, which was only possible because the director had become intrigued by her stubbornness. The picture was a success, and Claudia had to admit this was more because of the director's talent as a moviemaker than

hers as a writer. Quite simply she had not been able to see the director's vision. They fell into bed almost by accident, but the director
proved to be a disappointment. He refused to be naked, he made love
with his shirt on. But still Claudia had dreams of the two of them
making great movies together. One of the great director-writer
teams of all time. She was quite willing to be the subordinate partner, to make her talent serve his genius. They would create great art
together and become a legend. The affair lasted a month, until Claudia finished her "spec" script of *Messalina* and showed it to him. He
read it and tossed it aside. "A piece of feminist bullshit with tits and
ass," he said. "You're a clever girl but it's not a picture I want to
waste a year of my life making."

"It's only a first draft," Claudia said.

"Jesus, I hate people taking advantage of a personal relationship
to get a movie made," the director said.

In that moment Claudia fell completely out of love with him. She
was outraged. "I don't have to fuck you to make a movie," she said.

"Of course you don't," the director said. "You're talented and you
have your reputation of being one of the great pieces of ass in the
movie business."

Now Claudia was horrified. She never gossiped about her sexual
partners. And she hated his tone, as if women were somehow shameful for doing what men did.

Claudia said to him, "You have talent, but a man who fucks with
his shirt on has a worse reputation. And at least I never got laid by
promising someone a screen test."

That was the end of their relationship, and it had started her thinking of Dita Tommey as the director. She decided that only a woman
could do justice to her script.

Well, what the hell, Claudia thought. The bastard never got totally
naked and he didn't like to talk after sex. He was truly a genius in
film but he had no language. And for a genius he was a truly unin-
teresting man, except when he talked movies.

Now Claudia was approaching the great curve of the Pacific Coast
Highway that showed the ocean as a great mirror by reflecting the

cliffs to her right. It was her favorite spot in the world, natural beauty that always thrilled her. It was only ten minutes to the Malibu Colony, where Athena lived. Claudia tried to formulate her plea: to save the movie, to make Athena return. She remembered that at different times in their lives they had had the same lover, and she felt a flush of pride that the man who had loved Athena could love her.

The sun was at its most brilliant now. It polished the waves of the Pacific into huge diamonds. Claudia braked suddenly. She thought one of the gliders was coming down in front of her car. She could see the glider, a young girl with one tit hanging out of her blouse, give a demure wave as she sailed onto the beach. Why were they allowed, why didn't the police appear? She shook her head and pressed the gas pedal. Traffic was loosening and the highway swerved so that she could no longer see the ocean, though in a half mile it would reappear. Like true love, Claudia thought smilingly. True love in her life always reappeared.

When she truly fell in love, it was a painful but educational experience. And it was not really her fault, for the man was Steve Stalling, a Bankable Star and idol of women all over the world. He had a fearful masculine beauty, genuine charm, and an enormous vivacity that was fueled by the prudent use of cocaine. He also had great talent as an actor. More than anything else, he was a Don Juan. He screwed everything in sight—on location in Africa, in a small town in the American West, in Bombay, Singapore, Tokyo, London, Rome, Paris. He did this in the spirit of a gentleman giving alms to the poor, an act of Christian charity. There was never any question of a relationship, no more than a beggar would be invited to a benefactor's dinner party. He was so enchanted by Claudia that the affair lasted twenty-seven days.

It was a humiliating twenty-seven days for Claudia despite the pleasure. Steve Stallings was an irresistible lover, with the help of cocaine. He was more comfortable being naked than even Claudia. The fact that he had a perfectly proportioned body helped. Often Claudia caught him inspecting himself in the mirror in much the same way as a woman adjusting her hat.

Claudia knew she was just a lesser concubine. When they had dates he would always call her to say he would be an hour late and then would arrive six hours later. Sometimes he would cancel altogether. She was only his fallback position for the night. Also, when they made love he would always insist she use cocaine with him, which was fun but turned her brain into such mush she could not work the next few days, and what she did write, she distrusted. She realized that she was becoming what she detested more than anything else in the world: a woman whose whole life depended on the whims of a man.

She was humiliated by the fact that she was his fourth or fifth choice, but she didn't really blame him. She blamed herself. After all, at this point in his fame Steve Stallings could have almost any woman in America and he had chosen her. Stallings would grow old and less beautiful, he would become less famous and use more and more cocaine. He had to cash in during his prime. She was in love and, for one of the few times in her life, terribly unhappy.

So on the twenty-seventh day when Stallings called to say he would be an hour late, she told him, "Don't bother, Steve, I'm leaving your geisha house."

There was a pause, and when he answered he did not seem surprised. "We part friends I hope," he said. "I really enjoy your company."

"Sure," Claudia said and hung up. For the first time she did not want to remain friends at the end of an affair. What really bothered her was her lack of intelligence. It was obvious that all his behavior was a trick to make her go away, that it had taken her too long to take the hint. It was mortifying. How could she have been so dumb? She wept, but in a week she found she did not miss being in love at all. Her time was her own and she could work. It was a pleasure to get back to her writing with a head clear of cocaine and true love.


After her director genius of a lover had rejected her script, Claudia worked furiously for six months on the rewrite.

Claudia De Lena wrote her original screenplay of *Messalina* as a witty propaganda piece for feminism. But after five years in the movie business she knew that any message had to be coated with more basic ingredients, such as greed, sex, murder, and a belief in humanity. She knew she had to write great parts not only for her first choice, Athena Aquitane, but for at least three other female stars in lesser roles. Good female roles were so scarce that the script would attract top-name stars. And then, absolutely essential, the great villain—charming, ruthless, handsome, and witty. Here she drew on memories of her father.

Claudia at first wanted to approach a female independent producer with clout, but most studio heads who could green-light a picture were males. They would love the script but they would worry it would turn into too overt a propaganda piece with a female producer and a female director. They would want at least one male hand in there somewhere. Claudia had already decided that Dita Tommey would direct.

Tommey would certainly accept because it would be a megabudget film. Such a film if successful would put her in the Bankable class. Even if it failed it would enhance her reputation. A huge budget film that failed was sometimes more prestigious for a director than a small budget picture that made money.

Another reason was that Dita Tommey loved women exclusively and this picture would give her access to four beautiful famous women.

Claudia wanted Tommey because they had worked together on a picture a few years ago and it had been a good experience. She was very direct, very witty, very talented. Also she was not a "writer killer" director, who called in friends to rewrite and share credit. She never filed for writing credit on a film unless she contributed her fair share, and she was not a sexual harasser as were some directors and stars. Though the term "sexual harassment" could not really be used in the movie business, where the selling of sex appeal was part of the job.

Claudia made sure she sent the script to Skippy Deere on a Friday, he only read scripts carefully on weekends. She sent it to him because, despite his betrayals, he was the best producer in town. And because she could never let go completely on an old relationship. It worked. She got a call from him on Sunday morning. He wanted her to have lunch with him that very day.

Claudia threw her computer into her Mercedes and dressed to work: blue denim man's shirt, faded blue jeans, and slip-on sneakers. She tied her hair back with a red scarf.

She took Ocean Avenue in Santa Monica. In the Palisades Park that separated Ocean Avenue from Pacific Coast Highway, she saw the homeless men and women of Santa Monica gathering for their Sunday brunch. Volunteer social workers brought their food and drink to them every Sunday in the fresh air of the park at wooden tables and benches. Claudia always took this route to watch them, to remind herself of that other world where people did not have Mercedeses and swimming pools and did not shop on Rodeo Drive. In the early years she often volunteered to serve food in the park, now she just sent a check to the church that fed them. It had become too painful to go from one world to the other, it blunted her desire to succeed. She could not avoid watching the men, so shabbily dressed, their lives in ruins, yet some of them curiously dignified. To live so without hope seemed to her an extraordinary thing, and yet it was just a question of money, that money she earned so easily writing movie scripts. What she earned in six months was more money than these men saw in their entire lives.

At Skippy Deere's mansion in the Beverly Hills canyons, Claudia was led by the housekeeper to the swimming pool, with its bright blue-and-yellow cabanas. Deere was seated in a cushioned lounge chair. Beside him was the small marble table that held his phone and a stack of scripts. He was wearing his red-framed reading glasses that he only used at home. In his hand was a tall frosted glass of Evian water.

He sprang up and embraced her. "Claudia," he said, "we have business to do fast."

She was judging his voice. She could usually tell the reaction to her scripts by the tones of voices. There was the carefully modulated praise that meant a definite "no." Then there was the joyful, enthusiastic voice that expressed an unrestrained admiration and was almost always followed by at least three reasons why the script could not be bought; another studio was doing the same subject, the proper cast could not be assembled, the studios would not touch the subject matter. But Deere's voice was that of the determined business man latching onto a good thing. He was talking money and controls. That meant "Yes."

"This could be a very big picture," he told Claudia. "Very, very big. In fact it can't be small. I know what you're doing, you're a very clever girl, but I have to sell a studio on the sex. Of course I'll sell it to the female stars on feminism. The male star we can get if you soften him a little, give him more moments as a good guy. Now I know you want to be an associate producer on this, but I call the shots. You can have your say, I'm open to reason."

"I want to have my say on the director," Claudia said.

"You, the studio, and the stars," Deere said, laughing.

"I don't sell it unless I get approval of the director," Claudia said.

"Okay," Deere said. "So first tell the studio you want to direct, then back down, and they'll be so relieved that they'll give you the approval." He paused for a moment. "Who do you have in mind?"

"Dita Tommey," Claudia said.

"Good. Clever," Deere said. "Female stars love her. The Studio too. She brings everything in on budget, she doesn't live off the picture. But you and I do the casting before we bring her on."

"Who will you bring it to?" Claudia asked.

"LoddStone," Deere said. "They go with me pretty much so we won't have to fight too much about casting and directors. Claudia, you've written a perfect script. Witty, exciting, with a great point of view on early feminism and that's hot today. And sex. You justify Messalina and all women. I'll talk to Melo and Molly Flanders about your deal and she can talk to Business Affairs at LoddStone."

"You son of a bitch," Claudia said. "You've already talked to LoddStone?"

"Last night," Skippy Deere said with a grin. "I brought the script over to them and they gave me the green light if I can put everything together. And listen, Claudia, don't shit me. I know you've got Athena in your pocket on this, that's why you're being so tough." He paused for a moment. "That's what I told LoddStone. Now let's go to work."

That had been the beginning of the great project. She could not let it go down the drain now.

. . .

Claudia was approaching the traffic light where she would have to take a left turn onto the side road that would lead her to the Colony. For the first time, she felt a sense of panic. Athena was so strong-willed, as stars must be, that she would never change her mind. No matter; if Athena refused, she would fly to Vegas and ask her brother Cross to help. He had never failed her. Not when they were growing up, not when she went to live with her mother, not when their mother died.

Claudia had a memory of the great festive occasions at the Clericuzio mansion on Long Island. A setting from a Grimm's fairy tale, mansion enclosed by walls, she and Cross playing among the fig trees. There were two groups of boys ranging from eight to twelve years old. The opposing group was led by Dante Clericuzio, grandson of the old Don who had stationed himself at an upstairs window like a dragon.

Dante was an aggressive boy who loved to fight, who loved to be a general, and the only boy who dared to challenge her brother, Cross, in physical combat. Dante had Claudia on the ground, hitting her, trying to beat her into submission, when Cross appeared. Then Dante and Cross had fought. What had struck Claudia then was how confident Cross had been in the face of Dante's ferocity. And Cross won easily.

And so Claudia could not understand her mother's choice. How could she not love Cross more? Cross was so much more worthy. Proving his worth by electing to go with his father. And Claudia never doubted that Cross had wanted to stay with his mother and her.

In the years that followed the disruption, the family still maintained a relationship of sorts. Claudia came to know, by conversations, by the body language of the people around them, that her brother Cross had to some degree achieved their father's eminence. The affection between her and her brother remained constant, though they were now completely different. She realized that Cross was part of the Clericuzio Family, she was not.

Two years after Claudia moved to L.A., when she was twenty-three, her mother, Nalene, was diagnosed with cancer. Cross, then working with Gronevelt at the Xanadu after making his bones for the Clericuzio, came to spend the last two weeks with them in Sacramento. Cross hired nurses around the clock and a cook and housekeeper. The three of them lived together for the first time since the breakup of the family. Nalene forbade Pippi to visit her.

The cancer had affected Nalene's eyesight, so Claudia read to her constantly, from magazines, from newspapers and books. Cross went out to do the shopping. Sometimes he had to fly to Vegas for an afternoon to take care of Hotel business, but he always returned at evening.

During the night, Cross and Claudia would take turns holding their mother's hand, comforting her. And though she was heavily medicated, she continually pressed their hands. Sometimes she hallucinated and thought her two children were little again. One terrible night she wept and begged forgiveness of Cross for what she had done to him. Cross had to hold her in his arms and reassure her that everything had turned out for the best.

During the long evenings when their mother was deep into a drugged sleep, Cross and Claudia told each other the details of their lives.

Cross explained that he had sold the Collection Agency and left the Clericuzio Family, though they had used their influence to get him his job at the Xanadu Hotel. He hinted at his power and told Claudia that she was welcome at the Hotel anytime, RFB—room, food, and beverage free. Claudia asked how he could do that and Cross told her with just a touch of pride, "I have the Pencil."

Claudia found that pride comical and a little sad.

Claudia seemingly felt their mother's death far more strongly than Cross, but the experience had brought them together again. They regained their childhood intimacy. Claudia frequently went to Vegas over the years and met Gronevelt and observed the close relationship the old man had with her brother. During these years Claudia saw that Cross had a certain kind of power, but that he never linked his power with the Clericuzio Family. Since Claudia had severed all ties with the Family and never attended the funerals, weddings, and christenings, she didn't know that Cross still was part of the Family social structure. And Cross never spoke of it to her. She rarely saw her father. He had no interest in her.

New Year's Eve was the biggest event in Vegas; people all over the country flocked there, but Cross always had a suite for Claudia. Claudia was not a big gambler, but one New Year's Eve she got carried away. She had brought an aspiring actor with her and was trying to impress him. She lost control and signed fifty thousand dollars in markers. Cross had come down to the suite with the markers in his hand, and there was a curious look on his face. Claudia recognized it when he spoke. It was his father's face.

"Claudia," Cross said, "I thought you were smarter than me. What the hell is this?"

Claudia felt a little sheepish. Cross had often warned her to gamble only for small stakes. Also to never increase her bets when she was losing. And to spend no more than two or three hours gambling every day, because the length of time spent gambling was the greatest trap. Claudia had violated all his advice. . . .

She said, "Cross, give me a couple of weeks and I'll pay it off."

She was surprised by her brother's reaction. "I'll kill you before I let you pay off these markers." Very deliberately he tore up the slips of paper and put them in his pocket. He said, "Look, I invite you down here because I want to see you, not to take your money. Get this through your head, you cannot win. It has nothing to do with luck. Two and two make four."

"Okay, okay," Claudia said.

"I don't mind having to tear up these markers, but I hate your being dumb," Cross said.

They had left it at that, but Claudia wondered. Did Cross have that much power? Would Gronevelt approve or would he even know about this?

There had been other such incidents, but one of the most chilling involved a woman named Loretta Lang.

Loretta had been a singing and dancing star in the Xanadu Follies show. She had an abundance of verve and a natural humorous perkiness that charmed Claudia. Cross introduced them after the show.

Loretta Lang was as charming in person as she was on the stage. But Claudia noticed that Cross was not as charmed, in fact seemed a little irritated by her vivacity.

On Claudia's next visit, she brought along Melo Stuart for an evening in Vegas where they could catch the Follies show. Melo had come merely to indulge Claudia, not expecting much. He watched appraisingly and then told Claudia, "This girl has a real shot. Not singing or dancing, but she's a natural comic. A female with that is gold."

Backstage to meet Loretta, Melo put on his game face and said, "Loretta, I loved you. Loved you. Understand? Can you come to L.A. next week? I'll arrange to have you on film to show to a studio friend of mine. But first you have to sign a contract with my agency. You know I have to put in a lot of work before I make any money. That's the business, but remember I love you."

Loretta threw her arms around Melo. There was no witty mocking of devotion here, Claudia noted. A date was set and the three of them had dinner together to celebrate, before Melo caught his early morning plane back to L.A.

During supper Loretta confessed that she was already under an airtight contract with an agency that specialized in nightclub entertainment. A contract with three years to run. Melo assured Loretta that everything could be ironed out.

But things could not be ironed out. Loretta's showbiz agency insisted on controlling her career for the next three years. Loretta frantic, astonished Claudia by asking her to appeal to her brother, Cross.

"What the hell can Cross do?" Claudia asked.

Loretta said, "He has a lot of clout in this town. He can get a deal I can live with. Please?"

When Claudia went up to the penthouse suite on the roof of the Hotel and presented the problem to Cross, her brother looked at her with disgust. He shook his head.

"What the hell's the big deal?" Claudia asked. "Just put the word in, that's all I'm asking."

"You are dumb," Cross said. "I've seen dozens of dames like her. They ride friends like you up to the top and then you're history."

"So what?" Claudia said. "She's really talented. This could change her whole life for the better."

Cross shook his head again. "Don't ask me to do this," he said.

"Why not?" Claudia asked. She was used to asking people favors for other people, it was part of the movie business.

"Because once I get in to it, I have to succeed," Cross said.

"I'm not expecting you to succeed, I'm just asking you to do your best," Claudia said. "At least then I can tell Loretta we tried."

Cross laughed. "You really are dumb," he said. "Okay, tell Loretta and her agency to come and see me tomorrow. Ten A.M. sharp. And you might as well be there too."

At the meeting the next morning, Claudia met Loretta's showbiz agent for the first time. His name was Tolly Nevans, and he was dressed in the casual Vegas style, modified by the seriousness of the meeting. That is, he wore a blue blazer over a collarless white shirt and blue denim pants.

"Cross, a pleasure to see you again," Tolly Nevans said.

"We've met?" Cross asked. He never had handled the business details of the Follies show personally.

"A long time ago," Nevans said smoothly. "When Loretta opened her first time at the Xanadu."

Claudia noted the difference between the L.A. agents who dealt with big-time film talent and Tolly Nevans, who managed the much smaller-time world of nightclub entertainment. Nevans was a little more nervous, his physical appearance not so overpowering. He did not have the complete confidence of Melo Stuart.

Loretta pecked Cross on the cheek but did not say anything to him. Indeed she showed none of her usual vivacity. She sat next to Claudia, who sensed Loretta's tension.

Cross was in a golf outfit, white slacks, a white T-shirt, and white sneakers. He wore a blue baseball cap on his head. He offered drinks from the wet bar but they all refused. Then he said quietly, "Let's get this business settled. Loretta?"

Her voice trembled. "Tolly wants to keep his percentage of everything I earn. That includes any movie work. But the L.A. agency naturally wants their full percentage of any movie work they get me. I can't pay two percentages. And then Tolly wants to call the shots on anything I do. The L.A. people won't stand for that and neither will I."

Nevans shrugged. "We have a contract. We just want her to live up to that contract."

Loretta said, "But then my film agent won't sign me up."

Cross said, "It seems simple to me. Loretta, you just buy your way out of the contract."

Nevans said, "Loretta is a great performer, she makes a lot of money for us. We've always promoted her, we always believed in her talent. We've invested a lot of money. We can't just let her go now when she's paying off."

Cross said, "Loretta, buy him out."

Loretta almost wailed, "I can't pay two percentages. It's too cruel."

Claudia tried to control the smile on her face. But Cross did not. Nevans looked hurt.

Finally Cross said, "Claudia, go get your golf gear. I want you to shoot nine holes with me. I'll meet you downstairs at the Cashier's cage when I'm finished here."

Claudia had wondered at Cross being dressed for the meeting in such a cavalier way. As if he were not taking it seriously. It had offended her and she knew it offended Loretta. But it had reassured Tolly. The man had not proposed any compromise. So Claudia said to Cross, "I'll stick around, I want to see Solomon at work."

Cross could never get angry at his sister. He laughed and she smiled back at him. Then Cross turned to Nevans. "I see you're not bending. And I think you're right. How about a percentage of her movie earnings for one year? But you have to relinquish control or it won't work."

Loretta burst in angrily, "I'm not giving him that."

Nevans said, "And that's not what I want. The percentage is okay but what if we have a great booking for you and you're tied up in a movie? We lose money."

Cross sighed and said almost sadly, "Tolly, I want you to let this girl out of her contract. It is a request. Our hotel does a lot of business with you. Do me a favor."

For the first time Nevans seemed alarmed. He said in almost a pleading tone, "I'd love to do you this favor, Cross, but I have to check with my partners at the Agency." He paused for a moment. "Maybe I can arrange a buyout."

"No," Cross said. "I'm asking a favor. No buyout. And I want your answer now so I can go out and enjoy my golf game." He paused. "Just say yes or no."

Claudia was shocked by this abruptness. Cross was not threatening or intimidating as far as she could see. In fact he seemed to be giving up the whole affair, as if he had lost interest. But Claudia could see that Nevans was shaken.

What Nevans replied was surprising. "But that's unfair," he said. He shot a reproachful glance at Loretta, she lowered her eyes.

Cross pulled his baseball cap sideways in a swaggering manner. "It's just a request," he said. "You can refuse me. It's up to you."

"No, no," Nevans said. "I just didn't know you felt so strongly, that you were such good friends."

Suddenly Claudia saw an amazing change in her brother. Cross leaned over and gave Tolly Nevans a half hug of affection. His smile warmed his face. That bastard is handsome, she thought. And then Cross said in a voice full of gratitude, "Tolly, I won't forget this. Look, you have carte blanche here at the Xanadu for any new talent you want to showcase, third billing at the least. I'll even arrange to have a special night at the Follies with all the talent from you and on that night, I want you and your partners to have dinner with me at the hotel. Call me anytime and I'll leave word you get through. Direct. Okay?"

Claudia realized two things. Cross had deliberately shown his power. And that Cross had been careful to recompense Nevans to some degree but only after he had knuckled under, not before. Tolly Nevans would have his special night, would bask in power for that one night.

Claudia realized further that Cross had allowed her to see that power to show his love for her and that that love had a material force. And she saw in his beautifully planed face, in that beauty she had envied from childhood, of the sensual lips, the perfect nose, the oval eyes, all slightly hardening as if turning into the marble of ancient statues.

. . .

Claudia turned off the Pacific Coast Highway and drove to the gate of the Malibu Colony. She loved the Colony, the houses right on the beach, the ocean sparkling in front of them, and far off on the water, she saw again the reflections of the mountains behind them. She parked the car in front of Athena's house.


Boz Skannet was lying on the public beach south of the Malibu Colony fence. That fence of plain wire mesh ran down the beach for about ten steps into the water. But this fence was only a formal barrier. If you went out far enough, you could swim around it.

Boz was scouting for his next attack on Athena. Today would be a probing foray and so he had driven out to the public beach, bathing suit covered with a T-shirt and tennis slacks. His beach bag, really a tennis bag, held the vial of acid wrapped in towels.

From his spot on the beach he could look through the mesh fence at Athena's house. He could see the two private security guards on the beach. They were armed. If the back was covered, certainly the front of the house was covered. He didn't mind hurting the guards but he didn't want to make it seem like a madman slaughtering a whole bunch of people. That would detract from his justified destruction of Athena.

Boz Skannet took off his slacks and T-shirt and stretched out on his blanket, staring over the sand and the blue sheet of the Pacific Ocean beyond. The warmth of the sun made him drowsy. He thought of Athena.

In college he had heard a professor lecturing on Emerson's essays and quoting, "Beauty is its own excuse." Was it Emerson, was it Beauty? But he had thought of Athena.

It is so rare to find a human being so beautiful in physical form and so virtuous in other parts of her nature. And so he thought of Thena. Everybody had called her Thena in those days of her girlhood.

He had loved her so much in his youth that he lived in a dream of happiness that she loved him. He could not believe that life could be so sweet. And little by little everything had been tarnished with decay.

How did she dare to be so perfect? How did she dare to be so demanding of love? How did she dare to make so many people love her? Didn't she know how dangerous that would be?

And Boz wondered at himself. Why had his own love turned to hate? It was simple really. Because he knew he could not possess her to the end of their lives; that one day he must lose her. That one day she would lie down with other men, that one day she would disappear from his Heaven. And never think of him again.

He felt the sun's warmth move off his face and opened his eyes. Looming above him was a very large, well-dressed man who was carrying a folding chair. Boz recognized him. It was Jim Losey, the detective who had interrogated him after he threw the water in Thena's face.

Boz squinted up at him. "What a coincidence, both of us swimming on the same beach. What the fuck do you want?"

Losey unfolded the chair and sat on it. "My ex-wife gave me this chair. I was interrogating and arresting so many surfers she said I might as well be comfortable." He looked down at Boz Skannet almost kindly. "I just wanted to ask you a few questions. One, what are you doing so close to Miss Aquitane's house? You're violating the judge's restraining order."

"I'm on a public beach, there's a fence in between us, and I'm in a bathing suit. Do I look like I'm harassing her?" Boz said.

Losey had a sympathetic smile on his face. "Hey, look," he said, "if I was married to that broad, I couldn't stay away from her either. How about if I take a look in your beach bag?"

Boz put the beach bag beneath his head. "No," he said. "Unless you have a warrant."

Losey gave him a friendly smile. "Don't make me arrest you," he said. "Or just beat the shit out of you and take the bag."

This aroused Boz. He stood up, he offered the bag to Losey, but then he held it away from him. "Try and take it," he said.

Jim Losey was startled. In his own estimation he had never met anybody tougher than himself. In any other situation he would have drawn his blackjack or his gun and beaten the man to a pulp. Perhaps it was the sand under his feet that made him uncertain, or perhaps it was the utter fearlessness of Skannet.

Boz was smiling at him. "You'll have to shoot me," he said. "I'm stronger than you. Big as you are. And if you shoot me, you won't have probable cause."

Losey admired the man's perceptiveness. In a physical struggle the issue might be in doubt. And there was no cause to draw a weapon.

"Okay," he said. He folded up his chair and started to walk away. Then he turned and said admiringly, "You're really a tough guy. You win. But don't give me a good probable cause. You see I haven't measured your distance from the house, you may be just out of range of the judge's order. . . ."

Boz laughed. "I won't give you cause, don't worry."

He watched Jim Losey walk off the beach to his car and drive away. Boz put his blanket into the beach bag and returned to his own car. He put the beach bag in the trunk, took the car key off its ring, and hid it under the front seat. Then he went back to the beach for his swim around the fence.

# CHAPTER 5

A THENA AQUITANE had earned her way to stardom in the traditional way that the public seldom appreciates. She spent long years in training: acting classes, dance and movement classes, voice lessons, extensive reading in dramatic literature, all necessary to the art of acting.

And of course the scut work. She made the rounds of agents, casting directors, mildly lecherous producers and directors, the more dinosaur-like sexual advances of studio wheels and chiefs.

In her first year she earned her living by doing commercials, and some modeling, as a skimpily clad hostess for automotive expositions, but that was only her first year. Then her acting skills began to pay off. She had lovers who showered her with gifts of jewelry and money. Some of them offered marriage. The affairs were brief and ended on friendly terms.

None of this had been painful or humiliating to her, not even when the buyer of a Rolls-Royce assumed she came with the car. She had put him off with the joke that she had the same price as the car. She was fond of men, she enjoyed sex, but only as a treat and reward for more serious endeavor. Men were not a serious part of her world.

Acting was Life. Her secret knowledge of herself was serious. The dangers of the world were serious. But acting came first. Not the tiny movie roles that enabled her to pay expenses, but the great acting parts in great plays put on by local theater groups and then the plays at the Mark Taper Forum that finally propelled her toward major film roles.

Her real life was the parts she played, she felt more alive as she brought her characters to life, carried them around inside her while living out her ordinary existence. Her love affairs were like amusements, playing golf and tennis, dining with friends, dreamlike substances.

Real life was only in the cathedral-like theater: putting on makeup, adding one splash of color to her costume, her face contorting with emotions of the lines of the play running through her head, and then, looking into that deep blackness of the audience—God finally showing his face—she pleaded her fate. She wept, fell in love, screamed with anguish, begged forgiveness for her secret sins, and sometimes experienced the redemptive joy of happiness found.

She hungered for fame and success to obliterate her past, to drown her memories of Boz Skannet, of the child they had together, of the betrayal by her beauty; a sly fairy godmother's boon.

Like any artist, she wanted the world to love her. She knew she was beautiful—how could she not, her world constantly told her so—but she knew also she was intelligent. And so from the beginning she believed in herself. What she really could not believe, at the beginning, was that she had the indispensable ingredients of true genius: enormous energy and concentration. And curiosity.

Acting and music were Athena's true loves, and to be able to concentrate on these things she used her energy to make herself expert in everything else. She learned to fix a car, became a superb cook, excelled at sports. She studied lovemaking in the literature and in life, knowing how important it was in her chosen profession.

She had a flaw. She could not bear to inflict pain on a fellow human being, and since in this life this was impossible to avoid, she was an unhappy woman. Yet she made hard-nosed decisions that furthered her place in the world. She used her power as a Bankable Star; she sometimes had a coldness that was as intense as her beauty. Powerful men beseeched her to appear in their movies, men begged to climb into her bed. She influenced, even demanded, the choosing of directors and costars. She could commit minor crimes without punishment, outrage custom, defy nearly all moralities, and who was to say who was the real Athena? She had the inscrutability of all

Bankable Stars, she was a twin, you could not separate her real life from the lives she lived on screen.

All this and the world loved her, but that was not enough. She knew her inner ugliness. There was one person who did not love her and that caused her to suffer. It is part of the definition of an actress that she will despair if she gets one hundred positive reviews and a single hateful one.

At the end of her first five years in Los Angeles, Athena got her first starring role in film and made her greatest conquest.

Like all top male stars, Steven Stallings had a veto over the female leading role of each of his pictures. He saw Athena in a Mark Taper Forum play and recognized her talent. But even more he was struck by her beauty, and so he chose Athena to costar with him in his next film.

Athena was completely surprised and flattered. She knew this was her big break, and initially she did not know why she had been chosen. Her agent, Melo Stuart, enlightened her.

They were in Melo's office, a wonderfully decorated room with Oriental bric-a-brac, gold-threaded carpets, and heavy comfortable furniture all bathed in artificial lights since the curtains were closed to cut out daylight. Melo liked an English tea in his office rather than going out for lunch and picked up the little sandwiches and popped them into his mouth as he talked. He only went out to lunch with his really famous clients.

"You deserve this break," he told Athena. "You're a great actress. But you've only been in this town a few years and despite your intelligence you're a little green. So don't take offense about what I'm going to say—here's what happened." He paused for a moment. "Usually I would never explain this, usually it's not necessary."

"But I'm so green," Athena said smiling.

"Not green exactly," Melo said. "But you're so focused on your art, you sometimes seem unaware of the social complexities of the industry."

Athena was amused. "So tell me how I got the part."

Melo said, "Stalling's agent called me. He said Stallings saw you in the Taper play and was knocked out by your performance. He definitely wants you in the picture. Then the producer called me to negotiate and we made the deal. Straight salary, two hundred grand, no points, that comes later in your career, and no strings for any other picture. That's a really great deal for you."

"Thank you," Athena said.

"I really shouldn't have to be saying this," Melo said. "Steven has a habit of falling madly in love with his costars. Sincerely, but he's a very ardent wooer."

Athena interrupted him. "Melo, don't spell it out."

"I feel I must," Melo said.

He gazed at her fondly. He himself, usually so impervious, had fallen in love with Athena at the beginning, but since she had never acted seductively, he had taken the hint and not revealed his feelings. She was, after all, a valuable piece of property that would in the future earn him millions.

"Are you trying to tell me that I'm supposed to jump on his bones the first time we're alone?" Athena said dryly. "Isn't my great talent enough?"

"Absolutely not," Melo said. "And absolutely. A great actress is a great actress, no matter what. But you know how someone becomes a great star in film? At some time they have to get the great part at exactly the right moment. And this is that great part for you. You cannot afford to miss it. And what's so hard about falling in love with Steven Stallings? A hundred million women all over the world love him, why not you? You should be flattered."

"I'm flattered," Athena said coolly. "But if I really hate him, then what?"

Melo popped another tea sandwich into his mouth. "What's to hate? He's really a sweet man, I swear to you. But at least dally with him until they've shot you enough in the picture so they can't cut you out."

"What if I'm so good they won't want to cut me?" Athena said.

Melo sighed. "To tell the truth, Steven won't wait that long. If you're not in love with him after three days, you'll be out of the picture."

"That's sexual harassment," Athena said, laughing.

"There can be no sexual harassment in the movie business," Melo said. "In one form or another you're offering your ass for sale by just going in."

"I meant the part where I have to fall in love with him," Athena said. "Straight screwing is not enough for Steven?"

"He can get all the screwing he wants," Melo said. "He's in love with you so he wants love in return. Until the shoot is over." He sighed. "Then you'll both fall out of love because you'll be too busy working." He paused for a moment. "It won't be insulting to your dignity," he said. "A star like Steven indicates his interest. The recipient, yourself, responds or shows a lack of interest in that interest. Steven will send you flowers the first day. The second day after rehearsal he invites you to dinner to study the script. There's nothing forced about it. Except, of course, that you will be cut from the picture if you don't go. With a full payoff, I can do that for you."

"Melo, don't you think I'm good enough to make it without selling my body?" Athena said with mock reproach.

"Of course you are," Melo said. "You're young, only twenty-five. You can wait two or three, even four or five years. I have absolute faith in your talent. But give it a chance. Everybody loves Steven."


It went exactly as Melo Stuart predicted. Athena received flowers the first day. They second day they rehearsed with the whole company. It was a dramatic comedy where laughter led to tears, one of the hardest things to do. Athena was impressed with Steven Stallings's skill. He read his part in a monotone with no effort to impress but still the lines came alive, and on the variations he invariably picked the one most true. They played one scene a dozen different ways and responded to each other, followed each other like dancers. At the end, he muttered, "Good, good," and smiled at her with respectful acknowledgment that was purely professional.

At the end of the day Steven finally turned on his charm.

"I think this may be a great movie because of you," he said. "How about getting together tonight and really doing a number on this script?" He paused for a moment and then said with a boyish smile that was endearing, "We were really good together."

"Thank you," Athena said. "When and where?"

Immediately Steven's face expressed a polite, playful horror. "Oh, no," he said. "Your choice."

At that moment Athena decided to accept her role and to play it as a true professional. He was the superstar. She was the newcomer. But all the choices were his and it was her duty to choose what he wanted. Ringing in her ears was Melo saying, "you wait two, three, four, five years." She couldn't wait.

"Would you mind coming to my place?" Athena asked. "I'll make dinner simple so we can work while we eat." She paused for a moment, then said, "At seven?"


Because she was a perfectionist, Athena prepared for the mutual seduction physically and mentally. Dinner would be light so it would not affect their work or their sexual performance. Though she rarely touched alcohol, she bought a bottle of white wine. The meal would show off her talent as a cook, but she could prepare while they worked.

Clothes. She understood that the seduction was supposed to be accidental, with no prior intent. But they should not be used as a signal to ward him off either. As an actor, Steven would be looking to interpret every sign.

So she wore faded blue jeans that showed her buttocks to advantage, the mottled blue and faded white invitingly cheerful. No belt. Above, a frilly white silk blouse that though it showed no cleavage, indicated the milkier color of her breasts beneath. Her ears she decorated with small round clip-ons, green to match her eyes. Still it was just a little too severe, a little standoffish. It left room for doubt. Then she had a stroke of genius. She painted her toenails a scarlet red and greeted him barefoot.

Steven Stallings arrived carrying a bottle of good red wine, not super but very good. He was also dressed for business. Baggy brown corduroy trousers, blue denim shirt, white sneakers, his dark black hair carelessly combed. Under his arm was the script with yellow note slips peeking out demurely. The only thing that gave him away was the faint scent of cologne.

They ate casually at the kitchen table. He complimented her on the food, as well he should. And as they ate they leafed through their scripts, comparing notes, changing dialogue for smoother delivery.

After dinner they moved to the living room and played out specific scenes they had targeted as trouble areas in the script. Through all this they were very conscious of each other, and it affected their work.

Athena noticed that Steven Stallings was playing his part perfectly. He was professional, respectful. Just his eyes betrayed his genuine admiration of her beauty, his appreciation of her talent as an actress, of her mastery of the material. Finally he asked her if she was too tired to play the crucial love scene in the movie script.

By that time the dinner had been comfortably digested. By that time they had become close friends, like the characters in the script. They played the love scene, Steven kissing her slightly on the lips but leaving out the body gropings. After the first chaste kiss, he looked deeply and sincerely into her eyes, and with perfect husky emotion in his voice, he said, "I wanted to do that the first time I saw you."

Athena held his eyes with her own. Then she lowered them, pulled his head down gently and gave him a chaste kiss. The necessary signal. They were both surprised by the genuine passion with which he responded. Which proved she was the better actor, Athena thought. But he was skillful. As he undressed her, his hands smoothed her skin and his fingers probed, his tongue tickled the inside of her thigh and her body responded. This wasn't so terrible, she thought as they moved into the bedroom. And Steven was so startlingly handsome, his classic face, suffused with passion, had an intensity that could not be duplicated on film, indeed on film this would be degraded into lecherousness. When he made love on screen it was far more spiritual.

Athena had now worked herself into the part of a woman overcome with mad physical passion. They were perfectly in sync and in one blinding moment rose to a simultaneous climax. Lying back in exhaustion, both wondered how the scene would have appeared on film and decided it would not have been good enough for a take. It had not revealed character as it should, or advanced the story as it should. It had lacked the inner tender emotion of true love or even true lust. There would have to be another take.

Steven Stallings fell in love, but he often did that. Athena, despite the fact that it was in some sense professional rape, felt pleased that things had turned out so well. There was no real downside except the question of free will. And it could be said of any life that the suppression of free will, judiciously exercised, was often necessary for human survival.

Steven was happy that now in the shooting of his new film he had all his ducks in a row. He had a good working partner. They would have a pleasant relationship, he wouldn't have to look around for sex. Also, he had rarely had a woman so blessed with talent and beauty as Athena, and also so good in bed. And obviously madly in love with him, which of course could be a problem later on.

What happened next cemented their love. They both jumped out of bed and said, "Let's go back to work." They picked up their scripts and, naked, perfected their readings.

However, one disconcerting note for Athena was when Steven put on his shorts. They were scalloped pink, especially designed to show off his shapely buttocks, those buns that were the source of ecstasy to his female fans. Another odd note was when he proudly told her that he had used a condom made especially for him, manufactured by a company he had invested in. You could never detect he was wearing one. They were also absolutely impregnable. And he asked her what would be the best marketing name for them: Excalibur or King Arthur. He liked King Arthur. Athena thought it over for a moment.

Then she said with mock seriousness, "Maybe a more politically correct name?"

"You're right," Steven said. "They're so expensive to make we have to sell them to both sexes. Our tag marketing line will be 'Condom of the Stars.' How about that for a name? Star Condoms."

. . .

The movie and their affair were both huge successes. Athena had successfully climbed the first rung of the ladder to stardom, and each picture she made over the next five years solidified that success.

The affair, as most star affairs go, was also a success but naturally short-lived. Steven and Athena loved each other with help from the script, but their love had the humor and detachment made necessary by his fame and her ambition. Neither could afford to be more in love than the other and this equality in love was death to their passion. Also there was the question of geography. The affair ended when the picture ended. Athena went on location to India, Steven on location to Italy. There were phone calls and Christmas cards and gifts, they even flew to Hawaii for a weekend of ecstasy. Working together on a movie was like being Knights at the Round Table. Searching for fame and fortune was looking for the Holy Grail, you had to do it on your own.

There had been speculation that they might marry. Of this there was no possibility. Athena enjoyed the affair but always saw its comic side. Though she made it her business as a professional actor to appear more in love than Steven, it was almost impossible for her not to giggle. Steven was so sincere, so perfect as an ardent and sensitive lover, that she could just as well have gone to one of his films.

His physical beauty could be enjoyed but not constantly admired. His constant use of drugs and liquor was so controlled it was impossible to pass judgment. He treated cocaine as a prescription drug, alcohol made him more charming. Even his success had not made him willful or moody.

So it was a great surprise when Steven proposed marriage. Athena refused with good humor. She knew that Steven screwed everything that moved, on location, in Hollywood, and even at the rehabilitation clinic when his drug problem got out of control. He was not a man she wanted to have as a semipermanent part of her life.

Steven took her refusal well. It had been a momentary weakness springing from an excess of cocaine. He was almost relieved.

Over the next five years, as Athena shot up to the top rank of stardom, Steven began to fade. He was still an idol to his fans, especially women, but he was unlucky or unintelligent in picking his roles. Drugs and alcohol made him more careless in his work habits. Through Melo Stuart, Steven had asked Athena for the male lead in *Messalina.* The shoe was now on the other foot. Athena had approval of her costar and she gave him the role. She said yes out of a perverse sense of gratitude and because he was perfect for the part, however with the proviso that he did not have to sleep with her.

During the last five years Athena had had short affairs. One had been with a young producer, Kevin Marrion, the only son of Eli Marrion.

Kevin Marrion was her age but a veteran of the movie business. He had produced his first major film at the age of twenty-one and it had been a hit. Which convinced him he had a genius for movies. Since that time he had produced three flops, and now only his father gave him credibility in the industry.

Kevin Marrion was extremely good-looking; after all, Eli Marrion's first wife had been one of the greatest beauties in the business. Unfortunately his looks iced out in the camera and he failed all his screen tests. As a serious artist his future was as a producer.

Athena and Kevin met when he asked her to star in his new film. Athena listened to him in rapt wonder and horror. He talked with the particular innocence of the very serious-minded.

"This is the best movie script I have ever read," Kevin said. "I must tell you in all honesty that I helped rewrite it. Athena you are absolutely the only actress that deserves this role. I could have any actress in the industry but I want you." He looked sternly at her to convince her of his sincerity.

Athena was fascinated by his pitching of the script. It was the story of a homeless woman living on the streets who is redeemed by the finding of an abandoned infant in a garbage pail and who then goes on to become the leader of the homeless in America. Half of the film consisted of her pushing the shopping cart that held all her possessions. And after surviving alcohol, drugs, near starvation, rape, and a government attempt to take away her foundling, she goes on to run for president of the United States on an independent ticket. Not winning, however—that was the class of the script.

Athena's fascination had really been horror. This was a script that would require her to be a homeless, despairing woman in a desolate background in old clothes. Visually, a disaster. The sentimentality was rank, the intelligence level of dramatic construction, idiotic. It was a bewildering, hopeless mess.

Kevin said, "If you play this part, I will die happy."

And Athena thought, Am I crazy or is this guy a moron? But he was a powerful producer. Obviously sincere, and obviously a man who could get things done. She looked despairingly at Melo Stuart, and he smiled back at her encouragingly. But she could not speak.

"Wonderful. Wonderful idea," Melo said. "Classic. Rise and fall. Fall and rise. The very essence of drama. But Kevin, you know how important it is for Athena after her breakthrough to select the proper follow-up. Let us read the script and we'll get back to you."

"Of course," Kevin said and handed both of them copies of the script. "I know you'll love it."

Melo took Athena to a small Thai restaurant on Melrose. They ordered their meal and flipped through the script.

"I'll kill myself first," Athena said. "Is Kevin retarded?"

"You still don't understand the movie business," Melo said. "Kevin has intelligence. He's just doing something he is not equipped to do. I've seen worse."

"Where? When?" Athena said.

"I can't recall offhand," Melo said. "You're a big enough star to say no but you're not big enough to make unnecessary enemies."

"Eli Marrion is too smart to back his son up on this one," Athena said. "He must know how terrible this script is."

"Sure," Melo said. "He even jokes that he has a son who makes flop commercial movies and a daughter who makes serious movies that lose money. But Eli has to make his children happy. We don't. We say no to this movie. But there's a catch. LoddStone owns the rights to a big novel that has a great role for you. If you turn Kevin down, you may not get that other part."

Athena shrugged. "This time I'll wait."

"Why not take both parts? Make it a condition you do the novel first. Then we'll find an out on making Kevin's picture."

"And that won't make enemies?" Athena asked him smiling.

"The first picture will be a big hit so it won't matter. Then you can afford to make enemies."

"Are you sure I can get out of Kevin's picture afterwards?" Athena said.

"If I don't get you out, you can fire me," Melo said. He had already made the deal with Eli Marrion, who could not give the direct no to his son and had chosen this way out of the disaster. Eli wanted to make Melo and Athena the villains. And Melo didn't mind. Part of any movie agent's job was to be the villain in the script.

Everything worked out. The first part, the film of the novel, made Athena an absolutely first-rank star. But unfortunately the consequences made her decide on a period of celibacy.

During the sham of the preproduction of Kevin's movie that would never be made, it was predictable that he would fall in love with Athena. Kevin Marrion was a relatively innocent young man for a producer, and he pursued Athena with unabashed sincerity and ardor. His enthusiasm and his social conscience were his greatest charm. One evening, in a moment of weakness compounded by the guilt she felt about betraying the picture, Athena took him to bed. It was enjoyable enough and Kevin insisted on marriage.

Meanwhile Athena and Melo had persuaded Claudia De Lena to rewrite the script. She rewrote it as farce and Kevin fired her. He was so angry that he became a bore.

For Athena the affair was convenient. It fitted in nicely with her working schedule. And Kevin's enthusiasm was pleasurable in bed. And his insistence on marriage even without a prenuptial agreement was flattering, since he would inherit LoddStone Studios one day.

But one night after listening to him talk incessantly about the movies they were going to make together, a sudden insight flashed through Athena's mind: "If I have to listen to this guy one more minute, I will kill myself." Like many kind people exasperated into being unkind, she went all the way. Knowing she would feel guilty, she made it a package. In that moment, she told Kevin that not only would she not marry him, but she would not sleep with him anymore and that also she would not appear in his movie.

Kevin was stunned. "We have a contract," he said. "And we'll enforce it. You are betraying me in every way."

"I know," Athena said. "Just talk to Melo." She was disgusted with herself. Of course, Kevin was right, but she found it interesting that he was more worried about his movies than his love for her.

It was after this affair, her film career assured, that Athena lost interest in men. She remained celibate. She had more important things to do, things in which the love of men had no part.

Athena Aquitane and Claudia De Lena became close friends solely because Claudia was persistent in her pursuit of friendship with women she liked. She first met Athena while rewriting the script of one of her early movies, when Athena was not quite yet a great star.

Athena insisted on helping her with the script, and although this was usually a scary process for the writer, she proved to be intelligent and a great help. Her instincts on character and story were always good and nearly always unselfish. She was intelligent enough to know that the stronger the characters around her, the more she would have to play with in her own role.

They often worked in Athena's home in Malibu, and it was there they discovered they had many things in common. They were athletes: strong swimmers, top amateur golfers, and very good on the tennis court. The two of them played doubles together and beat most of the male doubles on the Malibu Beach tennis courts. So when the picture finished shooting, they continued their friendship.

Claudia told Athena everything about herself. Athena told Claudia little. It was that kind of friendship. Claudia recognized this but it didn't matter. Claudia told of her affair with Steve Stallings. Athena laughed delightedly and they compared notes. They agreed, yes, Steve had been great fun, great in bed. And so talented, he was a marvelously gifted actor and a really sweet man.

"He was almost as beautiful as you," Claudia said. She generously admired beauty in others.

Athena seemed not to have heard. It was a habit she had when somebody mentioned her beauty.

"Is he a better actor though?" Athena said teasingly.

"Oh no, you're a really great actor," Claudia said. And then to provoke Athena into revealing more of herself, she added, "But he's a lot happier person than you."

"Really?" Athena said. "That may be. But someday he will be a hell of a lot unhappier than I ever will be."

"Yeah," Claudia said. "The cocaine and booze will get him. He's not going to age well. But he's intelligent, maybe he'll adapt."

"I don't ever want to become what he's going to be," Athena said. "And I won't."

"You're my hero," Claudia said. "But you're not going to beat the aging process. I know you don't drink and booze or even fool around much but your secrets will get you."

Athena laughed. "My secrets will be my salvation," she said. "My secrets are so banal they're not even worth telling. We movie stars need our mystery."

Every Saturday morning when they were not working, they went shopping together on Rodeo Drive. Claudia was always amazed at how Athena could disguise herself so that she would not be recognized by fans or the clerks in the stores. She wore a black wig and loose clothes to disguise her figure. She changed her makeup so her jaw seemed to be thicker, her lips fuller, but most interesting of all, it seemed as if she could rearrange the features on her face. She also wore contact lenses that changed her brilliant green eyes to a demure hazel. Her voice became a soft Southern drawl.

When Athena bought something, she put it on one of Claudia's charge cards and then reimbursed her with a check when they had their late lunch. It was wonderful to relax in a restaurant as complete nobodies; as Claudia joked, no one ever recognized a screenwriter.

Twice a month Claudia spent the entire weekend at Athena's Malibu beach house for swimming and tennis. Claudia had let Athena read the second draft of *Messalina,* and Athena had asked for the lead role. As if she were not a top star and Claudia should not be begging her.

. . .

So when Claudia arrived in Malibu to persuade Athena to go back to work on the picture, she felt some hope for success. After all, Athena would not only ruin her own career but damage Claudia's.

The first thing that shook Claudia's confidence was the tight security around Athena's house, in addition to the usual guards at the Malibu Colony gates.

Two men with Pacific Ocean Security Company uniforms were at the gate of the house itself. Two additional guards patrolled the huge garden inside. When the little South American housekeeper led her to the Ocean Room, she could see two more guards on the beach outside. All the guards had batons and holstered guns.

Athena greeted Claudia with a tight hug. "I'll miss you," she said. "In a week I'll be gone."

"Why are you being so crazy?" Claudia said. "You're going to let some jerk of a macho man ruin your whole life. And mine. I can't believe you're so chicken. Listen, I'll stay with you tonight and tomorrow we'll get gun permits and start training. In a couple of days we'll be sharpshooters."

Athena laughed and gave her another hug. "Your Mafia blood is coming out," she said. Claudia had told her about the Clericuzio and her father.

They made drinks and sat in the stuffed chairs that gave them a view of the ocean that was like looking at some deep blue-green portrait of water.

"You can't change my mind and I'm not chickenshit," Athena said. "Now, I'll tell you the secret you wanted to know and you can tell the Studio and then maybe you'll both understand."

Then she told Claudia the whole story of her marriage. Of Boz Skannet's sadism and cruelty and deliberate humiliation and of her running away. . . .

With her astute, storyteller mind, Claudia felt there was something missing in Athena's story, that she was deliberately leaving out some important elements.

"What happened to the baby?" Claudia asked.

Athena's features arranged themselves into a movie-star mask. "I can't tell you anything more about that right now, in fact what I did tell you about me having a baby is just between you and me. That's the one part you mustn't tell the Studio. I trust you with that."

Claudia knew she couldn't press Athena on this. "But why are you quitting the picture?" Claudia asked. "You'll be protected. Then you can disappear."

"No," Athena said. "The Studio will only protect me while the picture's shooting. And that won't matter. I know Boz. Nothing will stop him. If I stay, I'll never finish the picture anyway."

At that moment they both noticed a man in bathing trunks walking up from the water to the house. The two security guards intercepted him. One of the guards blew a whistle and the two guards in the garden came running around. With the odds at four to one, the man in the bathing trunks seemed to retreat slightly.

Athena was standing up, obviously shaken. "It's Boz," she said to Claudia quietly. "He's doing this just to scare me. It's not his real move." She went out onto the deck and looked down at the five men. Claudia followed her.

Boz Skannet looked up at them, his eyes squinting, his bronzed face painted by the sun. His body, in the bathing trunks, looked lethal.

He smiled and said, "Hey, Athena, how about inviting me in for a drink?"

Athena gave him a brilliant smile. "I would if I had poison. You've broken the court order—I could have you locked up."

"Nah, you wouldn't," Boz said. "We're too close, we have too many secrets together." Though he smiled, he looked savage.

Claudia was reminded of the men who came to the Clericuzio feasts in Quogue.

One of the guards said, "He swam around the fence from the public beach. He must have a car there. Or we can have him locked up."

"No," Athena said. "Take him to his car. And tell the Agency I want four more guards around my house."

Boz still had his face tilted up, his body seemed to be a great statue rooted in the sand. "See you, Athena," he said. And then the guards led him away.

"He is frightening," Claudia said. "Maybe you're right. We would have to shoot cannons to stop him."

"I'll call you before I *flee*," Athena said, making it actressy. "We can have one last dinner together."

Claudia was almost in tears. Boz had really frightened her, had reminded her of her father. "I'm going to fly to Vegas and see my brother Cross. He's smart and knows a lot of people. I'm sure he can help. So don't leave until I come back."

"Why should he help?" Athena said. "And how? Is he in the Mafia?"

"Of course not," Claudia said indignantly. "He'll help because he loves me." She said this with pride in her voice. "And I'm the only person he really loves except for my father."

Athena looked at her with a frown. "Your brother sounds just a little shady. You're very innocent for a woman working in the movies. And, by the way, how come you sleep with so many men? You're not an actress and I don't think you're a tramp."

"That's no secret," Claudia said. "Why do men screw so many women?" Then she hugged Athena. "I'm off to Vegas," she said. "Don't move till I get back."

That night Athena sat on the deck and watched the ocean, black beneath the moonless sky. She went over her plans and thought fondly of Claudia. It was really funny that she could not see through her brother, but that's what love did.

When Claudia met with Skippy Deere later that afternoon and told him Athena's story, they both sat in silence for a while. Then Deere said, "She left some things out. I went to see Boz Skannet to buy him off. He refused. And he warned me that if we tried any funny stuff, he'd give the papers a story that would ruin us. How Athena dumped their kid."

Claudia flew into a rage. "That's not true," she said. "Anyone who knows Athena knows she couldn't do such a thing."

"Sure," Deere said. "But we didn't know Athena when she was twenty."

"Fuck you too," Claudia said. "I'm going to fly to Vegas and see my brother Cross. He has more brains and more balls than any of you guys. He'll straighten this out."

"I don't think he can scare Boz Skannet," Deere said. "We already gave it a good try." But now he saw another opportunity.

He knew certain things about Cross. Cross was looking to get into the movie business. He had invested in six of Deere's pictures and lost money overall, so Cross wasn't that smart. It was rumored Cross was "connected," that he had some influence in the Mafia. But everybody was connected with the Mafia, Deere thought. That didn't make them dangerous. He doubted that Cross could help them with Boz Skannet. But a producer always listened, a producer specialized in long shots. And besides he could always pitch Cross to invest in another picture. It was always a great help to have minor partners who had no control over the making of the picture and the finances.

Skippy Deere paused, then said to Claudia, "I'll go with you."


Claudia De Lena loved Skippy Deere despite the fact that Deere had once screwed her out of a half-million dollars. She loved Deere for his faults and the diversity of his corruption and because Skippy was always good company, all admirable qualities in a producer.

Years ago they had worked on a picture together and had been buddies. Even then, Deere had been one of the most successful and colorful producers in Hollywood. One time on a set, the star of the movie had boasted of fucking Deere's wife and Deere, listening off a ledge on the set three stories above him, had jumped and landed on the star's head and broken his shoulder in addition to then smashing his nose with a good right-hand punch.

Claudia had another memory. The two of them had been walking down Rodeo Drive and Claudia had seen a blouse in the window. It was the most beautiful blouse Claudia had ever seen. It was white with almost invisible stripes of green, so lovely it could have been painted by Monet. The store was one of those that required an appointment before you could even go in and shop, as if the owner were some great physician. No problem. Skippy Deere was a personal friend of the owner as he was a great friend of studio chiefs, the great corporate heads, the rulers of countries throughout the Western world.

When they were in the store, the clerk told them the blouse was five hundred dollars. Claudia staggered back, held her hands on her chest. "Five hundred dollars for one blouse?" she asked. "Don't make me laugh."

The clerk was staggered in his turn by Claudia's impudence. "It's of the finest fabric," he said, "handmade. . . . And the green stripe is a green like no other fabric in the entire world. The price is very reasonable."

Deere was smiling. "Don't buy it, Claudia," he said. "Do you know how much it costs to get it laundered? At least thirty bucks. Every time you wear it, thirty bucks. And you have to take care of it like a baby. No food stains, and definitely you can't smoke. If you burn a hole, bang, there goes your five hundred."

Claudia smiled at the clerk. "Tell me," she said, "do I get a free gift if I buy the blouse?"

The clerk, a beautifully dressed man, had tears in his eyes and said, "Please leave."

They walked out of the store.

"Since when can a store clerk throw a customer out?" Claudia asked, laughing.

"This is Rodeo Drive," Skippy said. "You're lucky you even got in."

The next day when Claudia arrived for work at the studio, there was a gift box on her desk. In it were a dozen of the blouses and a note from Skippy Deere: "Not to be worn except at the Oscars."

Claudia knew that the clerk at the store and Skippy Deere were both full of shit. She had later seen that same beautiful green stripe on a woman's dress and on a special hundred-dollar tennis bandanna.

And the picture she was working on with Deere was a schlock love-action film that would never come closer to an Academy Award than Deere's appointment to the Supreme Court. But she was touched.

And then there was the day that the picture they had worked on reached the magical one-hundred-million-dollar gross and Claudia had thought she would be rich. Skippy Deere invited her to dinner to celebrate. Skippy was bubbling over with good humor. "This is my lucky day," he said. "The picture goes over a hundred, I got a great blow job from Bobby Bantz's secretary, and my ex-wife got killed in a car accident last night."

There were two other producers at dinner with them and they both winced. Claudia thought Deere was making a joke. But then Deere said to the two producers, "I see your eyes green with envy. I save five hundred grand a year in alimony and my two kids inherit her estate, the settlement she got from me, so I don't have to support them anymore."

Claudia was suddenly depressed and Deere said to her, "I'm being honest, it's what every man would think but never say out loud."

Skippy Deere had paid his dues in the movie business. The son of a carpenter, he had helped his father work on the houses of movie stars in Hollywood. In one of those situations that are probable only in Hollywood, he became the lover of a middle-aged female star, who got him a job as an apprentice in her agent's company, a prelude to getting rid of him.

He worked hard, learning to control his fiery nature. Most of all, how to coddle Talent. How to beg hot new directors, fast-talk fresh young stars, become best friend and mentor to horseshit writers. He made fun of his own behavior, citing a great Renaissance cardinal pleading the Borgia Pope's cause with the King of France. When the King exposed his derriere, then defecated to show his contempt for the Pope, the Cardinal exclaimed, "Oh, the ass of an angel," and rushed to kiss it.

But Deere mastered the indispensable hardware. He learned the art of negotiation, which he simplified to "Ask for everything." He became literate, developing an eye for those novels that would make good movies. He could spot acting talent. He scrutinized the details of production, the different ways to steal money from the budget of a film. He became a successful producer, one who could put 50 percent of the script and 70 percent of the budget on the screen.

It was helpful that he enjoyed reading and also that he could screen-write. Not on a totally blank piece of paper, but he was adept at crossing out scenes and revising dialogue, and could actually create pieces of action, little set pieces, which sometimes played brilliantly but were seldom necessary to the story being told. What he prided himself on, what helped his pictures achieve financial success, was that he was especially good at endings, which were almost always triumphant, the exaltation of good over evil—and if that didn't fit, the sweetness of defeat. His masterpiece had been the ending of a film that dealt with the atom-bomb destruction of New York, in which all the characters came out as better human beings dedicated to the love of their fellow man, even the one who had exploded the bomb. He had to hire five extra writers to get that done.

All this would have been worth very little to him as a producer if he had not been especially astute about finance. He pulled investment money out of thin air. Rich men doted on his company, as did the beautiful women who hung on his arm. Stars and directors enjoyed his honest and bawdy appreciation of the good things in life. He charmed development money out of studios, and he learned that it was possible to get a green light out of some studio heads with an enormous bribe. His Christmas card and Christmas gift lists were endless, to stars, to critics on newspapers and magazines, even to high-ranking law enforcement people. He called them all dear friends and when they no longer became useful he cut them from the gift list but never from the card list.

One of the keys to being a producer was to own a property. It could be an obscure novel, unsuccessful in print, but it was something concrete you could talk about to the studio. Deere secured rights to these with five-year options at five hundred dollars a year. Or he would option a screenplay and work with the writer to shape it into something a studio would buy. That was real ditch-digging work, writers were so fragile. "Fragile" was his favorite word for people he thought jerks. It was especially useful with female stars.

One of his most successful relationships had been with Claudia De Lena, and one of the most enjoyable. He had really liked the kid, wanted to teach her the ropes. They had spent three months together working on the script. They went out to dinner together, they played golf together (Deere had been surprised when Claudia beat him). They went to the Santa Anita race track. They swam in Skippy Deere's pool with secretaries in bathing suits to take dictation. Claudia had even taken Deere to Vegas for a weekend at the Xanadu to meet her brother, Cross. They sometimes slept together, it was convenient.

The picture was a great financial success, and Claudia assumed she would earn a great deal of money on the back end. She had a percentage of Skippy Deere's percentage, and she knew that he was always positioned "upstream," as Deere liked to call gross percentage. But what Claudia did not know was that Deere had two different percentages, one on gross, the other on net. And Claudia's back end deal called for a piece of Skippy Deere's net position. Which, though the picture made over $100 million, came to nothing. The Studio's accounting procedure, Deere's percentage of the gross, and the cost of the picture easily wiped out net profits.

Claudia sued, and Skippy Deere settled for a small sum to preserve their friendship. When Claudia reproached him, Deere said, "This had nothing to do with our personal relationship, this is between our lawyers."

Skippy Deere often said, "I was human once, then I got married." More than that, he had fallen truly in love. His excuse was that he was young, and that he had married her because even then his keen eye knew she was a talented actress. In this he was correct, but his wife, Christi, did not have that magic quality on film that translated into a star. The best she could achieve was the third female lead.

But Deere really loved her. When he became a power in the movie industry, he did his best to make Christi a star. He called in favors from other producers, from directors, from studio chiefs, to get her big parts. In a few pictures he got her up to second female lead. But as she got older, she worked less. They had two children, but Christi became more and more unhappy and this took up a fair amount of Deere's work time.

Skippy Deere, like all successful producers, was insanely busy. He had to travel all over the world supervising his pictures, getting financing, developing projects. Coming in contact with so many beautiful, charming women, and needing companionship, he often had romantic liaisons, which he enjoyed with gusto, but still he loved his wife.

One day a Development girl brought him a script that she said was perfect for Christi, a foolproof star role that would exactly suit her talent. It was a dark movie, a woman who murdered her husband for love of a young poet and then had to escape the grief of her children and the suspicions of her in-laws. Then of course found redemption. It was very outrageous baloney, but it could work.

Skippy Deere had two problems: convincing a studio to make the movie and then convincing it to cast Christi in the part.

He called in all his favors. He took all his money on the back end. He persuaded a top male star to take a part that was really a featured role and got Dita Tommey to direct. Everything went like a dream. Christi played the part perfectly, Deere produced the film perfectly, that is to say, 90 percent of the budget actually got up on the screen.

During that time Deere was never unfaithful to his wife except for one night he spent in London arranging distribution, and then he fell only because the English girl was so thin he was intrigued by the logistics.

It worked. The picture was a commercial success, he made more on the sacrificial back end than he would have on a straight deal, and Christi won the Academy Award as best actress.

And, as Skippy Deere later said to Claudia, that was where the movie should have ended: Happily Ever After. But now his wife had found real self-esteem, now she sensed her true worth. The proof was that she became a vehicle star, she now received scripts delivered by messenger, with roles for beautiful, celluloid-magic personalities. Deere advised her to look for something more suited to her, the next picture would be crucial. He had never worried about her being faithful, indeed had conceded her the right to have fun when she was on location. But now in the few months after her Award—the toast of the town, invited to all the top parties, appearing in all the showbiz columns, courted by young actors struggling to get roles—she blossomed into a fresh young womanhood. She went out, openly, on dates with actors fifteen years her junior. The gossip journalists took note, the feminists among them cheering her on.

Skippy Deere seemingly took this very well. He understood the whole thing. After all, why did he himself keep screwing young girls? So why begrudge his wife equal pleasure? But then again why should he continue his extraordinary efforts to further Christi's career? Especially after she actually asked him for a role for one of her young lovers. He stopped looking for scripts for her, he stopped campaigning for her with other producers and directors and studio heads. And they, being older men, took umbrage for him in masculine brotherhood and no longer gave Christi any special consideration.

Christi made two more pictures in a starring role; both were flops because she was miscast. And so she spent the professional credit the Award had earned for her. In three years, she was back to playing third female leads.

By this time she had fallen in love with a young man who aspired to be a producer, indeed was very much like her husband, but he needed capital. So Christi sued for divorce, winning a huge settlement and $500,000 a year in alimony. Her lawyers never found out about Skippy's assets in Europe, so they parted friends. And now, seven years later, she had died in an automobile accident. By that time, although she had remained on Deere's Christmas card list, she was on his famous "Life Is Too Short" list, signifying he would not return her phone calls.

So Claudia De Lena had a twisted affection for Deere. For his exposing his true self to others, for his living his life so blatantly in his own self-interest, for his ability to look you in the eye and call you his friend while not caring that you knew he would never perform a true act of friendship. That he was such a cheerful, ardent hypocrite. And besides, Deere was a great persuader. And he was the only man she knew who could match wits with Cross. They took the next plane to Vegas.

# BOOK IV

# Cross De Lena
# The Clericuzio

# CHAPTER 6

**B**Y THE TIME Cross reached the age of twenty-one, Pippi De Lena was impatient for Cross to follow his destiny. The most important fact in a man's life, conceded by all, was that he must make a living. He must earn his bread, put a roof over his head and clothes on his back, and feed the mouths of his children. To do that without unnecessary misery, a man had to have a certain degree of power in the world. It followed then, as night the day, that Cross must take his place in the Clericuzio Family. To do that, it was absolutely necessary he "make his bones."

Cross had a good reputation in the Family. His answer to Dante when Dante told him that Pippi was a Hammer was quoted happily by Don Domenico himself, who savored the words almost with ecstasy. "I don't know that. You don't know that. Nobody knows that. Where did you get that fuckin' hat?" What an answer, the Don exclaimed with delight. So young a man to be so discreet, and so witty, what a credit to his father. We must give this boy his chance. All this had been related to Pippi, and so he knew the time was ripe.

He started to groom Cross. He sent him out on collection assignments that were difficult and required force. He discussed the old history of the Family and how operations were executed. Nothing fancy, he stressed. But when you had to get fancy, it must be planned in extreme detail. Simple was extreme simplicity. You sealed off a small geographic area and then you caught the target in that area. Surveillance first, then car and hit man, then blocking cars for any pursuers, then going to ground for a time afterward so that you could not be immediately questioned. That was simple. For fancy, you got fancy. You could dream up anything but you had to back it up with solid planning. You only got fancy when it was absolutely necessary.

He even told Cross certain code words. A "Communion" was when the victim's body disappeared. That was fancy. A "Confirmation" was when the body was found. That was simple.

Pippi gave Cross a briefing on the Clericuzio Family. Their great war with the Santadio Family, which established their dominance. Pippi said nothing of his part in that war and was indeed scarce on details. Rather he praised Giorgio and Vincent and Petie. But most of all he praised Don Domenico for his farsightedness.

The Clericuzio had spun many webs, but its most extensive was gaming. It dominated all forms of casino and illegal gambling in the United States. It had a very subtle influence on the Native American casinos, it had a serious influence on sports betting, legal in Nevada and illegal in the rest of the country. The Family owned slot machine factories, had an interest in the manufacture of dice and cards, the supply of chinaware and silverware, the laundries for the gambling hotels. Gambling was the great jewel of their empire, and they ran a public relations campaign to make gambling legal in every state of the union.

Legal gambling all over the United States by federal law was now the Holy Grail of the Clericuzio Family. Not only casinos and lotteries but also wagering on sports: baseball, football, basketball, and all others. Sports were holy in America, and once gambling was legalized that holiness would descend on gambling itself. The profits would be enormous.

Giorgio, whose company managed some of the state lotteries, had given the Family a breakdown on the expected numbers. A minimum of two billion dollars was bet on the Super Bowl all over the United States, most of it illegally. The sports books in Vegas, legal betting alone ran up over fifty million. The World Series, depending on how many games were played, totaled about another billion. Basketball was much smaller, but the many playoff games carried another billion, and this was not counting the everyday betting during the season.

Once made legal, all this could be easily doubled or tripled with special lotteries and combination betting, except for the Super Bowl, whose increase would be tenfold and might even provide a net revenue for one day of $1 billion. The overall total could reach $100 billion, and the beauty was that there was no productivity involved, the only expenses were marketing and administration. What a great deal of money for the Clericuzio Family to rack up, a profit of at least $5 billion a year.

And the Clericuzio Family had the expertise and the political connections and pure force to control a great deal of this market. Giorgio had charts to show the complicated prizes that could be constructed based on big sports events. Gambling would be a great magnet to draw the money from the huge gold mine that was the American people.

So gambling was low-risk and had great growth potential. To achieve legal gambling, cost was no object and even greater risks were considered.

The Family was also made rich with income from drugs, but only at a very high level, it was too risky. They controlled European processing, provided political protection and judicial intervention, and they laundered the money. Their position in drugs was legally impregnable and extremely profitable. They dropped the black money in a chain of banks in Europe and a few banks in the United States. The structure of the law was outflanked.

But then, Pippi cautiously pointed out, despite all this there came times when risks had to be taken, when an iron fist must be shown. This the Family did with the utmost discretion and with terminal ferocity. And that was when you must earn the good life you led, when you truly earned your daily bread.

Shortly after his twenty-first birthday, Cross was finally put to the test.

One of the most prized political assets of the Clericuzio Family was Walter Wavven, the governor of Nevada. He was a man in his early fifties, tall and lanky, who wore a cowboy hat but dressed in perfectly tailored suits. He was a handsome man and though married had a lusty appetite for the female sex. He also enjoyed good food and good drink, loved to bet sports, and was an enthusiastic casino gambler. He was too tender of public feelings to expose these traits, or to risk romantic seductions. So he relied on Alfred Gronevelt and the Xanadu Hotel to satisfy these appetites while preserving his political and personal image of the God-fearing, steadfast believer in old-fashioned family values.

Gronevelt had recognized Wavven's special gifts early on and provided the financial base that enabled Wavven to climb the political ladder. When Wavven became governor of Nevada and wanted a relaxing weekend, Gronevelt gave him one of the prized Villas.

The Villas had been Gronevelt's greatest inspiration. . . .

Gronevelt had come to Vegas early, when it was still basically a western cowboy gambling town, and he had studied gambling and gamblers as a brilliant scientist might study an insect important to evolution. The one great mystery that would never be solved was why very rich men still wasted time gambling to win money they did not need. Gronevelt decided they did so to hide other vices, or they desired to conquer fate itself, but more than anything it was to show some sort of superiority to their fellow creatures. Therefore he reasoned that when they gambled they should be treated as gods. They would gamble as the gods gambled or the kings of France in Versailles.

So Gronevelt spent $100 million to build seven luxurious Villas and a special jewel-box casino on the grounds of the Xanadu Hotel (with his usual foresight he had bought much more land than the Xanadu needed). These Villas were small palaces, each could sleep six couples in six separate apartments, not merely suites. The furnishings were lavish: hand-woven rugs, marble floors, gold bathrooms, rich fabrics on the walls; dining rooms and kitchens staffed by the Hotel. The latest audiovisual equipment turned living rooms into theaters. The bars of these Villas were stocked with the finest wines and liquors and a box of illegal Havana cigars. Each Villa had its own outdoor swimming pool and inside Jacuzzi. All free to the gambler.

In the special security area that held the Villas was the small oval casino called the Pearl, where the high rollers could play in privacy and where the minimum bet in baccarat was a thousand dollars. The chips in this casino were also different, the black one-hundred-dollar chip was the lowest denominator; the five hundred, pale white threaded with gold; a gold-barred blue chip for the thousand; and the specially designed ten-thousand-dollar chip, with a real diamond embedded in the center of its gold surface. However, as a concession to the ladies, the roulette wheel would change hundred-dollar chips into five-dollar chips.

It was amazing that enormously wealthy men and women would take this bait. Gronevelt figured that all these extravagant RFB comps ran the Hotel fifty thousand dollars a week on the cost sheet. But these were written off on tax reports. Plus the prices of everything were inflated on paper. Figures (he kept a separate accounting) showed that each Villa made an average profit of a million dollars a week. The very fancy restaurants that served the Villas' and other important guests also made a profit as tax write-offs. On the cost sheets, a dinner for four totaled over a thousand dollars, which since the guests were comped, was written off as business expense for that amount in taxes. Since the meal cost the Hotel no more than a hundred dollars counting labor, there was a profit right there.

And so, to Gronevelt, the seven Villas were like seven crowns that he bestowed on the heads of only those gamblers who risked or made a Drop of over a million dollars on their two- or three-day stay. It didn't matter that they won or lost. Just that they gambled it. And they had to be prompt in paying their markers or they would be relegated to one of the suites in the Hotel itself, which, however plush, were not comparable to the Villas.

Of course there was a little more. These were Villas where important public men could bring their mistresses or boyfriends, where they could gamble in anonymity. And strange to say there were many titans of business, men worth hundreds of millions of dollars, even with wives and mistresses, who were lonely. Lonely for care-free feminine company, for women of exceptional sympathy. And for these men, the Villas would be furnished by Gronevelt with the proper beauty.

Governor Walter Wavven was one of these men. And he was the only exception to Gronevelt's rule of the million-dollar Drop. He gambled modestly and then with a purse supplied privately by Gronevelt, and if his markers exceeded a certain amount they were put on hold to be paid by his future winnings.

Wavven came to the Hotel to relax, to golf on the Xanadu course, and to drink and court the beauties supplied by Gronevelt.

Gronevelt played it very long with the governor. In twenty years he had never asked an outright favor, just the special access to present his arguments for legislation that would help the casino business in Vegas. Most of the time his point of view prevailed; when it did not, the governor gave him a detailed explanation of the political realities that had denied him. But the governor provided a valuable service in that he introduced Gronevelt to influential judges and politicians who could be swayed with hard cash.

Gronevelt nurtured in his secret heart the hope that, against long odds, Governor Walter Wavven might someday be the president of the United States. Then the rewards could be enormous.

But Fate foils the most cunning of men, as Gronevelt always acknowledged. The most insignificant of mortals become the agents of disaster to the most powerful. This particular agent was a twenty-five-year-old young man who became the lover of the governor's eldest child, a young woman of eighteen.

The governor was married to an intelligent, good-looking woman who was more fair, more liberal in her political views than her husband, though they worked well as a team. They had three children, and this family was a great political asset for the governor. Marcy, the eldest, was attending Berkeley, her choice and her mother's, not the governor's.

Freed from the stiffness of a political household, Marcy was entranced by the freedom of the university, its orientation toward the political left, its openness to new music, the insights offered by drugs. A true daughter of her father, she had a frankness of sexual interest. With that innocence and the natural instinct for fair play in the young, her sympathies were with the poor, the working class, the suffering minorities. She also fell in love with the purity of art. It was therefore very natural for her to hang out with students who were poets and musicians. It was even more natural that after a few casual encounters she fell in love with a fellow student who wrote plays and strummed the guitar and was poor.

His name was Theo Tatoski and he was perfect for a college romance. He had dark good looks, he came from a family of Catholics who worked in Detroit's auto factories and, with a poet's alliterative wit, always swore he would rather fuck than fit a fender. Despite this he worked part-time jobs to pay his tuition. He took himself very seriously, but this was mitigated by the fact that he had talent.

Marcy and Theo were inseparable for two years. She brought Theo to meet her family in the governor's mansion and was delighted that he was unimpressed by her father. Later in their bedroom in the state mansion, he informed her that her father was a typical phony.

Perhaps Theo had detected their condescension; the governor and his wife had both been extra friendly, extra courteous, determined to honor their daughter's choice, while privately deploring so unsuitable a match. The mother was not worried; she knew Theo's charm would fade with her daughter's growth. The father was uneasy but tried to make up for it with a more-than-common affability, even for a politician. After all, the governor was a champion of the working class, per his political platform, the mother was an educated liberal. A romance with Theo could only give Marcy a broader view of life. Meanwhile Marcy and Theo were living together, and planned to get married after they graduated. Theo would write and perform his plays, Marcy would be his muse and a professor of literature.

A stable arrangement. The young people did not seem to be heavily into drugs, their sexual relationship was no big deal. The governor even thought idly that if worse came to worst their marriage would help him politically, an indication to the public that despite his pure WASP background, his wealth, his culture, he democratically accepted a blue-collar son-in-law.

They all made their adjustments to a banal situation. The parents just wished that Theo was not such a bore.

But the young are perverse. Marcy, in her final year of college, fell in love with a fellow student who was rich and socially more acceptable to her parents than Theo. But she still wanted to keep Theo as a friend. She found it exciting to juggle two lovers without committing the technical sin of adultery. In her innocence, it made her feel unique.

The surprise was Theo. He reacted to the situation not as a tolerant Berkeley radical, but like some beknighted Polack. Despite his poetic, musical bohemianism, the teachings of feminist professors, the whole Berkeley atmosphere of sexual laissez-faire, he became violently jealous.

Theo had always been moodily eccentric, it was part of his youthful charm. In conversation, he often took the extremely revolutionary position that blowing up a hundred innocent people was a small price to pay for a free society in the future. Yet Marcy knew Theo could never do such a thing. Once when they came to their apartment after a two-week vacation, they had found a litter of newborn mice in their bed. Theo had simply put the tiny creatures out into the street unharmed. Marcy found that endearing.

But when Theo found out about Marcy's other lover, he struck her in the face. Then he burst into tears and begged her forgiveness. She forgave him. She still found their lovemaking exciting, more exciting because now she held more power with his knowledge of her betrayal. But he became progressively more violent, they quarreled often, life together was no longer such fun, and Marcy moved out of their apartment.

Her other lover faded. Marcy had a few other affairs. But she and Theo remained friends and slept together occasionally. Marcy planned to go East and do her master's in an Ivy League university, Theo moved down to Los Angeles to write plays and look for movie-script work. One of his short musical plays was being produced by a small theater group for three performances. He invited Marcy to come to see it.

Marcy flew to Los Angeles to see the play. It was so terrible half the audience walked out. So Marcy stayed over that night in Theo's apartment to console him. What exactly happened that night could never be established. What was proven was that sometime in the early morning, Theo stabbed Marcy to death, knife wounds in each eye. Then he stabbed himself in the stomach and called the police. In time to save his life, but not Marcy's.

The trial in California was, naturally, a huge media event. A daughter of the governor of Nevada murdered by a blue-collar poet who had been her lover for three years and was then dumped.

The defense lawyer, Molly Flanders, successfully specialized in "passion" murders, though this case proved to be her last criminal case before she entered entertainment law. Her tactics were classic. Witnesses were brought in to show that Marcy had at least six lovers, while Theo believed they were to be married. The rich, socially prominent, sluttish Marcy had dumped her sincere blue-collar playwright, whose mind then snapped. Flanders pleaded "temporary insanity" on her client's behalf. The most relished line (written for Molly by Claudia De Lena) was "He is forever not responsible for what he has done." A line that would have incited Don Clericuzio into a fury.

Theo looked properly stricken during his testimony. His parents, devout Catholics, had persuaded powerful members of the California clergy to take up the cause, and they testified that Theo had renounced his hedonistic ways and was now determined to study for the priesthood. It was pointed out that Theo had tried to kill himself and was therefore self-evidently remorseful, thus proving his insanity, as if the two went together. All this was varnished by the rhetoric of Molly Flanders, who painted a picture of the great contribution Theo could make to society if he was not punished for a foolish act triggered by a woman of loose morals who broke his blue-collar heart. A careless rich girl, now unfortunately dead.

Molly Flanders loved California juries. Intelligent, well-educated enough to understand the nuances of psychiatric trauma, exposed to the higher culture of theater, film, music, literature, they pulsed with empathy. When Flanders got through with them, the outcome was never in doubt. Theo was found not guilty by reason of temporary insanity. He was immediately signed to appear in his life story for a miniseries, not as the primary actor but as a minor one who sang songs of his own composition to link the story together. It was a completely satisfactory ending to a modern tragedy.

But the effect on Governor Walter Wavven, the girl's father, was disastrous. Alfred Gronevelt saw his twenty-year investment going down the drain, for Governor Wavven in the privacy of his Villa announced to Gronevelt that he would not stand for reelection. What was the point of acquiring power when any son-of-a-bitch low-life white trash could stab his daughter to death, almost cut off her head, and live his life a free man? Even worse, his beloved child had been dragged through the papers and TV as a silly cunt who deserved to be killed.

There are tragedies in life that cannot be cured, and for the governor this was one of them. He spent as much time as possible at the Xanadu Hotel but was not his old jolly self. He was not interested in showgirls, or the roll of the dice. He simply drank and played golf. Which posed a very delicate problem for Gronevelt.

He was deeply sympathetic to the governor's problem. You cannot cultivate a man for over twenty years, even out of self-interest, without having some affection for him. But the reality was that Governor Walter Wavven, resigning from politics, was no longer a key asset, had no future potential. He was simply a man destroying himself with booze. Also, when he gambled he did so distractedly, Gronevelt held two hundred grand of his markers. So now had come the time when he must refuse the governor the use of a Villa. Certainly he would give the governor a luxury suite in the Hotel, but it would be a demotion, and before doing that Gronevelt took a last stab at rehabilitation.

Gronevelt persuaded the governor to meet him for golf one morning. To complete the foursome he recruited Pippi De Lena and his son, Cross. Pippi had a crude wit the governor always appreciated, and Cross was such a good-looking and polite young man that his elders were always glad to have him around. After they played they went to the governor's Villa for a late lunch.

Wavven had lost a great deal of weight and seemed to take no pride in his appearance. He was in a stained sweatsuit and wore a baseball cap with the Xanadu logo. He was unshaven. He smiled often, not a politician smile, but a sort of shameful grimace. Gronevelt noticed that his teeth were very yellow. He was also extremely drunk.

Gronevelt decided to take the plunge. He said, "Governor, you are letting your family down, you are letting your friends down, and you are letting the people of Nevada down. You cannot go on like this."

"Sure I can," Walter Wavven said. "Fuck the people of Nevada. Who cares?"

Gronevelt said, "I do. I care about you. I'll put the money together and you must run for senator in the next election."

"Why the hell should I?" the governor said. "It doesn't mean anything in this fucking country. I'm governor of the great state of Nevada and that little prick murders my daughter and goes free. And I have to take it. People make jokes about my dead kid and pray for the murderer. You know what I pray for? That an atom bomb wipes out this fucking country and especially the state of California."

Pippi and Cross remained silent during all this. They were a little shaken by the governor's intensity. Also, both understood Gronevelt was working to a purpose.

"You have to put all of that behind you," Gronevelt said. "Don't let this tragedy destroy your life." His unctuousness would have irritated a saint.

The governor threw his baseball cap across the room and helped himself to another whiskey at the bar.

"I can't forget," he said. "I lie awake at night and dream about squeezing that little cocksucker's eyes out of his head. I want to set him on fire, I want to cut off his hands and legs. And then I want him to be alive so I can do it again and again." He smiled drunkenly at them, almost fell, they could see the yellow teeth and smell the decay in his mouth.

Wavven now seemed less drunk, his voice became quiet, he spoke almost conversationally. "Did you see how he stabbed her?" he asked. "He stabbed her through the eyes. The judge wouldn't let the jury see the photos. Prejudicial. But I, her father, could see the photos. And so little Theo goes free, with that smirk on his face. He stabbed my daughter through the eyes but he gets up every morning and he sees the sun shining. Oh, I wish I could kill them all—the judge, the jurors, the lawyers, all of them." He filled his glass and then walked around the room furiously, his speech a crazy ramble.

"I can't go out there and bullshit about what I no longer believe. Not while the little bastard is alive. He sat at my dinner table, my wife and I treated him like a human being even though we disliked him. We gave him the benefit of the doubt. Never give anybody the benefit of the doubt. We took him into our home, gave him a bed to sleep in with our daughter and he was laughing at us all the time. He was saying, 'Who gives a fuck if you're the governor? Who gives a fuck if you have money? Who gives a fuck that you are civilized, decent human beings? I will kill your daughter whenever I like and there is nothing you can do. I'll bring you all down. I'll fuck your daughter, then I'll kill her, and then I'll stick it up your ass and go free.' " Wavven staggered and Cross quickly went to hold him. The governor looked up beyond Cross, to the high mural-decorated ceiling above, all pink angels and white-clad saints. "I want him dead," the governor said and burst into tears. "I want him dead."

Gronevelt said quietly, "Walter, it will all go away, give it time. File for senator. You have the best years of your life ahead of you, you can still do so much."

Wavven shook himself away from Cross and said quite calmly to Gronevelt, "Don't you see, I don't believe in doing good anymore. I'm forbidden to tell anyone how I really feel, not even my wife. The hatred I feel. And I'll tell you something else. The voting public has contempt for me, they perceive me as a weak fool. A man who lets his daughter get murdered, then can't get him punished. Who would trust the welfare of the great state of Nevada to such a man?" He was sneering now. "That little fuck could get elected easier than me." He paused for a moment. "Alfred, forget it. I'm not running for anything."

Gronevelt was studying him carefully. He was catching something that Pippi and Cross did not. Passionate grief so often led to weakness, but Gronevelt decided to take the risk. He said, "Walter, will you run for senator if the man is punished? Will you be the man you were?"

The governor seemed not to understand. His eyes rolled slightly toward Pippi and Cross, then stared into Gronevelt's face. Gronevelt said to Pippi and Cross, "Wait for me in my office."

Pippi and Cross quickly left. Gronevelt and Governor Wavven were alone. Gronevelt said to him gravely, "Walter, you and I must be very direct for the first time in our lives. We've known each other twenty years, have you ever found me to be indiscreet? So answer. It will be safe. Will you run again if that boy is dead?"

The governor went to the bar and poured whiskey. But he did not drink. He smiled. "I'll file the day after I go to that boy's funeral to show my forgiveness," he said. "My voters will love that."

Gronevelt relaxed. It was done. Out of relief, he indulged his temper. "First, go see your dentist," he told the governor. "You have to get those fucking teeth cleaned."

Pippi and Cross were waiting for Gronevelt back in his penthouse office suite. He led them into his living quarters so that they could be more comfortable, then told them what had been said.

"The governor is okay?" Pippi asked.

"The governor was not as drunk as he pretended," Gronevelt said. "He gave me the message without really implicating himself."

"I'll fly East tonight," Pippi said. "This must get the Clericuzio OK."

"Tell them I think the governor is a man who can go all the way," Gronevelt said. "To the very top. He would be an invaluable friend."

"Giorgio and the Don will understand that," Pippi said. "I just have to lay everything out and get the OK."

Gronevelt looked at Cross and smiled, then he turned to Pippi. He said gently, "Pippi, I think it's time Cross joined the Family. I think he should fly East with you."

But Giorgio Clericuzio decided to come West to Vegas for the meeting. He wanted to be briefed by Gronevelt himself, and Gronevelt had not traveled for the last ten years.

Giorgio and his bodyguards were established in one of the Villas, though he was not a high roller. Gronevelt was a man who knew how to make exceptions. He had refused the Villas to powerful politicians, financial giants, to some of the most famous movie stars in Hollywood, to beautiful women who had slept with him, to close personal friends. Even Pippi De Lena. But he gave a Villa to Giorgio Clericuzio, though he knew Giorgio had spartan tastes and did not really appreciate extraordinary luxuries. Every mark of respect counted, mounted up, and one breach, no matter how tiny, could be remembered someday.

They met in Giorgio's Villa. Gronevelt, Pippi, and Giorgio . . .

Gronevelt explained the situation. "The governor can be an enormous asset to the Family," Gronevelt said. "If he pulls himself together, he may go all the way. First, senator, then the presidency. That happens and you have a good shot at getting sports gambling legalized all over the country. That will be worth billions to the Family and those billions will not be black money. It will be white money. I say it's something we have to do."

White money was far more valuable than black money. But Giorgio's great asset was that he was never stampeded into rash decisions. "Does the governor know you are with us?"

"Not for sure," Gronevelt said. "But he must have heard rumors. And he's not a dummy. I've done some things for him that he knows I couldn't do if I were alone. And he's clever. All he said was that he would run for office if the kid were dead. He didn't ask me to do anything. He's a great con, he wasn't that drunk when he broke down. I think he figured the whole thing out. He was sincere, but he was faking it too. He couldn't figure out his revenge but he had the idea I could do something. He is suffering, but he's also scheming." He paused for a moment. "If we come through, he'll run for senator and he will be our senator."

Giorgio prowled uneasily in the room, avoiding the statues on their pedestals, the curtained Jacuzzi whose marble seemed to shine through the fabric. He said to Gronevelt, "You promised him without our OK?"

"Yes," Gronevelt said. "It was a matter of persuasion. I had to be positive to give him a sense that he still has power. That he could, still, cause things to happen, and so make power appeal to him again."

Giorgio sighed. "I hate this part of the business," he said.

Pippi smiled. Giorgio was so full of shit. He had helped wipe out the Santadio Family with a savageness that made the old Don proud.

"I think we need Pippi's expertise on this," Gronevelt said. "And I think it's time for his son, Cross, to join the Family."

Giorgio looked at Pippi. "Do you think Cross is ready?" he asked.

Pippi said, "He's had all the gravy, it's time for him to earn his living."

"But will he do it?" Giorgio asked. "It's a big step."

"I'll talk to him," Pippi said. "He'll do it."

Giorgio turned toward Gronevelt. "We do it for the governor, then what if he forgets about us? We take the risk and it's all for nothing. Here's a man who is governor of Nevada, his daughter gets killed and he lies down. He has no balls."

"He did do something, he came to me," Gronevelt said. "You have to understand people like the governor. That took a lot of balls for him."

"So he'll come through?" Giorgio said.

"We'll save him for the few big things," Gronevelt said. "I've done business with him for twenty years. I guarantee he comes through if he's handled right. He knows the score, he's very smart."

Giorgio said, "Pippi, it has to look like an accident. This will get a lot of heat. We want the governor to escape any innuendos from his enemies or the papers and that fucking TV."

Gronevelt said, "Yes, it's important that nothing can be implied about the governor."

Giorgio said, "Maybe this is too tricky for Cross to make his bones on."

"No, this is perfect for him," Pippi said. And they could not object. Pippi was the commander in the field. He had proved himself in many operations of this kind, especially in the great war against the Santadio. He had often told the Clericuzio Family, "It's my ass on the line, if I get stuck, I want it to be my fault, not somebody else's."

Giorgio clapped his hands. "Okay, let's get it done. Alfred, how about a round of golf in the morning? Tomorrow night I go on business to L.A. and the day after I go back East. Pippi, let me know who you want from the Enclave to help, and tell me if Cross is in or out."

And with that Pippi knew that Cross would never be admitted to the inside of the Clericuzio Family if he refused this operation.

Golf had become a passion for Pippi's generation of the Clericuzio Family; the old Don made malicious jokes that it was a game for *Brugliones*. Pippi and Cross were on the Xanadu course that afternoon. They didn't use driving carts; Pippi wanted the exercise of walking and the solitude of the greens.

Just off the ninth hole there was an orchard of trees with a bench beneath. They sat there.

"I won't live forever," Pippi said. "And you have to make a living. The Collection Agency is a big moneymaker but tough to keep. You have to be in solid with the Clericuzio Family." Pippi had prepared Cross, had sent him on some tough collecting missions where he had to use force and abuse, had exposed him to Family gossip; he knew the score. Pippi had waited patiently for the right situation, for a target that would not arouse sympathy.

Cross said quietly, "I understand."

Pippi said, "That guy that killed the governor's daughter. A punk prick and he gets away with it. That's not right."

Cross was amused by his father's psychology. "And the governor is our friend," he said.

"That's right," Pippi said. "Cross, you can say no, remember that. But I want you to help me on a job I have to do."

Cross looked down the rolling greens, the flags above the holes dead still in the desert air, the silvery mountain ranges beyond, the sky reflecting the neon signs of the Strip he could not see. He knew his life was about to change and he felt a moment of dread. "If I don't like it I can always go to work for Gronevelt," he said. But he let his hand rest on his father's shoulder for a moment to let him know it was a joke.

Pippi grinned at him. "This job is for Gronevelt. You saw him with the governor. Well, we're going to give him his wish. Gronevelt had to get the OK from Giorgio. And I said you would help me out."

Far away on one of the greens, Cross could see a foursome of two women and two men shimmering cartoonlike in the desert sun. "I have to make my bones," he said to his father. He knew he had to agree or live a completely different life. And he loved the life he led, working for his father, hanging out at the Xanadu, the direction of Gronevelt, the beautiful showgirls, the easy money, the sense of power. And once he did so he should never be subject to the fates of ordinary men.

"I'll do all the planning," Pippi said. "I'll be with you all the way. There's no danger. But you have to be the shooter."

Cross rose from the bench. He could see the flags on the seven Villas flapping, though there was no breeze on the golf course. For the first time in his young life he felt the ache of a world that was to be lost. "I'm with you," he said.

In the three weeks that followed, Pippi gave Cross an indoctrination. He explained that they were waiting for a surveillance team report on Theo, his movements, his habits, recent photos. Also, an operations team of six men from the Enclave in New York were moving into place in Los Angeles where Theo was still living. The whole operation plan would be based on the report of the surveillance team. Then Pippi lectured Cross on the philosophy.

"This is a business," he said. "You take all the precautions to prevent the downside. Anybody can knock somebody off. The trick is never to get caught. That is the sin. And never think of the personalities involved. When the head of General Motors throws fifty thousand people out of work, that's business. He can't help wrecking their lives, he has to do it. Cigarettes kill thousands of people, but what can you do? People want to smoke and you can't ban a business that generates billions of dollars. Same with guns, everybody has a gun, everybody kills everybody, but it's a billion-dollar industry, you can't get rid of it. What can you do? People must earn a living, that comes first. All the time. You don't believe that, go live in the shit."

The Clericuzio Family was very strict, Pippi told Cross. "You have to get their OK. You can't go around killing people because they spit on your shoe. The Family has to be with you because they can make you jailproof."

Cross listened. He only asked one question. "Giorgio wants it to look like an accident? How do we do that?"

Pippi laughed. "Never let anybody tell you how to run your operation. They can go fuck themselves. They tell me their maximum expectations. I do what is best for me. And the best is to be simple.

Very, very simple. And when you have to get fancy, get very, very fancy."

When the surveillance reports came, Pippi made Cross study all the data. There were some photos of Theo, photos of his car showing its license plates. A map of the road he traveled from Brentwood up to Oxnard to visit a girlfriend. Cross said to his father, "He can still get a girlfriend?"

"You don't know women," Pippi said. "If they like you, you can piss in the sink. If they don't like you, you can make them the Queen of England and they'll shit on you."

Pippi flew into L.A. to set up his operations team. He came back two days later and told Cross, "Tomorrow night."

The next day, before dawn, to escape the heat of the desert, they drove from Las Vegas to Los Angeles. Driving across the desert, Pippi told Cross to relax. Cross was mesmerized by the glorious sunrise that seemed to melt the desert sand into a deep river of gold lapping at the foot of the distant Sierra Nevadas. He felt anxious. He wanted to get the job done.

They arrived in a Family house in the Pacific Palisades where the six-man crew from the Bronx Enclave was awaiting them. In the driveway was a stolen car that had been repainted and had false license plates. Also at the house were the untraceable guns that were to be used.

Cross was surprised at the luxuriousness of the house. It had a beautiful view of the ocean across the highway, a swimming pool, and a huge sundeck. It also had six bedrooms. The men seemed to know Pippi well. But they were not introduced to Cross nor he to them.

They had eleven hours to kill before the operation started at midnight. The other men, ignoring a huge TV set, started a card game on the sundeck; they were all in bathing suits. Pippi smiled at Cross and said, "Shit, I forgot about the swimming pool."

"That's OK," Cross said. "We can go swimming in our shorts." The house was secluded, shielded by enormous trees and an encircling hedge.

"We can go bare-assed," Pippi said. "Nobody can see except the helicopters and they'll be looking at all the broads sunbathing outside their Malibu houses."

Both of them swam and sunbathed for a few hours and then ate a meal prepared by one of the six-man crew. The meal was steak, cooked on the sundeck grill, and a salad of arugula and lettuce. The other men drank red wine with their food, but Cross had a club soda. He noticed that all the men ate and drank sparingly.

After the meal, Pippi took Cross on a reconnaissance in the stolen car. They drove to the western-style restaurant and coffee shop farther down the Pacific Coast Highway where they would find Theo. The surveillance reports showed that on Wednesday nights Theo, on his way to Oxnard, had made a habit of stopping at the Pacific Coast Highway Restaurant at around midnight for coffee and ham and eggs. That he would leave about one in the morning. That night a surveillance team of two men would be tailing him and would report by telephone when he was on the way.

Back at the house Pippi rebriefed the men on the operation. The six men would have three cars. One car would precede them, another would bring up the rear, the third car would park in the restaurant lot and be prepared for any emergency.

Cross and Pippi sat on the sundeck waiting for the phone call. There were five cars in the driveway, all black, shining in the moonlight like bugs. The six men from the Enclave continued their card game, playing with silver coins: nickels, dimes, and quarters. Finally at eleven-thirty the phone call came: Theo was on his way from Brentwood to the restaurant. The six men got in three cars and drove away to take up their appointed posts. Pippi and Cross got into the stolen car and waited another fifteen minutes before they left. Cross had in the pocket of his jacket a small .22 pistol, which, though it had no silencer, only gave off a sharp little pop; Pippi carried a Glock that would make a loud report. Ever since his only arrest for murder, Pippi always refused to carry a silencer.

Pippi drove. The operation had been planned in the most specific detail. No member of the operations team was to go into the restaurant. Detectives would question the help about all the customers. The surveillance team had reported what Theo was wearing, the car he was driving, the license plates. They were lucky that Theo's car was a flaming red and that it was a cheap Ford, easily identifiable in an area where Mercedeses and Porsches were commonplace.

When Pippi and Cross arrived in the parking lot of the restaurant, they could see Theo's car was already there. Pippi parked next to it. Then he turned off the car lights and ignition and sat in the darkness. Across the Pacific Coast Highway they saw the ocean shimmering, parted with streaks of gold that were the moonlight. They saw one of their team cars parked on the far side of the lot. They knew their other two teams were at their stations on the highway waiting to shepherd them back to the house, ready to cut off any pursuers and intercept any problems before them.

Cross looked at his watch. It was twelve-thirty. They had to wait another fifteen minutes. Suddenly Pippi hit his shoulder. "He's early," Pippi said. "Go!"

Cross saw the figure emerging from the restaurant, caught in the glow of the door lights. He was struck by the boyishness of the figure, slight and short, a shock of curly hair above the pale, thin face. Theo looked too frail to be a murderer.

Then they were surprised. Theo, instead of going to his car, walked across the Pacific Coast Highway, dodging traffic. On the other side, he strolled out onto the open beach to the very edge, daring the waves. He stood there gazing at the ocean, the yellow moon setting on the horizon so far away. Then he turned and came back across the highway and into the parking lot. He had let the waves reach him, and there was the squish of water in his fashionable boots.

Cross slowly got out of the car. Theo was almost on him. Cross waited for Theo to go past, then smiled politely to let Theo get into his car. When Theo was inside, Cross drew the gun. Theo, about to put his key into the ignition, his car window down, raised his eyes, aware of the shadow. At the moment Cross fired, they looked into each other's eyes. Theo was frozen as the bullet smashed into his face, which instantly became a mask of blood, the eyes staring out. Cross yanked open the door and fired two more bullets into the top of Theo's head. Blood sprayed into his face. Then he threw a pouch of drugs on the floor of Theo's car. He slammed the door shut. Pippi had started up the motor of his car just as Cross fired. Now he opened the car door, and Cross hopped in. According to plan he had not dropped the pistol. That would have made it look like a planned hit instead of a drug deal gone sour.

Pippi drove out of the lot, and their cover car pulled out behind them. The two lead cars swung into position, and five minutes later they were back at the Family house. Ten minutes after that, Pippi and Cross were in Pippi's car heading toward Vegas. The operations team would get rid of the stolen car and the gun.

When they drove past the restaurant there were no signs of police activity. Obviously Theo was still undiscovered. Pippi turned the car radio on and listened to the news broadcasts. There was nothing. "Perfect," Pippi said. "When you plan right, it always goes perfect."

They arrived in Las Vegas as the sun was coming up, the desert a sullen red sea. Cross never forgot that ride through the desert, through the darkness, through the moonlight that never seemed to end. And then the sun coming up and then, a little later, the neon lights of the Vegas strip shining like a beacon heralding safety, the awakening from a nightmare. Vegas was never dark.

At almost that exact moment, Theo was discovered, his face ghostly in a paler dawn. Publicity centered on the fact that Theo was in possession of half a million dollars worth of cocaine. It was obviously a drug deal gone sour. The governor was in the clear.

Cross observed many things from this event. That the drugs he had planted on Theo cost no more than ten thousand dollars, although the authorities had placed the value at half a million; that the governor was praised for the fact that he sent condolences to Theo's family; that in a week the media never referred to the matter again.

Pippi and Cross were summoned East for an audience with Giorgio. Giorgio commended them both for an intelligent and well-executed operation, making no mention of the fact that it was supposed to look like an accident. And Cross was aware on this visit that the Clericuzio Family treated him with the respect due the Family Hammer. The primary evidence of this was that Cross was given a percentage of the income of the gambling books, legal and illegal, in Las Vegas. It was understood that he was now an official member of the Clericuzio Family, to be called to duty on special occasions with bonuses calculated on the risk of the project.

. . .

Gronevelt, too, had his reward. After Walter Wavven was elected senator, he took a weekend retreat at the Xanadu. Gronevelt gave him a Villa and went to congratulate him on his victory.

Senator Wavven was back in his old form. He was gambling and winning, he had little dinners with the showgirls of the Xanadu. He seemed completely recovered. He made only one reference to his earlier crisis. He said to Gronevelt, "Alfred, you have a blank check with me."

Gronevelt said, smiling, "No man can afford to carry blank checks in his wallet, but thank you."

He didn't want checks that paid off all the senator's debt. He wanted a long, continuing friendship, one that would never end.

In the next five years, Cross became an expert on gambling and running a casino hotel. He served as an assistant to Gronevelt, though his primary job was still working with his father, Pippi, not only in running the Collection Agency, which he was now certified to inherit, but also as the number two Hammer for the Clericuzio Family.

By the age of twenty-five, Cross was known in the Clericuzio Family as the Little Hammer. He himself found it curious that he was so cold about his work. His targets were never people he knew. They were lumps of flesh enclosed in defenseless skin; the skeleton beneath gave them the outline of wild animals he had hunted with his father when he was a boy. He did fear the risk but only cerebrally; there was no physical anxiety. There were moments in his life's repose, sometimes when he awoke in the morning with a vague terror as if he had some terrible nightmare. Then there were times when he was depressed, when he called up the memory of his sister and his mother, little scenes from childhood and some visits after the breakup of the family.

He remembered his mother's cheek, her flesh so warm, her satin skin so porous that he imagined he could hear the blood flow underneath, contained, safe. But in his dreams the skin crumbled like ash, blood washing over the obscene breaks into scarlet waterfalls.

Which triggered other memories. When his mother kissed him with cold lips, her arms embracing him for tiny moments of politeness. She never held his hand as she did Claudia's. The times he visited and left her house short of breath, his chest burning as if bruised. He never felt her loss in the present, he only felt her lost in his past.

When he thought of his sister, Claudia, he did not feel this loss. Their past together existed and she was still part of his life, though not enough. He remembered how they used to fight in the winter. They kept their fists in their overcoat pockets and swung at each other. A harmless duel. All was as it should be, Cross thought, except that sometimes he missed his mother and his sister. Still, he was happy with his father and the Clericuzio Family.

So in his twenty-fifth year Cross became involved in his final operation as a Hammer of the Family. The target was someone he had known all his life. . . .

A vast FBI probe destroyed many of the titular Barons, some true *Brugliones,* across the country, and among them was Virginio Ballazzo, now the ruler of the largest Family on the Eastern Seaboard.

Virginio Ballazzo was a Baron of the Clericuzio Family for over twenty years and had been dutiful in wetting the Clericuzio beak. In return the Clericuzio made him rich; at the time of his fall, Ballazzo was worth over $50 million. He and his family lived in very good style indeed. And yet the unforeseen happened. Virginio Ballazzo, despite his debt, betrayed those who had raised him so high. He broke the law of *omertà,* the code that forbade giving any information to the authorities.

One of the charges against him was murder, but it was not so much fear of imprisonment that made him turn traitor; after all, New York had no death penalty. And no matter how long his penalty, if indeed he was convicted, the Clericuzio would get him out in ten years, would ensure that even those ten years would be easy time. He knew the repertoire. At his trial, witnesses would perjure themselves in his behalf, jurors could be approached with bribes. Even after he had served a few years, a new case would be prepared, presenting new evidence, showing that he was innocent. There was one famous case in which the Clericuzio had done such a thing after one of their clients had served five years. The man had gotten out and the state had presented him with over a million dollars as reparation for his "false" imprisonment.

No, Ballazzo had no fear of prison. What made him turn traitor was that the Federal Government threatened to seize all his worldly goods under the RICO laws passed by Congress to crush crime. Ballazzo could not bear that he and his children would lose their palatial home in New Jersey, the luxurious condo in Florida, the horse farm in Kentucky that had produced three also-rans in the Kentucky Derby. For the infamous RICO laws permitted the government to seize all worldly goods of those arrested for criminal conspiracy. The stocks and bonds, the antique cars might be taken. Don Clericuzio himself had been angered by the RICO laws, but his only comment was "the rich will rue this thing, the day will come when they will arrest the whole of Wall Street under this RICO law."

It was not luck but foresight that the Clericuzio had removed their old friend Ballazzo from its confidence in the last few years. He had become too flashy for their tastes. *The New York Times* had run a story on his collection of antique cars, Virginio Ballazzo at the wheel of a 1935 Rolls-Royce, a debonair visored cap on his head. Virginio Ballazzo, on the TV at the running of the Kentucky Derby, riding crop in hand, talked about the beauty of the sport of kings. There he was identified as a wealthy importer of rugs. All this was too much for the Clericuzio Family, they became wary of him.

When Virginio Ballazzo opened discussions with the United States District Attorney, it was Ballazzo's lawyer who informed the Clericuzio family. The Don, who was semiretired, immediately took charge from his son Giorgio. This was a situation that required a Sicilian hand.

A Family conference was held: Don Clericuzio; his three sons, Giorgio, Vincent, and Petie; and Pippi De Lena. It was true that Ballazzo could damage the Family structure, but only the lower levels would suffer greatly. The traitor could give valuable information but no legal proof. Giorgio suggested that if worse came to worst, they could always set up headquarters in a foreign country, but the Don dismissed this angrily. Where else could they live but in America? America had made them rich, America was the most powerful country in the world and protected its rich. The Don often quoted the saying, "Rather a hundred guilty men go free than one innocent man be punished," then added, "What a beautiful country." The trouble was that everyone got soft because of such good living. In Sicily Ballazzo would never have dared become a traitor, would never even have dreamed of breaking the law of *omertà*. His own sons would have killed him.

"I'm too old to live in a foreign country," the Don said. "I will not be driven from my home by a traitor."

A small problem in and of himself, Virginio Ballazzo was a symptom, an infection. There were many more like him, who did not abide by the old laws that had made them all strong. There was a Family *Bruglione* in Louisiana, another in Chicago, and another in Tampa, who flaunted their wealth, who showed off their power for all the world to see. And then these *cafoni* when they were caught sought to escape the punishment they had earned by their own carelessness. By breaking the law of *omertà*. By betraying their fellows. This rot must be eradicated. That was the Don's position. But now he would listen to the others; after all, he was old, perhaps there were other solutions.

Giorgio outlined what was happening. Ballazzo was bargaining with the government attorneys. He would willingly go to jail if the government promised not to invoke the RICO laws, if his wife and children could keep his fortune. And of course he was bargaining not to go to jail, for that he would have to testify in court against the people he betrayed. He and his wife would be placed in a Witness Protection Program and would live the rest of their lives under false identities. Some plastic surgery would be performed. And his children would live the rest of their lives in respectable comfort. That was the deal.

Ballazzo, whatever his faults, was a doting father, they all agreed. He had three well-brought-up children. One son was graduating from the Harvard School of Business, the daughter, Ceil, had a fancy cosmetics store on Fifth Avenue, another son did computer work in the space program. They were all deserving of their good fortunes. They were true Americans and lived the American dream.

"So," the old Don said, "we will send a message to Virginio that will make sense to him. He can inform on everyone else. He can send them all to jail or to the bottom of the ocean. But if he speaks one word about the Clericuzio, his children are forfeit."

Pippi De Lena said, "Threats don't seem to scare anybody anymore."

"The threat will be from me personally," Don Domenico said. "He will believe me. Promise him nothing for himself. He understands."

It was Vincent who spoke up then. "We'll never be able to get near him once he's in the Protection Program."

The Don spoke to Pippi De Lena. "And you, *Martèllo* of mine, what do you say to that?"

Pippi De Lena shrugged. "After he testifies, after they hide him away in the Protection Program, sure we can. But there will be a lot of heat, a lot of publicity. Is it worth it? Does it change anything?"

The Don said, "The publicity, the heat, is what makes it worth doing. We will send the world our message. In fact when it is done it should be done a *bella figura*."

Giorgio said, "We could just let events take their course. No matter what Ballazzo says, it can't bury us. Pop, your answer is a short-term answer."

The Don pondered that. "What you say is true. But is there a long-term answer to anything? Life is full of doubts, of short-term answers. And you doubt that punishment will stop those others who will be trapped? It may or may not. It will certainly stop some. God himself could not create a world without punishment. I will talk personally to Ballazzo's lawyer. He will understand me. He will give the message. And Ballazzo will believe it." He paused for a moment and then sighed. "After the trials, we will do the job."

"And his wife?" Giorgio asked.

"A good woman," the Don said. "But she has become too American. We cannot leave a bereaved widow to shout her grief and secrets."

Petie spoke for the first time. "And Virginio's children?" Petie was the true assassin.

"Not if it's not necessary. We are not monsters," Don Domenico said. "And Ballazzo never told the children his business. He wanted the world to believe that he was a horse rider. So let him ride his horses at the bottom of the ocean." They were all silent. Then the Don said sadly, "Let the little ones go. After all, we live in a country where children do not avenge their parents."

The following day the message was transmitted to Virginio Ballazzo by his lawyer. In all these messages, the language was flowery. When the Don spoke to the lawyer he expressed his hope that his old friend Virginio Ballazzo had only the fondest memories of the Clericuzio, who would always look out for their unfortunate friend's interests. The Don told the lawyer that Ballazzo should never fear for his children where danger lurked, even on Fifth Avenue, but that the Don himself would guarantee their safety. He, the Don, knew how highly Ballazzo prized his children; that jail, the electric chair, the devils in hell, could not frighten his brave friend, only the specter of harm to his children. "Tell him," the Don said to the lawyer, "that I, personally, I, Don Domenico Clericuzio, guarantee that no misfortune will befall them."

The lawyer delivered this message word for word to his client, who responded as follows. "Tell my friend, my dearest friend, who grew up with my father in Sicily, that I rely on his guarantees with utmost gratitude. Tell him I have only the fondest memories of all the Clericuzio, so profound that I cannot even speak of them. I kiss his hand."

Then Ballazzo sang, "Tra la la . . ." at his lawyer. "I think we better go over our testimony very carefully," he said. "We do not want to involve my good friend. . . ."

"Yes," the lawyer said, as he reported later to the Don.

Everything proceeded according to plan. Virginio Ballazzo broke *omertà* and testified, sending numerous underlings to jail and even implicating a deputy mayor of New York. But not a word of the Clericuzio. Then the Ballazzos, man and wife, disappeared into the Witness Protection Program.

The newspapers and TV were jubilant, the mighty Mafia had been broken. There were hundreds of photos, live TV action shots of these villains being hauled off to prison. Ballazzo took up the whole centerfold of the *Daily News,* TOP MAFIA DON FALLS. It showed him with his antique cars, his Kentucky Derby horses, his impressive London wardrobe. It was an orgy.

When the Don gave Pippi the assignment of tracking down the Ballazzo couple and punishing them, he said, "Do it in such a way that it will get the same publicity as they are getting now. We don't want them to forget our Virginio." But it was to take the Hammer more than a year to complete this assignment.

Cross remembered Ballazzo and had fond memories of him as a jovial, generous man. He and Pippi had had dinner at the Ballazzo house, for Mrs. Ballazzo had a reputation as a fine Italian cook, particularly for her macaroni and cauliflower with garlic and herbs, a dish Cross still remembered. He had played with the Ballazzo children as a child and had even fallen in love with Ballazzo's daughter, Ceil, when they were teenagers. She had written him from college after that magical Sunday, but he had never answered. Alone with Pippi now, he said, "I don't want to do this operation."

His father looked at him and then smiled sadly. He said, "Cross, it happens sometimes, you have to get used to it. You won't survive otherwise."

Cross shook his head. "I can't do it," he said.

Pippi sighed. "OK," he said. "I'll tell them I'm going to use you for planning. I'll make them give me Dante for the actual operation."

Pippi set up the probe. The Clericuzio Family, with huge bribes, penetrated the screen of the Witness Protection Program.

The Ballazzos felt secure in their new identities, false birth certificates, new social security numbers, marriage papers, and the plastic surgery that had altered their faces so that they looked ten years younger. However, their body builds, their gestures, their voices, made them more easily identifiable than they realized.

Old habits die hard. On a Saturday night Virginio Ballazzo and his wife drove to the small South Dakota town near their new home to gamble in the small-time joint operating under the local option. On their way home, Pippi De Lena and Dante Clericuzio, with a crew of six other men, intercepted them. Dante, violating the plan, could not resist making himself known to the couple before he pulled the trigger of his shotgun.

No attempt was made to conceal the bodies. No valuables were taken. It was perceived as an act of retaliation, and it sent a message to the world. There was a torrent of rage from the press and television, the authorities promised justice would be done. Indeed, there was enough of a furor to make the whole Clericuzio Empire seem to be in jeopardy.

Pippi was forced to hide in Sicily for two years. Dante became the number one Hammer of the Family. Cross was made the *Bruglione* of the Western Empire of the Clericuzio. His refusal to take part in the Ballazzo execution had been noted. He did not have the temperament to be a true Hammer.


Before Pippi disappeared into Sicily for two years, he had a final meeting and bon voyage dinner with Don Clericuzio and his son Giorgio.

"I must apologize for my son," Pippi said. "Cross is young and the young are sentimental. He was very fond of the Ballazzos."

"We were fond of Virginio," the Don said. "I never liked a man better."

"Then why did we kill him?" Giorgio asked. "It's caused more trouble than it's worth."

Don Clericuzio gave him a stern look. "You cannot live a life without order. If you have power, you must use it for strict justice. Ballazzo committed a great offense. Pippi understands that, no, Pippi?"

"Of course, Don Domenico," Pippi said. "But you and I are of the old school. Our sons don't understand." He paused for a moment. "I wanted to thank you also for making Cross your *Bruglione* in the West while I'm gone. He will not disappoint you."

"I know that," the Don said. "I have as much trust in him as I have in you. He is intelligent and his squeamishness is that of youth. Time will harden his heart."

They were having a dinner cooked and served by a woman whose husband worked in the Enclave. She had forgotten the Don's bowl of grated Parmesan cheese, and Pippi went into the kitchen for the grater and brought the bowl to the Don. He carefully grated the cheese into the bowl and watched the Don dip his huge silver spoon into the yellowish mound, put it in his mouth, and then sip from his glass of powerful homemade wine. This was a man with a belly, Pippi thought. Over eighty years old and he could still order the death of a sinner, and also eat this strong cheese and harsh wine. He said casually, "Is Rose Marie in the house? I'd like to say good-bye to her."

"She's having one of her fucking spells," Giorgio said. "She's locked herself in her room, thank God, or else we wouldn't be able to enjoy our dinner."

"Ah," Pippi said. "I always thought she'd get better with time."

"She thinks too much," the Don said. "She loves her son Dante too much. She refuses to understand. The world is what it is, and you are what you are."

Giorgio said smoothly, "Pippi, how do you rate Dante after this Ballazzo operation? Did he show any nerves?"

Pippi shrugged and remained silent. The Don gave a little grunt and looked at him sharply. "You can be frank," the Don said. "Giorgio is his uncle and I am his grandfather. We are all of one blood and are permitted to judge each other."

Pippi stopped eating and looked directly at the Don and Giorgio. He said almost regretfully, "Dante has a bloody mouth."

In their world this was an idiom for a man who went beyond savageness, an intimation of bestiality while doing a necessary piece of work. It was strictly forbidden in the Clericuzio Family.

Giorgio leaned back in his chair and said, "Jesus Christ." The Don gave Giorgio a disapproving look for his blasphemy and then waved a hand at Pippi to continue. He did not seem surprised.

"He was a good pupil," Pippi said. "He has the temperament and the physical strength. He's very quick and he is intelligent. But he takes too much pleasure in his work. He took too much time with the Ballazzos. He talked to them for ten minutes before he shot the woman. Then he waited another five minutes before shooting Bal-lazzo. That's not to my taste but more important you never can tell when it might lead to danger, every minute might count. On other jobs he was unnecessarily cruel, a throwback to the old days when they thought it clever to hang a man on a meathook. I don't want to go into details."

Giorgio said angrily, "It's because that prick of a nephew is short. He's a fucking midget. And then he wears those fucking hats. Where the hell does he get them?"

The Don said good-humoredly, "The same place the blacks get their hats. In Sicily when I was growing up everybody wore a funny hat. Who knows why? Who cares? Now, stop talking nonsense. I wore funny hats, too. Maybe it runs in the family. It's his mother who put all kinds of nonsense in his head ever since he was little. She should have married again. Widows are like spiders. They spin too much."

Giorgio said with intensity, "But he's good at his job."

"Better than Cross could ever be," Pippi said diplomatically. "But sometimes I think he's crazy like his mother." He paused. "He even scares me sometimes."

The Don took a mouthful of cheese and wine. "Giorgio," he said, "instruct your nephew, repair his fault. It could be dangerous to all of us in the Family someday. But don't let him know it comes from me. He is too young and I am too old, I would not influence him."

Pippi and Giorgio knew this was a lie but also knew that if the old man wanted to hide his hand, he had a good reason. At that moment they heard steps overhead and then someone coming down the stairs. Rose Marie came into the dining room.

The three men saw with dismay that she was having one of her fits. Her hair was wild, her makeup was bizarre, and her clothing was twisted. Most serious, her mouth was open but no words were coming out. She used her body and hand flailing to take the place of speech. Her gestures were startlingly vivid, better than words. She hated them, she wanted them dead, she wanted their souls to burn in hell for eternity. They should choke on their food, go blind from the wine, their cocks should fall off when they slept with their wives.

Then she took Giorgio's plate and Pippi's plate and smashed them on the floor.

This was all permitted, but the first time, years ago, when she had her first fit, she treated the Don's plate in the same fashion and he had ordered her seized and locked in her room and then had her dispatched for three months to a special nursing home. Even now the Don quickly put the lid on his cheese bowl; she did a lot of spitting. Then suddenly it was over, she became very still. She spoke to Pippi. "I wanted to say good-bye. I hope you die in Sicily."

Pippi felt an overwhelming pity for her. He rose and took her in his arms. She did not resist. He kissed her on the cheek and said, "I wish to die in Sicily rather than come home and find you like this." She broke out of his arms and ran back up the stairs.

"Very touching," Giorgio said, almost sneering. "But you don't have to put up with her every month." He gave a slight leer with this, but they all knew that Rose Marie was far past menopause and she had the fits more than once a month.

The Don seemed the least upset by his daughter's fit. "She will get better or she will die," he said. "If not I will send her away."

Then he addressed Pippi. "I'll let you know when you can come back from Sicily. Enjoy the rest, we're all getting older. But keep your eyes open for new men to recruit for the Enclave. That is important. We must have men we can count on not to betray us, who have *omertà* in their bones, not like the rascals born in this country who want to lead a good life but not pay for it."


The next day, with Pippi on his way to Sicily, Dante was summoned to the Quogue mansion to spend the weekend. The first day Giorgio let Dante spend all his time with Rose Marie. It was touching to see their devotion to each other, Dante was a totally different person with his mother. He never wore one of his peculiar hats, he took her on walks around the estate, took her out for dinner. He waited on her like some eighteenth-century French gallant. When she broke into hysterical tears, he cradled her in his arms, and she never went into one of her fits. They spoke to each other constantly in low, confidential tones.

At supper time, Dante helped Rose Marie set the table, grate the Don's cheese, kept her company in the kitchen. She cooked his favorite meal of penne with broccoli and then roast lamb studded with bacon and garlic.

Giorgio was always struck by the rapport between the Don and Dante. Dante was solicitous, he spooned the penne and broccoli into the Don's plate and ostentatiously wiped and polished the great silver spoon he used to dip into the grated parmesan. Dante teased the old man. "Grandfather," he said, "if you got new teeth, we wouldn't have to grate this cheese. The dentists do great work now, they can plant steel in your jaw. A miracle."

The Don was playful in kind. "I want my teeth to die with me," he said. "And I'm too old for miracles. Why should God waste a miracle on an ancient like me?"

Rose Marie had prettied herself for her son, and traces of her young beauty could be seen. She seemed happy to see her father and her son on such familiar terms. It banished her constant air of anxiety.

Giorgio, too, was content. He was pleased that his sister seemed happy. She was not so nerve-racking and she was a better cook. She didn't stare at him with accusing eyes and she would not be subject to one of her fits.

When the Don and Rose Marie had both gone to bed, Giorgio took Dante into the den. It was the room that had neither phones nor TV and no communication lines to any part of the house. And it had a very thick door. Now it was furnished with two black leather couches and black studded leather chairs. It still contained a whiskey cabinet and a small wet bar equipped with a small refrigerator and a shelf of glasses. On the table rested a box of Havana cigars. Still, it was a room with no windows, like a small cave.

Dante's face, too sly and interesting for so young a man, always made Giorgio uneasy. His eyes were too cunningly bright and Giorgio didn't like it that he was short.

Giorgio made them both a drink and lit up one of the Havana cigars. "Thank God you don't wear those weird hats around your mother," he said. "Why do you wear them anyway?"

"I like them," Dante said. "And to make you and Uncle Petie and Uncle Vincent notice me." He paused for a moment and then said with a mischievous grin, "They make me look taller." It was true, Giorgio thought, that hats made him look handsomer. They framed his ferretlike face in a flattering way, his features were strangely uncoordinated when seen without his hat.

"You shouldn't wear them on a job," Giorgio said. "It makes an identification too easy."

"Dead men don't talk," Dante said. "I kill everybody who sees me on a job."

"Nephew, stop fucking me around," Giorgio said. "It's not smart. It's a risk. The Family doesn't take risks. Now one other thing. The word is getting around that you have a bloody mouth."

Dante for the first time reacted with anger. Suddenly he looked deadly. He put down his drink and said, "Does Grandfather know that? Does this come from him?"

"The Don knows nothing about it," Giorgio lied. He was a very expert liar. "And I won't tell him. You're his favorite, it would distress him. But I'm telling you, no more hats on the job and keep your mouth clean. You're the Family number one Hammer now and you take too much pleasure in the business. That's dangerous and against Family rules."

Dante seemed not to hear. He was thoughtful now and his smile reappeared. "Pippi must have told you," he said amiably.

"Yes," Giorgio said. He was curt. "And Pippi is the best. We put you with Pippi so you could learn the right way to do things. And do you know why he's the best? Because he has a good heart. It's never for pleasure."

Dante let himself go. He had a laughing fit. He rolled onto the sofa and then onto the floor. Giorgio watched him sourly, thinking he was as crazy as his mother. Finally Dante got to his feet, took a long swig from his drink, and said with great good humor, "Now you're saying I don't have a good heart."

"That's right," Giorgio said. "You're my nephew but I know what you are. You killed two men in some sort of personal quarrel without the Family OK. The Don wouldn't take action against you, he wouldn't even reprimand you. Then you killed some chorus girl you were banging for a year. Out of temper. You gave her a Communion so she wouldn't be found by the police. And she wasn't. You think you're a clever little prick, but the Family put the evidence together and found you guilty though you could never be convicted in a court of law."

Dante was quiet now. Not from fear but from calculation. "Does the Don know all this crap?"

"Yes," Giorgio said. "But you're still his favorite. He said to let it pass, that you're still young. That you will learn. I don't want to bring this bloody mouth business to him, he's too old. You're his grandson, your mother is his daughter. It would just break his heart."

Dante laughed again. "The Don has a heart. Pippi De Lena has a heart, Cross has a chickenshit heart, my mother has a broken heart. But I don't have a heart? How about you, Uncle Giorgio, do you have a heart?"

"Sure," Giorgio said. "I still put up with you."

"So, I'm the only one who doesn't have a fucking heart?" Dante said. "I love my mother and my grandfather and they both hate each other. My grandfather loves me less as I grow older. You and Vinnie and Petie don't even like me though we share family blood. You think I don't know these things? But I still love all of you though you put me down lower than that fucking Pippi De Lena. You think I don't have any fucking brains either?"

Giorgio was astonished by this outburst. He was also made wary by its truth. "You're wrong about the Don, he cares about you just as much. The same with Petie, Vincent, and me. Have we ever not treated you with the respect of family? Sure, the Don is a little remote but the man is very old. As for me, I'm just giving you a caution for your own safety. You're in a very dangerous business, you have to be careful. You cannot let personal emotions in. That's disaster."

"Do Vinnie and Pete know all this stuff?" Dante asked.

"No," Giorgio said. Which was another lie. Vincent had also spoken to Giorgio about Dante. Petie had not, but Petie was a born assassin. Yet he, too, had shown a distaste for Dante's company.

"Any other complaints about how I do my job?" Dante asked.

"No," Giorgio said, "and don't be so tough about this. I'm advising you as your uncle. But I'm telling you from my place in the Family. You do not anymore make anybody do their Communion or Confirmation without the Family OK. Got it?"

"OK," Dante said, "but I'm still the number one Hammer, right?"

"Until Pippi comes back from his little vacation," Giorgio said. "Depends on your work."

"I'll enjoy my work less if that's what you want," Dante said. "OK?" He tapped Giorgio on the shoulder affectionately.

"Good," Giorgio said. "Tomorrow night take your mother out to eat. Keep her company. Your grandfather will like that."

"Sure," Dante said.

"Vincent has one of his restaurants out by East Hampton," Giorgio said. "You could take your mother there."

Dante said suddenly, "Is she getting worse?"

Giorgio shrugged. "She can't forget the past. She holds on to old stories that she should forget. The Don always tells, 'The world is what it is and we are what we are,' his old line. But she cannot accept it." He gave Dante an affectionate hug. "Now let's just forget this little talk. I hate doing this stuff." As if he had not been specifically instructed by the Don.

After Dante left on Monday morning, Giorgio reported the whole conversation to the Don. The Don sighed. "What a lovely little boy he was. What could have happened?"

Giorgio had one great virtue. He spoke his mind when he really wanted to, even to his father, the great Don himself. "He talked too much to his mother. And he has bad blood." They were both silent for a time after this.

"And when Pippi comes back, what do we do with your grandson?" Giorgio asked.

"Despite everything, I think Pippi should retire," the Don said. "Dante must have his chance to be foremost, after all he is a Clericuzio. Pippi will be an advisor to his son's *Bruglione* in the West. If necessary he can always advise Dante. There is no one better versed in those matters. As he proved with the Santadio. But he should end his years in peace."

Giorgio muttered sarcastically, "The Hammer Emeritus." But the Don pretended not to understand the joke.

He frowned and said to Giorgio, "Soon you will have my responsibilities. Remember always that the task is that the Clericuzio must one day stand with society, that the Family must never die. No matter how hard the choice."

And so they left. But it was to be two years before Pippi returned from Sicily, the killing of Ballazzo receding into the bureaucratic mist. A mist manufactured by the Clericuzio.

# BOOK V

# Las Vegas
# Hollywood
# Quogue

# CHAPTER 7

CROSS DE LENA received his sister, Claudia, and Skippy Deere in the executive penthouse suite of the Xanadu Hotel. Deere was always impressed by the difference between the two siblings. Claudia, not quite pretty and yet so likable, and Cross, so conventionally handsome with a slim but athletic body. Claudia, so naturally amiable, and Cross, so rigidly affable and distant. There was a difference between amiable and affable, Deere thought. One was in the genes, the other, learned.

Claudia and Skippy Deere sat on the couch, Cross sat opposite them. Claudia explained about Boz Skannet and then leaned forward and said, "Cross, please listen to me. This isn't only business. Athena is my dearest friend. And she is truly one of the best people I have ever known. She helped me when I needed help. And this is the most important favor I've ever asked you to do. Help Athena out of this fix and I'll never ask you for anything again." Then she turned to Skippy Deere. "You tell Cross the money part."

Deere always took the offensive before he asked a favor. He said to Cross, "I've been coming to your hotel over ten years, how come you never give me one of the Villas?"

Cross laughed, "They've always been full."

Deere said, "Throw somebody out."

"Sure," Cross said. "When I get a profit statement from one of your pictures and when I see you lay down a ten-grand bet at baccarat."

Claudia said, "I'm his sister and I never got one of the Villas. Stop fucking around, Skippy, and lay out the money problem."

When Deere finished, Cross, reading off a pad on which he had made notes, said, "Let me get this straight. You and the Studio lose fifty million in cash, plus the two hundred million in projected profit, if this Athena doesn't go back to work. She won't go back to work because she's so afraid of an ex-husband called Boz Skannet. You can buy him off but she still won't go back to work because she doesn't believe he can be stopped. Is that the whole thing?"

"Yeah," Deere said. "We promised her she'd be protected better than the president of the United States while she's making this picture. We have surveillance on this guy Skannet even now. We have her guarded twenty-four hours. She still won't come back to work."

"I don't really see the problem," Cross said.

"This guy comes from a powerful political family in Texas," Deere said. "And he's a really tough guy, I tried to get our security people to lean on him . . ."

"Who's your security agency?" Cross asked.

"Pacific Ocean Security," Deere said.

"Why are you talking to me?" Cross asked.

"Because your sister said you could help," Deere said. "It wasn't my idea."

Cross said to his sister, "Claudia, what made you think I could help?"

Claudia's face twisted up in discomfort. "I've seen you solve problems in the past, Cross. You're very persuasive, and you always seem to come up with a solution." She smiled her innocent grin. "Besides you're my older brother, I have faith in you."

Cross sighed and said, "Same old bullshit," but Deere noticed the easy affection between the two.

The three of them sat silently for a while, then Deere said, "Cross, we came here as a long shot. But if you're looking for another investment, I have a project coming up that's very, very good."

Cross looked at Claudia, then at Deere, and said thoughtfully, "Skippy, I want to meet this Athena and after that maybe I can solve all your problems."

"Great," Claudia said, relieved. "We can all fly out tomorrow." She hugged him.

"OK," Deere said. He was already trying to figure out how he could get Cross to take some of his loss on the *Messalina* film.

The next day they flew into Los Angeles. Claudia had talked Athena into seeing them, then Deere had taken the phone. That conversation had convinced him that Athena would never return to the picture. He was infuriated by this, but he diverted himself on the plane by scheming how he would get Cross to give him one of his fucking Villas when he visited Vegas again.

The Malibu Colony, where Athena Aquitane lived, was a section of beach that was located about forty minutes north of Beverly Hills and Hollywood. The Colony held a little over a hundred dwellings, each one of which was worth from three to six million dollars but looked very ordinary and ramshackle from the outside. Each house was enclosed by fencing and sometimes ornate entry gates.

The Colony itself could only be entered through a private road guarded by security men in a large hut who controlled the swinging barriers. The security personnel screened all visitors by phone or checklist. Residents had special car stickers that were changed every week. Cross recognized this as a "nuisance" security barrier, not a serious one.

But the Pacific Ocean Security men around Athena's house were another matter. They were uniformed, armed, and looked to be in very tough physical condition.

They entered Athena's house from the sidewalk parallel to the beach. It had its own additional security controlled by Athena's secretary, who buzzed them in from a small guest house nearby.

There were two more men with Pacific Ocean uniforms, and another at the door of the house. Passing the guest house, they walked through a long garden filled with flowers and lemon trees, which scented the salty air. They finally arrived at the main house which looked out over the Pacific Ocean itself.

A tiny South American maid let them in and led them through a huge kitchen into a living room that seemed to be filled with the ocean filtered through the huge windows. A room with bamboo furniture, glass tables, and deep-sea-green sofas. The maid led them through this room to a glass door that opened onto a terrace overlooking the ocean, a wide, long terrace that had chairs and tables and an exercise bike that glittered like silver. Beyond all of this was the ocean itself, blue-green, slanting to the sky.

Cross De Lena, when he saw Athena on that terrace, felt a shock of fear. She was far more exquisite than on film, which was very rare. Film could not capture her coloring, the depth of her eyes or their shade of green. Her body moved as a great athlete's moved, with a physical grace that seemed effortless. Her hair, cut into a rough, golden crop that would have been ugly on any other woman, crowned her beauty. She was wearing a powder-blue sweat suit that should have concealed the shape of her body but did not. Her legs were long in proportion to her torso, her feet were bare, there was no polish on her toenails.

But it was the look of intelligence on her face, the focusing of attention, that impressed him most.

She greeted Skippy Deere with the customary kiss on the cheek, embraced Claudia with a warm hug, and shook hands with Cross. Her eyes reflected the ocean waters behind her. "Claudia always talks about you," she said to Cross. "Her handsome, mysterious brother who can make the earth stop when he wants to." She laughed, a completely natural laugh, not the laugh of a woman frightened.

Cross felt a wonderful delight, there was no other word. Her voice was throaty, pitched low, a bewitching musical instrument. The ocean framed her, the fine-planed cheekbones, the lips unadorned, generous and the color of red wine, the radiating intelligence. Flashing through Cross's mind was one of Gronevelt's short lectures. *Money can make you safe in this world, from everything except a beautiful woman.*

Cross had known many beautiful women in Vegas, as many as in Los Angeles and Hollywood. But in Vegas the beauty was beauty as of itself with only a slight degree of talent; many of those beauties had failed in Hollywood. In Hollywood, beauty was married to talent and, less often, artistic greatness. Both cities attracted beauty from all over the world. Then there were the actresses who became Bankable Stars.

These were the women who in addition to their charm and beauty had a certain childlike innocence and courage. A curiosity in their craft that could be raised to an art form, which gave them a certain dignity. Though beauty was commonplace in both cities, in Hollywood Goddesses arose and received the adoration of the world. Athena Aquitane was one of those rare Goddesses.

Cross said coolly to Athena, "Claudia told me you are the most beautiful woman in the world."

Athena said, "What did she say about my brain?"

She leaned over the balcony of the deck and stuck one leg in back of her in some sort of exercise. What would be an affectation in another woman seemed perfectly natural with her. And indeed throughout the meeting she continued doing exercises, bending her body forward and backward, stretching a leg over the railing, her arms pantomiming some of her words.

Claudia said, "Thena, you'd never think we were related, right?"

Skippy Deere said, "Never."

But Athena looked at them and said, "You both look very much alike," and Cross could see she was serious.

Claudia said, "Now you know why I love her."

Athena stopped her motions for a moment and said to Cross, "They tell me you can help. I don't see how."

Cross tried not to stare at her, tried not to look at the flaming-sun gold of her hair set against the green behind her. He said, "I'm good at persuading people. If it's true that the only thing keeping you from going back to work is your husband, maybe I can talk him into a deal."

"I don't believe in Boz keeping his deals," Athena said. "The Studio has already talked a deal."

Deere said in what was for him a subdued voice, "Athena you really have nothing to worry about. I promise you." But for some reason he was unconvincing even to himself. He watched them all carefully. He knew how Athena overwhelmed men, actresses were the most charming people in the world when they wanted to be. But Deere detected no change in Cross.

"Skippy just won't accept that I can leave movies," Athena said. "It's so important to him."

"And not to you?" Deere said angrily.

Athena gave a long, cool look. "It was once. But I know Boz. I have to disappear, I have to start a new life." She gave them a mischievous smile. "I can get along anywhere."

"I can make an agreement with your husband," Cross said. "And I can guarantee that he'll abide by it."

Deere said confidently, "Athena, in the movie business, there are hundreds of cases like this, harassment of stars by crazies. We have foolproof procedures. There really is no danger."

Athena continued her exercises. One leg flew improbably above her head. "You don't know Boz," she said. "I do."

"Is Boz the only reason you won't go back to work?" Cross asked.

"Yes," Athena said. "He'll track me forever. You can protect me until I finish the picture but then what?"

Cross said. "I've never failed to make a deal. I'll give him whatever he wants."

Athena stopped her exercises. For the first time, she looked Cross directly in the eye. "I'll never believe in any deal Boz makes," she said. She turned away in dismissal.

Cross said, "I'm sorry I wasted your time."

"I didn't waste my time," Athena said cheerfully. "I did my exercises." Then she looked directly into his eyes. "I do appreciate your trying. It's just that I'm trying to look fearless like in one of my movies. Really, I'm scared to death." Then she quickly regained her composure and said, "Claudia and Skippy are always talking about your famous Villas. If I come to Vegas, would you give me one to hide out in?"

Her face was grave, but her eyes were dancing. She was showing off her power to Claudia and Skippy. She obviously expected Cross to say yes, if merely out of gallantry.

Cross smiled at her. "The Villas are usually taken," he said. He paused for a moment then said, with an utmost seriousness that startled the others, "But if you come to Vegas, I can guarantee no one will harm you."

Athena spoke to him directly. "Nobody can stop Boz. He doesn't care if he gets caught. Whatever he does he'll do in public so everybody can see."

Claudia spoke out impatiently, "But why?"

Athena said laughingly, "Because he loved me once. And because my life turned out better than his." She looked at them all a moment. "Isn't it a shame," she said, "that two people in love can grow to hate each other?"

At this moment the meeting was interrupted by the South American maid, who was leading a man onto the terrace.

The man was tall, handsome, and formally dressed with a touch-all-bases style: an Armani suit, Turnbull & Asser shirt, Gucci tie, and Bally shoes. He immediately murmured his apologies. "She didn't tell me you were busy, Miss Aquitane," he said. "I guess she got scared by my shield." He showed her the badge. "I just came to get some information on that incident the other night. I can wait. Or come back."

His words were polite but his look was bold. He glanced at the other two men and said, "Hello, Skippy."

Skippy Deere looked angry. "You can't talk to her without a PR and legal person around," he said. "You know better than that, Jim."

The detective offered his hand to Claudia and Cross and said, "Jim Losey."

They knew who he was. The most famous detective in Los Angeles, whose exploits had even been the basis of a miniseries. He also had appeared in very minor roles in films, and he was on Deere's Christmas gift and card lists. So Deere was emboldened to say, "Jim, give me a call later and I'll arrange a meeting with Miss Aquitane properly."

Losey smiled at him amiably and said, "Sure, Skippy."

But Athena said, "I may not be here much longer. Why not ask me now? I don't mind."

Losey would have been suave except for that constant wariness in his eyes, an alertness of his body that many years of crime work had planted in him.

He said, "In front of them?"

Athena's body was no longer in motion, and she had erased all her charm when she said quietly, "I trust them far more than I do the police."

Losey took that in stride. It was familiar. "I just wanted to ask you why you dropped the charges against your husband. Did he threaten you in any way?"

"Oh, no," Athena said scornfully. "He just threw water in my face in front of a billion people and yelled 'acid.' The next day he was out on bail."

"OK, OK," Losey said, and held up his arms in a placating gesture. "I just thought I could help."

Deere said, "Jim, give me a call later."

This raised an alarm bell in Cross. He looked thoughtfully at Deere, avoided looking at Losey. And Losey avoided looking at him.

Losey said, "I will." He saw Athena's handbag on one of the chairs and picked it up. "I saw this on Rodeo Drive," he said. "Two thousand dollars." He looked directly at Athena and said with a contemptuous politeness, "Maybe you can explain it to me, why anyone would pay that kind of money for something like this?"

Athena's face was like stone, she moved out of the frame of the ocean. She said, "That's an insulting question. Get out of here."

Losey bowed to her and left. He was grinning. He had made the impression he wanted.

"So you're human after all," Claudia said. She put her arm around Athena's shoulders. "Why did you get so mad?"

"I wasn't mad," Athena said. "I was sending him a message."

After the three visitors left, they drove from Malibu to Nate and Al's in Beverly Hills. Deere insisted to Cross that it was the only place west of the Rockies where you could get edible pastrami, corned beef, and Coney Island–style hot dogs.

As they ate Deere said reflectively, "Athena won't get back to work."

"I always knew that," Claudia said. "What I don't get is why she got so mad at that detective."

Deere laughed and said to Cross, "Did you get it?"

"No," Cross said.

Deere said, "One of the great legends of Hollywood is how anybody can get to fuck the stars. Now, male stars it's true, that's why you see the girls hanging around locations and the Beverly Wilshire Hotel. Female stars, not so much . . . a guy works on their house, a carpenter, a gardener, can get lucky, maybe she gets horny, it happened to me. Stunt men score good and other guys on the crew can get lucky. But that's fucking below the line and hurts female stars in their careers. Unless, of course, they are Superstars. Us old guys who run the show don't like that. Hell, doesn't money and power mean anything?" He grinned at them. "Now, you take Jim Losey. He's a big, handsome guy. He really kills tough guys, he's glamorous to people who live in a make-believe world. He knows that. He uses it. So he doesn't beg a star, he intimidates her. That's why he made that crack. In fact that's why he came out. It was his excuse to meet Athena and he figured he could take a shot. That insulting question was a declaration he wanted to fuck her. And Athena froze him out."

"So she's the Virgin Mary?" Cross said.

"For a movie star," Deere said.

Cross said abruptly, "You think she's scamming the Studio, trying to get more money?"

"She would never do anything like that," Claudia said. "She's absolutely straight."

"She got any grudges she's paying off?" Cross asked.

"You don't understand the business," Deere said. "First thing, the Studio would let her scam them. Stars always do that. Second, if she has a grudge, it's right out in the open. She's just weird." He paused for a moment. "She hates Bobby Bantz and she's not crazy about me. We've both been after her ass for years but never a tumble."

"Too bad you couldn't help," Claudia said to Cross. But he didn't answer her.

All during the trip from Malibu, Cross had been thinking hard. That this was the opportunity he was looking for. It would be dangerous, but if it worked he could finally make a break from the Clericuzio.

"Skippy," Cross said, "I have a proposition I want to make to you and the Studio. I'll buy your picture right now. I'll give the fifty million you've invested, put up the money to complete it, and let the Studio distribute it."

"You've got a hundred million?" Skippy Deere and Claudia both asked in astonishment.

"I know people who have it," Cross said.

"You can't get Athena back. And without Athena, there's no picture," Deere said.

"I said I'm a great persuader," Cross said. "Can you get me a meeting with Eli Marrion?"

"Sure," Deere said, "but only if I stay on as producer of the picture."

The meeting was not so easy to arrange. LoddStone Studios, that is to say, Eli Marrion and Bobby Bantz, had to be convinced that Cross De Lena was not just another big-mouth hustler, that he had the money and the credentials. Certainly he owned part of the Xanadu Hotel in Vegas, but he had no personal recorded financial worth that indicated he could swing the deal he proposed. Deere would vouch for him, but the clincher was when Cross showed a fifty-million-dollar letter of credit.

On the advice of his sister, Cross De Lena hired Molly Flanders as his lawyer for the deal.

Molly Flanders received Cross in her cave of an office. Cross was very alert, he knew certain things about her. In the world he had lived all his life, he had never met a woman who wielded power in any way, and Claudia had told him that Molly Flanders was one of the most powerful people in Hollywood. Studio chiefs took her calls, monster agents like Melo Stuart sought her help on the biggest deals. Stars like Athena Aquitane used her in their quarrels with studios. Flanders had once stopped production of the top miniseries on TV when her star client's check had been delayed in the mail.

She was much better looking than Cross had expected. She was large but well-proportioned and dressed beautifully. But on that body was the face of an elfin blond witch, the aquiline nose, the generous mouth and fierce brown eyes that seemed to squint with intense, intelligent combativeness. Her hair was braided into snakes around her head. She was forbidding until she smiled.

Molly Flanders, for all her toughness, was susceptible to handsome men and liked Cross as soon as she saw him. She was surprised because she had expected Claudia's brother to be homely. More than the handsomeness, she saw a force that Claudia did not have. He had a look of awareness that the world held no surprises. All this, however, did not convince her that she wanted to take Cross on as a client. She had heard rumors about certain connections, she didn't like the world of Vegas, and she was dubious as to the extent of his determination to take such a horrendous gamble.

"Mr. De Lena," she said, "let me make one thing clear. I represent Athena Aquitane as a lawyer not an agent. I've explained the consequences she must bear if she persists in her course of action. I'm convinced she will persist in it. Now, if you make your deal with the Studio and Athena still doesn't go back to work, I will represent her if you pursue legal action against her."

Cross looked at her intently. He had no way he could read a woman like this. He had to put most of his cards on the table. "I'll sign a waiver that I won't sue Miss Aquitane if I do buy the picture," he said. "And I have a check for two hundred thousand dollars here if you take me on. That's just for openers. You can bill me for more."

"Let's see if I understand this," Molly said. "You pay the Studio the fifty million they invested. Right now. You put up the money to complete the picture, minimum another fifty million. So you're going to gamble a hundred million that Athena goes back to work. Plus you're gambling that the picture will be a hit. It could be a flop. That's an awful risk."

Cross could be charming when he wanted to be. But he sensed that charm would not help with this woman. "I understand that with the foreign money, video, and TV sales, the picture can't lose money even if it's a flop," he said. "The only real problem is getting Miss Aquitane back to work. And maybe you can help on that."

"No, I can't," Molly said. "I don't want to mislead you. I've tried and failed. Everybody tried and failed. And Eli Marrion doesn't ever bullshit. He'll close down the picture and take the loss, then he'll try to ruin Athena. But I won't let him."

Cross was intrigued. "How will you do that?"

"Marrion has to get along with me," she said. "He's a smart man. I'll fight him in the courts, I'll make his Studio miserable on every deal. Athena won't be able to work again but I won't let them take her to the cleaners."

"If you represent me, you can save your client's career," Cross said. From the inside of his jacket he took an envelope and handed it to her. She opened it, studied it, then picked up the phone and made some calls that established the check was good.

She smiled at Cross and said, "I'm not insulting you, I do this with the biggest movie producers in town."

"Like Skippy Deere?" Cross said, laughing. "I invested in six of his pictures, four of them were hits and still I haven't made money."

"Because you didn't have me representing you," Molly said. "Now before I agree, you have to tell me how you can get Athena back to work." She paused. "I've heard some rumors about you."

Cross said, "And I've heard about you. I remember years ago when you were a criminal defense lawyer, you got some kid off a murder rap. He killed his girlfriend and you got an insanity plea. He was walking the streets less than a year later." He paused for a moment, deliberately letting his irritation show. "You didn't worry about his reputation."

Molly looked at him coldly. "You have not answered my question."

Cross decided that a lie should carry a little charm. "Molly," he said. "May I call you Molly?" She nodded her head. Cross went on. "You know I run a hotel in Vegas. I've learned this. Money is magic, you can overcome any kind of fear with money, so I'm going to offer Athena fifty percent of any money I make from the movie. If you structure the deal right and we're lucky, that means thirty million for her." He paused for a minute and said earnestly, "Come on, Molly, would you take a chance for thirty million?"

Molly shook her head. "Athena doesn't really care about money."

"The only thing that puzzles me is why the Studio doesn't give her the same deal," Cross said.

For the first time in their meeting, Molly smiled at him. "You don't know movie studios," she said. "They worry that all the stars will pull the same stunt if they set such a precedent. But let's go on. The Studio will take your deal, I think, because they will make a great deal of money just distributing the film. They will insist on that. Also, they will want a percentage of the profits. But I'm telling you again, Athena will not take your offer." She paused, then said with a teasing smile, "I thought you Vegas owners never gambled."

Cross smiled back at her. "Everybody gambles. I do when the percentages are right. And besides I plan to sell the Hotel and make a living in the movie business." He paused for a minute, letting her look into him to see the desire to be part of that world. "I think it's more interesting."

"I see," Molly said. "So this is not just a passing fancy."

"A foot in the door," Cross said. "Once I do that, I'll need your help further on."

Molly was amused by this. "I'll represent you," she said. "But as for us doing business further on, let's see first if you lose that hundred million."

She picked up the phone. She spoke into it. Then she hung up and said to Cross, "We have our meeting with their Business Affairs people to set out the rules before then. And you have three days to reconsider."

Cross was impressed. "That was fast," he said.

"Them, not me," Molly said. "It's costing them a fortune to tread water on this picture."

"I don't have to say this, I know," Cross said. "But the offer I plan to make Miss Aquitane is confidential, between you and me."

"No, you didn't have to say it," Molly said.

They shook hands, and after Cross left, Molly remembered something. Why had Cross De Lena mentioned that long-ago case when she had gotten that kid off, that famous victory of hers. Why that particular case? She had gotten plenty of murderers off.

Three days later Cross De Lena and Molly Flanders met in her office before going to LoddStone Studios so that she could check over the financial papers that Cross was bringing to the meeting. Then Molly drove both of them to the Studio in her Mercedes SL 300.

When they had been cleared through the gate, Molly said to Cross, "Check the lot. I'll give you a dollar for any American car you see."

They passed a sea of sleek cars of all colors, Mercedeses, Aston Martins, BMWs, Rolls-Royces. Cross saw one Cadillac and pointed it out. Molly said cheerily, "Some poor slob of a writer from New York."

LoddStone Studios was a huge area on which were scattered small buildings housing independent production companies. The main building was only ten floors and looked like a movie set piece. The Studio had kept the flavor of the 1920s when it had started up, with only the necessary repairs being done. Cross was reminded of the Enclave in the Bronx.

The offices in the Studio Administration Building were small and crowded except for the tenth floor, where Eli Marrion and Bobby Bantz had their executive suites. Between the two suites was a huge conference room with a bar and bartender far off to one side and a small kitchen adjoining the bar. The seats around the conference table were plush armchairs of dark red. Framed posters of Lodd-Stone movies hung on the wall.

Waiting for them were Eli Marrion, Bobby Bantz, Skippy Deere, the chief counsel of the Studio, and two other lawyers. Molly handed the chief counsel the financial papers, and the three opposing lawyers sat down to read them through. The bartender brought them drinks of their choice, then disappeared. Skippy Deere made the introductions.

Eli Marrion, as always, insisted that Cross call him by his first name. Then told them one of his favorite stories, which he often used to disarm opponents in a negotiation. His grandfather, Eli Marrion said, had started the company in the early 1920s. He had wanted to call the firm Lode Stone Studios, but he still had a severe German accent that confused the lawyers. It was only a ten-thousand-dollar company then and when the mistake was discovered, it didn't seem worth the trouble to change it. And here now it was a seven-billion-dollar company with a name that didn't make sense. But, as Marrion pointed out—he never told a joke that didn't make a serious point—

the printed word was not important. It was the visual image with the lodestone attracting light from every corner of the universe that made the company logo so powerful.

Then Molly presented the offer. Cross would pay the Studio the fifty million it had spent, would give the Studio distribution rights, keep Skippy Deere as producer. Cross would put up the money to finish the picture. LoddStone Studios would also get 5 percent of the profits.

They all listened intently. Bobby Bantz said, "The percentage is ridiculous, we would have to have more. And how do we know that you people and Athena are not in a conspiracy? That this isn't a stickup?"

Cross was astonished by Molly's reply. For some reason he had assumed that negotiations would be much more civil than he had been used to in his Vegas world.

But Molly was almost screaming, her witchlike face blazing with fury. "Fuck you, Bobby," she said to Bantz. "You have the fucking balls to accuse us of a conspiracy. Your insurance doesn't cover you on this, you take this meeting to get off the hook and then insult us. If you don't apologize, I'll take Mr. De Lena right out of here and you can eat shit."

Skippy Deere broke in, "Molly, Bobby, come on. We're trying to save a picture here. Let's talk this through at least. . . ."

Marrion had observed all this with a quiet smile but did not say anything. He would speak only to give a yes or no.

"I think it's a reasonable question," Bobby Bantz said. "What can this guy offer Athena to make her come back that we can't?"

Cross sat there smiling. Molly had told him to let her answer whenever possible.

She said, "Mr. De Lena obviously has something special to offer. Why should he tell you? If you offer him ten million to give you that information I'll confer with him. Ten million would be cheap."

Even Bobby Bantz laughed at this.

Skippy Deere said, "They think Cross wouldn't be risking all that money unless he had a sure thing. That makes them a little suspicious."

"Skippy," Molly said, "I've seen you lay out a million for a novel that you never made into a picture. How is this different?"

Bobby Bantz broke in. "Because Skippy gets our studio to put up the million."

They all laughed. Cross wondered about this meeting. He was losing patience. Also, he knew he must not look too eager, so it wouldn't hurt if he showed his irritation. He said in a low voice, "I'm going on a hunch. If it's too complicated, we can just forget the whole thing."

Bantz said angrily, "We are talking about a lot of money here. This picture could gross a half billion worldwide."

"If you could get Athena back," Molly shot in quickly. "I can tell you I talked with her this morning. She already cut off all her hair to show she's serious."

"We can wig her. Fucking actresses," Bantz said. Now he was glowering at Cross, trying to read him. He was pondering something. He said, "If Athena does not come back and you lose your fifty million and can't go on to finish the picture, who gets the footage already done?"

"I do," Cross said.

"Aha," Bantz said. "Then you just release it the way it is. Maybe as soft porn."

"That's a possibility," Cross said.

Molly shook her head at Cross, warning him to keep quiet. "If you agree to this deal," she said to Bantz, "everything can be negotiated on foreign, video, TV, and profit participation. There's only one deal-breaker. The agreement must be secret. Mr. De Lena only wants credit as a coproducer."

"That's OK with me," Skippy Deere said. "But my money deal with the Studio still stands."

For the first time Marrion spoke. "That's separate," he said, meaning no. "Cross, do you give your lawyer full discretion on negotiations?"

"Yes," Cross said.

"I want to go on record on this," Marrion said. "You must know we planned to scrap the picture and take the loss. We are convinced Athena will not come back. We do not represent to you that she may come back. If you make this deal and pay us fifty million, we are not liable. You would have to sue Athena and she doesn't have that kind of money."

"I would never sue her," Cross said. "I'd forgive and forget."

Bantz said, "You don't have to answer to your money people?"

Cross shrugged.

Marrion said, "That is a corruption. You can't let your personal attitude betray the money people who trust you. Just because they're rich."

Cross said, straight-faced, "I never think it's a good idea to get on the wrong side of rich people."

Bantz said in exasperation, "This is some kind of trick."

Masking his face with benign confidence, Cross said, "I've spent my whole life convincing people. In my Vegas hotel I have to convince very smart men to gamble their money against the odds. And I do that by making them happy. That means I give them what they really want. I'll do that with Miss Aquitane."

Bantz disliked the whole idea. He was sure his studio was being screwed. He said bluntly, "If we find out Athena has already agreed to work with you, we will sue. We will not honor this agreement."

"I want to be in the movie business for the long haul," Cross said. "I want to work with LoddStone Studios. There's money enough for everyone."

Eli Marrion had been studying Cross all during the meeting, trying to come to an assessment. The man was very low key, not a bluffer or a bullshit artist. Pacific Ocean Security could not establish any real link with Athena, there was no likely conspiracy. A decision had to be made, but it was not really as difficult a decision as the people in this room were pretending. Marrion was so weary now he could feel the weight of his clothing on his skeletal frame. He wanted this to be over.

Skippy Deere said, "Maybe Athena is just nuts, maybe she's gone over the edge. Then we can bail out with the insurance."

Molly Flanders said, "She's saner than anyone in this room. I can have all of you certified before you get her."

Bobby Bantz looked Cross directly in the face. "Will you sign papers that you have no agreement with Athena Aquitane at this point in time?"

"Yes," Cross said. He let his dislike for Bantz show.

Marrion, observing this, felt satisfaction. At least this part of the meeting was going according to plan. Bantz was now established as the bad guy. It was amazing how people almost instinctively disliked him, and it really wasn't his fault. It was the role chosen for him to play, though admittedly it suited his personality.

"We want twenty percent of the profits of the picture," Bantz said. "We distribute it domestic and foreign. And we will be partners in any sequel."

Skippy Deere said in exasperation, "Bobby, they are all dead at the end of the picture, there can be no sequel."

"OK," Bantz said, "rights in any prequel."

"Prequel, sequel, bullshit," Molly said. "You can have them. But you get no more than ten percent of the profits. You'll make a fortune on distribution. And you have no risk. Take it or leave it."

Eli Marrion could endure no more. He rose, standing very straight, and spoke in a measured, serene voice. "Twelve percent," he said, "We have a deal."

He paused and then looking directly at Cross, he said, "It's not so much the money. But this could be a great picture and I don't want to scrap it. Also, I'm very curious to see what will happen." He turned to Molly. "Now, yes or no?"

Molly Flanders, without even looking at Cross for a sign, said, "Yes."

Later, Eli Marrion and Bobby Bantz sat alone in the conference room. They were both silent. They had learned over the years that there were things that must not be said aloud. Finally Marrion said, "There's a moral question here."

Bantz said, "We've signed to keep the agreement secret, Eli, but if you feel we must, I could make a call."

Marrion sighed. "Then we lose the film. This man Cross is our only hope. Plus if he found out the leak came from you there might be some danger."

"Whatever he is, he doesn't dare touch LoddStone," Bantz said. "What I worry about is letting him get a foot in the door."

Marrion sipped his drink, puffed his cigar. The thin, woody-smelling smoke made his body tingle.

Eli Marrion was really tired now. He was getting too old to worry about long-term future disasters. The great universal disaster was closer.

"Don't make the call," he said. "We have to keep the agreement. And besides, maybe I'm getting into my second childhood, but I'd love to see what the magician pulls out of his hat."

Skippy Deere, after the meeting, went back to his house and made a call summoning Jim Losey to meet with him. At their meeting he swore Losey to secrecy and told him what had happened. "I think you should put a surveillance on Cross," he said. "You might find out something interesting."

But he said this only after he had agreed to sign Jim Losey to play a small part in a new movie he was making about serial murders in Santa Monica.

As for Cross De Lena, he returned to Las Vegas and in his penthouse suite pondered the new course of his life. Why had he taken the risk? Most important, the winnings could be huge: not only the money but a new way of life. But what he questioned was an underlying motive, the vision of Athena Aquitane framed by the sea-green water, her constantly moving body, the notion that one day she might come to know him and love him, not forever, but just for a moment of time. What had Gronevelt said? "Women are never more dangerous to men than when they have to be saved. Beware, beware," Gronevelt said, "of Beauty in Distress."

But he dismissed all this from his mind. Looking down on the Vegas Strip, the wall of colored light, the throngs moving through that light, ants carrying bales of money to bury in some great nest, he analyzed the whole problem for the first time in a coldly neutral way.

If Athena Aquitane was such an angel, why then was she demanding, in effect if not in words, that the price for her returning to the picture was that someone kill her husband? Surely that had to be clear to anyone. The Studio's offer to protect her while she completed the picture was worth less because she would be working toward her own death. After the picture was done and she was alone, Skannet would come after her.

Eli Marrion, Bobby Bantz, Skippy Deere, they knew the problem and knew the answer. But no one would dare speak it aloud. For people like them, the risk was too great. They had risen so high, lived so well, that they had too much to lose. For them the gain did not equal the risk. They could accommodate the loss of the picture, for them it was only a minor defeat. They could not afford the great tumble from the highest level of society to the lowest. That risk was mortal.

Also, to give them their due, they had made an intelligent decision. They were not expert in this field of endeavor; they could make mistakes. Better to treat the fifty million dollars like a loss of points in their stock on Wall Street.

So now there were two main problems. The execution of Boz Skannet in a manner that would not injure the picture or Athena in any way. Problem number two, and far more important, was winning the approval of his father, Pippi De Lena, and the Clericuzio Family. For Cross knew the whole arrangement would not remain secret to them very long.

# CHAPTER 8

C ROSS DE LENA pleaded for Big Tim's life for many different reasons. One, he contributed between five hundred grand and one million to the Xanadu cage every year. Second, he had a sneaking affection for the man, for his lust for life, his outrageous buffooneries.

Tim Snedden, known as the Rustler, was the owner of a string of shopping malls that stretched over the northern part of the state of California. He was also a Las Vegas high roller who usually stayed at the Xanadu. He was particularly fond of and extraordinarily lucky at sports betting. The Rustler made big bets, fifty grand on football and sometimes ten grand on basketball. Thinking he was being clever, he lost small bets but almost invariably won his big bets. Cross was on to that immediately.

The Rustler was very big, nearly six and a half feet and over three hundred fifty pounds. His appetite matched his physique, he ate everything in sight. He boasted he had had a partial stomach bypass so that food passed directly through his system and he never gained weight. He was gleeful about this as an ultimate scam on nature itself.

For the Rustler was a natural-born scam artist, which was how he earned his nickname. At the Xanadu he fed his friends free under his comp, he absolutely destroyed room service. He tried to pay his call girls and the purchases at the gift shop under his comp. And then when he lost and had a cage full of markers, he stalled payment until his next visit to the Xanadu, instead of paying them within a month as a gentleman gambler would do.

Though he was very lucky with his sports gambling, the Rustler was less fortunate with casino games. He was skillful, he knew the odds and bet correctly, but his natural exuberance carried him away, and his winnings on sports would be wiped out and more. So it wasn't because of the money but because of long-range strategic reasons that the Clericuzio took an interest.

Since the Family's ultimate goal was the legalization of sports gambling all over the United States, any gambling scandal involving sports would hurt that aim. So an inquiry into the life of Big Tim Snedden the Rustler was launched. The results wcrc so alarming that Pippi and Cross were summoned East to the mansion in Quogue for a conference. It was Pippi's first operation after his return from Sicily.

Pippi and Cross took the flight back East together. Cross worried that the Clericuzio had already found out about his movie deal on *Messalina* and that his father would be angry he had not been consulted. For Pippi, at fifty-seven, though retired, still was consigliere to his son the *Bruglione.*

So on the plane Cross told his father about the movie and reassured him that he still valued his counsel but had not wanted to put him in a bad light with the Clericuzio. He also voiced his anxiety about being summoned back East because the Don had learned about his Hollywood plans.

Pippi listened without saying a word, then sighed with disgust. "You're still too young," he said. "It won't be about the movie deal. The Don would never show his hand this quick. He'd wait to see what happened. It looks like Giorgio runs things, that's what Vincent and Petie and Dante think. But they're wrong. The old man is smarter than all of us. And don't worry about him, he's always fair in these things. It's Giorgio and Dante you have to worry about." He paused for a moment as if reluctant to talk about the Family even with Cross.

"You notice that Giorgio and Vincent and Petie's kids know nothing about Family business? The Don and Giorgio have all planned that the children will be strictly legit. The Don planned that for Dante too, but Dante was too smart, figured everything out, and he wanted in. The Don couldn't stop him. Think of all of us—Giorgio, Vincent, and Petie, you and me and Dante—as the rear guard, fighting so that the Clericuzio clan can escape to safety. That's the Don's planning. It's his strength, what makes him great. So he may even be glad you're making your escape, it's what he hoped Dante would do. That's what it is, isn't it?"

"I think so," Cross said. Not even to his father would he confess his terrible weakness. That he was doing it for the love of a woman.

"Always play it long, like Gronevelt," Pippi said. "When the time comes, tell the Don directly and make sure the Family wets its beak on the deal. But watch out for Giorgio and Dante. Vincent and Petie won't give a shit."

"Why Giorgio and Dante?" Cross asked.

"Because Giorgio is a greedy prick," Pippi said. "And Dante, because he's always jealous of you and because you're my son. Besides, he's a fucking lunatic."

Cross was surprised. It was the first time he had heard his father criticize any of the Clericuzio. "And why won't Vincent and Petie care?" he asked.

"Because Vincent has his restaurants and Petie has his construction business and the Bronx Enclave. Vincent wants to enjoy his old age and Petie likes the action. And both of them like you and respect me. We did jobs together when we were young."

Cross said, "Pop, you're not mad I didn't clear it with you?"

Pippi gave him a sardonic look. "Don't bullshit me," he said. "You knew I would disapprove and the Don would disapprove. Now when are you going to kill this Skannet guy?"

"I don't know yet," Cross said. "It's very tricky, has to be a Confirmation so that Athena will know she doesn't have to worry about him anymore. Then she can come back to the picture."

"Let me plan it for you," Pippi said. "And what if this broad, Athena, doesn't come back to work? Then you lose fifty mil."

"She'll come back to work," Cross said. "She and Claudia are close friends and Claudia says she will."

"My darling daughter," Pippi said. "She still doesn't want to see me?"

"I don't think so," Cross said. "But you can always drop around when she's staying at the Hotel."

"No," Pippi said. "If this Athena doesn't come to work after you do the job, I'll plan her Communion for her, no matter how big a movie star she is."

"No, no," Cross said. "You should see Claudia. She's much prettier now."

"That's good," Pippi said. "She had such an ugly mug when she was a kid. Like me."

"Why don't you make up with her?" Cross asked.

"She wouldn't let me go to my ex-wife's funeral, and she doesn't like me. So what's the point? In fact, when I die I want you to bar her from my funeral. Fuck her." He paused for a moment. "She was a ballsy little kid."

"You should see her now," Cross said.

"Remember," Pippi said. "Don't volunteer anything to the Don. This meeting is about something else."

"How can you be sure?" Cross asked.

"Because he would have met with me first to see if I would give you away," Pippi said.

As it turned out, Pippi was right.


At the mansion, Giorgio, Don Domenico, Vincent, Petie, and Dante waited to greet them in the garden by the fig trees. As was the custom they all had lunch together before they got down to business.

Giorgio laid it out. An investigation had shown that Rustler Snedden was fixing certain college games in the Midwest. That he possibly shaved points in the pro football and pro basketball games. He did this by bribing the officials and certain players, a very tricky and dangerous business. If this came out, it would cause a tremendous scandal and uproar that would give a near fatal blow to the Clericuzio Family's effort to have sports gambling legalized in the United States. And it would eventually be found out.

"The cops throw more manpower into a sports fix than into a serial murder," Giorgio said. "Why, I don't know. What the hell difference does it make who wins or loses? It's a crime that hurts nobody except the bookmakers and the cops hate them anyway. If the Rustler fixed all the Notre Dame games so that they always won, the whole country would be happy."

Pippi said impatiently, "Why are we even talking about this? Just have somebody warn him off."

Vincent said, "We already tried that. This guy is a special piece of work. He doesn't know what fear is. He's been warned, he still keeps doing it."

Petie said, "They call him Big Tim, and they call him the Rustler, and he loves all that shit. He never pays his bills, he even stiffs the IRS, he fights with the California state authorities because he won't pay the sales tax of the stores he owns in his malls. Hell, he even stiffs his ex-wife and his kids on support payments. He's a thief in his heart. You cannot talk sense to him."

Giorgio said, "Cross, you know him personally from his gambling in Vegas. What do you say?"

Cross considered. "He's very late paying his markers. But he finally pays. He's smart gambling, not degenerate. He's one of those guys who is hard to like, but he's very rich so he has lots of friends that he brings to Vegas. Actually even fixing the games and winning some of our money, he is a big plus for us. Just let it go." As he said this he noticed Dante smiling, knowing something he didn't know.

"We can't let it go," Giorgio said. "Because this Big Tim, this Rustler, is fucking nuts. He's laying down some crazy scheme to fix the Super Bowl game."

Don Domenico spoke for the first time and directly to Cross, "Nephew, is that possible?"

The question was a compliment. It was the Don acknowledging that Cross was the expert in the field.

"No," Cross said to the Don. "You can't fix the Super Bowl officials because no one knows who they will be. You can't fix the players because the important ones make too much money. Also, you can never fix one game in any sport a one hundred percent sure thing. If you are a fixer you have to be able to fix fifty or a hundred games. That way if you lose three or four, you don't get hurt. And so unless you can do a lot of them it's not worth the risk."

"Bravo," the Don said. "Then why does this man, who is rich, want to do something so foolhardy?"

"He wants to be famous," Cross said. "To fix the Super Bowl he would have to do something so risky he is sure to be found out. Something so crazy I can't even think what it will be. The Rustler will think it clever. And he is a man who believes he can get out of every jam he gets in."

"I have never met a man like that," the Don said.

Giorgio said, "They grow them only in America."

"But then he is very dangerous to what we want to do," the Don said. "From what you tell me, he is a man who will not listen to reason. So there is no choice."

Cross said, "Wait. He means at least a half million dollars' profit every year to the casino."

Vincent said, "It's a matter of principle. The Books pay us money to protect them."

Cross said, "Let me talk to him. Maybe he'll listen to me. The whole thing is small potatoes. He can't fix the Super Bowl. It's not worth our taking action." But then he got a look from his father and he realized that in some way it was not proper for him to make such arguments.

The Don said with a terminal determination, "The man is dangerous. Don't talk to him, nephew. He doesn't know who you really are. Why give him the advantage? The man is dangerous because he is stupid, he is stupid as an animal is stupid, he wants to feed on everything. And then when he is caught he wants to wreak as much havoc as he can. He will implicate everyone whether true or not." He paused for a moment and then looked at Dante. "Grandson," he said, "I think you should do the job. But let Pippi do the planning on this one, he knows the territory."

Dante nodded.

Pippi knew he was on dangerous ground. If anything happened to Dante, he would be held responsible. And another thing was clear to him. The Don and Giorgio were determined some day Dante would head the Clericuzio Family. But at present they did not trust his judgment.

. . .

In Vegas Dante registered in a suite at the Xanadu. The Rustler, Snedden, was not due in Vegas for a week, and during that time Cross and Pippi indoctrinated Dante.

"Rustler is a high roller," Cross said. "But not high enough to rate a Villa. Not in the class of Arabs and Asians. His RFB is enormous, he wants everything free he can get. He puts friends on restaurant tabs, orders the best wines, he even tries to put the gift shop on his tab. We don't give that even to the Villa guys. He's a claim artist, so the dealers have to watch him. He'll claim he made a bet just before the number hit on the crap table. He'll try to make a bet in baccarat after the first card shows. At blackjack he'll claim he wanted to hit an eighteen when the next card is three. He's very late paying his markers. But he gives us a half million a year, even after we take off what he beats the sports book for. He's cute. He even draws chips for his friends and puts them on his marker so we'll think he gambles bigger than he actually does. All that chickenshit stuff like the garment center guys used to pull in the old days. But then he goes berserk when his luck goes bad. Last year he dropped two million and we made him a party and gave him a Cadillac. He bitched that it wasn't a Mercedes."

Dante was outraged. "He draws chips and money from the cage and doesn't gamble it?"

"Sure," Cross said. "A lot of guys do it. We don't mind. We like to look stupid. It gives them more confidence at the tables. They outsmart us again."

"Why do they call him the Rustler?" Dante asked.

"Because he takes things without paying for them," Cross said. "When he has girls he bites them as if he wants to take a chunk of their flesh. And he gets away with it. He's a great, great bullshit artist."

Dante said dreamily, "I can't wait to hear him."

"He could never talk Gronevelt into giving him a Villa," Cross said. "So I don't."

Dante looked at him sharply. "How come I didn't get a Villa?"

"Because it could cost the Hotel a hundred grand to a million bucks a night," Cross said.

Dante said, "But Giorgio gets a Villa."

"OK," Cross said, "I'll clear it with Giorgio." They both knew Giorgio would be outraged by Dante's request.

"Fat chance," Dante said.

"When you get married," Cross said, "you'll get a Villa for your honeymoon."

Pippi said, "My operational plan depends on Big Tim's character. Cross you have to cooperate just here in Vegas to set the guy up. You have to let Dante draw unlimited credit in the cage and then make his markers disappear. Timewise, the arrangements in L.A. are set. You have to make sure the guy gets here and doesn't cancel his reservation. So you give him a party to present him with a Rolls-Royce. Then when he's here you have to introduce him to Dante and me. After that you're through."

It took Pippi more than an hour to tell the plan in detail. Dante said admiringly, "Giorgio always said you were the best. I was pissed off when the Don put you over me on this. But I can see he was right."

Pippi took this flattery stone-faced. He said to Dante, "Remember this is a Communion not a Confirmation. It has to look as if he took it on the lam. With his record and all the lawsuits against him, that will be plausible. Dante, don't wear one of your fucking hats on this operation. People have funny memories. And remember that the Don said he would like the guy to give information about the fix, but it's not really necessary. He's the ringleader, when he's gone the whole fix will disappear. So don't do anything crazy."

Dante said coolly, "I feel unlucky without my hat."

Pippi shrugged. "Another thing, don't try to cheat on your unlimited credit. That comes from the Don himself, he doesn't want the Hotel to lose a fortune on this operation. They already have to put up the Rolls."

"Don't worry," Dante said. "My work is my pleasure." He paused for a moment and then said with a sly grin, "I hope you give me a good report on this one."

This surprised Cross. It was plain that there was some hostility between them. And he was also surprised that Dante would try to intimidate his father. That could be disastrous, grandson of the Don or not.

But Pippi seemed not to have noticed. "You're a Clericuzio," he said. "Who am I to report on you?" He clapped Dante on the shoulder. "We have a job to do together. Let's make it fun."

When Rustler Snedden arrived, Dante studied him. He was big and fat but the fat was hard, it stuck to his bones and didn't roll. His shirt was blue denim with large pockets on each breast, a white button in the middle. In one pocket he stuffed the black hundred-dollar chips, and in the other, the white-and-gold five hundreds. The red fives and green twenty-fives he stuffed into the pocket of his wide-trousered white canvas pants. On his feet were floppy brown sandals.

The Rustler played mostly craps, the best percentage game. Cross and Dante knew that he had already bet ten grand on two college basketball games and placed a five-thousand-dollar bet with the illegal books in town on a horse race in Santa Anita. The Rustler was not going to pay the taxes. And he seemed not to be worrying about his bets. He was having a grand time shooting craps.

He was the mayor of the crap table, telling other gamblers to ride with his dice, shouting good-humoredly at them not to be chicken. He was betting the blacks, stacks of them covering all the numbers, betting right all the way. When the dice came to him he hurled them vigorously so that they bounced off the opposite wall of the table and came back to his easy reach. He would then try to grab them, but the stickman was always alert to catch them in the claw of his stick and hold them so that other players could make their bets.

Dante took his place at the crap table and bet with Big Tim to win. Then he made all the ruinous side bets that would, unless he was very lucky, make him a sure loser. He bet the hard four and the hard ten. He bet the boxcars in one roll and the aces and eleven in one roll at odds of thirty and fifteen to one. He called for a twenty-thousand-dollar marker and, after signing for the black chips, spread them all over the table. He called for another marker. By this time, he had caught Big Tim's attention.

"Hey, you with the hat. Learn to play this game," Big Tim said.

Dante waved to him cheerily and continued his wild betting. When Big Tim sevened out, Dante took the dice and called for a fifty-thousand-dollar marker. He spread black chips all over the table hoping he wouldn't get lucky. He didn't. Now Big Tim was watching him with more than ordinary interest.

Big Tim the Rustler ate in the coffee shop, which was also the restaurant that served plain American fare. Big Tim rarely ate in the Xanadu's fancy French restaurant or its Northern Italian Restaurant or its authentic English Royal Pub restaurant. Five friends joined him for dinner, and Big Tim the Rustler made out Keno tickets for everybody so they could watch the numbers board while eating. Cross and Dante sat in a corner booth.

His short-cut blond hair made the Rustler resemble a Brueghel painting of a jolly German burgher. He ordered a great variety of dishes, the equivalent of three dinners, but to his credit he ate most of them while also dipping into his companions' plates.

"It's really too bad," Dante said. "I never saw a guy who enjoyed life so much."

"That's one way to make enemies," Cross said. "Especially when you enjoy it at other people's expense."

They watched Big Tim sign the check, which he did not have to pay, and order one of his companions to tip in cash. After they left, Cross and Dante relaxed over their coffee. Cross loved this huge room with glass walls showing the night lit outside by pink lamps, green from the grass and trees outside reflecting into the room, softening the chandeliers.

"I remember one night about three years ago," Cross said to Dante. "The Rustler had a great streak at the crap table. I think he won over a hundred grand. It was about three in the morning. And when the pit boss took his chips to the cage, the Rustler jumped up on the crap table and pissed all over it."

"What did you do?" Dante asked.

"I had the security guards take him to his room and charged him five grand for the piss on the table. Which he never paid."

"I would have ripped his fucking heart out," Dante said.

"If a man gives you a half million a year, wouldn't you let him piss on a table?" Cross said. "But to tell the truth, I always held it against him. In fact, if he had done that in the Villas' casino, who knows?"

The next day Cross had lunch with Big Tim to brief him on his party and the presentation of the Rolls-Royce. Pippi joined them and was introduced.

Big Tim always pushed for more. "I appreciate the Rolls but when do I get one of your Villas?"

"Yeah, you deserve it," Cross said. "The next time you come to Vegas, you get a Villa. That's a promise, even if I have to kick somebody out."

Big Tim the Rustler said to Pippi, "Your son is a much nicer man than that old prick, Gronevelt."

"He was a little funny in his last years," Pippi said. "I was maybe his best friend and he would never give me a Villa."

"Well, fuck him," Big Tim said. "Now that your son is running the Hotel, you can get a Villa whenever you want."

"Never," Cross said, "he's not a gambler." They all laughed.

But now Big Tim was on another tack. "There's a weird little guy who wears a funny hat and is the worst crapshooter I ever saw," he said. "This guy signed nearly two hundred grand in markers in less than an hour. What can you tell me about him? You know I'm always looking for investors."

"I can't tell you anything about my players," Cross said. "How would you like it if I gave out information about you? I can tell you he can get a Villa anytime, but he never asks. He likes to keep a low profile."

"Just give me an intro," Big Tim said. "If I make a deal, you'll get a piece."

"No," Cross said. "But my father knows him."

"I could use some dough," Pippi said.

Big Tim said, "Good. Give me a big buildup."

Pippi turned on his charm. "You two guys would make a great team. This guy has a lot of money but he doesn't have your flair for big business. I know you're a fair guy, Tim, so just give me what you think I deserve."

Big Tim beamed at this. Pippi would be another of his suckers. "Great," he said. "I'll be at the crap table tonight, so bring him around."

When the introductions were made at the crap table, Big Tim the Rustler startled both Dante and Pippi by snatching Dante's Renaissance cap off his head and replacing it with a Dodger baseball cap he was wearing. The result was hilarious. The Renaissance cap on Big Tim's head made him look like one of Snow White's dwarfs.

"To change our luck," Big Tim said. They all laughed but Pippi didn't like the malevolent gleam in Dante's eyes. Also, he was angry that Dante had ignored his instructions and was wearing the hat. He had introduced Dante as Steve Sharpe and had pumped Big Tim up with stories that Steve was the overlord of a drug empire on the Eastern Seaboard and had to "wash" many millions. Also that Steve was a degenerate gambler who had bet a million on the Super Bowl and had lost without batting an eye. And his markers in the casino cage were pure gold. Paid them right up.

So now Big Tim threw his massive arm over Dante's shoulders and said, "Stevie, we have to talk. Let's have a little bite in the coffee shop."

There, Big Tim took a secluded booth. Dante ordered coffee but Big Tim ordered a whole array of desserts: strawberry ice cream, napoleons, and banana cream pie plus a dish of assorted cookies.

Then he launched into an hour-long selling speech. He owned a small mall he wanted to get rid of, a long-term moneymaker, and he could arrange that the payment would be mostly under-the-table cash. There was a meat-packing plant and carloads of fresh produce that could be sold for undercover cash, then resold for a profit for white money. He had an "in" with the movie business so that he could help finance pictures that went direct to video or to porno theaters. "Great business," Big Tim said. "You get to meet the stars and fuck the starlets and turn your money white."

Dante enjoyed the performance. Everything Big Tim said was with such confidence and brio that the victim could only believe in future riches. He asked questions that betrayed his eagerness but made a show of coyness.

"Give me your card," he said. "I'll give you a call or have Pippi call you and then we can set up a dinner meeting and have a full discussion so I can make a commitment."

Big Tim gave him his card. "Let's do it real quick," he said. "I have one particular 'no lose' deal I'll cut you in on. But we would have to move fast." He paused for a moment. "It's a sports thing."

Now Dante showed an enthusiasm he had not shown before. "Jesus, that has always been my dream. I love sports. You mean maybe buy a major league baseball team?"

"Not that big," Big Tim said hastily. "But big enough."

"So when do we meet?" Dante asked.

Big Tim said proudly, "Tomorrow the Hotel is giving me a party and a Rolls. For being one of their best suckers. I go back to L.A. the day after. How about that night?"

Dante pretended to give the question some thought. "Okay," he said. "Pippi's coming to L.A. with me and I'll have him give you a call to set it up."

"Great," Big Tim said. He wondered a bit about the man's cautiousness but knew better than to queer a deal with unnecessary questions. "And tonight I'm going to show you how to shoot craps so that you have some chance of winning."

Dante made himself look sheepish. "I know the odds, I just like to fuck around. And then the word gets out and I can get a whack at the chorus girls."

"Then there's no hope for you," Big Tim said. "But you and me, we'll make some money together anyway."


The next day the party for Big Tim the Rustler was held in the great ballroom of the Xanadu Hotel, which was often used for special events: the New Year's Eve party, Christmas buffets, weddings for high rollers, presentations of special awards and gifts, Super Bowl parties, the World Series, and even political conventions.

It was a huge, high-ceilinged room, with balloons floating everywhere and two enormous buffet tables, splitting the room in half. The buffets were shaped like huge ice glaciers, and encrushed in the ice were exotic fruits of all colors. Crenshaw melons, split open to show their yellow-gold flesh, great purple grapes with their juice bursting against the skin, porcupine pineapples, kiwi and kumquat, nectarines and lichee nuts, and a huge log of watermelon. Buckets of twelve different kinds of ice cream were buried like submarines. Then there was a passageway of hot dishes: a baron of beef as big as a buffalo, a huge turkey, a white, fat-ringed ham. Then there was a tray of different pastas, sprinkled green with pesto and red with tomato sauce. And then a great red pot, as big as a garbage can, with silver handles and steaming with a "wild boar" stew that was really a pork, beef, and veal mixture. Then came bread of all kinds and rolls heavy with flour. Another bank of ice held desserts, cream puffs, whipped-cream-filled doughnuts, an assortment of tiered cakes decorated with replicas of the Hotel Xanadu. Coffee and hard liquor would be served to the guests by the best-looking waitresses at the Hotel.

Big Tim the Rustler was already wreaking havoc on these tables before the first guest arrived.

In the full center of the room, mounted on a ramp separated by ropes from the crowd, was the Rolls-Royce. Creamy, white, luxurious, with true elegance and a certain genius in design, it stood in sharp contrast to the pretensions of this Vegas world. A wall of the room had been replaced by heavy golden draperies to allow its entrance and departure. Then off in a corner of the room was a purple Cadillac that was to be awarded as a door prize to those with numbered invitations: high rollers invited to the party and casino managers of the biggest hotels. This had been one of Gronevelt's best ideas. These parties increased the Drop at the Hotel significantly.

The party was a huge success because Big Tim was so flamboyant. Attended by his two waitresses, he almost single-handedly destroyed the buffet table. He loaded up three plates and gave an exhibition of eating that nearly made Dante's mission unnecessary.

Cross made the presentation speech for the Hotel. Then Big Tim made his acceptance speech.

"I want to thank the Xanadu Hotel for this wonderful gift," he said. "That two-hundred-thousand-dollar car is now mine for nothing. It's my reward for coming to the Xanadu the last ten years, during which they treated me like a prince and emptied my wallet. I figure if they give me fifty Rolls we would be about even but what the hell, I can only drive one car at at time."

Here he was interrupted by applause and cheers. Cross grimaced. He was always embarrassed by these rituals that exposed the falseness of the Hotel's goodwill.

Big Tim threw his arms around the two waitresses flanking him. He squeezed their breasts in a friendly way. He waited like an experienced comic for the applause to die down.

"No kidding, I'm truly grateful," he said. "This is one of the happiest days of my life. Right up there with my divorce. One little thing. Who's going to give me gas money to drive this car back to L.A.? The Xanadu cleaned me out again."

Big Tim knew when to stop. As the applause and cheers broke out again, he climbed the ramp and got into the car. The golden draperies that had replaced the wall now parted, and Big Tim drove out.

The party speedily broke up after the Cadillac was won by a high roller. The festivities had lasted for four hours and everybody wanted to get back to the gambling tables.

That night Gronevelt's ghost would have been overjoyed with the results of the party. The Drop was nearly double the average. Sexual coupling could not be confirmed but the smell of semen seemed to seep out into the hallways. The great-looking call girls that had been invited to Big Tim's party had quickly snuggled into relationships with less dedicated high rollers, who gave them black chips to gamble.

Gronevelt had often remarked to Cross that male and female gamblers had different sex patterns. And that it was important for casino owners to know them.

First Gronevelt proclaimed the primacy of pussy, as he called it. Pussy could overcome anything. It could even make a degenerate gambler go straight. There had been many important men of the world who had been guests at the Hotel. Nobel Prize–winning scientists, billionaires, great religious revivalists, eminent literary icons. A Nobel Prize–winner in physics, the best brain maybe in the world, had frolicked with a whole line of chorus girls during his six-day stay. He didn't gamble much but it was an honor for the Hotel. Gronevelt himself had to give gifts to each of the girls, it had never occurred to the Nobel Prize–winner to do so. The girls had reported he was the best screw in the world, eager, ardent, and skillful, no tricks, with one of the most beautiful cocks they had ever seen. And best of all, amusing, never boring them with serious talk. As gossipy and bitchy as any of the girls. For some reason this cheered Gronevelt up. That such a brain could please the opposite sex. Not like Ernest Vail, such a great writer but a middle-aged kid with a perpetual hard-on and no small talk to go with it. Then there was Senator Wavven, a possible future president of the United States, who treated sex like a game of golf. To say nothing of the dean of Yale, the cardinal of Chicago, the leader of the Civil Rights National Committee, and the crusty Republican bigwigs. All of them reduced to children by pussy. The only possible exceptions were the gays or druggies, but after all they were not typically gamblers.

Gronevelt noted that male gamblers called for hookers *before* they set out to gamble. Women, however, preferred sex *after* they gambled. Since the Hotel had to cater to the sexual needs of everyone and there were no male hookers, just gigolos, the Hotel used barmen croupiers and junior pit boys for the women, and that was their report. So Gronevelt made a jump. Males need sex to prepare them to go into battle with confidence. Women need sex to assuage the sorrow of losing or as part of the reward for their victory.

It was true that Big Tim called for a hooker an hour before his party and then went to bed with his two waitresses in the early morning after losing a big sum of money. They were reluctant, they were straight girls. Big Tim solved the problem in his own particular way. He put up ten thousand dollars worth of black chips and told them it was theirs if they spent the night with him. Accompanied with his usual vague promise of more if they had a really good night. He loved the way they studied the chips thoughtfully before agreeing. The joke was they got him so drunk that he fell asleep, gorged with food and drink, before he got past the fondling stage. He fell asleep between the two of them, his huge frame pushing them to the edges, both girls clinging to him until finally they fell on the floor to sleep.

Late that night Cross received a call from Claudia. "Athena disappeared," she said. "The Studio is frantic and I'm worried. Except ever since I've known her Athena has disappeared at least one weekend a month. But this time I thought you should know. You better do something before she runs away forever."

"It's OK," Cross said. He didn't tell her he had his own men covering Skannet.

But that call focused his mind on Athena. That magical face, which seemed to show her every emotion; the long, beautiful stretch of her legs. And the intelligence of her eyes, the vibration from some invisible instrument of inner being.

He picked up the phone and called a chorus girl he sometimes dated called Tiffany.

Tiffany was the captain of the chorus line of the Xanadu's big cabaret show. This entitled her to extra pay and perks for keeping discipline and preventing the usual quarrels and outright fights the girls fell into. She was a statuesque beauty who had failed screen tests because she simply was too big for celluloid. Where on the stage her beauty was commanding, on film she looked huge.

When she arrived, she was surprised at the quickness of Cross's lovemaking. He simply grabbed her and stripped her of her clothes and then seemed to devour her body with kisses. He entered her quickly and came to a climax quickly. This was so different from his usual style that she said, almost ruefully, "This time it must be true love."

"It sure is," Cross said, and began to make love to her again.

"Not me, you dope," Tiffany said. "Who's the lucky girl?"

Cross was annoyed that he was so easy to read. And yet he could not stop his devotion to the flesh beside him. He could not have enough of her succulent breasts, her silky tongue, the velvet mound between her thighs, all radiating an irresistible heat. When finally, hours later, the lustful fever was gone, he could not stop thinking about Athena.

Tiffany picked up the phone and ordered room service for them both. "I pity that poor girl when you finally get her," Tiffany said.

After she left, Cross felt free. It was a weakness to be so much in love, but satisfied lust gave him confidence. At three in the morning he made his last tour of the casino.

In the coffee shop he saw Dante with three good-looking, vivacious women. Though one of them was Loretta Lang, the singer he had helped to break her contract, he did not recognize her. Dante waved him over, but he declined with a shake of his head. Up in his penthouse suite he took two sleeping pills before going to bed, but he still dreamed of Athena.

The three women at Dante's table were famous ladies of Hollywood, wives of Bankable Stars and minor stars in their own right. They had been guests at Big Tim's party, not by invitation but by having wangled their way in on their charms.

The oldest was Julia Deleree, who was married to one of the most famous Bankable Stars in the movies. She had two children, and the family often appeared in magazines as the exceptional couple that had no problems, were ecstatic with their marriage.

The second was Joan Ward. She was still very attractive, nearly fifty. She played second leads now, usually as the intelligent woman, the suffering mother of a doomed child, or in the role of a deserted woman whose tragedy leads to a second happy marriage. Or as a fiery fighter for the feminist viewpoint. She was married to the head of a studio who paid her charge cards without complaint, no matter how huge, and whose only demand on her was to be the hostess for the many social-business parties he gave. She had no children.

The third star was Loretta, who by now was first choice as the comedy lead in kooky comedies. She, too, had married well, to a Bankable Star of empty-headed action films that took him on location in other countries for the best part of the year.

These three had become friends by being cast in the same movies and by shopping on Rodeo Drive and having lunches at the Beverly Hills Hotel's Polo Lounge, where they compared notes on their husbands and their charge cards. About the cards, they had no complaints. It was like having a shovel to dig in a gold mine, and their husbands never questioned their bills.

Julia complained that her husband didn't spend enough time with her kids. Joan, whose husband was acclaimed as a discoverer of new stars, complained she was childless. Loretta complained that her husband should branch out into more serious roles. But there came a day when Loretta, with her usual vivaciousness, said, "Let's stop bullshitting ourselves. We're all happily and very suitably married to very important guys. What we really hate is that our husbands send us out on Rodeo Drive so they feel less guilty about fucking other women." The three of them laughed. It was so true.

Julia said, "I love my husband but he's been in Tahiti for a month shooting a picture. And I know he's not sitting on the beach masturbating. But I don't want to spend a month in Tahiti, so he's either screwing his leading lady or the local talent."

"Which he would be doing even if you were there," Loretta said.

Joan said wistfully, "And even though my husband hasn't the sperm of a fucking ant, his cock is like a water wand. How come most of the stars he discovers are females? He screen-tests them by finding out how much of his cock they can swallow."

They were all half tipsy by now. They believed that wine had no calories.

Loretta said crisply, "We can't blame our husbands. The most beautiful women in the world show it to them. They really have no choice. But why should we suffer? Fuck the charge cards, let's have some fun."

And so had followed their sacred once-a-month girl's night out. When their husbands were gone, which was often, they would go on overnight adventures.

Since they were recognizable to most Americans, they had to disguise themselves. This proved to be extraordinarily easy to do. They used wigs to change the style and color of their hair. They used makeup, thickened their lips or thinned them. They dressed in the style of middle-class women. They downgraded their beauty, which didn't matter because, like most actresses, they could be enormously charming. And they delighted in the role playing. They loved to listen to different kinds of men bare their hearts to them in hope of getting into bed with them, often successfully. It was a breath of real life, the characters still mysterious, not doomed to a written script. And there were delightful surprises. Sincere offers of marriage and true love; men sharing their pain because they thought they would never see them again. The admiration they received not because of their hidden status, but because of their innate charms. And they loved creating new personas for themselves. Sometimes they would be computer operators on vacation, sometimes off-duty nurses or dental technicians or social workers. They would bone up for their parts by reading about their new professions. Sometimes they would pretend to be legal secretaries in the office of a big showbiz lawyer in L.A. and spread scandal about their own husbands and other of their actor friends. They had great times but always went out of town; Los Angeles was too dangerous, they might run into friends who would easily recognize them despite their disguise. They discovered that San Francisco was also risky. Some gay men seemed to know their true identity at a glance. Their favorite place was Las Vegas.

Dante had picked them up at the Xanadu Club Lounge, where tired gamblers took a break and listened to a band, a comic, and a girl singer. Loretta had once performed there at the beginning of her career. There was no dancing. The Hotel wanted their customers to get back to the tables as soon as they were rested.

Dante was attracted to them by their vivaciousness, their natural charm. They were attracted to him because they had watched him gamble and lose enormous amounts of money with his unlimited credit. After the drinks, he took them to the roulette wheel and staked them each to a thousand dollars' worth of chips. They were charmed by his hat and the extravagant courtesy showed to him by the croupiers and the pit boss. And his sly charm, which was touched by a vicious humor. Dante was witty in a vulgar and sometimes chilling way. And the extravagance of his gambling excited them. Of course they themselves were rich, they earned enormous amounts of money, but his was hard cash and that had its own magic. Certainly they had spent tens of thousands on Rodeo Drive in one day, but they had received luxurious goods in return. When Dante signed a hundred-thousand-dollar marker, they were awed, though their husbands had bought them cars that cost more. But Dante was throwing away money.

They didn't always sleep with men they picked up, but when they went to the ladies room they conferred on which one would get Dante. Julia begged and she said she had a real yen to pee in Dante's funny hat. The others gave in.

Joan had hoped to score five or ten grand. Not that she really needed it, but it was cash, real money. Loretta was not as charmed as the others by Dante. Her life in Las Vegas cabaret had partly inured her to such men. They were too full of surprises, most of them not pleasant.

The women had a three-bedroom suite in the Xanadu. They always stuck close together on these outings, for reasons of safety and so they could gossip together about their adventures. They made it a rule not to spend the entire night with the men they picked up.

So Julia wound up with Dante, who had no say in the matter, though he preferred Loretta. But he insisted Julia go to his suite, which was just below hers. "I'll walk you up to your suite," he said coolly. "We'll just be an hour. I have to get up early in the morning." It was then Julia realized he thought they were soft hookers.

"Come up to my suite," Julia said. "I'll walk you down."

Dante said, "You got your two horny buddies up there. How do I know you won't all jump me and sodomize me? I'm just a little guy."

That amused Julia enough to go to his suite. She had missed the slyness of his smile. On their way to his room, she said jokingly, "I want to pee in your hat."

Dante said to her, stone-faced, "If it's fun for you, it's fun for me."

Once in his suite there was very little chitchat. Julia threw her purse on the sofa and then pulled down the top of her dress so that her breasts showed, they were her best feature. But Dante seemed to be the exception, a male who was not interested in breasts.

He led her into the bedroom and then pulled off her dress and underclothes. When she was naked, he shed his own clothes. She could see his penis was short, stubby, and uncircumcised. "You have to use a condom," she said.

Dante threw her on the bed. Julia was a robust woman, but he picked her up and threw her without seeming to make an effort. Then he straddled her.

"I insist you use a condom," she said. "I mean it."

In the next moment there was an explosion of light in her head. She realized he had slapped her so hard that she had almost lost consciousness. She tried to wriggle away but for so small a man he was incredibly strong. She felt two more slaps that suffused her face with a hot glow and made her teeth ache. Then she felt him enter her. His driving thrusts lasted for only a few seconds and then he slumped over her.

They lay entwined and then he began to turn her over. She could see that he still had an erection and she knew he wanted to penetrate her anally. She whispered to him, "I love that but I have to get some Vaseline from my purse."

He let her slide out from under him and she went into the living room. Dante came to the door of the bedchamber. They were both still naked and he still had an erection.

Julia fumbled in her purse and then, with a dramatic flourish, took out a tiny silver handgun. It was a prop from a movie she had worked in and she had always fantasized about using it in a real-life situation. She pointed it at Dante, took the crouch stance she had been taught in the movie, and said, "I'm going to dress and leave. If you try to stop me, I'll shoot."

To her surprise, the naked Dante burst out in a good-humored laugh. But Julia noted with satisfaction that he immediately lost his erection.

She was enjoying the situation. She was imagining that she was back upstairs with Joan and Loretta and how they would laugh about this. She tried to get up the courage to ask for his hat so she could pee in it.

But now Dante surprised her. He started walking toward her slowly. He was smiling, he said gently, "That's such a small caliber, it won't even stop me unless you get a lucky shot to the head. Never use a small gun. You can put three bullets to my body and then I'll strangle you. Also, you're holding that gun wrong, you don't need that stance, there's no kick in it. Plus the chances are you won't even hit me, those little bitty things are inaccurate. So throw it away and we'll talk this over. Then you can leave."

He continued walking toward her so she threw the gun on the sofa. Dante picked it up and looked at it, shook his head. "A fake gun?" he said. "That's the sure way to get killed." He shook his head in an almost affectionate disapproval. "Well, if you were a real hooker, this would be a real gun. So who are you?"

He pushed Julia down on the sofa and imprisoned her there with his leg, his toes pushed against her pubic hair. Then he opened her purse and spilled the contents onto the coffee table. He fished into the purse pockets and took out her wallet of credit cards and her driver's license. He studied them carefully and then grinned in pure delight. He said to her, "Take off that wig." Then he reached over with a doily from the sofa and wiped her face clean of makeup.

"Jesus Christ, you are Julia Deleree," Dante said. "I'm fucking a movie star." He gave another delighted laugh. "You can pee in my hat anytime."

His toes were searching her crotch. Then he pulled her to her feet. "Don't be scared," he said. He kissed her and then turned her around and pushed her so that she was bent over the back of the sofa, breasts hanging down, her buttocks presented, tilted up to him.

Julia said to him tearfully, "You promised to let me leave."

Dante was kissing her buttocks, his fingers probing. Then he entered her savagely and she gave a yell of pain. When he finished, he patted her buttocks tenderly.

"You can get dressed now," he said. "I'm sorry I broke my word. I just couldn't miss the chance of telling my friends that I fucked Julia Deleree up her great ass."


The next morning Cross had a wakeup call push him out of bed early. It would be a busy day. He had to pull all of Dante's markers out of the casino cage and do the necessary paperwork to make them disappear. He had to get the pit bosses' marker books out of their hands and have them redone. Then he had to make arrangements so that the papers on the Rolls for Big Tim would be revoked. Giorgio had had the legal papers prepared so that the official change of ownership would not be valid until a month in the future. That was vintage Giorgio.

In the middle of all this he was interrupted with a call from Loretta Lang. She was in the Hotel and urgently wanted to see him. Because he thought it might be something about Claudia, he had Security bring her up to the penthouse.

Loretta kissed him on both cheeks and then told him the whole story about Julia and Dante. She said the man had introduced himself as Steve Sharpe and had lost a hundred grand at the crap table. They were impressed, and Julia decided to sleep with him. The three of them had only come to relax and have a night of gambling. Now they were terrified that Steve might cause a scandal.

Cross nodded sympathetically. He was thinking, What a stupid thing for Dante to do before a big operation, and the son of a bitch was giving away black chips for his pickups to gamble with. He said to Loretta calmly, "I know the man, of course. Who are the two women with you?"

Loretta knew better than to dally with Cross. She told him the two names. Cross smiled. "Do you three do this often?"

"We have to have a little fun," Loretta said. Cross gave her a sympathetic smile.

"OK," he said. "Your friend went to his room. She undressed. She wants to scream rape? What?"

Loretta said hastily, "No, no. We just want him to keep quiet. If he talks it could be absolute disasters for our careers."

"He won't talk," Cross said. "He's a funny kind of guy. Keeps a low profile. But take my advice, don't get mixed up with him again. You girls should be more careful."

Loretta was annoyed by this last remark. The three women had decided to continue their outings. They were not going to be frightened by one mishap. Nothing really terrible had happened. She said, "How do you know he won't talk?"

Cross looked at her gravely. "I'll ask him the favor," he said.

When Loretta left, Cross called for the secret camera file that showed all the guests at the registration desk. He studied them. Now that he had the information, it was easy to penetrate the disguises of the two women with Loretta Lang. It was dumb for Dante not to have gotten that info.

Pippi came by the penthouse office to have lunch before he left for Los Angeles to check off the logistics of the Big Tim operation. Cross told him the story Loretta had told.

Pippi shook his head. "The little bastard could have ruined the whole operation by throwing the timing off. And he keeps wearing that fucking hat after I told him not to."

Cross said, "Be careful on this operation. Keep your eye on Dante."

"I planned it, he can't fuck it up," Pippi said. "And when I see him in L.A. tonight, I'll give him another briefing."

Cross told him about how Giorgio had prepared the papers on the Rolls so that Big Tim would not acquire legal ownership for a month and so that after his death, the Hotel could regain the car.

"Typical Giorgio," Pippi said. "The Don would have let the estate keep his car for his kids."


Big Tim the Rustler Snedden left Vegas two days later, owing sixty grand in markers to the Xanadu Hotel. He took the late-afternoon plane to Los Angeles, went to his office and worked for a few hours, and then drove to Santa Monica to have dinner with his ex-wife and his two children. His pockets had wads of five-dollar bills, which he gave to his kids along with a cardboard container, a quart of silver dollars. To his wife he gave the support and alimony check due, without which he would not be allowed to visit. He conned his wife with sweet talk after the children went to bed but she wouldn't give him a screw, which he didn't really want after Vegas. But he had to try, it was something for nothing.

The next day Big Tim the Rustler had a very busy day indeed. Two Internal Revenue Agents tried to frighten him into paying some disputed taxes. He told them he would go to tax court and threw them out. Then he had to visit a warehouse of canned foods and another warehouse of over-the-counter drugs, all acquired at rock-bottom prices because their expiration dates were coming up. Those expiration dates would have to be changed. At lunch he met with a supermarket-chain vice president who would accept the shipment of these goods. During lunch he slipped the executive an envelope that held ten thousand dollars.

After lunch he received a surprise call from two FBI agents who wanted to ask him about his relationship with a congressman who was under indictment. Big Tim told them to go fuck themselves.

Big Tim the Rustler had never known fear. Perhaps because of his bulk, or maybe there was a piece of his brain missing. For he not only lacked physical fear, he lacked mental fear. He had not only taken the offensive against man but against nature itself. When the doctors told him he was eating himself to death and he should seriously diet, he had opted instead for the stomach bypass operation, which was more hazardous. And it had turned out perfectly. He ate as he wished without apparent harmful effect.

He had built his financial empire the same way. He made contracts that he refused to honor when they became unprofitable, he betrayed partners and friends. Everybody sued him, but they always had to settle for less than they would have received on the original terms. It was a life of success for one who took no precautions for the future. He always thought he would win in the end. He could always collapse corporate entities, shmooze over personal animosities. With women he was even more merciless. He promised them whole malls, apartments, boutiques. Then they settled for a small piece of jewelry at Christmas, a small check on their birthdays. Significant sums but not up to the original promises. Big Tim did not want a relationship. He just wanted to make sure he could have a friendly screw when he needed it.

Big Tim loved all this rustling, it made life interesting. There had been an independent bookmaker in L.A. that he had stiffed for a seventy-grand bet on football games. The bookmaker held a gun to his head and Big Tim said, "Go fuck yourself," then offered ten grand to settle the debt. The bookmaker took it.

His fortune, his ruddy health, his imposing bulk, his lack of guilt made Big Tim successful in everything he touched. His belief that all humanity was corruptible gave him a certain air of innocence that was useful not only in a woman's bed but also in the courts of law. And his gusto for life gave him a certain charm. He was a con man who let you peek at his cards.

So Big Tim did not wonder at the mystery of the arrangement Pippi De Lena had made with him for that night. The man was a hustler like himself and could be dealt with appropriately. Big promises and small rewards.

As for Steve Sharpe, Big Tim smelled a great opportunity, a multi-year scam. The little guy had dropped at least a half million in one day at the tables that he observed. Which meant he had an enormous credit line at the casino and must be in a position to earn a great deal of black money. He would be perfect in the Super Bowl fix. Not only could he supply the betting money, but he had the confidence of bookmakers. After all, those guys didn't take mammoth bets from just anybody.

Then Big Tim daydreamed about his next visit to Vegas. Finally he would get a Villa. He pondered on who to bring with him as guests. Business or pleasure? Future scam victims or maybe all women? Finally it was time to go to dinner with Pippi and Steve Sharpe. He called his ex-wife and his two kids for a chat and then was on his way.

The dinner was at a small fish restaurant down in the L.A. dock area. There was no valet service, so Big Tim put his car in a parking lot.

In the restaurant he was greeted by a tiny maître d' who took one look at him and ushered him to a table where Pippi De Lena was waiting.

Big Tim was an expert of the *abraccio* and he took Pippi into his arms. "Where's Steve? Is he jerking me around? I haven't the time for that kind of bullshit."

Pippi turned on all his charm. He clapped Big Tim on the shoulder. "What am I, chopped liver?" he said. "Sit down and have the best fish dinner you ever ate. We'll be seeing Steve after."

When the maître d' came to take their order, Pippi told him, "We want the best of everything and the most of everything. My friend here is a champion eater and if he gets up from this table hungry, I'll talk to Vincent."

The maître d' smiled confidently; he knew the quality of his kitchen. His restaurant was part of Vincent Clericuzio's empire. When the police backtracked Big Tim's trail, they would meet a blank wall here.

They ate a progression of clams, mussels, shrimps, and then lobsters: three for Big Tim and one for Pippi. Pippi was finished long before Big Tim. He said to him, "This guy is a friend of mine and I can tell you now he is tops in drugs. If that scares you off, tell me now."

"That scares me as much as this lobster," Big Tim said, waving its huge, nibbled claws in Pippi's face. "What else?"

"He always has to launder black money," Pippi said. "Your deal will have to include that."

Big Tim was enjoying the food; all the briney spices of the ocean filled his nostrils. "Great, I know all that," he said. "But where the fuck is he?"

"He's on his yacht," Pippi said. "He doesn't want anybody to see you with him. That's to your interest. He's a very cautious guy."

"I don't give a flying fuck who sees me with him," Big Tim said. "I want to see *me* with *him*."

Finally Big Tim was finished. His dessert was fruit, with a cup of espresso. Pippi skillfully skinned a pear for him. Tim ordered another espresso. "To keep me awake," he said. "That third lobster nearly put me away."

No check was presented. Pippi left a twenty-dollar bill on the table and the two left the restaurant, the maître d' silently applauding Tim's performance at the table.

Pippi guided Big Tim to a small rental car that Tim squeezed into with difficulty. "Christ, can't you afford a bigger car?" Big Tim said.

"It's only a short distance," Pippi said soothingly. And indeed it was a five-minute ride. By that time it was really dark except for the lights of a small yacht moored to the pier.

The gangplank was down, guarded by a man almost as big as Tim. There was another man on the far deck. Pippi and Big Tim went up the gangplank and onto the deck of the yacht. Then Dante appeared

243 • THE LAST DON

on the deck and came forward to shake their hands. He was wearing his Renaissance hat, which he guarded good-naturedly from Big Tim's swipe.

Dante led them below deck to a cabin decorated as a dining room. They sat around a table in comfortable chairs screwed into the floor.

On the table was an array of liquor bottles, a bucket of ice, and a tray with drinking glasses. Pippi poured them all a brandy.

At that moment the engines started and the yacht began to move. Big Tim said, "Where the hell are we going?"

Dante said smoothly, "Just a little spin for some fresh air. Once we're out on the open sea, we can go up on the deck and enjoy it."

Big Tim was not that unsuspicious, but he had faith in himself, that he could handle anything that happened in the future. He accepted the explanation.

Dante said, "Tim, my understanding is that you want to go into business with me."

"No, I want you to go into business with *me*," Big Tim said with boastful good humor. "I run the show. You get your money washed without paying a premium. And make a good bit extra. I have a mall I'm building outside Fresno and you can get a piece for five million or ten. I have a lot of other deals all the time."

"That sounds very good," Pippi De Lena said.

Big Tim gave him a cold stare. "Where do you shine in? I've been meaning to ask."

"He's my junior partner," Dante said. "My advisor. I have the money but he has the brains." He paused and then said sincerely, "He's told me a lot of good things about you, Tim, that's why we're talking."

The yacht was moving very swiftly now, the glasses trembled on the tray. Big Tim debated whether he should cut this guy in on the Super Bowl fix. Then he had one of his hunches, and they were never wrong. He leaned back in his chair, sipped his brandy, and gave both men a serious questioning look, which he often gave and had in fact rehearsed. The look of a man about to bestow his trust. In a best friend. "I'm going to let you guys in on a secret," he said. "But first, are we going to do business? You want a piece of the mall?"

"I'm in," Dante said. "Our lawyers will get together tomorrow and I'll put up some good faith money."

Big Tim emptied his brandy glass and then leaned forward. "I can fix the Super Bowl," he said. With a dramatic flourish he signaled to Pippi to fill his glass. He was gratified to see the look of astonishment on their faces. "You think I'm full of shit, right?" he said.

Dante took off his Renaissance hat and looked at it thoughtfully. "I think you're peeing in my hat," he said with a reminiscing smile. "A lot of people try. But Pippi is the expert on this stuff. Pippi?"

"Can't be done," Pippi said. "The Super Bowl is eight months away and you don't even know who'll be in it."

"Then fuck you," Big Tim said. "You don't want part of a sure thing, that's okay with me. But I'm telling you I can fix it. If you don't want it okay, let's do the mall. Turn this boat around and stop wasting my fucking time."

"Don't be so touchy," Pippi said. "Just tell us how the fix works."

Big Tim gulped his brandy and said in a regretful voice, "I can't tell you that. But I'll give you a guarantee. You bet ten million and we split the winnings. If anything goes wrong, I'll give you ten million back. Now is that fair?"

Dante and Pippi looked at each other with amused grins. Dante ducked his head, and his Renaissance hat made him look like a cunning squirrel. "You give me the money back in cash?" he asked.

"Not exactly," Big Tim said. "I'll make it up on another deal. Take ten million off the price."

"Do you fix the players?" Dante asked.

"He can't," Pippi said. "They make too much money. It must be the officials."

Big Tim was enthusiastic now. "I can't tell you but it's foolproof. And never mind the money. Think of the glory. It will be the biggest fix in sports history."

"Sure, they'll toast us in jail," Dante said.

"That's the beauty of me not telling you anything," Big Tim said. "I go to jail, you guys don't. And my lawyers are too good and I have too many connections."

For the first time, Dante varied Pippi's script. He said, "Are we far enough out?"

Pippi said, "Yeah, but I think if we talk a little more, Tim will tell us."

"Fuck Tim," Dante said pleasantly. "You hear that, Big Tim? Now I want to hear how the fix works and no bullshit." His tone was so contemptuous that Big Tim's face flushed red.

"You little prick," he said, "you think you can scare me? You think you're tougher than the FBI, and the IRS, and the toughest shylock on the West Coast? I'll *shit* in your hat."

Dante leaned back in his chair and banged on the wall of the cabin. A few seconds later two large, tough-looking men opened the door, then stood guard. In answer, Big Tim stood up and swept the table clean with one huge arm. Liquor bottles, the bucket of ice, and the tray of glasses crashed to the cabin floor.

"No Tim, listen to me," Pippi shouted. He wanted to spare the man unnecessary suffering. Also, he did not want to be the shooter, that was not part of the plan. But Big Tim was rushing toward the door, ready to do battle.

Then suddenly Dante was slipping inside Big Tim's arms, nestled against his huge body. They broke apart and Big Tim sagged to his knees. It was a frightening sight. Half his shirt had been sliced away and where once his hairy right breast had been there was just a huge red patch from which an enormous gush of blood poured, staining half the table.

In Dante's hand was the knife he had used, the blood crimson on its broad blade up to the hilt.

"Put him in a chair," Dante said to the guards, and then he took the cloth off the table to staunch Big Tim's bleeding. Big Tim was nearly unconscious with shock.

Pippi said, "You could have waited."

"No," Dante said. "He's a tough guy. Let's see how tough."

"I'll get things ready on the deck," Pippi said. He didn't want to watch. He had never done torture. There were really no secrets so important that justified that kind of work. When you killed a man, you merely separated him from this world so that he could do you no harm.

Up on the deck he saw that two of his men had already prepared. The steel cage was ready on its hook, the slatted bars closed. The deck was covered with a plastic sheet.

He felt the balmy air fragrant with salt, the night ocean purple and still. The yacht was slowing down and then it stopped.

Pippi gazed down at the ocean for a full fifteen minutes before the two men who had stood guard at the door appeared, carrying Big Tim's body. It was so terrible a sight that Pippi averted his eyes.

The four men put Big Tim's body into the cage and then lowered it over the water. One of the men adjusted the slats so that the cage was open for the denizens of the ocean deep to slide between the bars and feast on the body. Then the hook was released and the cage plunged to the bottom of the sea.

Before the sun rose, there would be only the skeleton of Big Tim's body swimming eternally in its cage on the ocean floor.

Dante came up on deck. He had obviously taken a shower and changed his clothes. Underneath the Renaissance hat his hair was slick and wet. There was no trace of blood.

"So he already made his Communion," Dante said. "You could have waited for me."

Pippi said, "Did he talk?"

"Oh yeah," Dante said. "The fix was really simple. Except maybe he was full of shit right up to the end."

The next day Pippi flew East to give the Don and Giorgio a full report. "Big Tim was crazy," he said. "He bribed the caterer who supplies the food and drink to the teams in the Super Bowl. They were going to use drugs to make the team they bet against weaker as the game went on. The coaches and players would notice even if the fans didn't, and the FBI, too. You were right, Uncle, the scandal would have set back our program maybe forever."

"Was he an idiot?" Giorgio asked.

"I think he wanted to be famous," Pippi said. "Rich wasn't enough."

"What about the others involved in the scheme?" the Don asked.

"When they don't hear from the Rustler, they'll be scared off," Pippi said.

Giorgio said, "I agree."

"Very good," the Don said. "And my grandson, did he perform well?"

It seemed an offhand remark, but Pippi knew the Don well enough to understand that this was a very serious question. He answered as carefully as he could but with a certain purpose.

"I told him not to wear his hat on this operation in Vegas and L.A. He did anyway. Then he didn't follow the script of the operation. We could have got the information with more talk but he wanted blood. He cut the guy to pieces. He cut off his cock and nuts and breasts. That wasn't necessary. He enjoys doing it and that is very dangerous for the Family. Somebody really has got to talk to him."

"It will have to be you," Giorgio said to the Don. "He doesn't listen to me."

Don Domenico pondered this a long time. "He's young, he'll grow out of it."

Pippi saw that the Don would not do anything. So he told them about Dante's indiscretion with the movie star the night before the operation. He saw the Don flinch and Giorgio grimace with distaste. There was a long silence. Pippi wondered if he had gone too far.

Finally, the Don shook his head and said, "Pippi, you have planned well, as always, but you can set your mind at rest. You will never have to work with Dante again. But you must understand, Dante is my daughter's only child. Giorgio and I must do our best with him. He will grow wiser."


Cross De Lena sat on the balcony of his executive penthouse suite in the Xanadu Hotel and examined the dangers of the course of action he was taking. From his vantage point he could see the full length of the Strip, the line of luxury casino hotels on either side, the crowds of people in the street. He could see the gamblers on the Xanadu golf course, superstitiously trying for a hole in one to ensure the victory at the gaming tables later.

First danger: In this Boz operation he was making a crucial move without consulting the Clericuzio Family. It was true that he was the administrative Baron of the Western District, which comprised

Nevada and the southern part of California. It was true that the Barons operated independently in many areas and were not strictly under the Clericuzio Family as long as they wet the Clericuzio beak with a percentage of earnings. But there were very strict rules. No Baron, or *Bruglione,* could embark on an operation of such magnitude without the approval of the Clericuzio. For one simple reason. If a Baron did so and got into trouble, he would receive no prosecutorial indulgence, no judicial intervention. In addition, he would receive no support against any rising chief in his own territories, and his money would not be laundered and tucked away for his old age. Cross knew he should see Giorgio and the Don for an OK.

This operation could be enormously sensitive. And he was putting up part of his 51 percent equity in the Xanadu, left to him by Gronevelt, to finance the movie deal. It was true it was his own money, but it was money allied to the hidden interest that the Clericuzio shared in the Hotel. And it was money that the Clericuzio had helped him earn. It was a peculiar and yet somehow very human quirk of the Clericuzio that they felt a proprietary interest in the fortunes of their subordinates. They would resent his investing this money without their advice. Their quirk, though it had no legal foundation, resembled a medieval courtesy: no baron could sell his castle without royal consent.

And the magnitude of the money involved was a factor. Cross had inherited Gronevelt's fifty-one points, the Xanadu was worth a billion dollars. But he was gambling fifty million, investing another fifty million for a total of a C million. The economic risk was enormous. And the Clericuzio were notoriously prudent and conservative, as indeed they had to be to survive the world they moved in.

Cross remembered another thing. Long ago, when the Santadio and Clericuzio Families were on good terms, they had gained a foothold in the movie business. But it had not turned out well. When the Santadio Empire was crushed, Don Clericuzio had ordered that all attempts to infiltrate the movie business be halted. "Those people are too clever," the Don said. "And they have no fear because the rewards are so high. We should have to kill them all and then we would not know how to run the business. It is more complicated than drugs."

No, Cross decided. If he asked permission it would be denied. And then it would be impossible to proceed. When it was done he could do penance, he could let the Clericuzio beak drown itself in his profits, success often excused the most impudent of sins. And if he failed, then most likely he would be finished anyway, approval or not. Which brought up a final doubt.

Why was he doing this? He thought of Gronevelt's "Beware of damsels in distress." Well, he had met damsels in distress before and had left them to their dragons. Vegas was full of damsels in distress.

But he knew. He yearned for the beauty of Athena Aquitane. It wasn't just for the loveliness of her face, her eyes, her hair, her legs, her breasts. He yearned to see the look of intelligence and warmth in her eyes, in the very bones of her face, in the delicate curve of her lips. He felt that if he could know her, be in her presence, the whole world would take on a different light, the sun a different heat. He saw the ocean behind her, rolling green and capped with white flume, like a halo around her head. And the thought strayed into his mind: Athena was the woman his mother had dreamed of becoming.

Astonished, he felt a well of longing to see her, to be with her, to listen to her voice, to watch her move. And then he thought, Oh shit, is this why I'm doing this?

He accepted it and was pleased that finally he knew the real reason for his actions. It made him resolute and it made him focus. At the present time the main problem was operational. Forget Athena. Forget the Clericuzio. There was the difficult problem of Boz Skannet, a problem that had to be solved quickly.

Cross knew he had put himself in too naked a position, another complication. To publicly profit if anything happened to Skannet was dangerous.

Cross resolved on the three people he needed for the planned operation. The first was Andrew Pollard, who owned Pacific Ocean Security and was already involved in the whole mess. The second was Lia Vazzi, the caretaker of the Clericuzio hunting lodge in the Nevada mountains. Lia headed a crew of men who also served as caretakers but were on call for special duties. The third man was Leonard Sossa, a retired counterfeiter on Family retainer to do odd jobs. All three came under Cross De Lena's control as the Western *Bruglione.*

It was two days later that Andrew Pollard got the phone call from Cross De Lena. "I hear you're working too hard," Cross said. "How about coming to Vegas for a little vacation? I'll comp you RFB— room, food, beverage. Bring the wife. And if you get bored pop up to my office for a chat."

"Thanks," Pollard said, "I'm pretty busy right now, but how about next week?"

"Sure," Cross said. "But then I'll be out of town, so I'll miss you."

"I'll come tomorrow then," Pollard said.

"Great," Cross said and hung up.

Pollard leaned back in his chair, pondering. The invitation had been a command. He would have to walk a very thin line.

Leonard Sossa enjoyed life as only a man reprieved from a terrible death sentence can enjoy life. He enjoyed the sunrise, he enjoyed the sunset. He enjoyed the grass growing and the cows who ate the grass. He enjoyed the sight of beautiful women and confident young men and clever children. He enjoyed a crust of bread, a glass of wine, a knob of cheese.

Twenty years before, the FBI had arrested him for making hundred-dollar bills for the now-extinct Santadio Family. His confederates had copped a plea, sold him out, and he had believed the flower of his manhood would wither in prison. Counterfeiting money was a far more dangerous crime than rape, murder, arson. When you counterfeited money, you attacked the machinery of government itself. When you committed the other crimes you were only some scavenger taking a bite out of the carcass of the huge beast that composed the expendable human chain. He expected no mercy and was given none. Leonard Sossa was sentenced to twenty years.

Sossa did only a year. A fellow inmate, overcome with admiration for Sossa's skills, his genius with ink and pencil and pen, recruited him for the Clericuzio Family.

Suddenly he had a new lawyer. Suddenly he had an outside doctor he had never met. Suddenly there was a hearing for clemency on the ground that his mental capacity had deteriorated to that of a child and he was no longer a menace to society. Suddenly Leonard Sossa was a free man and an employee of the Clericuzio Family.

The Family had a need for a first-rate forger. Not for currency, they knew that to the authorities counterfeiting was an unforgivable crime. They needed a forger for far more important tasks. In the mountains of paperwork Giorgio had to handle, juggling different national and international corporations, signing legal documents by nonexistent corporate officers, making deposits and withdrawals of vast sums of money, a variety of signatures and imitations of signatures were needed. Then, as time went on, other uses were found for Leonard.

The Xanadu Hotel used his skills very profitably. When a very rich high roller died and had markers in the cage, Sossa was brought in to sign another million dollars. Of course the dead man's estate would not pay the markers. But then the whole amount could be charged as loss on the Xanadu's taxes. This happened far more often than was natural. There seemed to be a high mortality rate in pleasure. The same was done to high rollers who reneged on their debts or settled dimes on the dollar.

For all this Leonard Sossa was paid a hundred thousand dollars a year and barred from doing any other kind of work, especially counterfeiting currency. This fit in with Family policy in general. The Clericuzio had an edict that prohibited all crime-family members from engaging in counterfeiting and kidnapping. These were the crimes that made all the Federal enforcement agencies come down with crushing force. The rewards were simply not worth the risk.

So for twenty years Sossa enjoyed life as an artist in his little house that nestled in Topanga Canyon, not far from Malibu. He had a small garden, a goat, a cat, and a dog. He painted during the day and drank at night. There was an endless supply of young girls who lived in the Canyon and were free spirits and fellow painters.

Sossa never left the Canyon except to shop in Santa Monica or when he was called to duty by the Clericuzio Family, which was usually twice a month for a period of no more than a few days. He did the work they wanted him to do and never asked questions. He was a valued soldier in the Clericuzio Family.

So when a car came to pick him up and the driver told him to bring his tools and clothes for a few days, Sossa turned his goat, dog, and cat loose into the Canyon and locked his house. The animals could take care of themselves; after all, they were not children. It was not that he was not fond of them, but animals had a short life span, especially in the Canyon, and he had gotten used to losing them. His year in prison had made Leonard Sossa a realist, and his unexpected release had made him an optimist.

Lia Vazzi, the caretaker of the Clericuzio Family's hunting lodge in the Sierra Nevada, had arrived in the United States when he was only thirty years old and the most wanted man in Italy. In the ten years since then he had learned to speak English with only a very slight accent and could read and write it to a fair degree. In Sicily he had been born to one of the most learned and powerful Families on the island.

Fifteen years before, Lia Vazzi had been the leader of the Mafia in Palermo, a Qualified Man of the first rank. But he had reached too far.

In Rome, the government had appointed an examining magistrate and given him extraordinary powers to wipe out the Mafia in Sicily. The examining magistrate had arrived in Palermo with his wife and children, protected by army troops and a horde of police. He gave a fiery speech, promising to show no mercy to those criminals who had ruled the beautiful island of Sicily for centuries. The time had come for the law to rule, for the elected representatives of the people of Italy to decide the fate of Sicily, not the ignorant thugs with their shameful secret societies. Vazzi took his speech as a personal insult.

The examining magistrate was heavily guarded day and night, as he heard the testimony of witnesses and issued arrest orders. His court was a fortress, his living quarters rimmed by a perimeter of army troops. He was seemingly impregnable. But after three months Vazzi learned the magistrate's itinerary, which had been kept secret to prevent surprise attacks.

The magistrate traveled to the big towns in Sicily to gather evidence and issue arrest warrants. He was scheduled to return to

Palermo to be given a medal for his heroic attempt to rid the island of its Mafia scourge. Lia Vazzi and his men mined a small bridge that the magistrate had to pass over. The magistrate and his guards were blown into such tiny bits that the bodies had to be brought out of the water with sieves. The government in Rome, infuriated, replied with a massive search for the culprits responsible, and Vazzi had to go underground. Though the government had no proof, he knew that if he fell into their hands he would be better off dead.

Now the Clericuzio sent Pippi De Lena to Sicily every year to recruit men to live in the Bronx Enclave and soldier for the Clericuzio Family. The bedrock of the Don's faith was that only Sicilians with their centuries-long tradition of *omertà* could be trusted not to turn traitor. The young men in America were too soft, too lightheaded with vanity, could be too easily turned into informants by the more ferocious of the district attorneys who were sending so many of the *Brugliones* to prison.

As a philosophy, *omertà* was quite simple. It was a mortal sin to talk to the police about anything that would harm the Mafia. If a rival Mafia clan murdered your father before your eyes, you were forbidden to inform the police. If you yourself were shot and lay dying, you were forbidden to inform the police. If they stole your mule, your goat, your jewelry, you were forbidden to go to the police. The authorities were the Great Satan a true Sicilian could never turn to. Family and the Mafia were the avengers.

Ten years before, Pippi De Lena had taken his son, Cross, on his trip to Sicily as part of his training. The task was not so much recruiting as screening, there were hundreds of willing men whose greatest dream was to be picked to go to America.

They went to a little town fifty miles from Palermo, into the countryside of villages built of stone, decorated with the bright flowers of Sicily. There they were welcomed into the home of the mayor himself.

The mayor was a short man with a rounded belly, the belly figurative as well as literal, for "a man with a belly" was the Sicilian idiom for a Mafia chief.

The house had a pleasant garden with fig and olive and lemon trees, and it was here that Pippi did his interviews. The garden strangely resembled the Clericuzio garden in Quogue, except for the brilliantly colored flowers and the lemon trees. The mayor was obviously a man who loved beauty, for in addition he had a comely wife and three lusciously pretty daughters who, though in their early teens, were fully developed women.

But Cross saw that his father, Pippi, was a different man in Sicily. There was none of his carefree gallantry here, he was soberly respectful to the women, his charm erased. Late that night, in the room they shared, he lectured Cross. "You have to be careful with Sicilians. They distrust men who are interested in women. You screw one of their daughters, we'll never get out of here alive."

Over the next few days men came to be interviewed and screened by Pippi. He had criteria. The men could not be older than thirty-five or younger than twenty. If they were married, they could not have more than one child. Finally, they had to be vouched for by the mayor. He explained this. If the men were too young, they might be too influenced by the American culture. If they were too old, they could not make the adjustment to America. If they had more than one child, they would be of too cautious a temperament to take the risks their duties would demand.

Some of the men who came were so seriously compromised in the eyes of the law that they had to leave Sicily. Some were simply seeking a better life in America no matter the cost. Some were too clever to rely on fate and desperately wanted to soldier for the Clericuzio, and these were the best.

At the end of the week Pippi had his quota of twenty men, and he gave his list to the mayor, who would approve them and then arrange for their emigration. The mayor crossed out one name on the list.

Pippi said, "I thought he would be perfect for us. Have I made a mistake?"

"No, no," the mayor said. "You have done cleverly as always."

Pippi was puzzled. All of the recruits would be treated very well. The single men would be given apartments, the married men with a child a small house. They would all have steady jobs. They would all live in the Bronx Enclave. And then some would be chosen as soldiers in the Clericuzio Family and make a handsome living with a bright future. The man whose name had been crossed out by the mayor had to be in very bad odor. But then why had he been cleared for an interview? Pippi sensed a Sicilian rat.

The mayor was observing him shrewdly, seeming to read his mind and pleased by what he read.

"You are too much of a Sicilian for me to deceive you," the mayor said. "The name I crossed out is a man my daughter intends to marry. I want to keep him here a year longer for my daughter's happiness, then you can have him. I could not refuse his interview. The other reason is that I have a man who I think you should take in his place. Will you do me the favor of seeing him?"

"Of course," Pippi said.

The mayor said, "I don't want to mislead you, but this is a special case and he must leave immediately."

"You know I have to be very careful," Pippi said. "The Clericuzio are particular."

"It will be to your interest," the mayor said. "But it is a little dangerous." He then explained about Lia Vazzi. The assassination of the magistrate had made world headlines, so Pippi and Cross were familiar with the case.

"If they have no proof, why is this situation so desperate for Vazzi?" Cross said.

The mayor said, "Young man, this is Sicily. The police are also Sicilians. The magistrate was a Sicilian. Everybody knows it was Lia. Never mind your legal proof. If he falls into their hands, he will be dead."

Pippi said, "Can you get him out of the country and into America?"

"Yes," said the mayor. "The difficulty is keeping him hidden in America."

Pippi said, "He sounds like he's more trouble than he's worth."

The mayor shrugged. "He's a friend of mine, I confess. But put that aside." He paused and smiled benignly to make sure that it was not put aside. "He is also an ultimate Qualified Man. He is expert in explosives and that is always a very tricky business. He knows the rope, an old and very useful skill. The knife and gun of course. Most important of all he is intelligent, a man of all parts. And steadfast.

Like a rock. He never talks. He listens and has the gift of loosening tongues. Now tell me, can you not use a man like that?"

"An answer to my prayers," Pippi said smoothly. "But still why does such a man run away?"

"Because in addition to all his other virtues," the mayor said, "he is prudent. He does not challenge fate. His days are numbered here."

"And a man who's qualified," Pippi said, "can he be happy as a mere soldier in America?"

The mayor bowed his head in a sorrowful commiseration. "He is a true Christian," he said. "He has the humility that Christ has always taught us."

"I must meet such a man," Pippi said, "if only for the pleasure of the experience. But I can guarantee nothing."

The mayor made a wide, expansive gesture. "Of course he must suit you," he said. "But there is another thing I must tell you. He forbade me to deceive you about this." For the first time the mayor was not so confident. "He has a wife and three children and they must go with him."

At that moment Pippi knew his answer would be no. "Ah," he said, "that makes it very difficult. When do we see him?"

"He will be in the garden after dark," the mayor said. "There is no danger, I have seen to that."


Lia Vazzi was a small man but with that wiry toughness that many Sicilians inherited from long-ago Arab ancestors. He had a handsome, hawklike face, a dark brown, dignified mask, and he spoke English to a degree.

They sat around the mayor's garden table with a bottle of homemade red wine, a dish of olives from the nearby trees, and bread, crusty and freshly baked that evening, round, still warm, and beside it a whole leg of prosciutto, studded with grains of whole pepper, like black diamonds. Lia Vazzi ate and drank and said nothing.

"I have received the highest recommendations," Pippi said respectfully. "But I worry. Can a man of your education and qualification be happy in America in the service of another man?"

Lia looked at Cross and then said to Pippi, "You have a son. What would you do to save him? I want to have my wife and children safe and for that I will do my duty."

"There will be some danger for us," Pippi said. "You understand that I have to think of the benefits that justify the risk."

Lia shrugged. "I can't be the judge of that." He seemed resigned to being refused.

Pippi said, "If you come by yourself, it will be easier."

"No," Vazzi said. "My family will live together or die together." He paused for a moment. "If I leave them here, Rome will make it very difficult for them. I would rather give myself up."

Pippi said, "The problem is how to hide you and your family."

Vazzi shrugged. "America is vast," he said. He offered the plate of olives to Cross and said almost mockingly, "Would your father ever desert you?"

"No," Cross said. "He is old-fashioned, like yourself." He said it gravely but with a tiny trace of a smile. Then he said, "I hear you're a farmer also."

"Olives," Vazzi said. "I have my own press."

Cross said to Pippi, "How about the Family hunting lodge in the Sierras? He could take care of it with his family and earn his keep. It's isolated. His family can help." He turned to Lia. "Would you live in the woods?" Woods as the idiom for anything not urban. Lia shrugged.

It was the personal force of Lia Vazzi that persuaded Pippi De Lena. Vazzi was not a big man, but his body put out an electric dignity. He had a chilling effect, a man who was not daunted by death, feared neither Hell nor Heaven.

Pippi said, "It's a good idea. Perfect camouflage. And we can call on you for special jobs and let you earn extra money. Those jobs will be your risk."

They could see the muscles on Lia's face loosen when he realized that he had been chosen. His voice trembled slightly when he spoke. "I want to thank you for saving my wife and children," he said, and looked directly at Cross De Lena.

. . .

Since then Lia Vazzi had more than earned the mercy that had been shown to him. He had risen from soldier to leader of all of Cross's operational crews. He supervised the six men who helped him care for the Hunting Lodge estate, on whose grounds he owned his own house. He had prospered, he had become a citizen, his children went away to the university. All this earned by his courage and good sense, and most of all, his loyalty. So when he received the message to meet Cross De Lena in Las Vegas, it was with a goodwill that he packed his suitcase in his new Buick and made the long drive to Vegas and the Xanadu Hotel.

Andrew Pollard was the first to arrive in Las Vegas. He flew from L.A. on the noon flight, relaxed by one of the Hotel Xanadu's huge pools, gambled small-time craps for a few hours, then was secretly whisked into Cross De Lena's penthouse office suite.

They shook hands and Cross said, "I won't keep you long. You can fly back tonight. What I need is all the information you have on the Skannet guy."

Pollard briefed him on everything that had happened and informed him that Skannet was now staying in the Beverly Hills Hotel. He told of his conversation with Bantz.

"So they don't really give a shit about her, they just want to get the picture done," he told Cross. "Also, the Studio doesn't take characters like that seriously. I have a twenty-man section in my company that just handles harassers. Movie stars really have to worry about people like him."

"What about the cops?" Cross asked. "Can't they do something?"

"No," Pollard said. "Not until after the damage."

"What about you?" Cross asked. "You have some good personnel working for you."

"I have to be careful," Pollard said. "I could lose my business if I get tough. You know how the courts are. Why should I stick my neck out?"

"This Boz Skannet, what kind of guy is he?" Cross said.

"He won't scare," Pollard said. "In fact he scares me. He's one of those genuinely tough guys who doesn't care about consequences.

His family has money and political power so he figures he can get away with anything. And he really enjoys trouble, you know, how some guys do. If you're going to get into this you have to be serious."

"I'm always serious," Cross said. "You have Skannet under surveillance now?"

"I sure have," Pollard said. "He is definitely capable of pulling bad shit."

Cross said, "Pull off your surveillance. I don't want anyone watching him. Understand?"

"OK, if you say so," Pollard said. He paused for a moment, then said, "Watch out for Jim Losey, he's keeping an eye out on Skannet. Do you know Losey?"

"I've met him," Cross said. "I want you to do one other thing. Lend me your Pacific Ocean Security ID for a couple of hours. You'll have it back in time to catch the midnight flight to L.A."

Pollard was worried. "You know I'll do anything for you Cross, but be careful; this is a very touchy case. I've built up a very good life out here and I don't want it to go down the drain. I know I owe it all to the Clericuzio Family, I'm always grateful, I'm always paid back. But this is a very complicated business."

Cross smiled at him reassuringly. "You're too valuable to us. One other thing, if Skannet calls up to check on men from your office talking to him, you just verify it."

At this, Pollard's heart sank. This was going to be real trouble.

Cross said, "Now tell me anything else you can about him." When Pollard hesitated, Cross added, "I'll do something for you. Later on."

Pollard thought for a moment. "Skannet claims he knows a big secret that Athena would do anything not to have anyone find out. That's why she dropped the charges against him. A terrific secret, Skannet loves that secret. Cross, I don't know how or why you're involved, but maybe knowing that secret can solve your problem."

For the first time Cross looked at him without affability and suddenly he knew why Cross had acquired his reputation. The look was cold, judging, a judging that could result in death.

Cross said, "You know why I'm interested. Bantz must have told you the story. He hired you to do a background on me. Now do you have any of this big secret or does the Studio?"

"No," Pollard said. "Nobody knows. Cross, I'm doing my best for you, you know that."

"I do know that," Cross said, suddenly gentle. "Let me make it easier for you. The Studio is hot to know how I'm going to get Athena Aquitane back to work. I'll tell you. I'm going to give her half the profits of the movie. And it's okay by me for you to tell them. You can make points, they may even give you a bonus." He reached into his desk and took out a round leather bag and put it in Pollard's hand. "Five grand of black chips," he said. "I always worry when I ask you up here on business that you'll lose money in the casino."

He need not have worried. Andrew Pollard always turned the chips into the casino cage for cash.

Leonard Sossa was just getting settled into a secured business suite at the Xanadu when Pollard's ID was brought to him. With his own equipment he carefully forged four sets of Pacific Ocean Security IDs, complete with special flap-open billfolds. They would not have passed an inspection by Pollard, but that was not necessary, Pollard would never see these IDs. When Sossa finished the job several hours later, two men drove him to the Sierra Nevada Hunting Lodge, where he was installed in a bungalow deep in the woods.

On the porch of the bungalow that afternoon, he watched a deer and bear that wandered by. At night he cleaned his tools and waited. He didn't know where he was or what he was going to do and he didn't want to know. He got his hundred grand a year and lived the life of a free man in the open air. He killed time by sketching the bear and the deer he had seen on a hundred sheets of paper and then riffling them together to give the impression of the deer chasing the bear.

Lia Vazzi was greeted in an altogether different fashion. Cross embraced him, gave him dinner in his suite. During Vazzi's years in America, Cross had been his operational chief many times. Vazzi, despite his own force of character, had never tried to usurp authority, and Cross in turn had treated him with the respect that a man gave his equal.

Over the years Cross had gone to the Hunting Lodge for weekend vacations and the two of them had gone hunting together. Vazzi told stories of the troubles in Sicily and the difference in living in America. Cross had reciprocated by inviting Vazzi and his family to Vegas, comped RFB at the Xanadu plus a credit rating of five thousand in the casino, which Lia was never asked to pay.

Over dinner they talked generally. Vazzi marveled still at his life in America. His oldest son was taking a degree at the University of California and had no knowledge of his father's secret life. Vazzi was uneasy with this. "Sometimes I think he has none of my blood," he said. "He believes everything his professors tell him. He believes women are equal to men, he believes peasants should be given free land. He belongs to the swimming team at college. In all my life in Sicily, and Sicily is an island, I have never seen a Sicilian swimming."

"Except a fisherman thrown off his boat," Cross said laughing.

"Not even then," Vazzi said. "They all drowned."

When they had finished eating, they talked business. Vazzi never really enjoyed the food in Vegas, but he loved the brandy and Havana cigars. Cross always sent him a case of good brandy and a box of thin Havana cigars once a year at Christmas.

"I have something very difficult for you to do," Cross said. "Something that must be done very intelligently."

"That is always difficult," Vazzi said.

"It must be at the Hunting Lodge," Cross said. "We will bring a certain person there. I want him to write some letters, I want him to give a piece of information." He paused to smile at Vazzi's dismissive gesture. Vazzi had often commented on American movies where the hero or villain refused to give information. "I could make them speak Chinese," Vazzi would say.

"The difficulty," Cross said, "is that there must be no mark on his body, no drugs inside his body. Also this certain person is very strong-willed."

"Only women can make a man talk with kisses," Vazzi said amiably, savoring his cigar. "It sounds to me that you are going to be personally involved in this story."

Cross said, "There is no other way. The men working will be your crew but first the Lodge must be cleared of the women and children."

Vazzi waved his cigar. "They will go to Disneyland, that blessing in happiness and trouble. We always send them there."

"Disneyland?" Cross asked, and laughed.

"I have never been," Vazzi said. "I hope to go there when I die. Will this be a Communion or a Confirmation?"

"Confirmation," Cross said.

Then they got down to business. Cross explained the operation to Vazzi and why and how it should be done. "How does it sound to you?" he asked.

"You are far more Sicilian than my son and you were born in America," Vazzi said. "But what happens if he remains stubborn and won't give you what you want."

"Then the fault will be mine," Cross said. "And his. And then we must pay. In that, America and Sicily are the same."

"True," Vazzi said. "As in China and Russia and Africa. As the Don often says, then we can all go swim in the bottom of the ocean."

# CHAPTER 9

E LI MARRION, Bobby Bantz, Skippy Deere, and Melo Stuart assembled in emergency session in Marrion's home. Andrew Pollard had reported to Bantz Cross De Lena's secret scheme to get Athena back to work. This information had been corroborated by the detective Jim Losey, who refused to divulge his source.

"This is a stickup," Bantz said. "Melo, you're her agent, you're responsible for her and all your clients. Does this mean when we are in the middle of a big picture your star refuses to go to work until they get half the profits?"

"Only if you're crazy enough to pay it," Stuart said. "Let this De Lena guy do it. He won't stay in the business long."

Marrion said, "Melo, you're talking strategy, we're talking right this minute. If Athena goes back to work, then you and your client are sticking us up like bank robbers. Will you permit that?"

They were all astonished. It was rare that Marrion cut so quickly to the bone, at least since his younger days. Stuart was alarmed.

"Athena knows nothing about this," he said. "She would have told me."

Deere said, "Would she take the deal if she knew?"

Stuart said, "I would advise her to take it and then in a side letter split her half with the studio."

Bantz said crisply, "Then all her protestations of fear would be a mockery. Bullshit, in short. And Melo, you're full of shit. You think this studio would settle for half of what Athena gets from De Lena? All that money rightfully belongs to us. And she may get away rich with De Lena but it means the end of her career in the movies. No studio will ever hire her again."

"Foreign," Skippy said. "Foreign would take a chance."

Marrion picked up the phone and handed it to Stuart. "This is all to no purpose. Call Athena. Tell her what Cross De Lena is going to offer and ask if she is going to accept."

Deere said, "She disappeared over the weekend."

"She's back," Stuart said. "She often disappears on weekends." He pushed the buttons on the phone.

The conversation was very brief. Stuart hung up and smiled. "She said she has received no such offer. And no such offer would make her come back to work. She doesn't give a shit about her career." He paused for a moment and then said admiringly, "I'd like to meet this guy Skannet. Any man who can scare an actress out of her career has some good in him."

Marrion said, "It's settled then. We've recouped our loss out of a hopeless situation. But it's a pity. Athena was such a great star."

Andrew Pollard had his instructions. The first had been to inform Bantz of Cross De Lena's intention regarding Athena. The second was to pull the surveillance team off Skannet. The third was to visit Boz Skannet and offer a proposition.

Skannet was in his undershirt when he let Pollard into his Beverly Hills Hotel suite, and he smelled of cologne. "Just finished shaving," he said. "This hotel has more bathroom perfumes than a whorehouse."

"You are not supposed to be in this town," Pollard said reproachfully.

Skannet slapped him on the back. "I know, but I'll leave tomorrow. I just have a few loose ends to tie up." His malicious glee while saying this, his massive torso, would have frightened Pollard before, but now that Cross was involved it only evoked pity. But he would have to be careful.

"Athena is not surprised that you haven't left," he said. "She feels the Studio doesn't understand you but she does. So she would like to meet with you personally. She thinks that just the two of you alone can strike a deal."

When he saw the momentary rush of joy on Skannet's face, he knew that Cross had been right. This guy was still in love, he would buy the story.

Boz Skannet was suddenly wary. "That doesn't sound like Athena. She can't stand the sight of me, not that I blame her." He laughed. "She needs that pretty mug of hers."

Pollard said, "She wants to make a serious offer. A lifetime annuity. A percentage of her earnings for the rest of her life if you want. But she wants to talk to you personally and secretly. There's something else she wants."

"I know what she wants," Skannet said. Skannet had a curious look on his face. Pollard had seen that look on the faces of wistfully repentant rapists.

"Seven o'clock," Pollard said. "Two of my men will come to pick you up and bring you to the meeting place. They will stay with her to be her bodyguards. Two of my best men, armed. Just so you won't get any funny ideas."

Skannet smiled. "Don't worry about me," he said.

"Right," Pollard said and left.

When the door closed, Skannet shot his right hand up in the air. He would see Athena again with only two half-assed private detectives to protect her. And he would have proof that she initiated the meeting, he would not be violating the judge's restraining order.

For the rest of the day he dreamed of their reunion. It was really a surprise to him, and thinking about it he knew that Athena would use her body to persuade him into the bargain. He lay on his bed imagining how it would be to be with her again. The image of her body was clear. Her white skin, the gentle curve of her belly, her breasts with their pink nipples, her eyes so green they were another kind of light, her warm delicate mouth, her breath, her flaming hair like the sun turning into smoky brass under a night sky. For a moment his old love swept over him, his love of her intelligence and her brave character that he had broken down into fear. Then for the first time since he was sixteen, he was fondling himself. His mind formed clear figures of Athena urging him on, until he climaxed. For that one moment he was happy and he loved her.

And then everything turned around. He felt a sense of shame, of humiliation. He hated her again. Suddenly he was convinced it was some sort of trap. What did he really know about this guy Pollard, anyway. Skannet dressed hurriedly and studied the card Pollard had given him. The office was only a twenty-minute drive from the hotel. He rushed down to the hotel entrance and a valet brought his car.

When he entered the Pacific Ocean Security Building, he was surprised at the size and opulence of the operation. He made his way to the reception desk and stated his business. An armed security guard escorted him to Pollard's office. Skannet noticed that the walls were decorated with awards from the L.A. Police Department, the Association to Help the Homeless, and other organizations, including the Boy Scouts of America. There was even some sort of a movie award.

Andrew Pollard was regarding him with surprise, and a little concern. Skannet reassured him.

"I just wanted to tell you," he said, "I'll drive to the meeting in my car. Your men can ride with me and give me directions."

Pollard shrugged. This would be none of his business. He had done what he had been instructed to do. "Fine," he said. "But you could have called me."

Skannet grinned at him. "Sure, but I just wanted to check on your offices. Also, I want to call Athena to make sure this is on the up-and-up. I figured you can get her on the phone for me. She might not take my call."

"Sure," Pollard said agreeably. He picked up the phone. He didn't know what was going on and in his heart he hoped that Skannet would abort the meeting and he would no longer be involved in whatever Cross was planning to do. He also knew Athena would not speak to him directly.

He dialed the number and asked for Athena. He put the loudspeaker on so that Skannet could hear the call. Athena's secretary told him that Miss Aquitane was out and was not expected back until the next day. He put down the phone and raised an eyebrow to Skannet. Skannet looked happy.

And Skannet was. He had been right. Athena was planning to use her body to make the deal. She was planning to spend the night with him. The red skin of his face took on an almost bronze sheen with the rush of blood to his brain, remembering when she was young, when she had loved him, when he had loved her.

At seven that evening, when Lia Vazzi arrived at the hotel with one of his soldiers, Skannet was waiting for him and ready to go immediately. Skannet was dressed very neatly in a boyish way. He wore heavy blue jeans, a faded blue denim shirt, and a white sports jacket. He had shaved carefully, and his blond hair was combed straight back. His red skin seemed paler, his face softened by the paleness. Lia Vazzi and his soldier showed Skannet their forged Pacific Ocean Security IDs.

Skannet was not impressed by the men. Two runts, one with a slight accent he thought might be Mexican. They would give him no trouble. These private dick agencies were so full of shit, what kind of protection was this for Athena?

Vazzi said to Skannet, "I understand you want to drive your own car. I will go with you and my friend will follow in our car. Is that agreeable to you?"

"OK," Skannet said.

When they got out of the elevator and entered the lobby, they were stopped by Jim Losey. The detective had been waiting on a sofa by the fireplace and intercepted them on just a hunch. He had staked out there to keep an eye on Skannet just in case. Now he held his ID out to the three men.

Skannet looked at the ID and said, "What the fuck do you want?"

Jim Losey said, "Who are these two men with you?"

"None of your fucking business," Skannet said. Vazzi and his companion remained silent as Losey studied their faces.

"I'd like to have a few words with you in private," Losey said.

Skannet brushed him aside and Losey grabbed his arm. They were both big men. Skannet was frantic to be away. He said to Losey, his voice furious and loud, "The charges were dropped, I don't have to talk to you. And if you don't get your hands away, I'm going to kick the shit out of you."

Losey dropped his hand. He was in no way intimidated, but his mind was working. The two men with Skannet seemed strange to him, there was something going on. He stepped aside but followed them to the archway where cars were brought to hotel guests. He watched Skannet get into his car with Lia Vazzi. Somehow the other man had vanished. Losey noted this and waited to see if another car pulled out of the parking lot, but there was none.

There was no use trying to follow and there was equally no purpose to be served in putting out an alert for Skannet's car. He debated on whether to report this incident to Skippy Deere and decided against it. One thing was for certain, if Skannet got out of line again, he would regret his insults today.

It was a long drive, Skannet kept complaining and asking questions and even threatening to turn back. But Lia Vazzi was reassuring. Skannet had been told that the meeting place was a hunting lodge Athena owned in the Sierra Nevada, and the instructions were that they were to spend the night. Athena had insisted she wanted the meeting a secret from everyone, that she would settle the whole problem to everyone's satisfaction. Skannet didn't know what that meant. What could she do to dissolve the hatred that had grown over the last ten years? Was she stupid enough to think that a night of lovemaking and a bundle of cash would soften him? Did she think he was that simple? He had always admired her intelligence but maybe now she was just one of those arrogant Hollywood actresses who thought she could buy anything with her body and her money? And yet the thought of her beauty haunted him. Finally after all these years, she would smile at him, charm him, submit to him. No matter what happened he would have this coming night.

Lia Vazzi was not worried about Skannet's threats to turn back. He knew there were three cars on the road behind him as escort and he had his instructions. As a last resort he could simply have Skannet killed. But his instructions were also clear that Skannet should not suffer any injury short of death.

They drove through the open gate, and Skannet was surprised at the size of the Hunting Lodge. It looked like a small hotel. He got out and stretched his arms and legs. There were five or six cars parked alongside the lodge, which made him wonder for a moment.

Vazzi led him to the door and opened it. At that moment Skannet heard more cars pulling into the driveway. He turned thinking that Athena had arrived. What he saw were three cars parking and two men getting out of each one. Then Lia led him through the main entry of the lodge and into the living room with its huge fireplace. There, sitting on the sofa waiting for him, was a man he had never seen. The man was Cross De Lena.

What happened next was very quick. Skannet asked angrily, "Where's Athena?" then two men grabbed his arms, another two men put guns to his head, and the seemingly harmless Lia Vazzi pulled his legs out from under him so that he toppled to the floor.

Vazzi said, "You can die now if you don't do exactly as you are told. Don't struggle. Lie still."

Still another man shackled Skannet's legs together and then they pulled him to his feet so that he was facing Cross. Skannet was surprised how helpless he felt even when the men released his arms. His imprisoned feet seemed to neutralize all his physical powers. He reached out to at least punch the little bastard, but Vazzi stepped back, and though Skannet gave a little hop he could not get leverage with his arms.

Vazzi regarded him with quiet contempt. "We know you are a violent man," he said, "but now is the time to use your brain. Strength is of no use here. . . ."

Skannet seemed to take his advice. He was thinking hard. If they had wanted to kill him they would have done so. This was some process of intimidation to make him agree to something. Well and good, he would agree. And then he would take precautions in the future. One thing he was sure of. Athena was not involved in such an operation. He disregarded Vazzi and turned to the man sitting on the sofa.

"Who the hell are you?" he said.

Cross said, "I have a few things I want you to do and then you will be allowed to drive home."

"And if I don't, you'll torture me, right?" Skannet laughed. He was beginning to think this was some jerk-off Hollywood scene, some bad movie the Studio was using.

"No," Cross said simply. "No torture. No one will touch you. I want you to sit down at that table and write four letters for me. One to Lodd-Stone Studios promising never to go near their lot. One to Athena Aquitane apologizing for your previous conduct and swearing never to go near her again. Another to the police authorities admitting you purchased acid to be used in another attack on your wife, and another letter to me stating what secret you hold over your wife. Simple."

Skannet took a hobbling leap toward Cross and was pushed by one of the men so that he went sprawling onto the opposite sofa.

"Don't touch him," Cross said sharply.

Skannet used his arms to push himself to his feet.

Cross pointed to the desk where there was a stack of paper.

"Where's Athena?" Skannet said.

"She's not here," Cross said. "Everybody out of the room, except Lia," he said. The other men went out the door.

"Go sit at the desk," Cross said to Skannet. Skannet did so.

Cross said to him, "I want to talk to you very seriously. Stop trying to show how tough you are. I want you to listen. Don't do anything foolish. You have your hands free and that may give you illusions of grandeur. All I want you to do is write those letters and you'll be free."

Skannet said contemptuously, "You can go fuck yourself."

Cross turned to Vazzi and said, "No use wasting time. Kill him."

Cross had kept his voice even and yet there was something terrible in his casualness. In that moment Skannet felt a fear he had not known since he was a child. He realized for the first time the significance of all the men in the lodge, all the forces that were arrayed against him. Lia Vazzi had not yet made a move. Skannet said, "OK. I'll do it." He picked up a sheet of paper and began to write.

Cunningly, he wrote the letters with his left hand; like some good athletes, he could perform almost equally well with either hand. Cross came up behind him and watched. Skannet, ashamed of his sudden cowardice, braced his feet against the floor. Confident of his physical coordination, he switched the pen to his right hand and sprang up to stab Cross in the face, hoping to get the bastard in the eye. He exploded into action, his arm coming around, the whole torso of his body propelled, and was surprised that Cross had easily moved out of range. Still Skannet tried to move with his leg shackles.

Cross regarded him quietly and said, "Everybody is entitled to his once. You've had that. Now put down the pen and give me those sheets."

Skannet did so. Cross studied the sheets of paper and said, "You haven't told me the secret."

"I won't put it on paper. Get rid of that guy," he motioned to Vazzi, "and I'll tell you."

Cross handed the sheets of paper to Lia and said, "Take care of these."

Vazzi went out of the room.

"OK," Cross said to Skannet, "let's hear this big secret."

When Vazzi left the Hunting Lodge he ran the hundred yards to the bungalow that housed Leonard Sossa. Sossa was waiting. He looked at the two sheets of paper and said disgustedly, "This is left-handed. I can't do left-handed script. Cross knows that."

"Look at it again," Vazzi said. "He tried to stab Cross with his right hand."

Sossa studied the pages again. "Yeah," he said. "This guy is not a real lefty. He's just dicking you around."

Vazzi took the sheets and went back to the Hunting Lodge and entered the library. By Cross's face he knew something had gone wrong. Cross had a look of bewilderment, and Skannet was lying down on the sofa, his shackled legs extended over the arm, smiling happily up at the ceiling.

"These letters are no good," Vazzi said. "He wrote them left-handed and the analyst says he's a rightie."

Cross said to Skannet, "I think you're too tough for me to handle. I can't scare you, I can't make you do what I want. I give up."

Skannet rose from the sofa and said malevolently to Cross, "But what I told you is true. Everybody falls in love with Athena, but nobody knows her the way I do."

Cross said quietly, "You don't know her. And you don't know me." He went to the door and motioned. Four men came into the room. Then Cross turned to Lia. "You know what I want. If he doesn't give it to me, then just get rid of him." He walked out of the room.

Lia Vazzi gave a visible sigh of relief. He admired Cross, had been a willing subordinate all these years, but Cross was too patient. It was true that all the great Dons in Sicily excelled in patience, but they knew when to stop. Vazzi suspected that there was an American softness in Cross De Lena that would prevent his rise to greatness.

Vazzi turned to Skannet and said silkily, "You and I, we begin." He turned to the four men. "Secure his arms, but gently. Don't hurt him."

The four men pounced on Skannet. One of the men produced handcuffs, and in a moment Skannet was completely helpless. Vazzi pushed him to the floor on his knees, the other men forced Skannet to stay in place.

"The comedy is finished," Vazzi said to Skannet. His wiry body seemed relaxed, his voice was conversational. "You will scribble those letters with your right hand. Or you can refuse." One of the men produced a huge revolver and a box of bullets and handed them to Lia. He loaded the revolver, showing each of the bullets to Skannet. He went to the window and fired into the forest until the gun was empty. Then he went back to Skannet and put one bullet in. Spinning the cylinder, he put the gun under Skannet's nose.

"I don't know where the bullet is," Lia said. "You don't know where it is. If you still refuse to write the letters, I pull the trigger. Now is it yes or no?"

Skannet looked into Lia's eyes and did not answer. Lia pulled the trigger. There was just the click of an empty chamber. Lia nodded approvingly. "I was rooting for you," he said to Skannet.

He looked into the cylinder and put the bullet in the first chamber. He went to the window and fired. The explosion seemed to rock the room. Lia went back to the table, took another bullet from the box, loaded the gun with it, spinning the cylinder.

"We will try again," Lia said. He put the revolver beneath Skannet's chin. But this time Skannet flinched.

"Call back your boss," Skannet said. "I have a few more things I can tell him."

"No," Lia said, "that foolishness is over. Now answer yes or no."

Skannet looked into Lia's eyes and saw not a threat but a mournful regret. "OK," Skannet said. "I'll write."

He was immediately hauled to his feet and seated at the writing desk. Vazzi sat on the sofa while Skannet busied himself writing. He took the papers from Skannet and went to Sossa's bungalow. "Is that OK?" he asked.

"This will do fine," Sossa said.

Vazzi went back to the Hunting Lodge and reported to Cross. Then he went to the library and said to Skannet, "It's all over. I'll drive you back to L.A. as soon as I'm ready." Then Lia walked Cross out to his car.

Cross said, "You know everything you have to do. Wait until morning, I should be back in Vegas by then."

"Don't worry," Vazzi said. "I thought he would never write. What an animal." He could see that Cross was preoccupied. "What did he tell you when I was away?" Vazzi asked. "Something I should know?"

Cross said, with savage bitterness Vazzi had never seen before, "I should have killed him straight out. I should have taken my chances. I hate being so fucking clever."

"Ah well," Vazzi said, "it's done now."

He watched Cross drive through the gates. For one of the few times in ten years, he was homesick for Sicily. In Sicily men never became so distraught about a woman's secret. And in Sicily there would never have been all this fuss. Skannet would have been swimming at the bottom of the ocean a long time ago.


As dawn broke, a closed van pulled up to the Hunting Lodge.

Lia Vazzi collected the forged suicide notes from Leonard Sossa and put him into the car that would take him back to Topanga Canyon. Vazzi cleaned up the bungalow, burned the letters Skannet had written, removing all traces of occupancy. Leonard Sossa had never seen either Skannet or Cross during his stay.

Then Lia Vazzi prepared for the execution of Boz Skannet.

Six men were involved in this operation. They had blindfolded and gagged Skannet and put him in the van. Two of the men got into the van with him. Skannet was completely helpless, shackled hand and foot. Another man drove the van, and another man rode shotgun for the driver. The fifth man drove Skannet's car. Lia Vazzi and the sixth man drove another car that went in front.

Lia Vazzi watched the sun slowly rise from the shadows of the mountains. The caravan drove nearly sixty miles and then turned into a road deep in the woods.

Finally the caravan halted. Vazzi directed exactly how Skannet's car should be parked. Then he had Skannet taken out of the van. Skannet made no resistance, he seemed to have accepted his fate. Well, he's finally figured it all out, Vazzi thought.

Vazzi took the rope out of the car. He measured the length carefully and hung one end to the thick limb of a nearby tree. Two men were holding Skannet up straight so that he could slip the noose around the man's neck. Vazzi took out the two suicide notes that Leonard Sossa had forged and slipped them into Skannet's jacket pocket.

It took four of the men to lift Skannet to the roof of the van and then Lia Vazzi threw his fist out in the direction of the driver. The van shot ahead and Skannet flew off the roof and dangled in the air. The sound of his neck cracking resounded through the forest. Vazzi checked the corpse and removed the shackles from the body. The other men removed the blindfold and the gag. There were little scrapes around the mouth, but a couple of days hanging in the forest and they would not be significant. He checked the arms and legs for signs of restraint. Again, there were slight marks, but they would not be conclusive. He was satisfied. He did not know if it would work, but everything Cross ordered had been done.


Two days later, alerted by an anonymous tip, the county sheriff found Skannet's body. He had to scare off an inquisitive brown bear who was hitting the rope to make the body sway back and forth, and when the coroner and his assistants arrived, they found the body's rotting skin eaten by insects.

# BOOK VI

# A
# Hollywood
# Death

# CHAPTER 10

TEN BARE female asses rose in harmony to greet the camera's blinking eye. Despite the picture still being in limbo, Dita Tommey was auditioning actresses on the *Messalina* soundstage for an ass to double for Athena Aquitane's.

Athena had refused to do nudes, that is, she would not show full tits and ass, an astonishing modesty in a star but not a fatal one. Dita would simply substitute tits and ass from some of the different actresses she was now auditioning.

Of course she had given the actresses full scenes with dialogue, she wouldn't demean them by posing them as if they were pornography. But the determining factor would be in the culminating sex scene, when rolling around in bed they would thrust their bare buttocks up to the camera eye. Her sex-scene choreographer was sketching out the rolls and twists with the male actor, Steve Stallings.

Watching the tests with Dita Tommey were Bobby Bantz and Skippy Deere. The only other people on the set were the necessary crew members. Tommey didn't mind Deere watching, but what the hell was Bobby Bantz doing here. She had considered briefly barring him from the set, but if *Messalina* was abandoned she would be in a very weak power position. She could use his goodwill.

Bantz asked fretfully, "What exactly are we looking for here?"

The sex-scene choreographer, a young man named Willis, who was also the head of the Los Angeles Ballet Company, said cheerfully, "The most beautiful ass in the world. But also with great muscles. We don't want sleaze, we don't want the crack open."

"Right," Bantz said, "Nothing sleazy."

"How about the tits?" Deere asked.

"They cannot be allowed to bounce," the choreographer said.

"We audition tits tomorrow," Tommey said. "No woman has perfect tits and a perfect ass, except maybe Athena, and she won't show them."

Bantz said slyly, "You should know, Dita."

Tommey forgot her weak power position. "Bobby, you're the perfect asshole, if that's what we're looking for. She won't fuck you so you assume she's a dyke."

"OK, OK," Bantz said. "I've got a hundred phone calls I have to return."

"Me too," Deere said.

"I don't believe you guys," Tommey said.

Deere said, "Dit, have a little sympathy. Bobby and I, what recreation do we get? We're too busy to play golf. Watching movies is work. We don't have the time to go to the theater or opera. We can squeeze maybe an hour a day for fun after we spend time with our families. What can you do with just one hour a day? Screw. It's the least labor-intensive recreation."

"Wow, Skippy, look at that," Bantz said. "That's the most beautiful ass I have ever seen."

Deere shook his head in wonder. "Bobby's right. Dita, that's the one. Sign her up."

Tommey shook her head in disbelief. "Jesus, you guys are morons," she said. "That's a black ass."

"Sign her up anyway," Deere said with exuberant joy.

"Yeah," Bantz said. "An Ethiopian slave girl for Messalina. But why the hell is she auditioning?"

Dita Tommey observed both men with curiosity. Here were two of the toughest men in the movie business, with over a hundred phone calls to return, and they were like two teenagers looking for their first orgasm. She said patiently, "When we send out casting calls we're not allowed to say we just want white asses."

Bantz said, "I want to meet that girl."

"Me too," Deere said.

But all this was interrupted by Melo Stuart coming on the set. He was smiling triumphantly. "We can all go back to work," he said.

"Athena is going back on the picture. Her husband, Boz Skannet, hung himself. Boz Skannet, off the picture." As he said this he clapped his hands as the crew always clapped when an actor finished work on a movie, his part finished. Skippy and Bobby clapped with him. Dita Tommey stared at the three of them with disgust.

"Eli wants the two of you right away," Melo said. "Not you, Dita," he smiled apologetically. "This will just be a business discussion, no creative decisions." The men left the soundstage.

When they were gone, Dita Tommey summoned the girl with the beautiful ass to her trailer. She was very pretty, truly black rather than tan, and she had an impudent vivacity that Dita identified as natural and not an actor's put-on.

"I'm giving you the part of an Ethiopian slave girl to the Empress Messalina," Dita said. "You'll have one line of dialogue but mainly we'll be showing your ass. Unfortunately we need a white ass to double for Miss Aquitane and yours is too black, otherwise you might steal the picture. She gave the girl a friendly smile. "Falene Fant, that's a movie name."

"Whatever," the girl said. "Thank you. For both the compliments and the job."

"One more thing," Dita said. "Our producer, Skippy Deere, thinks you have the most beautiful ass in the world. So does Mr. Bantz, the president and head of production for the Studio. You'll be hearing from them."

Falene Fant gave her a wicked grin. "And what do you think?" she said.

Dita Tommey shrugged. "I'm not into asses as much as men are. But I think you're charming and a very good actress. Good enough so that I think you can carry more than one line in this picture. And if you come to my house tonight, we can talk about your career. I'll give you dinner."

That night, after Dita Tommey and Falene Fant spent two hours in bed, Dita cooked dinner and they discussed Falene's career.

"It was fun," Dita said, "but I think from now on we should just be friends and keep this night a secret."

"Sure," Falene said. "But everyone knows you're dykey. Is it my black ass?" She was grinning.

Dita ignored the word *dykey*. That was a deliberate impudence to pay back for the seeming rejection. "It's a great ass, black, white, green, or yellow," Dita said. "But you have real talent. If I keep casting you in my pictures, you won't get credit for your talent. And I only make a picture every two years. You have to work more than that. Most directors are male and when they cast somebody like you they're always hoping for a little screw. If they think you're dykey, they may pass."

"Who needs directors if I have a producer and the head of a studio," Falene said cheerfully.

"You do," Dita said. "The other guys can get you a foot in the door, but the director can leave you on the cutting-room floor. Or he can shoot you so that you look and sound like shit."

Falene shook her head woefully. "I have to fuck Bobby Bantz, Skippy Deere, and I've already fucked you. Is this absolutely necessary?" She opened her eyes wide, innocently.

Dita really felt fond of her at the moment. Here was a girl who didn't try to be indignant. "I had a very good time tonight," she said. "You hit exactly the right note."

"Well, I never understood the fuss people make about sex," Falene said. "It's no hardship for me. I don't do drugs, I don't drink a lot. I have to have a little fun."

"Fine," Dita said. "Now, about Deere and Bantz. Deere is the better bet and I'll tell you why. Deere is in love with himself and he loves women. He will really do something for you. He'll find you a good part, he's smart enough to see your talent. Now Bantz doesn't like anybody except Eli Marrion. Also he has no taste, no eye for talent. Bantz will sign you to a studio contract and then let you rot. He does that with his wife to keep her quiet. She gets a lot of work for top dollar but never a decent part. Skippy Deere, if he likes you, will do something for your career."

"This sounds a little cold-blooded," Falene said.

Dita tapped her on the arm. "Don't bullshit me. I'm a dyke but I'm a woman too. And I know actors. They will do anything, male or female, to go up the ladder. We all play for big stakes. Do you want to go to a nine-to-five job in Oklahoma or do you want to become a movie star and live in Malibu? I see by your sheet that you're twenty-three years old. How many have you fucked already?"

"Counting you?" Falene said. "Maybe fifty. But all for fun," she said in mock apology.

"So a few more won't traumatize you," Dita said. "And who knows, it may be fun again."

"You know," Falene said, "I wouldn't do it if I wasn't so sure I'd be a star."

"Of course," Dita said. "None of us would."

Falene laughed. "What about you?" she asked.

"I didn't have the option," Dita said. "I made it on sheer overwhelming talent."

"Poor you," Falene said.

At LoddStone Studios, Bobby Bantz, Skippy Deere, and Melo Stuart were meeting with Eli Marrion in his office. Bantz was enraged. "That silly prick, he scares everybody to death and then commits suicide."

Marrion said to Stuart, "Melo, your client is coming back to work I assume."

"Of course," Melo said.

"She has no further requests, she doesn't need any extra inducements?" Marrion asked in a quiet, deadly voice. For the first time, Melo Stuart became aware that Marrion was in a rage.

"No," Melo said. "She can start work tomorrow."

"Great," Deere said. "We may still come in under budget."

"I want you all to shut up and listen to me," Marrion said. And this rudeness, so unprecedented in him, made them silent.

Marrion spoke in his usual low, pleasant voice, but there was now no mistaking his anger.

"Skippy, what do we give a fuck if the picture comes in on budget? We don't own the picture anymore. We panicked, we made a stupid mistake. All of us are at fault. We do not own this film, an outsider does."

Skippy Deere tried to interrupt him. "LoddStone will make a fortune on distribution. And you get a percentage on profits. It's still a very good deal."

"But De Lena makes more money than we do," Bantz said. "That's not right."

"The point is that De Lena did nothing to solve the problem," Marrion said. "Surely our studio has some sort of legal basis to regain the picture."

"That's right," Bantz said. "Fuck him. Let's go to court."

Marrion said, "We threaten him with court and then we cut a deal. We give him his money back and ten percent of the adjusted gross."

Deere laughed. "Eli, Molly Flanders won't let him take your deal."

"We'll negotiate directly with De Lena," Marrion said. "I think I can persuade him." He paused for a moment. "I called him as soon as I got the news. He will be joining us very shortly. And you know he has a certain background, this suicide is too fortunate for him, I don't think he will care for the publicity of a court case."


Cross De Lena, in his penthouse suite at the Xanadu Hotel, read the newspaper reports of Skannet's death. Everything had gone perfectly. It was a clear case of suicide, the two farewell notes on the body clinched it. There was no possibility the handwriting experts could detect the forgery, Boz Skannet had not left any great body of correspondence and Leonard Sossa was too good. The shackles on Skannet's legs and arms had been purposely loose and had left no marks. Lia Vazzi was an expert.

The first call Cross received was expected. Giorgio Clericuzio summoning him to the Family mansion in Quogue. Cross had never deceived himself that the Clericuzio would not find out what he was doing.

The second call Cross received was from Eli Marrion asking him to come to Los Angeles and without his lawyer. Cross said he would. But before he left Las Vegas he called Molly Flanders and told her about the phone call from Marrion. She was enraged. "Those slimy bastards," she said. "I'll pick you up at the airport and we'll go in together. Never even say good morning to a studio head unless you've got a lawyer with you."

When the two of them walked into LoddStone Studios and Marrion's office they knew there was trouble. The four men waiting there had the seriously truculent look of men about to commit strong-arm.

"I decided to bring my lawyer," Cross said to Marrion. "I hope you don't mind."

"As you wish," Marrion said. "I merely wanted to save you a possible embarrassment."

Molly Flanders, stern-faced and angry, said, "This is going to be really good. You want the picture back but our contract is iron."

"You're correct," Marrion said. "But we are going to appeal to Cross's sense of fair play. He did nothing to solve the problem, whereas LoddStone Studios has invested considerable time and money and creative talent without which this movie would not have been possible. Cross will get his money back. He gets ten percent of the adjusted gross and we will be generous in determining the adjustments. He will not be at risk."

"He has already survived the risk," Molly said. "Your offer is insulting."

"Then we will have to go to court," Marrion said. "Cross, I'm sure you will find that as distasteful as I do." He smiled at Cross. It was a kindly smile that made his gorilla-like face angelic.

Molly was furious. "Eli, you go to court twenty times a year and give depositions because you're always pulling crap like this." She turned to Cross and said, "We're leaving."

But Cross knew that a long court case was something he could not afford. His buying the film followed by Skannet's opportune death would be held up to scrutiny. They would dig up everything about his background, they would paint him in such a way that he would become too much of a public figure, and that was something the old Don had never tolerated. There was no mistaking that Marrion knew all this.

"Let's stick around," Cross said to Molly. Then he turned to Marrion, Bantz, Skippy Deere, and Melo Stuart. "If a gambler comes into my hotel and plays a long shot and wins, I pay him the full odds. I don't say I'll pay him even money. That's what you gentlemen are doing here. So why don't you reconsider this?"

Bantz said with contempt, "This is business not gambling."

Melo Stuart said soothingly to Cross, "You will make conservatively ten million dollars on your investment. Surely that's fair."

"And you didn't even do anything," Bantz said.

Only Skippy Deere seemed to be on his side. "Cross, you deserve more. But what they offer is better than a court fight, the risk of losing. Let this one go and you and I will do business again without the Studio. And I promise you'll get a fair shake."

Cross knew it was important to seem nonthreatening. He smiled in resignation. "Maybe you're all right," he said. "I want to stay in the movie business on good terms with everybody and ten million profit is not a bad start. Molly, take care of the papers. Now I have to catch a plane so please excuse me." He left the room and Molly followed him.

"We can win in court," Molly told him.

"I don't want to go to court," Cross said. "Make the deal."

Molly studied him carefully, then she said, "OK, but I'll get more than ten percent."

When Cross arrived at the mansion in Quogue the next day, Don Domenico Clericuzio, his sons Giorgio, Vincent, and Petie, and the grandson, Dante, were waiting for him. They had lunch in the garden, a lunch of cold Italian hams and cheeses and an enormous wooden bowl of salad, long loaves of crispy Italian bread. There was the bowl of grated cheese for the Don's spoon. As they ate, the Don said conversationally, "Croccifixio, we hear you have become involved in the moving picture business." He paused to sip his red wine. He then took a spoonful of the grated Italian Parmesan cheese.

"Yes," Cross answered.

Giorgio said, "Is it true that you pledged some of your shares in the Xanadu to finance a movie?"

"That is within my right," Cross said. "I am, after all, your *Bruglione* in the West." He laughed.

" *'Bruglione'* is right," Dante said.

The Don shot a disapproving look at his grandson. He said to Cross, "You got involved in a very serious affair without Family consultation. You did not seek our wisdom. Most important of all, you carried out a violent action that might have severe official repercussions. On that, custom is clear, you must have our consent or go your own way and suffer consequences."

"And you used resources of the Family," Giorgio said harshly. "The Hunting Lodge in the Sierra. You used Lia Vazzi, Leonard Sossa, and Pollard with his Security Agency. Of course, they are your people in the West but they are also Family resources. Luckily everything went perfectly but what if it had not? We would all have been at risk."

Don Clericuzio said impatiently, "He knows all that. The question is why. Nephew, years ago you asked not to take part in that necessary work some men must do. I granted your request despite the fact that you were so valuable. Now you do it for your own profit. That is not like the beloved nephew I have always known."

Cross knew then that the Don was sympathetic to him. He knew he could not tell the truth, that he had been seduced by Athena's beauty; that would not be a reasonable explanation, indeed it would be insulting. And possibly fatal. What could be more inexcusable than that the attraction to a strange woman outweighed his loyalty to the Clericuzio Family. He spoke carefully. "I saw an opportunity to make a great deal of money," he said. "I saw a chance to get a foothold in a new business. For me and the Family. A business to bc used to turn black money white. But I had to move quickly. Certainly I did not wish to keep it a secret and the proof is that I used Family resources which you must come to know. I wanted to come to you with the deed done."

The Don was smiling at him when he asked gently, "And is the deed done?"

Cross immediately sensed that the Don knew everything. "There is another problem," Cross said, and explained the new deal he had made with Marrion. He was surprised when the Don laughed aloud.

"You did exactly right," the Don said. "A court case might be a disaster. Let them have their victory. But what rascals they are. It's a good thing we always stayed out of that business." He paused for a moment. "At least you've made your ten million. That's a tidy sum."

"No," Cross said. "Five for me and five for the Family, that is understood. I don't think we should be discouraged so easily. I have some plans but I must have Family help."

"Then we must discuss better shares," Giorgio said. He was like Bantz, Cross thought, always pressing for more.

The Don interrupted impatiently. "First catch the rabbit then we will share it. You have the Family blessing. But one thing. Full discussion on everything drastic that is done. You understand me, nephew?"

"Yes," Cross said.

He left Quogue with a feeling of relief. The Don had shown his affection.


Don Domenico Clericuzio, in his eighties, still commanded his Empire. A world he had created with great endeavor and at great cost and so therefore felt he had earned.

At a venerable age, when most men are obsessed with sins inevitably committed, the regrets of lost dreams, and even doubts of their own righteousness, the Don was still as unshakable in his virtue as when he was fourteen.

Don Clericuzio was strict in his beliefs and strict in his judgments. God had created a perilous world, and mankind had made it even more dangerous. God's world was a prison in which man had to earn his daily bread, and his fellow man was a fellow beast, carnivorous and without mercy. Don Clericuzio was proud that he had guarded his loved ones safely in their journey through life.

He was content that, at his advanced age, he had the will to pass the sentence of death on his enemies. Certainly he forgave them, was he not a Christian who maintained a holy chapel in his own home? But he forgave his enemies as God forgives all men while condemning them to inevitable extinction.

In the world Don Clericuzio had created, he was revered. His family, the thousands who lived in the Bronx Enclave, the *Bru-*

*gliones* who ruled territories and entrusted their money to him and came for his intercession when they got into trouble with the formal society. They knew that the Don was just. That in time of need, sickness, or any trouble, they could go to him and he would address their misfortunes. And so they loved him.

The Don knew that love is not a reliable emotion no matter how deep. Love does not ensure gratitude, does not ensure obedience, does not provide harmony in so difficult a world. No one understood this better than Don Clericuzio. To inspire *true* love, one also had to be feared. Love alone was contemptible, it was nothing if it did not also include trust and obedience. What good was love to him if it did not acknowledge his rule?

For he was responsible for their lives, he was the root of their good fortune, and so he could not falter in his duty. He must be strict in his judgment. If a man betrayed him, if a man damaged the integrity of his world, that man must be punished and restrained even if it meant a sentence of death. There could be no excuse, no mitigating circumstance, no appeal to pity. What must be done must be done. His son Giorgio had once called him archaic. He accepted that this could not be otherwise.

Now he had many things to ponder. He had planned well over the last twenty-five years since the Santadio war. He had been farsighted, cunning, brutal when necessary, and merciful when it was safe to be so. And now the Clericuzio Family was at the height of its power, seemingly safe from any attack. Soon it would disappear into the legal fabric of society and become invulnerable.

But Don Domenico had not survived so long by being optimistically shortsighted. He could spot a malignant weed before it popped its head above the ground. The great danger now was internal, the rise of Dante, his growing into manhood in a manner not entirely satisfactory to the Don.

Then there was Cross, enriched by the Gronevelt legacy, actually making a major move without Family supervision. The young man had started so brilliantly, nearly becoming a Qualified Man, like his father, Pippi. Then the Virginio Ballazzo job had turned him finicky. And after being excused from operational duties by the Family because of his tender heart, he had gone back into the field for his own personal gain and executed that man Skannet. Without the permission of the Don himself. But Don Clericuzio excused himself for condoning these actions, for his rare sentimentalities. Cross was trying to escape his world and enter another. Though these actions were or could be the seeds of treason, Don Clericuzio understood. Still, Pippi and Cross combined would be a threat to the Family. Also, the Don was not unaware of Dante's hatred for the De Lenas. Pippi was too clever not to know this also, and Pippi was a dangerous man. An eye must be kept on him despite his proven loyalty.

The Don's forbearance sprang from a fondness for Cross and a love for Pippi, his old and faithful soldier, his sister's son. After all, they had Clericuzio blood. He was truly more worried about the danger to the Family presented by Dante.

Don Clericuzio had always been a fond and loving grandfather to Dante. The two had been very close until the boy was about ten years old and a certain disenchantment had settled in. The Don detected traits in the boy's character that troubled him.

Dante at the age of ten was an exuberant, slyly humorous child. He was a good athlete with great physical coordination. He loved to talk, especially with his grandfather, and he had long secret conversations with his mother, Rose Marie. But then, after the age of ten, he became malicious and crude. He fought with boys his own age with inappropriate intensity. He teased girls mercilessly and with an innocent lewdness that was shocking though funny. He tortured small animals—not necessarily significant with small boys, as the Don knew— but he tried once to drown a smaller boy in the school swimming pool.

Not that the Don was particularly judgmental of these things. After all, children were animals, civilization had to be drummed into their brains and backsides. There had been children like Dante who had grown up to be saints. What disturbed the Don was his loquacity, his long conversations with his mother, and most of all, his small disobediences to the Don himself.

Perhaps what disturbed the Don as well, who was in awe of the vagaries of nature, was that at the age of fifteen, Dante stopped growing. He remained at the height of five feet three inches. Doctors were consulted and agreed that at the most he would grow three more inches, and not to the usual Clericuzio family height of six feet. The Don considered Dante's short stature to be a danger signal, as he also considered twins. He claimed that while birth was a blessed miracle, twins were going too far. There had been a soldier in the Bronx Enclave who had fathered triplets, and the Don, horrified, bought them a grocery store in Portland, Oregon, a good living but a lonely one. The Don also had superstitions about left-handed people, and those who stuttered. Whatever anyone said, these could not be good signs. Dante was naturally left-handed.

But even all this would not have been enough to make the Don wary of his grandchild or lessen his affection; anyone of his blood was naturally exempt. But as Dante grew older he grew more contrary to the Don's dreams of his future.

Dante quit school in his sixteenth year and immediately pushed his nose into Family affairs. He worked for Vincent in his restaurant. He was a popular waiter and earned huge tips because of his quickness and his wit. Tiring of that, he worked for two months in Giorgio's Wall Street office but hated it and showed no aptitude, despite Giorgio's earnest attempts to teach him the intricacies of paper wealth. Finally he settled in with Petie's construction company and loved working with the Enclave soldiers. He was proud of his body, which grew more and more muscular. But in all this he acquired to some degree certain characteristics of his three uncles, which the Don noted with pride. He had Vincent's directness, Giorgio's coolness, and Petie's ferocity. Somewhere along the way, he established his own personality, what he truly was: sly, cunning, devious, but with a sense of fun that could be charming. And it was then he began wearing his Renaissance hats.

The hats—nobody knew where he got them—were made of colorful iridescent thread; some were round, some were rectangular, and they rode on his head as if they were on water. They seemed to make him taller, handsomer, and more likable. Partly because they were clownlike and disarming, partly because they balanced his two profiles. The hats suited him. They disguised his hair, jet black and ropey as with all the Clericuzio.

One day in the den, where Silvio's photo still occupied the place of honor, Dante asked his grandfather, "How did he die?"

The Don said shortly, "An accident."

"He was your favorite son, right?" Dante asked.

The Don was startled by all this. Dante was still only fifteen. "Why would this be true?" the Don asked.

"Because he's dead," Dante said with a sly grin, and it took the Don a few moments to realize that this raw youth had dared to make such a joke.

The Don also knew that Dante roamed and searched his office suite in the house when the Don was down at dinner. This did not disturb him, children were always curious about the old and the Don never had anything on paper that would divulge information of any kind. Don Clericuzio had a huge blackboard in a corner of his brain that was chalked with all necessary information, including the totals of all the sins and virtues of those dearest to him.

But as Don Clericuzio became more wary of Dante, he showed him even more affection, assuring the boy he was to be one of the heirs to his Family Empire. And rebukes and admonitions were given the boy by his uncles, primarily Giorgio.

Finally, the Don despaired of Dante joining the retreat into a legal society and gave his permission for Dante to train to be a Hammer.

The Don heard his daughter, Rose Marie, calling him to dinner in the kitchen where they ate when it was just the two of them. He went in, sat in the chair in front of the large, colorful bowl of angel hair pasta covered with tomatoes and fresh basil from his garden. She put the silver bowl of grated cheese before him, the cheese was very yellow, which proved its nutty sweetness. Rose Marie came to sit opposite him. She was gay and cheerful, and he was delighted by her good humor. Tonight there would be none of her terrible fits. She was as she had been before the Santadio War.

What a tragedy that had been, one of the few mistakes he had made, one that proved a victory was not always a victory. But who would have thought that Rose Marie would remain forever a widow?

Lovers always loved again, he'd always believed that. At that moment the Don felt an overpowering affection for his daughter. She would excuse Dante's small sins. Rose Marie leaned over and gave the Don's grizzled head an affectionate caress.

He took a huge spoonful of the grated cheese and felt its nutty heat against his gums. He sipped his wine and watched Rose Marie carve the leg of lamb. She served him three crusty brown potatoes, glossy with fat. His troubled mind cleared. Who was better than him?

He was in such a good mood that he let Rose Marie persuade him to watch television with her in the sitting room for the second time that week.

After watching four hours filled with horror, he said to Rose Marie, "Is it possible to live in such a world where everyone does what he pleases? No one is punished by God or man and no one has to earn a living? Are there such women who follow every whim? Men such foolish weaklings, who succumb to every little desire, every little dream of happiness? Where are the honest husbands who work to earn their bread, who think of the best ways to protect their children from fate and the cruel world? Where are the people who understand a piece of cheese, a glass of wine, a warm house at the end of the day is reward enough? Who are these people who yearn for some mysterious happiness? What an uproar they make of life, what tragedies they brew up out of nothing." The Don patted his daughter on the head and waved at the television screen with a dismissive hand. He said, "Let them all swim at the bottom of the ocean." Then he gave her a final piece of wisdom. "Everyone is responsible for everything he does."

That night, alone in his bedroom, the Don stepped out on his balcony. The houses in the compound were all brightly illuminated; he could hear the thwack of tennis balls on the tennis court and see the players underneath its bank of lights. There were no children playing outdoors so late. He could see the guards on the gate and around the house.

He pondered what steps he could take to prevent future tragedy. His love for his daughter and grandson washed over him, that was what made old age worthwhile. He would simply have to protect them as best he could. Then he was angry with himself. Why was he always foreseeing tragedy? He had solved all the problems in his life and he would solve this one.

Still, his mind whirled with plans. He thought of Senator Wavven. For years he had given the man millions of dollars to get legislation passed to ensure legalized gambling. But the senator was slippery. It was too bad that Gronevelt was not still alive; Cross and Giorgio did not have the necessary skill to prod him. Perhaps the gambling empire would never come to pass.

Then he thought of his old friend David Redfellow, now living so comfortably in Rome. Perhaps it was time to bring him back into the Family. It was all very well for Cross to be so forgiving of his Hollywood partners. After all, he was young. He could not know that one sign of weakness might be fatal. The Don decided he would summon David Redfellow from Rome to do something about the movie business.

# CHAPTER 11

**A** WEEK AFTER the death of Boz Skannet, Cross received, through Claudia, a dinner invitation to Athena Aquitane's house in Malibu.

Cross flew from Vegas to L.A., rented a car, and arrived at the Malibu Colony guarded gatehouse as the sun began to fall into the ocean. There was no longer any special security, though there was still the secretary in the guest house who checked and buzzed him in. He walked through the longitudinal garden to the house on the beach. There was still the little South American maid, who led him to the sea-green living room that seemed just out of reach of the Pacific Ocean waves.

Athena was waiting for him, and she was even more beautiful than he remembered. She was dressed in a green blouse and slacks, and she seemed to melt and become part of the mist over the ocean behind her. He could not take his eyes off her. She shook his hand in greeting, not the usual Hollywood kiss on both cheeks. She had drinks ready and she handed him one. It was Evian water with lime. They sat in the large, mint green upholstered chairs that faced the ocean. The descending sun scattered gold coins of light in the room.

Cross was so aware of her beauty that he had to bow his head to avoid looking at her. The golden helmet of hair, the creamy skin, the way her long body sprawled in her chair. Some of the gold coins fell into her green eyes, fleeting shadows. He felt an urgent desire to touch her, to be closer to her, to own her.

Athena seemed unaware of the emotions she was causing. She sipped her drink and said quietly, "I wanted to thank you for keeping me in the movie business."

The sound of her voice further entranced Cross. It was not sultry or inviting. But it had such a velvet tone, it had such regal confidence and yet was so warm, that he just wanted her to keep talking. Jesus Christ, he thought, what the hell is this? He was ashamed of her power over him. His head still down, he murmured, "I thought I could get you back to work by appealing to your greed."

"That is not one of my many weaknesses," Athena said. Now she turned her head from the ocean so that she could look directly into his eyes. "Claudia told me the Studio reneged on their deal once my husband killed himself. You had to give them back the picture and take a percentage."

Cross kept his face impassive. He hoped to banish everything he was feeling about her. "I guess I'm not a very good businessman," he said. He wanted to give her the impression that he was ineffective.

"Molly Flanders wrote your contract," Athena said. "She's the best. You could have held on."

Cross shrugged. "A matter of politics. I want to get into the movie business permanently and didn't want enemies as powerful as Loddstone Studios."

"I could help you," Athena said. "I could refuse to return to the picture."

Cross felt a thrill that she would do that for him. He considered the offer. The Studio might still take him to court. Also, he could not bear to make Athena put him in her debt. And then it occurred to him that though Athena was beautiful that didn't mean she was not clever.

"Why would you do that?" he asked.

Athena got up from her chair and moved to stand close to the picture window. The beaches were gray shadows, the sun had disappeared, and the ocean seemed to reflect the mountain ranges behind her house and the Pacific Coast Highway. She gazed out toward the now blue-black water, the small waves rippling in slyly. She did not turn her head to him when she said, "Why would I do that? Simply because I knew Boz Skannet better than anybody. And I don't care if he left a hundred suicide notes, he would never kill himself."

Cross shrugged. "Dead is dead," he said.

"That's true," Athena said. She turned to face him, looked directly at him. "You buy the picture and suddenly Boz conveniently commits suicide. You're my candidate as the killer." Even stern, her face was so beautiful to Cross that his voice was not as steady as he would have wished.

"How about the Studio?" Cross said. "Marrion is one of the most powerful men in the country. What about Bantz and Skippy Deere?"

Athena shook her head. "They understood what I was asking them. Just as you did. They didn't do it, they sold the picture to you. They didn't care if I was killed after the picture was finished, but you did. And I knew you would help me even when you said you couldn't. When I heard about you buying the picture, I knew exactly what you would do, but I must say I didn't think you could be so clever."

Suddenly she came toward him and he rose from his chair. She took his hands in hers. He could smell her body, her breath.

Athena said, "That was the only evil thing I have ever done in my life. Making somebody commit murder. It was terrible. I would have been a much better person if I had done it myself. But I couldn't."

Cross said, "Why were you so sure I would do something?"

Athena said, "Claudia told me so much about you. I understood who you were but she's so naïve, she still hasn't caught on. She thinks you're just a tough guy with a lot of clout."

Cross became very alert. She was trying to get him to admit his guilt. Something he would never do even to a priest, not even to God himself.

Athena said, "And the way you looked at me. A lot of men have looked at me that way. I'm not being immodest, I know I'm beautiful, people have been telling me that since I was a child. I always knew I had power, but I could never really understand that power. I'm not really happy with it but I use it. What they call 'love.' "

Cross let go of her hands. "Why were you so afraid of your husband? Because he could ruin your career?"

For one moment there was a flash of anger in her eyes. "It wasn't my career," she said, "and it wasn't out of fear, though I knew he would kill me. I had a better reason." She paused, then said, "I can make them give you the picture back. I can refuse to keep working."

"No," Cross said.

Athena smiled and said with a brilliant, gay cheerfulness, "Then we can just go to bed together. I find you very attractive and I'm sure we'll have a good time."

His first reaction was one of anger, that she could think she could just buy him off. That she was acting a part, using her skill as a woman the same way a man would use physical force. But what really bothered him was that he could hear a faint bit of mockery in her voice. Mockery of his gallantry, and turning his true love into a simple screw. As if she was telling him that his love for her was as fake as her love for him.

He said to her coolly, "I had a long talk with Boz, trying to make a deal. He said he used to fuck you five times a day when you were married."

He was pleased that she seemed startled. She said, "I wasn't counting, but it was a lot. I was eighteen and I really loved him. Isn't it funny that now I wanted him dead?" She frowned a moment and said, casually, "What else did you talk about?"

Cross looked at her grimly. "Boz told me the terrible secret you had between you. He claims you confessed that when you ran away, you buried your baby in the desert."

Athena's face became a mask, her green eyes went dull. For the first time that night, Cross felt she could not possibly be acting. Her face had a pallor no actress could achieve. She whispered to him, "Do you really believe I murdered my baby?"

"Boz said that's what you told him," Cross said.

"I did tell him that," Athena said. "Now, I'm asking you again. Do you believe I murdered my baby?"

There is nothing so terrible as to condemn a beautiful woman. Cross knew that if he answered truthfully, he would lose her forever. Suddenly he put his arms around her very gently. "You're too beautiful. Nobody as beautiful as you could do that." The eternal worship of men for beauty against all evidence. "No," he said. "I don't believe you did."

She stepped away from him. "Even though I'm responsible for Boz?"

"You're not responsible," Cross said. "He killed himself."

Athena was gazing at him intently. He took her hands. "Do you believe I killed Boz?" he asked.

And then Athena smiled, an actress who finally realized how to play a scene. "No more than you believe I killed my baby."

They smiled, they had declared each other innocent. She took his hand and said, "Now, I'm cooking dinner for you and then we're going to bed." She led him into the kitchen.

How many times had she played this scene, Cross thought jealously. The beautiful Queen performing housewifely duties like an ordinary woman. He watched her cook. She wore no protective clothing and she was extraordinarily professional. She spoke to him as she chopped vegetables, prepared a skillet, and set the table. She gave him a bottle of wine to open, holding his hand and brushing against his body. She saw him looking with admiration when the table was laden after just a half hour.

She said, "I played a woman chef in one of my first roles, so I went to school to get everything right. And one critic wrote, 'When Athena Aquitane acts as well as she cooks, she will be a star.' "

They ate in the alcove of the kitchen so they could look at the rolling ocean. The food was delicious, little squares of beef covered with vegetables and then a salad of bitter greens. There was a platter of cheeses and warm short loaves of bread, plump as pigeons. Then there was espresso with a small, light lemon tart.

"You should have been a cook," Cross said, "My cousin Vincent would hire you for his restaurants any day."

"Oh, I could have been anything," Athena said with mock boastfulness.

All through dinner she had touched him casually in a way that was sexual, as if she were searching for some spirit in his flesh. Cross with every touch yearned to feel her body on his. By the end of the meal, he no longer could taste what he was eating. Finally they were done and Athena took him by the hand and led him out of the kitchen and up the two flights of stairs to her bedroom. She did it gracefully, almost shyly, almost blushing, as if she were an eager virginal bride. Cross marveled at her acting ability.

The large bedroom was at the very top of the house and had a small balcony that looked out over the ocean. The walls were covered with a weird, garish painting that seemed to light up the room.

They stood on the balcony and watched the room illuminate the beach sand with a spooky yellow glow, the other Malibu houses squatted along the water showing little boxes of light. Tiny birds, as if playing a game, ran in and out of the incoming waves to escape getting wet.

Athena put her hand on Cross's shoulder, around his body, the other hand reaching out to pull his mouth down to hers. They kissed for a long time as the warm ocean air washed over them. Then Athena led him inside the bedroom.

She undressed quickly, slipping out of her green blouse and slacks. Her white body flashed in the moon-ridden darkness. She was as beautiful as he had imagined. The rising breasts with their raspberry nipples seemed spun of sugar. Her long legs, the curve of her hips, the blond hair at her crotch, her absolute stillness, limned by misty ocean air.

Cross reached out for her body and her flesh was velvet, her lips filled with the scent of flowers. The sheer joy of touching her was so sweet he could not do anything else. Athena began to undress him. She did so gently, running her hands over his body as he had over hers. Then, kissing him, she gently pulled him onto the bed.

Cross made love with a passion he had never known or even dreamed existed. He was so urgent that Athena had to stroke his face to gentle him. He could not let loose of her body, even after they climaxed. They lay intertwined until they began again. She was even more ardent than before, as if it was some sort of contest, some sort of avowal. Finally they both drifted off into slumber.

Cross awoke just as the sun showed above the horizon. For the first time in his life, he had a headache. Naked, he moved onto the balcony and sat on one of the straw chairs. He watched the sun slyly rise slowly from the ocean and begin its ascent to the sky.

She was a dangerous woman. The murderer of her own child, whose bones were now filled with desert sand. And she was too skillful in bed. She could be the end of him. At that moment he decided he would never see her again.

Then he felt her arms around his neck and his face twisted around to kiss her. She was in a white fluffy bathrobe, and her hair was held in place by pins that glittered like jewels in a crown. "Take a shower and I'll make you breakfast before you go," she said.

She led him into the double bathroom, two sinks, two marble counters, two bathtubs, and two showers. It was stocked with men's toilet articles, razors, shaving cream, skin toners, brushes, and combs.

When he had finished and was out on the balcony again, Athena brought a tray with croissants, coffee, and orange juice to the table. "I can make you bacon and eggs," she said.

"This is fine," Cross said.

"When will I see you again?" Athena asked.

"I have lots of things to do in Las Vegas," Cross said. "I'll call you next week."

Athena gave him an appraising look. "That means good-bye, doesn't it?" she asked. "And I really enjoyed last night."

Cross shrugged. "You paid off your obligation," he said.

She gave him a good-humored grin and said, "And with amazing goodwill, don't you think? It wasn't begrudging."

Cross laughed. "No," he said.

She seemed to read his mind. Last night they had lied to each other, this morning the lies had no power. She seemed to know that her beauty was too much for him to trust. That he felt in danger with her, and with her confessed sins. She seemed deep in thought and ate silently. Then she said to him, "I know you're busy but I have something to show you. Can you spare this morning and catch an afternoon plane? It's important. I want to take you someplace."

Cross could not resist spending one last time with her and so he said yes.

Athena drove them in her car, a Mercedes SL 300, and took the highway south to San Diego. But just before they reached the city, she turned off into a thin road that led inland through the mountains.

In fifteen minutes they came to a compound enclosed by barbed wire. Inside the compound were six redbrick buildings separated by green lawns and connected by sky blue painted walkways. In one of the green squares, a group of about twenty children were playing with a soccer ball. On another green about ten children were flying kites. There was a group of three or four adults standing around watching them, but something seemed odd about the scene. When the soccer ball flew through the air, it seemed most of the children ran away from it, while on the other square the kites flew up, up, into the sky and never returned.

"What is this place?" Cross asked.

Athena looked pleadingly at him. "Just come with me please for now. Later, you can ask your questions."

Athena drove to the entry gate and showed a gold ID badge to the security guard. Passing through, she drove to the largest building and parked.

Once inside at the reception desk, Athena asked the attendant something in a low voice. Cross stood back, but still he heard the answer. "She was in a mood so we gave her a hug in her room."

"What the hell was that?" Cross asked.

But Athena didn't answer. She took his hand and led him through a long, shiny tile hallway to an adjoining building and into some sort of dormitory.

A nurse sitting at the entrance asked their names. When she nodded, Athena led Cross down another long hallway of doors. Finally, she opened one.

They were standing in a pretty bedroom, large and full of light. There were the same strange, dark paintings as on the wall in Athena's house, but here they were strewn on the floor. On the wall a small shelf held a row of pretty dolls dressed in starched Amish costumes. Also on the floor were several other scraps of drawings and paintings.

There was a small bed covered with a pink fuzzy blanket, the pillows white with red roses stitched all over them. But there was no child in the bed.

Athena walked toward a large box that was open at the top, its walls and base covered with a thick, soft pad colored light blue, and when Cross looked inside he saw the child lying there. She didn't notice them. She was fiddling with a knob at the head of the box, and Cross watched as she forced the pads together, almost crushing herself.

She was a small girl of ten, a tiny copy of Athena, but without emotion, devoid of all expression, and her green eyes were as unseeing as those of a porcelain doll. Yet each time she turned the controls to make the panels squeeze her tight, her face shone with complete serenity. She did not acknowledge them in any way.

Athena moved to the top of the wooden box. She switched the controls so that she could lift the child out of the box. The child seemed to weigh almost nothing.

Athena held her like an infant and bent her head to kiss the child's cheek, but the child flinched and pulled away.

"It's your mommy," Athena said. "Won't you give me a kiss?"

The tone of her voice broke Cross's heart. It was an abject pleading, but now the child was churning wildly within her arms. Finally Athena gently put her down on the floor. The child scrambled to her knees and immediately picked up a box of paints and a huge cardboard sheet. Completely absorbed, she began to paint.

Cross stood back and watched as Athena tried all her acting skill to establish a rapport with the child. First she kneeled down next to the little girl and was the loving playmate helping her daughter paint, but the child took no notice.

Athena then sat up, tried to be a confiding parent telling the child what was happening in the world. Then Athena became a fawning adult praising the child's paintings. To all this the child merely kept moving away. Athena picked up one of the brushes and tried to help, but when the child did see, she grabbed the brush away. She never said a word.

Finally Athena gave up.

"I'll come back tomorrow, darling," she said. "I'll take you for a ride and I'll bring a new paint box. See," she said, tears welling in her eyes, "you're running out of reds." She tried to give the child a farewell kiss but was held away by two small, beautiful hands.

Finally Athena rose and led Cross out of the room.

Athena gave him the keys to the car so he could drive back to Malibu, and during the ride, she held her head in her hands and wept. Cross was so stunned he could not say a word.

When they got out of the car, Athena seemed to have control of herself. She pulled Cross into the house and then turned and faced him. "That was the baby I told Boz I buried in the desert. Now do you believe me?" And for the first time Cross really believed she might love him.

Athena led him into the kitchen and made coffee. They sat in the alcove to watch the ocean. As they drank their coffee, Athena started speaking. She talked casually, no emotion in her voice or on her face.

"When I ran away from Boz, I left my baby with some distant cousins, a married couple in San Diego. She seemed a normal baby. I didn't know she was autistic then, maybe she wasn't. I left her there because I was determined to be a successful actress. I had to make money for both of us. I was sure I was talented and God knows everybody told me how beautiful I was. I always thought that when I was successful, I could take my baby back."

"So I worked in Los Angeles and visited her in San Diego whenever I could. Then I began to break through and I didn't see her that often, maybe once a month. Finally when I was ready to bring her home I went to her third birthday party with all kinds of presents, but Bethany seemed to have slipped into another world. She was a blank. I couldn't reach her at all. I was frantic. I thought maybe she had a brain tumor, I remembered when Boz had let her fall on the floor, that maybe her brain had been injured and it was now beginning to show. For months after that I brought her to doctors, she underwent a battery of tests of all kinds, I took her to specialists and they checked everything. Then someone, and I don't remember whether it was the doctor in Boston or the psychiatrist in Texas Children's Hospital, told me she was autistic. I didn't even know what that meant except that I thought it was some kind of retardation. 'No,' the doctor said. It meant she lived in her own world, was unaware of other people's existence, had no interest in them, could feel nothing for anything or anyone. It was when I brought her to the clinic here to be close to me that we found she could respond to that hugging machine you saw. That seemed to help, so I had to leave her there."

Cross sat without a word, while Athena continued. "Being autistic meant she could never love me. But the doctors told me some autistic people are talented, even geniuslike. And I think Bethany is a genius. Not only with her painting. Something else. The doctors tell me that after many years of hard training some autistic people can be taught to care for some things, then some people. A few can even live a near-to-normal life. Right now, Bethany can't stand listening to music or any noise. But at first she couldn't bear to have me touch her, and now she's learned to tolerate me, so she's better than she used to be.

"She still rejects me but not as violently. We've made some progress. I used to think it was punishment for my neglect of her because I wanted to be a success. But the specialists say that sometimes though it seems hereditary, it can be acquired, but they don't know what really makes it happen. The doctors told me it had nothing to do with Boz dropping her on her head or me deserting her, but I don't know if I believe that. They kept trying to reassure me that we were not responsible, that it was one of the mysteries of life, maybe it was preordained. They insisted nothing could have prevented it from happening and nothing can ever change it. But again something inside me refuses to believe any of that.

"Even when I first found out, I thought about it constantly. I had to make some hard decisions. I knew I would be helpless to rescue her until I made a lot of money. So I put her in the clinic and visited her at least one weekend a month and some weekdays. Finally, I got rich, I was famous and nothing that mattered before mattered any longer. All I wanted was to be with Bethany. Even if this hadn't happened, I was going to quit after *Messalina* anyway."

"Why?" Cross asked. "What were you going to do?"

"There's a special clinic in France with this great doctor," Athena explained. "And I was going to go there after the picture. Then Boz showed up and I knew he would kill me and Bethany would be all alone. That's why I sort of put a contract out on him. She has nobody but me. And well, I'll bear that sin." Athena paused now and smiled at Cross. "It's worse than the soaps, isn't it?" she said with a small smile.

Cross looked out over the ocean. It was a very bright oily blue in the sunlight. He remembered the little girl and her blank, masklike face that would never open up to this world.

"What was that box she was lying in?" he asked.

Athena laughed. "That's what gives me hope," she said. "Sad, isn't it? It's a hug box. A lot of autistic children use it when they get depressed. It's just like a hug from a person but they don't have to connect or relate to another human being." Athena took a deep breath and said, "Cross, someday I'm going to take the place of that box. That's the whole purpose of my life now. My life has no meaning except for that. Isn't that funny? The Studio tells me that I get thousands of letters from people who love me. In public people want to touch me. Men keep telling me they love me. Everybody but Bethany, and she's the only one I want."

Cross said, "I'll help you in any way I can."

"Then call me next week," Athena said. "Let's be together as much as we can until *Messalina* is finished."

"I'll call," Cross said. "I can't prove my innocence, but I love you more than anything in my life."

"And are you truly innocent?" Athena asked.

"Yes," Cross said. Now that she had been proven innocent, he could not bear for her to know.

Cross thought about Bethany, her blank face so artistically beautiful with its sharp planes, its mirror eyes; the rare human being totally free of sin.

As for Athena, she had been judging Cross. Of all the people she knew, he was the only one who had ever seen her daughter since the child had been diagnosed as autistic. It had been a test.

One of the greatest shocks of her life came when she found out that though she was so beautiful, though she was so talented (and, she thought with self-mockery, so kind, so gentle, so generous), her closest friends, men who loved her, relatives who adored her, sometimes seemed to relish her misfortunes.

It was when Boz had given her a black eye, and though everyone called Boz a "no-good bastard," she caught in all of them a fleeting look of satisfaction. At first she thought she had imagined it, was too sensitive. But when Boz had given her the second black eye, she caught those looks again. And she had been terribly hurt. For this time she had understood completely.

Of course they all loved her, she did not doubt that. But it seemed no one could resist a little touch of malice. Greatness in any form arouses envy.

One of the reasons she loved Claudia was because Claudia had never betrayed her with that look.

It was why she kept Bethany so secret from her day-to-day life. She hated the idea that people she loved would have that fleeting look of satisfaction, that she had been punished for her own beauty.

So though she knew the power of her beauty and used that power, she despised it. She longed for the day when lines would cut deep into her perfect face, each showing a path she had taken, a journey survived, when her body would fill out, soften and enlarge her to provide comfort for those she'd hold and care for, and her eyes would grow more liquid with mercy from all the suffering she'd witnessed and all the tears she'd never shed. She'd grow smile lines around her mouth from laughing at herself, and at life itself. How free she would be when she no longer feared the consequences of her physical beauty and instead delighted in its loss as it was replaced by a more enduring serenity.

And so she had kept careful watch on Cross De Lena when he met Bethany, saw his slight recoil at first but then afterward nothing. She knew he was helplessly in love with her and she saw he did not have that certain look of satisfaction when he knew of her misfortune with Bethany.

# CHAPTER 12

CLAUDIA WAS DETERMINED to cash in on her sexual marker with Eli Marrion; she would shame him into giving Ernest Vail the points he wanted on his novel. It was a long shot, but she was willing to compromise her principles. Bobby Bantz was implacable on gross points, but Eli Marrion was unpredictable and had a soft spot for her. Besides, it was an honorable custom in the movie business that sexual congress, no matter how brief, demanded a certain material courtesy.

Vail's threat of suicide had been the trigger for this meeting. If carried out, the rights to his novel would revert to his former wife and her children, and Molly Flanders would drive a hard bargain. Nobody believed in the threat, not even Claudia, but Bobby Bantz and Eli Marrion, operating from their knowledge of what they would do for money, always had to worry.

When Claudia, Ernest, and Molly arrived at LoddStone, they found only Bobby Bantz in the executive suite. He looked uncomfortable, though he tried to disguise it with effusive greetings, especially to Vail. "Our National Treasure," he said and hugged Ernest with respectful affection.

Molly was immediately alert, wary. "Where's Eli?" she said. "He's the only one who can make the final decision on this."

Bantz's voice was reassuring. "Eli's in the hospital, Cedar Sinai, nothing serious, just a checkup. That's confidential. The LoddStone stock goes up and down on his health."

Claudia said dryly, "He's over eighty, everything is serious."

"No, no," Bantz said. "We do business every day in the hospital. He's even sharper. So present your case to me and I'll tell him your story when I visit."

"No," Molly said curtly.

But Ernest Vail said, "Let's talk to Bobby."

They presented their case. Bantz was amused but did not laugh outright. He said, "I've heard everything in this town but this is a beauty. I ran it by my lawyers and they say that Vail's demise does not affect our rights. It's a complicated legal point."

"Run it by your PR people," Claudia said. "If Ernest does it and the whole story comes out LoddStone will look like shit. Eli won't like that. He has more moral sense."

"Than me?" Bobby Bantz said politely. But he was furious. Why didn't people understand that Marrion approved everything he did. He turned to Ernest and said, "How would you knock yourself off? Gun, knife, out the window?"

Vail grinned at him. "Hara-kiri on your desk, Bobby." They all laughed.

"We're getting nowhere," Molly said. "Why can't we all go to the hospital and see Eli?"

Vail said, "I'm not going to a sick man's hospital bed and argue about money."

They all looked at him sympathetically. Of course in conventional terms it seemed insensitive. But men in sickbeds planned murders, revolution, frauds, studio betrayals. A hospital bed was not a true sanctuary. And they knew that Vail's protest was basically a romantic convention.

Molly said coldly, "Keep your mouth shut, Ernest, if you want to remain my client. Eli has screwed a hundred people from his hospital bed. Bobby, let's make a sensible deal. LoddStone has a gold mine in the sequels. You can afford to give Ernest a couple of gross points, for insurance."

Bantz was horrified, a hot stab went through his bowels. "*Gross points?*" he shouted incredulously. "Never."

"OK," Molly said. "How about a structured five percent of the net? No advertising charges, no interest deductions or gross points to the stars."

Bantz said contemptuously, "That's almost gross. And we all know that Ernest won't kill himself. That's too stupid and he is too intelligent." What he really wanted to say was that the guy didn't have the balls.

"Why gamble?" Molly said. "I've gone over the figures. You plan at least three sequels. That's at least a half billion in rentals including foreign but not the videos and TV. And God knows how much money you fucking thieves make in video. So why not give Ernest points, a measly twenty million. You would give that to any half-assed star."

Bantz thought it over. Then he turned on the charm. "Ernest," he said, "as a novelist you are a National Treasure. No one respects you more than me. And Eli has read every one of your books. He absolutely adores you. So we want to come to an accommodation."

Claudia was embarrassed at how Ernest obviously swallowed this bullshit, though to his credit, he shuddered a bit at the "National Treasure."

"Be specific," he said. Now Claudia was proud of him.

Bantz spoke to Molly. "How about a five-year contract at ten grand a week to write original scripts and do some rewrites and of course on the originals we only get first look. And for every rewrite he gets an additional fifty grand a week. In five years he could make as much as ten million."

"Double the money," Molly said. "Then we can talk."

At this point Vail seemed to lose his almost angelic patience. "None of you are taking me seriously," he said. "I can do simple arithmetic. Bobby, your deal is only worth two and a half. You'll never buy an original script from me and I'll never do one. You'll never give me rewrites. And what if you make six sequels? Then you make a billion." Vail began to laugh with genuine enjoyment. "Two and a half million dollars doesn't help me."

"What the fuck are you laughing about?" Bobby said.

Vail was almost hysterical. "I never dreamed in my life of even one million and now it doesn't help me."

Claudia knew Vail's sense of humor. She said, "Why doesn't it help you?"

"Because I'll still be alive," Vail said. "My family needs the points. They trusted me and I betrayed them."

They would have been touched, even Bantz, except that Vail sounded so false, so self-satisfied.

Molly Flanders said, "Let's go talk to Eli."

Vail lost his temper completely and stormed out of the door shouting, "I can't deal with you people. I won't beg a man on a hospital bed."

When he was gone, Bobby Bantz said, "And you two want to stick up for that guy?"

"Why not?" Molly said. "I represented a guy who stabbed his mother and his own three kids. Ernest is no worse than him."

"And what's your excuse?" Bantz asked Claudia.

"We writers have to stick together," she said wryly. They all laughed.

"I guess that's about it," Bobby said. "I did the best I could, right?"

Claudia said, "Bobby, why can't you give him a point or two, it's only fair."

"Because over the years he's screwed a thousand writers and stars and directors. It's a matter of principle," Molly said.

"That's right," Bantz said. "And when they have the muscle they screw us. That's business."

Molly said to Bantz with fake concern, "Eli is okay? Nothing serious?"

"He's fine," Bantz said. "Don't sell your stock."

Molly pounced. "Then he can see us."

Claudia said, "I want to see him anyway. I really care about Eli. He gave me my first break."

Bantz shrugged them off. Molly said, "You will really kick yourself if Ernest knocks himself off. Those sequels are worth more than I said. I softened him up for you."

Bantz said scornfully, "That schmuck won't kill himself. He doesn't have the balls."

"From 'National Treasure' to 'schmuck,' " Claudia said musingly.

Molly said, "The guy is definitely a little crazy. He'll croak out of sheer carelessness."

"Does he do drugs?" Bantz asked, a little worried.

"No," Claudia said, "but Ernest is full of surprises. He's a true eccentric who doesn't even know he's eccentric."

Bantz pondered this for a moment. There was some merit in their argument. And besides he never believed in making unnecessary enemies. He didn't want Molly Flanders to carry a grudge against him. The woman was a terror.

"Let me call Eli," he said. "If he gives the okay, I'll take you to the hospital." He was sure that Marrion would refuse.

But to his surprise, Marrion said, "By all means, they can all come to see me."

They drove to the hospital in Bantz's limo, which was a big stretch job but by no means luxurious. It was fitted with a fax, a computer, and a cellular phone. A bodyguard supplied by Pacific Ocean Security sat next to the driver. Another security car with two men followed behind.

The brown-tinted windows of the limo presented the city in a beige monochrome of old-time cowboy movies. As they progressed inward, the buildings became taller, as if they were penetrating a deep stone forest. Claudia was always amazed how in the short space of ten minutes she could go from a mildly bucolic small-town green to a metropolis of concrete and glass.

In Cedars Sinai, the hospital corridors seemed as vast as the halls of an airport, but the ceiling compressed like a bizarre camera shot in a German impressionist movie. They were met by a hospital co-ordinator, a handsome women dressed in a severe but high-couture suit who reminded Claudia of the "Hosts" in Vegas hotels.

She led them to a special elevator that took them nonstop to the top penthouse suites.

These suites had huge carved black oak doors that reached from floor to ceiling, with shiny brass knobs. The doors opened like gates, to a suite of a hospital bedroom, a larger, open-walled room with dining table and chairs, a sofa and lounge chairs, and a secretarial niche that held a computer and fax. There was also a small kitchen space and guest bathroom in addition to the bathroom for the patient. The ceiling was very high and the absence of walls between the kitchen niche, the living room area, and the business nook gave the whole room the look of a movie set.

Lying on a crisp, white hospital bed, propped up by huge pillows, was Eli Marrion. He was reading an orange-covered script. On the table beside him were business folders with budgets of movies in production. A pretty young secretary seated on the other side of the bed was taking notes. Marrion always liked pretty women around him.

Billy Bantz kissed Marrion on the cheek and said, "Eli, you look great, just great." Molly and Claudia also kissed him on the cheek. Claudia had insisted on bringing flowers, and put them on the bed. Such familiarities were excused because the great Eli Marrion was ill.

Claudia was noting all the details as if researching a script. Medical dramas were almost financially foolproof.

In fact, Eli Marrion was not looking "great just great." His lips were ridged with blue lines that seemed drawn with ink, he gasped for air when he spoke. Two green prongs grew from his nostrils, the prongs attached to a thin plastic tube that ran to a bubbling bottle of water that was plugged into the wall, all connected to some oxygen tank hidden there.

Marrion noted her gaze. "Oxygen," he said.

"Only temporary," Bobby Bantz said hurriedly. "Makes it easier for him to breathe."

Molly Flanders ignored them. "Eli," she said, "I've explained the situation to Bobby and he needs your OK."

Marrion seemed to be in good humor. "Molly," he said, "you were always the toughest lawyer in this town. Are you going to harass me on my deathbed?"

Claudia was distressed. "Eli, Bobby told us you were okay. And we really wanted to see you." She was so obviously ashamed that Marrion raised his hand with acceptance and benediction.

"I understand all the arguments," Marrion said. He made a motion of dismissal to the secretary and she left the room. The private duty nurse, a handsome, tough-looking woman, was reading a book at the dining room table. Marrion gestured to her to leave. She looked at him and shook her head. She resumed reading.

Marrion laughed, a low wheezing laugh. He said to the others, "That is Priscilla, the best nurse in California. She's an intensive care nurse, that's why she's so tough. My doctor recruited her especially for this case. She's the boss."

Priscilla acknowledged them with a nod of her head and resumed reading.

Molly said, "I'll be willing to limit his points to a maximum of twenty million. It will be insurance. Why take the risk? And why be so unfair?"

Bantz said angrily, "It's not unfair. He signed a contract."

"Fuck you, Bobby," Molly said.

Marrion ignored them. "Claudia, what do you think?"

Claudia was thinking many things. Obviously Marrion was sicker than anyone was admitting. And it was terribly cruel to put pressure on this old man who had to make such an effort to even speak. She was tempted to say that she was leaving, then she remembered that Eli would never have let them come except for some purpose of his own.

"Ernest is a man who does surprising things," Claudia said. "He is determined to provide for his family. But Eli, he's a writer and you always loved writers. Think of it as a contribution to art. Hell, you gave twenty million to the Metropolitan Museum. Why not do it for Ernest?"

"And have all the agents on our ass?" Bantz said.

Eli Marrion took a deep breath, the green prongs seemed to go deeper into his face. "Molly, Claudia, we will have to keep this our little secret. I'll give Vail two gross points to a max of twenty million. I'll give him a million up front. Will that satisfy you?"

Molly thought it over. Two gross points on all the pictures should yield a minimum of fifteen million but maybe more. It was the best she could do, and she was surprised that Marrion had gone so far. If she haggled he was quite capable of withdrawing the offer.

"That's wonderful, Eli, thank you." She leaned over to kiss him on the cheek. "I'll send your office a memo tomorrow. And Eli, I do hope you get well soon."

Claudia could not restrain her emotion. She clasped Eli's hand in hers. She noticed the brown specks that mottled the skin, the hand chilly with approaching death. "You saved Ernest's life."

At that moment Eli Marrion's daughter came into the room with her two small children. The nurse, Priscilla, rose from her chair like a cat scenting mice and moved toward the children, interposing herself between them and the bed. The daughter had been twice divorced and did not get on with her father, but she had a production company on the LoddStone lot because Eli was so fond of his grandchildren.

Claudia and Molly took their leave. They drove to Molly's office and called Ernest to tell him the good news. He insisted on taking them out to dinner to celebrate.


Marrion's daughter and two grandchildren stayed only a short time. But long enough for the daughter to get her father to promise to buy her a very expensive novel for her next movie.

Bobby Bantz and Eli Marrion were alone. "You're a soft touch today," Bantz said.

Marrion felt the weariness in his body, the air being sucked into it. He could relax with Bobby, he never had to act with him. They had been through so much together, used power together, won wars, traveled and schemed through the wide world. They could read each other's minds.

"That novel I'm buying for my daughter, will it make a movie?" Marrion asked.

"Low-budget," Bantz said. "Your daughter makes quote-unquote 'serious' movies."

Marrion made a weary gesture. "Why do we always have to pay for other people's good intentions? Give her a decent writer but no stars. She'll be happy and we won't lose too much money."

"Are you really going to give Vail gross?" Bantz asked. "Our lawyer says we can win in court if he dies."

Marrion said smilingly, "If I get well. If not, it will be up to you. You'll be running the show."

Bantz was astonished at this sentimentality. "Eli, you'll get well, of course you will." And he was absolutely sincere. He had no desire to succeed Eli Marrion, indeed he dreaded the day that inevitably had to come. He could do anything as long as Marrion approved it.

"It's going to be up to you, Bobby," Marrion said. "The truth is that I'm not going to make it. The doctors tell me I need a heart transplant and I've decided not to get one. I can live maybe six months, maybe a year, maybe much less with this lousy heart I have. And besides, I'm too old to qualify for a transplant."

Bantz was stunned. "They can't do a bypass?" he asked. When Marrion shook his head, Bantz went on. "Don't be ridiculous, of course you'll get a transplant. You built half the hospital, they have to give you a heart. You have another good ten years." He paused for a moment. "You're tired, Eli, we'll talk about this tomorrow." But Marrion had dozed off. Bantz left to check with the doctors and then to tell them to start all procedures to harvest a new heart for Eli Marrion.

Ernest Vail, Molly Flanders, and Claudia De Lena celebrated by having dinner at La Dolce Vita on Santa Monica. It was Claudia's favorite restaurant. She had memories of herself as a little girl being brought there by her father and being treated like royalty. She had memories of the bottles of red and white wine being stacked in all the window alcoves, on the back rails of banquettes, and in every vacant space. The customers could reach out and pluck a bottle as if they were grapes.

Ernest Vail was in good spirits, and Claudia wondered again how anybody could believe he would commit suicide. He was bubbling over with glee that his threat had worked. And the very good red wine put them all into a merry mood that was slightly boastful. They were very pleased with themselves. The food itself, robustly Italian, fueled their energy.

"Now what we have to think about," Vail said, "is two points good enough or should we push for three?"

"Don't get greedy," Molly said. "The deal is made."

Vail kissed her hand movie-star style and said, "Molly you're a genius. A ruthless genius, true. How could you two browbeat a guy sick on his hospital bed?"

Molly dipped bread into tomato sauce. "Ernest," she said, "you will never understand this town. There is no mercy. Not when you're drunk, or on coke, or in love, or broke. Why make an exception for sick?"

Claudia said, "Skippy Deere once told me that when you're buying, take people to a Chinese restaurant, but when you're selling, take them to an Italian restaurant. Does that make any sense?"

"He's a producer," Molly said. "He read it someplace. It doesn't mean anything without a context."

Vail was eating with the gusto of a reprieved criminal. He had ordered three different kinds of pasta just for himself but gave small portions to Claudia and Molly and demanded their opinions. "The best Italian food in the world outside Rome," he said. "About Skippy, it makes a certain kind of movie sense. Chinese food is cheap, it brings the price down. Italian food can put you to sleep and make you less sharp. I like both. Isn't it nice to know that Skippy is always scheming?"

Vail always ordered three desserts. Not that he ate all of them, but he wanted to taste many different things at one dinner. In him it did not seem eccentric. Not even the way he dressed, as if clothes were to shield skin from wind or sun, or the way he carelessly shaved, one sideburn cut lower than the other. Not even his threat to kill himself seemed illogical or strange. Nor his complete and childish frankness, which often hurt people's feelings. Claudia was not unused to eccentricity. Hollywood abounded with eccentrics.

"You know, Ernest, you belong to Hollywood. You're eccentric enough," she said.

"I am not an eccentric," Vail said. "I'm not that sophisticated."

"You don't call wanting to kill yourself over a dispute about money eccentric?" Claudia said.

"That was an extremely cool-headed response to our culture," Vail said. "I was tired of being a nobody."

Claudia said impatiently, "How can you think that? You've written ten books, you've won the Pulitzer. You're internationally famous."

Vail had polished off his three pastas and was looking at his entrée, three pearly slices of veal covered with lemon. He picked up a fork and knife. "All that means shit," he said. "I have no money. It took me fifty-five years to learn that if you have no money, you're shit."

Molly said, "You're not eccentric, you're crazy. And stop whining because you're not rich. You're not poor either. Or we wouldn't be here. You're not suffering too much for your art."

Vail put down his knife and fork. He patted Molly's arm. "You're right," he said. "Everything you say is true. I enjoy life from moment to moment. It's the arc of life that gets me down." He drank his glass of wine and then went on matter-of-factly. "I'm never going to write again," he said. "Writing novels is a dead end, like being a blacksmith. It's all movies and TV now."

"That's nonsense," Claudia said. "People will always read."

"You're just lazy," Molly said. "Any excuse not to write. That's the real reason why you wanted to kill yourself." They all laughed. Ernest helped them to the veal on his dish and then to the extra desserts. The only time he was courtly was over dinner, he seemed to take pleasure in feeding people.

"That's all true," he said. "But a novelist can't make a good living unless he writes simple novels. And even that is a dead end. A novel can never be as simple as a movie."

Claudia said angrily, "Why do you put movies down? I've seen you cry at good movies. And they are art."

Vail was enjoying himself. After all, he had won his fight against the Studio, he had his points. "Claudia, I really agree," he said. "Movies are art. I complain out of envy. Movies are making novels irrelevant. What's the point of writing a lyrical passage about nature, painting the world in red heat, a beautiful sunset, a mountain range coated with snow, the awe-inspiring waves of great oceans." He was declaiming, waving his arms. "What can you write about passion and the beauty of women? What's the use of all that when you can see it on the movie screen in Technicolor? Oh, those mysterious women with full red lips, their magical eyes, when you can see them bare-assed, tits as delicious-looking as beef Wellington. All much better than real life even, never mind prose. And how can we write about the amazing deeds of heroes who slay their enemies by the hundred, who conquer great odds and great temptation, when you can get it all in gouts of blood before your eyes, tortured, agonized faces on the screen. Actors and cameras doing all the work without processing through the brain. Sly Stallone as Achilles in the Iliad. Now the one thing the screen can't do is get into the minds of their characters, it cannot duplicate the thinking process, the complexity of life." He paused for a moment, then said wistfully, "But you know what's worst of all? I'm an elitist. I wanted to be an artist to be something special. So what I hate is that movies are such a democratic art. Anybody can make a movie. You're right, Claudia, I've seen movies that moved me to tears and I know for a fact that the people who made them are moronic, insensitive, uneducated, and with not an iota of morality. The screenwriter is illiterate, the director an ego-maniac, the producer a butcher of morality and the actors smash their fists into the wall or a mirror to show the audience they are upset. But then the movie works. How can that be? Because a movie uses sculpture, painting, music, human bodies, and technology to form itself, while a novelist only has a string of words, black print on white paper. And to tell the truth that's not so terrible. That's progress. And the new great art. A democratic art. And art without suffering. Just buy the right camera and meet with your friends."

Vail beamed at the two women. "Isn't it wonderful, an art that requires no real talent? What democracy, what therapy, to make your own movie. It will replace sex. I go to see your movie and you come to see mine. It's an art that will transform the world and for the better. Claudia, be happy that you are in an art form that is the future."

"You are a condescending prick," Molly said. "Claudia fought for you, defended you. And I've been more patient with you than any murderer I've defended. And you buy us dinner to insult us."

Vail seemed genuinely astonished. "I'm not insulting, I'm just defining. I am grateful and I love you both." He paused for a moment and then said humbly, "I'm not saying I'm better than you."

Claudia burst out laughing. "Ernest, you're so full of shit," she said.

"Just in real life," Vail said amiably. "Can we talk business a little bit? Molly, if I were dead and my family regained all the rights, would LoddStone pay five points?"

"At least five," Molly said. "Now you're going to kill yourself over extra points? You lose me entirely."

Claudia was looking at him, troubled. She distrusted his high spirits. "Ernest, are you still unhappy? We got you a wonderful deal. I was so thrilled."

Vail said fondly, "Claudia, you have no idea what the real world is all about. Which makes you perfect to do screenplays. What the hell difference does it make if I'm happy? The happiest man who ever lived is going to have terrible times in his life. Terrible tragedies. Look at me now. I've just won a great victory, I don't have to kill myself. I'm enjoying this meal, I'm enjoying the company of you two beautiful, intelligent, compassionate women. And I love it that my wife and children will have economic security."

"Then why the fuck are you whining?" Molly asked him. "Why are you spoiling a good time?"

"Because I can't write," Vail said. "Which is no great tragedy. It's not really important anymore but it's the only thing I know how to do." As he was saying this, he was finishing the three desserts with such evident enjoyment that the two women burst out laughing. Vail grinned back at them. "We sure bluffed out old Eli," he said.

"You take writer's block too seriously," Claudia said. "Just take some speed."

"Screenwriters don't have writer's block because they don't write," Vail said. "I cannot write because I have nothing to say. Now let's talk about something more interesting. Molly, I've never understood how I can have ten percent of the profit of a picture that grosses one hundred million dollars and costs only fifteen million to make, and then never see a penny. That's one mystery I'd like to solve before I die."

This put Molly in good spirits again; she loved to teach the law. She took a notebook out of her purse and scribbled down some figures.

"It's absolutely legal," she said. "They are abiding by the contract, one you should not have signed in the first place. Look, take the one-hundred-million gross. The theaters, the exhibitors, take half, so now the studio only gets fifty million, which is called rentals.

"OK. The studio takes out the fifteen million dollars the picture costs. Now there's thirty-five million left. But by the terms of your contract and most studio contracts, the studio takes thirty percent of the rentals for distribution costs on the film. That's another fifteen mil in their pockets. So you're down to twenty mil. Then they deduct the cost of making prints, the cost for advertising the picture, which could easily be another five. You're down to fifteen. Now here's the beauty. By contract, the studio gets twenty-five percent of the budget for studio overhead, telephone bills, electricity, use of soundstages etc. Now you're down to eleven. Good, you say. You'll take your piece of eleven million. But the Bankable Star gets at least five percent of the rentals, the director and producer another five percent. So that comes to another five million. You're down to six million. At last you'll get something. But not so fast. They then charge you all the costs of distribution, they charge fifty grand for delivering the prints to the English market, another fifty to France or Germany.

And then finally they charge the interest on the fifteen million they borrowed to make the picture. And there they lose me. But that last six million disappears. That's what happens when you don't have me for a lawyer. I write a contract that really gets you a piece of the gold mine. Not gross for a writer but a very good definition of net. Do you understand it now?"

Vail was laughing. "Not really," he said. "How about TV and video money?"

"TV you'll see a little," Molly said. "Nobody knows how much money they make in video."

"And my deal with Marrion now is straight gross?" Vail asked. "They can't screw me again?"

"Not the way I'll write the contract," Molly said. "It will be straight gross all the way."

Vail said mournfully, "Then I won't have a grievance anymore. I won't have an excuse for not writing."

"You really are so eccentric," Claudia said.

"No, no," Vail said. "I'm just a fuckup. Eccentrics do odd things to distract people from what they do or are. They are ashamed. That's why movie people are so eccentric."


Who would have dreamed that dying could be so pleasant, that you could be so at peace, that you could be so without fear? That best of all you had solved the one great common myth?

Eli Marrion, in the long hours of the sick at night, sucked oxygen from the tube in the wall and reflected on his life. His private duty nurse, Priscilla, working a double shift, was reading a book by the dim lamp on the other side of the room. He could see her eyes dart quickly up and then down, as if checking him after every line she read.

Marrion thought how different this scene was from how it would be in a movie. In a movie there would be a great deal of tension because he was hovering between life and death. The nurse would be crouched over his bed, doctors would be coming in and out. There should sure as hell be a lot of noise, a lot of tension. And here he was in a room absolutely quiet, the nurse reading, Marrion easily breathing through his plastic tube.

He knew this penthouse floor held only these huge suites for very important people. Powerful politicians, real estate billionaires, stars who were the fading myths of the entertainment world. All kings in their own right and now, here in the night in this hospital, vassals to death. They lay helpless and alone, comforted by mercenaries, their power scattered. Tubes in bodies, prongs in nostrils, waiting for surgeon's knives to scour the debris from their failing hearts or, like himself, for a completely edited heart to be inserted. He wondered if they were as resigned as he.

And why that resignation? Why had he told the doctors he would not have a transplant, that he preferred to live only the short time his failing heart would give him. He thought that, thank God, he could still make intelligent decisions devoid of sentiment.

Everything was clear to him, like making a deal on a film: figuring the cost, the percentage of return, the value of subsidiary rights, the possible traps with stars, directors, and cost overages.

Number one: He was eighty years old and not a robust eighty. A heart transplant would disable him for a year, at the very best. Certainly he would never run LoddStone Studies again. Certainly most of his power over his world would vanish.

Number two: Life without power was intolerable. After all, what could an old man like himself do even with a fresh new heart? He could not play sports, run after women, take pleasure from food or drink. No, power was an old man's only pleasure, and why was that so bad? Power could be used for the good. Had he not granted mercy to Ernest Vail, against all prudent principles, against all his lifelong prejudices? Had he not told his doctors that he did not want to deprive a child or some young man the chance to have a new life by taking a heart? Was that not a use of power for the higher good?

But he had had a long life of dealing with hypocrisy and recognized it now in himself. He had declined a new heart because it was not a good deal; a bottom-line decision. He had granted Ernest Vail his points because he desired the affection of Claudia and the respect of Molly Flanders, a sentimentality. Was it so terrible that he wanted to leave an image of goodness?

He was satisfied in the life he had lived. He had fought his way from poverty to riches, he had conquered his fellow man. He had enjoyed all the pleasure of human life, loved beautiful women, lived in luxurious homes, worn the finest silks. And he had helped in the creation of art. He had earned enormous power and a great fortune. And he had tried to do good for his fellow man. He had contributed tens of millions to this very hospital. But most of all he had enjoyed struggling against his fellow man. And what was so terrible about that? How else could you acquire the power to do good? Even now he regretted the last act of mercy to Ernest Vail. You could not simply give the spoils of your struggle to your fellow man, especially under threat. But Bobby would take care of that. Bobby would take care of everything.

Bobby would plant the necessary publicity stories featuring his refusal of a heart transplant so that someone younger could have it. Bobby would recover all the gross points that existed. Bobby would get rid of his daughter's production company, which was a losing proposition for LoddStone. Bobby would take the rap.

Far off he could hear a tiny bell, then the snakelike rattling of the fax machine transmitting the box office receipts compiled in New York. The stuttering making a refrain for his failing heart.

The truth now. He had enough of life at its best. It was not his body that had ultimately betrayed him but his mind.

The truth now. He was disappointed in human beings. He had seen too many betrayals, too many pitiful weaknesses, too much greed for money and fame. The falseness between lovers, husbands, and wives, fathers, sons, mothers, daughters. Thank God for the films he had made that gave people hope and thank God for his grandchildren and thank God he would not see them grow up into the human condition.

The fax machine stilled its stutter, and Marrion could feel the fluttering of his failing heart. Early morning light filled his room. He saw the nurse flick off her lamp and close her book. It was so lonely to die with only this stranger in this room when he was loved by so many powerful people. Then the nurse was prying open his eyelids, putting her stethoscope to his chest. The huge doors to his hospital suite opened like the great door of some ancient temple and he could hear the rattling of dishes on the breakfast trays. . . .

Then the room filled with bright lights. He could feel fists thumping his chest and wondered why they were doing this to him. A cloud was forming in his brain, filling it with mist. Through that mist voices were screaming. A line from a movie penetrated his oxygen-starved brain. "Is this how the Gods die?"

He felt the electric shocks, the pummeling, the incision made to massage his heart with bare hands.

All of Hollywood would mourn but none more than the night duty nurse, Priscilla. She had done a double shift because she supported two small children, and it displeased her that Marrion had died on her shift. She prided herself on her reputation as one of the finest nurses in California. She hated death. But the book she had been reading had excited her and she had been planning how to talk with Marrion about making it into a movie. She would not be a nurse forever, she was a screenwriter on the side. Now she did not give up hope. This top floor of the hospital with its huge suites received the greatest men of Hollywood and she would stand guard for them against death forever.

But all this had happened in Marrion's mind before he died, a mind saturated with thousands of movies he had watched.

In reality, the nurse had gone to his bed some fifteen minutes after he was dead, so quietly had he died. She debated for maybe thirty seconds about calling an alert to try to bring him back to life. She was an old hand with death and more merciful. Why try to revive him to all the torture of reclaiming life? She went to the window and watched the sun rise and the pigeons strutting lustfully on the stone ledges. Priscilla was the final power deciding Marrion's fate . . . and his most merciful judge.

# CHAPTER 13

S ENATOR WAVVEN had great news, and it would cost the Clericuzio five million dollars. So said Giorgio's courier. That demanded a mountain of paperwork. Cross would have to extract five
million from the casino cage and leave a long record to account for
its disappearance.

Cross also had a message from Claudia and Vail. They were in the
Hotel occupying the same suite. They wanted to see him as soon as
possible. It was urgent.

There was also a call from Lia Vazzi in the Hunting Lodge. He requested to see Cross personally as soon as possible. He did not have
to say it was urgent, any request from him had to be urgent or he
would not call, and he was already on his way.

Cross started on the paperwork for the transfer of the five million
dollars to Senator Wavven. The cash itself would have too much bulk
for a suitcase or large overnight bag. He called the Hotel gift shop; he
remembered an antique Chinese trunk for sale that was big enough to
hold the money. It was dark green decorated with red dragons and su-
perimposed false green gems, and it had a strong locking mechanism.

Gronevelt had taught him how to make the paper trail that legit-
imized money skimmed from the Hotel casino. It was long and labo-
rious work that involved transfers of money to different accounts,
the payment of different suppliers for liquor and food, special training projects and publicity stunts, and a roster of players who did not
exist as debtors to the cage.

Cross worked an hour on this. Senator Wavven was not due in
until the next day, a Saturday, and the five million had to be put in his

hands before he left early Monday morning. Finally his concentration began to wander and he had to take a break.

He called down to Claudia and Vail's suite. Claudia picked up the phone. She said, "I'm having a terrible time with Ernest. We have to talk to you."

"OK," Cross said. "Why don't the two of you go down and gamble and I'll pick you up in the dice pit an hour from now." He paused. "Then we can go for dinner and you can tell me your troubles."

"We can't gamble," Claudia said. "Ernest went over his credit limit and you won't give me credit anymore except for a lousy ten grand."

Cross sighed. That meant Ernest Vail owed the casino a hundred grand that was just so much toilet paper. "Give me an hour and then come up to my suite. We'll have dinner here."

Cross had to make another phone call, to Giorgio to confirm the payment to the senator, not that the courier was suspect but it was one of the built-in routines. This they did with verbal code already established. The name was in arbitrary prearranged numbers, the money designated in arbitrary prearranged alphabetical letters.

Cross tried to continue his paperwork. But again his mind wandered. For five million, Senator Wavven was going to have something important to say. For Lia to make the long drive to Vegas, he had to have serious trouble.

There was a ring at the doorbell, Security had brought Claudia and Ernest to the penthouse. Cross gave Claudia an extra warm hug because he didn't want her to think he was mad at her for losing in the casino.

In the living room of his suite, he handed them the room service menu and then ordered for them. Claudia sat stiffly on the sofa, Vail slouched back disinterestedly.

Claudia said, "Cross, Vail is in terrible shape. We have to do something for him."

Vail didn't look so bad to Cross. He seemed truly relaxed, his eyes half closed, a pleased smile on his lips. This irritated Cross.

"Sure, first thing I'll do is cut off all his credit in this town. That will save money, he's the most incompetent gambler I've ever seen."

"It's not about gambling," Claudia said. And she told him the whole story about Marrion promising to give Vail gross on all the sequels to his book, and then dying.

"So?" Cross asked.

"Now Bobby Bantz won't honor that promise," Claudia said. "Since Bobby became head of LoddStone Studios, he's gone crazy with power. He's trying his best to be like Marrion but he just hasn't got the intelligence or the charisma. So Ernest is out in the cold again."

"Just what the hell do you think I can do?" Cross asked.

"You're partners with LoddStone in *Messalina*," Claudia said. "You must have some clout with them. I want you to ask Bobby Bantz to keep Marrion's promise."

It was at times like this that Cross despaired of Claudia. Bantz would never give way, that was part of his job and his character.

"No," Cross said. "I've explained to you before. I can't take a position unless I know the answer will be yes. And here there's no chance."

Claudia frowned. "I never understood that," she said. She paused for a moment. "Ernest is serious, he will kill himself so that his family can get back the rights."

At this, Vail took an interest. He said, "Claudia, you dumbbell, don't you understand about your brother? If he asks somebody for something and they say no, then he has to kill them." He gave Cross a big grin.

Cross was enraged that Vail would dare to speak that way in front of Claudia. Luckily, at that moment room service arrived with their rolling tables and set dinner up in the living room. Cross controlled himself as they sat down to eat, but he couldn't help saying, with a cold smile, "Ernest, you can solve everything if you knock yourself off, as I understand it. Maybe I can help. I'll move your suite up to the tenth floor and you can just step out the window."

Now Claudia was angry. "This is not a joke," she said. "Ernest is one of my best friends. And you're my brother who always claims to love me and will do anything for me." She was in tears.

Cross got up and went over to hug her. "Claudia, there's nothing I can do. I'm not a magician."

Ernest Vail was enjoying his dinner. No man looked less likely to kill himself. "You're too modest, Cross," he said. "Look, I haven't got the nerve to jump out of a window. I have too much imagination, I'd die a thousand deaths on the way down thinking how I would look splattered all over the place. And I might even land on some innocent person. I'm too chicken to cut my wrists, I can't stand the sight of blood and I'm scared to death of guns and knives and traffic. I don't want to end up a vegetable with nothing accomplished. I don't want that fuckin' Bantz and Deere laughing at me and keeping all my money. There is one thing you can do: Hire somebody to kill me. Don't tell me when. Just get it done."

Cross began laughing. He gave Claudia a reassuring pat on the head and went back to his chair. "Do you think this is a fuckin' movie?" he said to Ernest. "You think killing somebody is sort of a joke?"

Cross left the table and went to his office desk. He unlocked the drawer and took out a purse of black chips. He threw the purse at Ernest and said, "Here's ten grand. Take your last shot at the tables, maybe you'll get lucky. Just stop insulting me in front of my sister."

Vail was cheerful now. "Come on Claudia," he said. "Your brother is not going to help." He put the purse of black chips into his pocket. He seemed anxious to get started gambling.

Claudia seemed abstracted. She was adding up everything in her head but refused to come to a sum total. She looked at the serene handsome face of her brother. He could not be what Vail was saying he was. She kissed Cross on the cheek, and said, "I'm sorry, but I'm worried about Ernest."

"He'll be all right," Cross said. "He likes to gamble too much to die. And he is a genius, isn't he?"

Claudia laughed. "So he always says, and I agree," she said. "And he's such a terrible coward." But she reached out to touch Vail affectionately.

"Why the hell do you stick with him?" Cross said. "Why are you sharing a suite with him?"

"Because I'm his best and last friend," Claudia said angrily. "And I love his books."

. . .

After the two left, Cross spent the rest of the night completing the plan to transfer the five million to Senator Wavven. When he finished, he called the casino manager, a high-ranking member of the Clericuzio Family, and told him to bring the money to his penthouse suite.

The money was brought up in two huge sacks by the manager and two security guards who were also of the Clericuzio. They helped Cross stack the money into the Chinese trunk. The casino manager gave Cross a little grin and said, "Nice trunk."

After the men left, Cross took the huge quilt from his bed and wrapped it around the trunk. Then he ordered room service to bring two breakfasts. Within a few minutes, Security called to tell him Lia Vazzi was waiting to see him. He gave the OK to bring him up.

Cross embraced Lia. He was always delighted to see him.

"Good news or bad news?" Cross asked him after room service delivered breakfast.

"Bad," Lia said. "That detective who stopped me in the lobby of the Beverly Hills Hotel when I was with Skannet. Jim Losey. He showed up at the Hunting Lodge and asked me questions about my relationship with Skannet. I brushed him off. The bad part is how he knew who I was and where I was. I'm not in any police file, I've never been in trouble. So that means there's an informer."

That startled Cross. A turncoat was rare in the Clericuzio Family and was always mercilessly rooted out.

"I'll report it to the Don himself," Cross said. "How about you? Do you want to take a vacation down in Brazil until we find out what it's all about?"

Lia had eaten very little. He helped himself to the brandy and Havana cigars Cross put out.

"I'm not nervous, not yet," Lia said. "I'd just like your permission to protect myself against this man."

Cross was alarmed. "Lia, you can't do that," he said. "It's very dangerous to kill a police officer in this country. This is not Sicily. So I have to tell you something you shouldn't know. Jim Losey is on the Clericuzio pad. Big money. I think he's just nosing around to claim a bonus for laying off you."

"Good," Vazzi said. "But it remains a fact. There must be an informer."

"I'll take care of it," Cross said. "Don't worry about Losey."

Lia puffed on his cigar. "He's a dangerous man. Be careful."

"I will," Cross said. "But no preemptive strikes on your part, OK?"

"Of course," Lia said. He seemed to relax. Then he said casually, "What's under that quilt?"

"A little gift to a very important man," Cross said. "Do you want to spend the night in the Hotel?"

"No," Lia said. "I'll go back to the Lodge and you can tell me what you learn at your leisure. But my advice would be to get rid of Losey right now."

"I'll talk to the Don," Cross said.

Senator Warren Wavven and his entourage of three male aides were checked into their Xanadu Villa at three in the afternoon. As usual, he had traveled in an unmarked limo and without any sort of escort. At five, he summoned Cross to his Villa.

Cross had two of the security guards put the quilt-wrapped trunk in the back of a motorized golf cart. One of the guards drove and Cross sat in the passenger seat keeping an eye on the trunk, which rested in the cargo space that usually held golf clubs and ice water. It was only a five-minute run through the grounds of the Xanadu to the separately secured compound that held the seven Villas.

Cross always loved the sight of them, the sense of power. Small palaces of Versailles, each with a diamond-shaped emerald swimming pool, and in the center a square holding the pearl-shaped private casino for the Villa occupants.

Cross carried the trunk into the Villa himself. One of the senator's aides led him into the dining room where the senator was enjoying a sumptuous array of cold food and iced jugs of lemonade. He no longer drank alcohol.

Senator Wavven was as handsome and affable as ever. He had risen high in the political councils of the nation, was the head of several important committees, and was a dark horse in the next presidential race. He sprang up to greet Cross.

Cross whipped the quilt off the trunk and put it on the floor.

"A little gift from the Hotel, Senator," he said. "Have a pleasant stay."

The senator clasped Cross's hand with both of his. His hands were smooth. "What a delightful present," he said. "Thank you, Cross. Now, could I have a few confidential words with you?"

"Of course," Cross said and gave him the key to the trunk. Wavven slipped it into his trouser pocket. Then he turned to his aides and said, "Please put the trunk in my bedroom and one of you stay with it. Now, let me have a few moments alone with my friend Cross."

They left and the senator began to pace the room. He frowned, "I have good news naturally, but I also have bad news."

Cross nodded and said amiably, "That's usually the case." He thought that for the five mil the good news had to be a hell of a lot better than the bad.

Wavven chuckled. "Isn't that the truth? The good news first. And very good news it is. I've devoted my attention in the last few years to passing legislation that would make gambling legal all over the United States. Even the provision to make sports gambling legal. I think I finally have the votes in the Senate and the House. The money in the trunk will swing some key votes. It is five, isn't it?"

"It's five," Cross said. "And money well spent. Now, what's the bad news?"

The senator shook his head sadly. "Your friends won't like this," he said. "Especially Giorgio, who is so impatient. But he's a fabulous fellow, truly fabulous."

"My favorite cousin," Cross said dryly. Of all the Clericuzio he liked Giorgio least, and it was obvious the senator felt the same way.

Then Wavven delivered the bombshell. "The president has told me he will veto the bill."

Cross had been feeling jubilant over the final success of Don Clericuzio's master plan. To build a legitimate empire based on legal

gambling. Now, he was confused. What the hell was Wavven bab-
bling about?

"And we don't have enough votes to overcome a veto," Wavven
said.

Just to give himself time to recover his composure, Cross said,
"So the five mil is for the president?"

The senator was horrified. "Oh, no, no," he said. "We're not even
in the same party. And besides, the president will be a very rich man
when he retires into private life. Every board of directors of every
big company will want him. He has no need for petty cash." Wavven
gave Cross a satisfied smile. "Things work differently when you are
the president of the United States."

"So we're nowhere unless the president drops dead," Cross said.

"Exactly," Wavven said. "He is a very popular president, I must
say, though we are in opposing parties. He will surely be reelected.
We must be patient."

"So we have to wait five years and then hope to get a president
who won't veto?"

"That's not exactly true," the senator said, and here he faltered a
bit. "I must be honest with you. In five years the composition of the
Congress may change, I may not have the votes I have now." He
paused again. "There are many factors."

Cross was completely bewildered now. What the hell was Wavven
really saying? Then the senator tipped his hand. "Of course if something happens to the president, the vice president will sign the bill.
So, as malicious as it sounds, you have to hope that the president has
a heart attack or his plane crashes, or he has an incapacitating stroke.
It could happen. All of us are mortal." The senator was beaming at
him and then suddenly it all became clear to Cross.

He felt a flash of anger. This bastard was giving him a message for
the Clericuzio: The senator had done his part, now they had to kill
the president of the United States to get the bill passed. And he was
so slick and so sly, he had not implicated himself in any concrete
way. Cross was sure the Don would not go for it, and if he did, Cross
would refuse to be part of the Family ever after.

Wavven was going on with an affable smile. "It looks pretty hopeless but you never know. Fate may take a hand and the vice president

is a very close friend of mine, even though we're from different parties. I know for a fact, he will approve my bill. We just have to wait and see."

Cross could scarcely believe what the senator was saying. Senator Wavven was the personification of the virtuous All-American politician, though admittedly with a weakness for women and innocent golf. His face was honorably handsome and his voice patrician. He presented himself as one of the most likable men on earth. Yet he was implying that the Clericuzio Family assassinate his own president. This is a piece of work, Cross thought.

The senator was now picking at the food on the table. "I'm only staying for one night," he said. "I hope you have some girls in your show who would like to have dinner with an old geezer like me."

Back in his penthouse suite Cross called Giorgio and told him he would be in Quogue the next day. Giorgio told him the Family driver would pick him up at the airport. He didn't ask any questions. The Clericuzio never talked business on the phone.

When Cross arrived at the Quogue mansion, he was surprised to find a full attendance. Assembled in the windowless den were not only the Don, but also Pippi, and the Don's three sons, Giorgio, Vincent, and Petie, and even Dante, wearing a sky-blue Renaissance hat.

There was no food in the den, dinner was to come later. As usual the Don made everyone look at the photos of Silvio and the christening of Cross and Dante on the mantelpiece. "What a happy day," the Don always said. They all settled in on chairs and sofas, Giorgio handed out drinks, and the Don lit up his twisted black Italian cheroot.

Cross gave a detailed report: how he had delivered the five million to Senator Wavven and then, word for word, his conversation with him.

There was a long silence. None of them needed Cross's interpretation. Vincent and Petie looked the most concerned. Now that Vincent had his chain of restaurants, he was less inclined to take risks. Petie, though he was head of the soldiers in the Bronx Enclave, had his enormous construction business as his primary concern. They did not relish such a terrible mission at this stage of their lives.

"That fucking senator is crazy," Vincent said.

The Don said to Cross, "Are you sure that was the message the senator was sending us? That we should actually assassinate the leader of our country, one of his colleagues in government?"

Giorgio said dryly, "They're not in the same political party, the senator says."

Cross answered the Don. "The senator would never incriminate himself. He just presented the facts. I think he assumes we will act on it."

Dante spoke up. He was excited by the idea, by the glory, by the profit. "We can get the whole gambling business, legal. That would be worth it. That's the biggest prize."

The Don turned to Pippi. "And what do you think, *Martèllo* of mine?" he asked affectionately.

Pippi was obviously angry. "It can't be done and it shouldn't be done."

Dante said in a taunting voice, "Cousin Pippi, if you can't do it, I can."

Pippi looked at him contemptuously. "You're a butcher, not a planner. You couldn't plan something like this in a million years. This is too big a risk. This is too much heat. And the execution is too difficult. You cannot get away free."

Dante said arrogantly, "Grandfather, give me the job. I'll get it done."

The Don was respectful to his grandson. "I'm sure you could," he said. "And the rewards would be very great. But Pippi is right. The aftermath would be too risky for our Family. One can always make mistakes, but never make a fatal mistake. Even if we were successful and achieved our aim, the deed would hang over us forever. It is too great a crime. Also, this is not a situation that endangers our existence, it is simply one that achieves a purpose. A purpose that can be achieved with patience. Meanwhile, we sit in a pretty position. Giorgio, you have your seat on Wall Street, Vincent, you have your restaurants, Petie, you have your construction business. Cross, you have your hotel and Pippi, you can retire and spend your last years in peace. And Dante, my grandson, you must have patience, some day you will have your gambling empire, that shall be your legacy. And when you do, it will be without the shadow of a terrible deed hanging over your head. So—let the senator swim to the bottom of the ocean."

Everyone in the room relaxed, the tension broken; except for Dante, all were happy with the decision. And all agreed with the Don's curse that the senator should drown. That he had dared to put them in this dangerous dilemma.

Only Dante seemed to disagree. He said to Pippi, "You've got a lot of balls, calling me a butcher. What are you, a fucking Florence Nightingale?"

Vincent and Petie laughed. The Don shook his head disapprovingly. "Another thing," Don Clericuzio said. "I think we for now should continue all our ties with the senator. I don't begrudge him the extra five million, but I take it as an insult that he thinks we would kill the president of our country to further a business venture. Also, what other fish does he have to fry? How does this act benefit him? He seeks to manipulate us. Cross, when he comes to your hotel, build up his markers. Make sure he has a good time. He is too dangerous a man to have as an enemy."

Everything was settled. Cross was hesitant about bringing up another sensitive problem. But he told the story of Lia Vazzi and Jim Losey. "There could be an informer inside the Family," Cross said.

Dante said coolly, "That was your operation, that's your problem."

The Don shook his head decisively. "An informer cannot be," he said. "The detective found something by accident and he wants a bonus to stop. Giorgio, take care of it."

Giorgio said sourly, "Another fifty grand. Cross, that's your deal. You'll have to pay it out of your hotel."

The Don relit his cigar. "Now that we are all here together, are there any other problems? Vincent, how is your restaurant business?"

Vincent's granite features softened. "I'm opening three more," he said. "One in Philly, one in Denver, and another in New York City. High class. Pop, would you believe I charge sixteen dollars for a plate of spaghetti? When I make it at home, I figure out the cost is half a buck a plate. No matter how hard I try, I can't make it more than that. I even put in the cost of the garlic. And meatballs, I'm the only high-class Italian restaurant that serves meatballs, I don't know why, but I get eight dollars for them. And not big ones. They cost me twenty cents."

He would have gone on but the Don cut him off. He turned to Giorgio and said, "Giorgio, how goes your Wall Street?"

Giorgio said cautiously, "It goes up and down. But the commissions we get for trading are as good as the shylocks get on the streets if we churn it enough. And with no risk of deadbeats or jail. We should forget about all our other business, except maybe gambling."

The Don was enjoying these recitals, success in the legitimate world was dear to him. He said, "And Petie, your construction business? I hear you had a little trouble the other day . . ."

Petie shrugged. "I got more business than I can handle. Everybody's building something and we have a lock on the highway contracts. All my soldiers are on the payroll and make a good living. But a week ago, this eggplant shows up on my biggest construction job. He's got a hundred black guys behind him with all kinds of civil rights banners. So I take him into my office and all of a sudden he's charming. I just have to put ten percent blacks on the job and pay him twenty grand under the table."

That tickled Dante. "We're getting strong-armed?" he said with a giggle. "The Clericuzio?"

Petie said, "I tried to think like Pop. Why shouldn't they make a living? So I gave the eggplant his twenty grand and told him I'd put five percent on the job."

"You did well," the Don told Petie. "You kept a small problem from becoming a big problem. And who are the Clericuzio not to pay their share in the advancement of the other people and civilization itself?"

"I would have killed the black son of a bitch," Dante said. "Now, he'll come back for more."

"And we will give him more," the Don said. "Just so long as they are reasonable." He turned to Pippi and said, "And what troubles do you have?"

"None," Pippi said. "Except that now the Family is nearly nonoperational and I'm out of a job."

"That is your good fortune," the Don said. "You've worked hard enough. You've escaped many perils, so now enjoy the flower of your manhood."

Dante didn't wait to be questioned. "I'm in the same boat," he said to the Don. "And I'm too young to retire."

"Play golf like the *Brugliones,*" Don Clericuzio said dryly. "And don't worry, life always provides work and problems. Meanwhile, be patient. I fear your time will come. And mine."

# CHAPTER 14

O N   T H E   M O R N I N G   O F  Eli Marrion's funeral, Bobby Bantz
was screaming at Skippy Deere.

"This is fucking crazy, this is what's wrong with the movie business. How the fuck can you allow this to happen?" He was waving a stapled bundle of pages in Deere's face.

Deere looked at it. It was the transportation schedule for a picture shooting in Rome. "Yeah, so what?" Deere said.

Bantz was in rage. "Everyone in the picture is booked first class on the flight to Rome . . . the crew, the bit players, the fucking cameo roles, the gofers, the interns. There is only one exception. You know who that is? The LoddStone accounting officer we sent there to control the spending. He flew economy."

"Yeah, again, so what?" Deere said.

Bantz became deliberate in his anger. "And the picture has on budget a school to be set up for the children of everybody on the picture. The budget has the renting of a yacht for two weeks. I just read the script carefully. There are twelve actors and actresses who have maybe two, three minutes in the film. The yacht is listed for just two days' shooting. Now explain to me how you allowed this."

Skippy Deere was grinning at him. "Sure," he said. "Our director is Lorenzo Tallufo. He insists his people travel first class. The bit players and cameo roles were written into the script because they were screwing the vehicle stars. The yacht is booked for two weeks because Lorenzo wants to visit the Cannes Film Festival."

"You're the producer, talk to Lorenzo," Bantz said.

"Not *me*," Deere told him. "Lorenzo has four one-hundred-million-dollar-grossing pictures, he has two Academy Awards. I'll kiss his ass when I help him onto the yacht. You talk to him."

There was no answer to this. Technically, in the hierarchy of the industry, the head of the Studio outranked everybody. The producer was the person who got all the elements together and oversaw the budget and script development. But the reality was that once the picture started shooting, the director was the supreme power. Especially if he had a record of successful movies.

Bantz shook his head. "I can't talk to Lorenzo, not when I don't have Eli to back me up. Lorenzo would tell me to go fuck myself and we'd lose the picture."

"And he'd be right," Deere said. "What the hell, Lorenzo always steals five million off a picture. They all do it. Now calm down so we can show ourselves at the funeral."

But Bantz was now looking at another cost sheet. "On your picture," he said to Deere, "there's a charge of five hundred thousand dollars for Chinese take-out food. Nobody, *nobody*, not even my wife can spend a half million dollars on Chinese food. French food maybe. But Chinese? Chinese take-out?"

Skippy Deere had to think fast, Bobby had him there. "It's a Japanese restaurant, the food is sushi. That's the most expensive food in the world."

Bantz was suddenly calm. People were always complaining about sushi. The head of a rival studio had told him about taking a Japanese investor to dinner at a restaurant that specialized in sushi. "A thousand bucks for two people for twenty fucking fish heads," he had said. Bantz was impressed.

"OK," Bantz said to Skippy Deere, "but you have to cut down. Try to get more college interns on your next picture." Interns worked for free.


The Hollywood funeral of Eli Marrion was more newsworthy than even that of a Bankable Star. He had been revered by studio heads, producers, and agents, he had even been respected and sometimes loved by Bankable Stars, directors, and even screenplay writers. What had inspired this was his civility and an overpowering intelligence that had solved many problems in the movie business. He also had had the reputation of being fair, within reason.

In his later years, he was an ascetic, did not wallow in power, did not command sexual favors from starlets. Also, LoddStone had made more great movies than any other studio, and there was nothing more precious to people who actually made movies.

The president of the United States sent his chief of staff to give a brief eulogy. France sent its minister of culture, though he was an enemy of Hollywood movies. The Vatican sent a papal envoy, a young cardinal, handsome enough to receive offers for cameo roles. A Japanese group of business executives magically appeared. The highest executives of movie corporations from the Netherlands, Germany, Italy, and Sweden did Eli Marrion honor.

The eulogies began. First a male Bankable Star, then a female Bankable Star, then an A director; even a writer, Benny Sly, gave Marrion tribute. Then the president's chief of staff. Then, just so the show would not be judged pretentious, two of the movie's greatest comics made jokes about Eli Marrion's power and business acumen. Finally, Eli's son, Kevin, and his daughter, Dora, and Bobby Bantz.

Kevin Marrion extolled Eli Marrion as a caring father, not only to his own children, but to everyone who worked at LoddStone. He was a man who carried the torch of Art on a film. A torch, Kevin assured the mourners, that he would pick up.

Eli Marrion's daughter, Dora, gave the most poetic speech, written by Benny Sly. It was eloquent, spiritual, and addressed Eli Marrion's virtues and accomplishments with a humorous respect. "I loved my father more than any man I have ever known," she said, "but I'm glad I never had to negotiate with him. I only had to deal with Bobby Bantz and I could outsmart him."

She got her laugh and it was Bobby Bantz's turn. Secretly he resented Dora's joke. "I spent thirty years building LoddStone Studios with Eli Marrion," he said. "He was the most intelligent, the kindest man I have ever known. Under him, my service of thirty years has been the happiest time of my life. And I will continue to serve his dream. He showed his faith in me by leaving me in control of the Studio for the next five years and I will not fail him. I cannot hope to equal Eli's achievements. He gave dreams to billions of people all over the world. He shared his wealth and love with his family and all the people of America. He was indeed a lodestone."

The assembled mourners knew that Bobby Bantz had written the speech himself, because he had given an important message to the whole movie industry. That he was to rule LoddStone Studios for the next five years and that he expected everyone to give him the same respect they had given Eli Marrion. Bobby Bantz was no longer a Number Two man, he was a Number One.

Two days after the funeral, Bantz summoned Skippy Deere to the studio and offered him the job of head of production of LoddStone, the job he had held himself. Now he was moving up to Marrion's job as chairman. The rewards he offered Deere were irresistible. Deere would get a share of profits of every movie made by the Studio. He would be able to green-light any picture budgeted for less than thirty million dollars. He would be able to fold his own production company into LoddStone as an independent, and name the head of that company.

Skippy Deere was astounded by the richness of the offer. He analyzed this as a mark of insecurity on Bantz's part. Bantz knew he was weak on the creative side and counted on Deere to cover him.

Deere accepted the offer and appointed Claudia De Lena to head his production company. Not only because she was creative, not only because she really knew movie making, but because he knew she was too honest to undercut him. With her, he would not have to watch his back. In addition, and this was no small thing in making movies, he always enjoyed her company, her good humor. And their sex thing had been gotten out of the way a long time ago.

It gave Skippy Deere a glow to think of how rich they would all become. For Deere had been around long enough to know that even Bankable Stars sometimes came to old age in semipoverty. Deere was already very wealthy, but he thought that there were ten levels of being rich and he was only on the first level. Certainly he could live in luxury the rest of his life, but he could not have his own private jet, he could not have five homes and keep them up. He could not keep a harem. He could not afford to be a degenerate gambler. He could not afford another five divorces. He could not afford to keep a hundred servants. He could not even afford to finance his own pictures over any period of time. And he couldn't afford an expensive collection of art, a major Monet or Picasso, as Eli had done. But now someday he would move up from the first level to perhaps as high as the fifth level. He would have to work very hard and be very cunning, and most important, study Bantz very carefully.

Bantz outlined his plans, and Deere was surprised at how daring they were. Obviously Bantz was determined to take his place in the world of power.

For starters, he was going to make a deal with Melo Stuart so that Melo would give LoddStone preferential access to all the Talent in his agency.

"I can handle that," Deere said. "I'll make it clear to him that I'll give him the green light on his favorite projects."

"I'm particularly interested that we have Athena Aquitane do our next picture," Bobby Bantz said.

Aha, Deere thought. Now that Bantz controlled LoddStone, he hoped to get Athena into bed. Deere thought that as head of production he had a shot, too.

"I'll tell Claudia to work on a project for her right away," Deere said.

"Great," Bantz said. "Now remember I always knew what Eli really wanted to do but couldn't because he was too soft. We are going to get rid of Dora and Kevin's production companies. They always lose money and besides I don't want them on the lot."

"You have to be careful on that one," Deere said. "They own a lot of stock in the company."

Bantz grinned. "Yeah, but Eli left me in control for five years. So you're going to be the fall guy. You will refuse to green-light their projects. I figure that after a year or two, they'll leave in disgust and blame you. That was Eli's technique. I always took the rap for him."

"I think you'll have a hard time moving them off the lot," Deere said. "It's their second home, they grew up on it."

"I'll try," Bantz said. "Another thing. The night before he died, Eli agreed to give Ernest Vail gross with some money up front on all the pictures we made from his shitty novel. Eli made that promise because Molly Flanders and Claudia nagged him on his deathbed, which was really a lousy thing to do. I've notified Molly in writing that I'm not bound legally or morally to keep that promise."

Deere pondered the problem. "He'll never kill himself but he could die a natural death in the next five years. We should ensure ourselves against that."

"No," Bantz said. "Eli and I consulted our lawyers and they say Molly's argument would lose in the courts. I'll negotiate some money but not gross. That's sucking our blood."

"So, has Molly answered?" Deere asked.

"Yeah, the usual bullshit lawyer letter," Bantz said. "I told her to go fuck herself."

Bantz picked up the phone and called his psychoanalyst. His wife had insisted for years that he go into therapy to become more likable.

Bantz said into the phone, "I just wanted to confirm our appointment for four P.M. Yes, we'll talk about your script next week." He hung up the phone and gave Deere a sly smile.

Deere knew that Bantz had a rendezvous with Falene Fant at the Studio's Beverly Hotel Bungalow. So Bobby's therapist served as his beard because the Studio had taken an option on the therapist's original screenplay about a serial murder psychiatrist. The joke was that Deere had read the script and thought it would make a nice low-budget movie, although Bantz thought it was shit. Deere would make the movie and Bantz would believe Deere was just doing him a favor.

Then Bantz and Deere chatted about why spending time with Falene made them so happy. They both agreed that it was childish for important men like themselves. They also agreed that sex with Falene was so pleasurable because she was so much fun, and because she made no claims on them. Of course there were implied claims, but she was talented and when the right time came she would be given her chance.

Bantz said, "The thing that worries me is that if she becomes some sort of half-assed star our fun may be over."

"Yeah," Deere said. "That's the way Talent reacts. But what the hell, then she'll make us a lot of money."

The two of them went over the production and release schedules. *Messalina* would be finished in two months and would be the Locomotive for the Christmas season. A Vail sequel was in the can and would be released in the next two weeks. These two LoddStone pictures combined might gross a billion dollars worldwide, including video. Bantz would see a twenty-million-dollar bonus, Deere probably five million. Bobby would be hailed as a genius in his first year as successor to Marrion. He would be acknowledged as a true Number One exec.

Deere said thoughtfully, "It's a shame we have to pay Cross fifteen percent of the adjusted gross on *Messalina*. Why don't we just pay him back his money with interest and if he doesn't like it, he can sue. Obviously, he's leery about going to court."

"Isn't he supposed to be Mafia?" Bantz asked. And Deere thought, This guy is really chickenshit.

"I know Cross," Deere said. "He's not a tough guy. His sister Claudia would have told me if he was truly dangerous. The one I worry about is Molly Flanders. We're screwing two of her clients at the same time."

"OK," Bobby said. "Christ, we really did a good day's work. We save twenty mil on Vail and maybe ten on De Lena. That will pay our bonuses. We'll be heroes."

"Yeah," Deere said. He looked at his watch. "It's getting close to four o'clock. Shouldn't you be on your way to Falene?"

At that moment the door to Bobby Bantz's office burst open and there stood Molly Flanders. She was in fighting garb, trousers, jacket, and white silk blouse. And in flat heels. Her beautiful complexion was a blushing red with rage. There were tears in her eyes and yet she had never looked more beautiful. Her voice was filled with gleeful malice.

"OK, you two cocksuckers," she said. "Ernest Vail is dead. I've got an injunction pending to prevent you from releasing your new sequel to his book. Now are you two fuckheads ready to sit down and make a deal?"

Ernest Vail knew his greatest problem in committing suicide was how to avoid violence. He was far too cowardly to use the most popular methods. Guns frightened him, knives and poisons were too direct and not foolproof. Head in a gas oven, death in his car by carbon monoxide, again left too much uncertainty. Slitting his wrists involved blood. No, he wanted to die a pleasurable death, quick, certain, leaving his body intact and dignified.

Ernest prided himself that his was a rational decision that would benefit everyone except LoddStone Studios. It was purely a matter of personal financial gain and the restoration of his ego. He would be regaining control of his life; that made him laugh. Another proof of sanity: He still had his sense of humor.

Swimming out into the ocean was too "movies," throwing himself in front of a bus was also too painful and somehow demeaning, as if he were some homeless bum. One notion appealed to him for a moment. There was a sleeping pill, no longer popular, a suppository, which you just slipped into your rectum. But again, it was too undignified and was not completely certain.

Ernest rejected all these methods and searched for something that would give him a happy certain death. This process cheered him up so much that he almost abandoned the whole idea. So did writing rough drafts of suicide notes. He wanted to use all his art not to sound self-pitying, accusatory. Most of all he wanted his suicide to be accepted as a completely rational act and not one of cowardice.

He started with the note to his first wife, whom he thought of as his only true love. The first sentence he tried to make objective and practical.

"Get in touch with Molly Flanders, my lawyer, as soon as you get this note. She will have important news for you. I thank you and the children for the many happy years you've given me. I do not want you to think that what I've done is a reproach to you in any way. We were sick of each other before we parted. Please do not think my action is because of a diseased mind, or any unhappiness. It is completely rational, as my lawyer will explain. Tell my children that I love them."

Ernest pushed the note aside. It would need a lot of rewrite. He wrote notes to his second and third wives, which sounded cold even to him, informing them that they were being left small portions of his estate and thanking them for the happiness they had given him and reassuring them they also were in no way responsible for his action. It seemed he was not really in a loving mood. So he wrote a short note to Bobby Bantz, a simple "Fuck you."

Then he wrote a note to Molly Flanders that read, "Go get the bastards." This put him in a better mood.

To Cross De Lena, he wrote, "I finally did the right thing." He had sensed De Lena's contempt for his waffling.

Finally his heart opened up when he wrote to Claudia. "You gave me the happiest times of my life and we weren't even in love. How do you figure that? And how come everything you did in life was right and everything I did was wrong? Until now. Please disregard everything I've said about your writing, how I demeaned your work, that's just the envy of an old novelist as out of date as a blacksmith. And thank you for fighting for my percentage even though finally you failed. I love you for trying."

He stacked up the notes, which he had written on yellow second sheets. They were terrible but he would rewrite them, and rewriting was always the key.

But composing the notes had stirred his subconscious. Finally he thought of the perfect way to kill himself.


Kenneth Kaldone was the greatest dentist in Hollywood, as famous as any Bankable Star within that small milieu. He was extremely skillful in his profession, he was colorful and daring in his private life. He detested the portrayal in literature and movies of dentists as extremely bourgeois and did everything to disprove it.

He was charming in dress and manner, his dental office was luxurious and had a rack of a hundred of the best magazines published in

America and England. There was another, smaller rack for magazines in foreign languages, German, Italian, French, and even Russian.

First-rate modern art hung on the walls of the waiting room, and when you went into the labyrinth of treatment rooms, the corridors were decorated with autographed pictures of some of the greatest names in Hollywood. His patients.

He was always bubbly with cheerful good humor and vaguely effeminate in a way that was strangely misleading. He loved women but did not understand in any way a commitment to women. He regarded sex as no more important than a good dinner, a fine wine, wonderful music.

The only thing Kenneth believed in was the art of dentistry. There, he was an artist, he kept up with all technical and cosmetic developments. He refused to make removable bridges for his clients, he insisted on steel implants to which an artificial series of teeth could be attached permanently. He lectured at the dental conventions, he was such an authority that he had once been summoned to treat the teeth of one of the royal bloods of Monaco.

No patient of Kenneth Kaldone's would be forced to put his teeth in a water glass at night. No patient would ever feel pain in his elaborately outfitted dental chair. He was generous in his use of drugs and especially in the use of "sweet air," the combination of nitrous oxide and oxygen inhaled by patients though a rubber mask, which remarkably killed any pain to the nerves and transported his patient into a semiconsciousness as nearly pleasurable as opium.

Ernest and Kenneth had become friends on Ernest's first visit to Hollywood almost twenty years before. Ernest had suffered an excruciating toothache at the dinner of a producer who was courting him for the rights to one of his books. The producer had called Kenneth at midnight, and Kenneth had rushed to the party to drive Ernest to his office to treat the infected tooth. Then he had driven Ernest to his hotel, instructing him to come back to the office the next day.

Ernest later commented to the producer that he must have a lot of clout for a dentist to make a house call at midnight. The producer said no, Kenneth Kaldone was just that kind of a guy. A man with a toothache was to him like a man drowning, he had to be rescued. But also Kaldone had read all of Ernest's books and loved his work.

The next day when Ernest visited Kenneth in his office, he was effusively grateful. Kenneth stopped him with an upraised hand and said, "I'm still in your debt for the pleasure your books have given me. Now let me tell you about steel implants." He gave a long lecture that argued it was never too early to take care of your mouth. That Ernest would soon lose some other teeth, and steel implants would save him from putting his teeth in a water glass at night.

Ernest said, "I'll think about it."

"No," Kenneth said, "I can't treat a patient who disagrees with me about my work."

Ernest laughed. "It's a good thing you're not a novelist," he said. "But OK."

They became friends. Vail would call him for dinner whenever he came to Hollywood and sometimes he made a special trip to L.A. just to be treated with sweet air. Kenneth spoke intelligently about Ernest's books, he knew literature almost as well as he knew dentistry.

Ernest loved sweet air. He never felt pain and he had some of his best ideas while he was in the semiconscious state it induced. In the next few years he and Kenneth built a friendship so strong it resulted in Ernest having a new set of teeth with roots of steel, which would accompany him to the grave.

But Ernest's main interest in Kenneth was as a character for a novel. Ernest had always believed that in every human being there was one startling perversity. Kenneth had revealed his, and it was sexual but not in the usual pornographic style.

They always chatted a bit before a treatment, before Ernest was given sweet air. Kenneth mentioned that his primary girlfriend, his "significant other," was also having sex with her dog, a huge German shepherd.

Ernest, just beginning to succumb to the sweet air, took the rubber mask off his face and said without thinking, "You're screwing a woman who screws her dog? Don't you worry about that?" He meant the medical and psychological complications.

Kenneth did not grasp what was implied. "Why should I worry?" he said. "A dog is no competition."

At first Ernest thought he was joking. Then he realized Kenneth was serious. Ernest put his mask back on and submerged himself in the dreaminess of the nitrous oxide and oxygen, and his mind, stimulated as usual, made a complete analysis of his dentist.

Kenneth was a man who had no conception of love as a spiritual exercise. Pleasure was paramount, similar to his skills in killing pain. Flesh was to be controlled while indulged.

They had dinner together that night, and Kenneth more or less confirmed Ernest's analysis. "Sex is better than nitrous," Kenneth said. "But like nitrous, you must have at least thirty percent oxygen mixed in." He gave Ernest a sly look. "Ernest, you really like sweet air, I can tell. I give you the maximum—seventy percent—and you tolerate it well."

Ernest asked, "Is it dangerous?"

"Not really," Kenneth said. "Unless you keep the mask on for a couple of days and maybe not even then. Of course, pure nitrous oxide will kill you in fifteen to thirty minutes. In fact about once a month I have a little midnight party in my office, carefully selected 'beautiful people.' All my patients, so I have their blood work. All healthy. The nitrous turns them on. Haven't you felt sexual under the gas?"

Ernest laughed. "When one of your technicians goes by I want to grab her ass."

Kenneth said with wry humor, "I'm sure she'd forgive you. Why don't you come by the office tomorrow at midnight? It's really a lot of fun." He saw Ernest looking scandalized and said, "Nitrous is not cocaine. Cocaine makes women sort of helpless. Nitrous just loosens them up. Just come as you would go to a cocktail party. You're not committed to any action."

Ernest thought maliciously, Are dogs allowed? Then he said he would drop in. He excused himself by thinking it would only be research for a novel.

He did not have any fun at the party and did not really participate. The truth was, the nitrous oxide made him feel more spiritual than sexy, as if it were some sacred drug only to be used to worship a merciful God. The copulation of the guests was so animal-like that for the first time he understood Kenneth's casualness about his significant other and the German shepherd. It was so devoid of human content that it was boring. Kenneth himself did not participate, he was too busy operating the controls on the nitrous.

But now, years later, Ernest knew he had a way of killing himself. It would be like painless dentistry. He would not suffer, he would not be disfigured, he would not be afraid. He would float from this world to the other in a cloud of benign reflections. As the saying goes, he would die happy.

The problem now was how to get into Kenneth's office at night and how to figure out how the controls operated. . . .

He made an appointment with Kenneth for a checkup. While Kenneth was studying his X rays, Ernest told him that he was using a dentist as a character in his new novel and asked to be shown how the controls for the sweet air worked.

Kenneth was a natural-born pedagogue and showed him how to work the controls on the tanks of nitrous oxide and oxygen, stressing the safe ratios, lecturing all the while.

"But couldn't it be dangerous?" Ernest asked. "What if you got drunk and screwed up? You could kill me."

"No, it's automatically regulated so that you always get at least thirty percent oxygen," Kenneth explained.

Ernest hesitated a moment, trying to look embarrassed. "You know I enjoyed that party years ago. Now I have a beautiful girlfriend who is acting a little coy. I need some help. Could you let me have the key to your office so I could bring her here some night? The nitrous would just tip the balance."

Kenneth studied the X rays carefully. "Your mouth is in terrific shape," he said. "I'm really a great dentist."

"The key?" Ernest said.

"A really beautiful girl?" Kenneth asked. "Tell me which night and I'll come and work the controls."

"No, no," Ernest said. "This is a really straight girl. She wouldn't do even the nitrous if you were around." He paused for a moment. "She really is old-fashioned."

"No shit," Kenneth said and looked directly into Ernest's eyes. Then he said, "I'll just be a minute," and he left the treatment room.

When he returned, he had a key in his hand. "Take this to a hardware store and get it duplicated," Kenneth said. "Make sure you let them know who you are. Then come back and give me my key."

Ernest was surprised. "I don't mean right now."

Kenneth packed away the X rays and turned to Ernest. For one of the few times since Ernest had known him, the cheerfulness in his face was gone.

"When the cops find you," Kenneth said, "dead in my chair, I don't want to be implicated in any way. I don't want my professional status jeopardized, or my patients deserting me. The cops will find the duplicate and track it down to the store. They will assume trickery on your part. I assume you're leaving a note?"

Ernest was stunned and then ashamed. He had not thought of harming Kenneth. Kenneth was looking at him with a reproachful smile tinged with sadness. Ernest took the key from Kenneth, then in a rare show of emotion, he gave Kenneth a tentative hug. "So you understand," he said. "I'm being completely rational."

"Sure I do," Kenneth said. "I've often thought about it for myself in my old age or if things go bad." He smiled cheerfully and said, "Death is no competition." They both laughed.

"You really know why?" Ernest asked.

"Everybody in Hollywood knows," Kenneth said. "Skippy Deere was at a party and someone asked if he was really going to do the picture. He said, 'I will try until Hell freezes over or Ernest Vail commits suicide.' "

"And you don't think I'm crazy?" Ernest said. "Doing it for money I can't spend . . ."

"Why not?" Kenneth said. "It's smarter than killing yourself for love. But the mechanics are not that simple. You have to disconnect this hose in the wall that supplies the oxygen, that disables the regulator and you can make the mixture more than seventy percent. Do it on Friday night after the cleaning people leave so you won't be discovered until Monday. There's always a chance you can be revived. Of course if you use pure nitrous oxide you'll be gone in thirty minutes." Again he smiled a little sadly. "All my work on your teeth wasted. What a shame."

Two days later, on a Saturday morning, Ernest woke very early in his Beverly Hills Hotel room. The sun was just coming up. He showered and shaved and dressed in slacks, a T-shirt, and comfortable jeans. Over that he wore a tan linen jacket. His room was strewn with clothes and newspapers, but it would be pointless to tidy up.

Kenneth's office was a half-hour walk from the hotel, and Ernest stepped out feeling a sense of freedom. Nobody walked in L.A. He was hungry but was afraid to eat anything because it might make him throw up when he was under the nitrous.

The office was on the fifteenth floor of a sixteen-story building. There was only a single civilian guard in the lobby and no one in the elevator. Ernest turned the key in the door of the dental suite and entered. He locked the door behind him and put the key in his jacket pocket. The suite of rooms was ghostly still, the receptionist's window glinted in the early morning sun and her computer was ominously dark and silent.

Ernest opened the door that led to the work area. As he walked down the corridor, he was greeted by the photos of Bankable Stars. There were six treatment rooms, three on each side of the corridor. At the end was Kenneth's office and conference room where they had chatted many times. Kenneth's own treatment room was attached, with his special hydraulic dental chair, where he cared for his high-ranking patients.

That chair was extra luxurious, the padding thicker and the leather softer. On the mobile table beside the chair was the sweet air mask. The console, with its hose linked to the hidden nitrous oxide and oxygen tanks, had its two control knobs turned to zero.

Ernest adjusted the dials so that he would get half nitrous oxide and half oxygen. Then he sat in the chair and put the mask over his face. He relaxed. After all, Kenneth would not be sticking knives into his gums now. All the aches and pains left his body, his brain roamed over the entire world. He felt wonderful, it was ridiculous to think of death.

Ideas for future novels floated through his head, insights into many people he knew, none of them malicious, which was what he loved about nitrous. Shit, he had forgotten to rewrite the suicide notes, and he realized how, despite his good intentions and language, they were in essence insulting.

Ernest was now in a huge, sailing colored balloon. He floated over the world he had known. He thought about Eli Marrion, who had followed his destiny, achieved great power, was regarded with awe for his ruthless intelligence in using that power. And yet, when Ernest's best book came out and was bought for the movies, the one that earned him the Pulitzer, Eli had come to the cocktail party his publishers gave him.

Eli had put out his hand and said, "You are a very fine writer." His coming to the party was sensational Hollywood gossip. And the great Eli Marrion had shown him the final and absolute mark of respect, he had given him gross. No matter that Bantz had taken it away after Marrion died.

And Bantz was not a villain. His relentless pursuit of profit was a result of his experience in a special world. If truth be told, Skippy Deere was worse, because Deere, with his intelligence, his charm and his elemental energy, and his instinctive moves to betrayal in a personal sense, was more lethal.

Another insight came to Ernest. Why was he always knocking Hollywood and films, sneering at them? It was jealousy. Film was now the most revered art form, and he himself loved movies, good ones anyway. But he envied more the relationships in making a movie. The cast, the crew, the director, the Bankable Stars and even the "Suits," those crass execs, seemed to come together in a close if not ever-loving family, at least until the picture was finished. They gave each other presents then and kissed and hugged and swore eternal devotion. What a wonderful feeling that must be to have. He remembered when he wrote his first script with Claudia, he thought he might be admitted to this family.

But how that could be with his personality, his malicious wit, his constant sneering? But under the sweet nitrous oxide, he could not even judge himself harshly. He had a right, he had written great books (Ernest was an oddity among novelists because he really loved his books), and he had deserved to be treated with more respect.

Benignly saturated with forgiving nitrous, Ernest decided he really didn't want to die. Money was not that important, Bantz would relent or Claudia and Molly would find a way out.

Then he remembered all his humiliation. None of his wives had ever truly loved him. He had always been the mendicant, never enjoyed requited love. His books had been respected but never aroused the adoration that made a writer rich. Some critics had reviled him and he had pretended to take it in good sport. After all, it was wrong to get angry with critics, they were only doing their job. But their remarks hurt. And all his male friends, though they sometimes enjoyed his company, his wit and honesty, never became close, not even Kenneth. While Claudia was truly fond of him, he knew Molly Flanders and Kenneth felt pity for him.

Ernest reached over and turned off the sweet air. It took just a few minutes for his head to clear and then he went to sit in Kenneth's office.

His depression came back. He tilted back in Kenneth's lounge chair and watched the sun rise over Beverly Hills. He was so angry at the studio screwing him out of his money that he couldn't enjoy anything. He hated the dawning of a new day; at night he took sleeping pills early and tried to sleep as long as he could. . . . That he could be humiliated by such people, people he held in contempt. And now he could no longer even read, a pleasure that had never before betrayed him. And of course, he could no longer write. That elegant prose, so often praised, was now false, inflated, pretentious. He no longer enjoyed writing it.

For a long time now, he had awakened every morning dreading the coming day, too tired to even shave and shower. And he was broke. He had earned millions and had pissed it away on gambling, women, and booze. Or given it away. Money had never been important until now.

The last two months he had not been able to send his kids their support payments or his wives their alimony. Unlike most men, sending those checks made Ernest happy. He had not published a book for five years, and his personality had become less pleasant even to himself. He was always whining about his fate. He was like a sore tooth in the face of society. And this image itself depressed him. What kind of soapy metaphor was this for a writer of his talent? A wave of melancholy swept over him; he was completely powerless.

He sprang up and walked into the treatment room. Kenneth had told him what he must do. He pulled out the cable that held the two plugs, one for oxygen and one for the nitrous oxide. Then he plugged back only one. Nitrous. He sat in the dental chair, reached over and turned the dial. At that moment he thought that there must be some way to get at least a ten percent oxygen flow so that death would not be so certain. He picked up the mask and put it over his face.

The pure nitrous hit his body and he experienced a moment of ecstasy, a washing away of all pain and a dreamy content. The nitrous hit and scrubbed out the brain in his skull. There was one last moment of pure pleasure before he ceased to exist, and in that moment, he believed there was a God and a Heaven.

Molly Flanders savaged Bobby Bantz and Skippy Deere; she would have been more careful if Eli Marrion was still alive.

"You have a new sequel to Ernest's book coming out. My injunction will stop that. The property now belongs to Ernest's heirs. Sure, maybe you can override the injunction and release the picture but then I sue. If I win, Ernest's estate will own that picture and most of what it earns. And for a certainty we can prevent you from making other sequels based on the characters in his books. Now, we can save all that and years of trouble in court. You pay five million up front and ten percent of the gross of each picture. And I want a true and certified account of the money on home video."

Deere was horrified and Bantz enraged. Ernest Vail, a writer, would have a greater percentage of the profit on the pictures than anyone except a Bankable Star ever got, and that was a fucking outrage.

Bantz immediately called Melo Stuart and the chief counsel for LoddStone Pictures. They were in the meeting room within a half hour. Melo was necessary to the meeting because he was the packager of the sequels and earned a commission on the Bankable Star, the director, and the rewriter, Benny Sly. This was a situation that could require him to give up some points.

The chief counsel said, "We studied the situation when Mr. Vail made his first threat against the Studio."

Molly Flanders broke in angrily. "You call killing himself a threat to the Studio?"

"And blackmail," the chief counsel said smoothly. "Now we've completely researched the law in this situation, which is very tricky, but even then I advised the Studio we could fight your claim in court and win. In this particular case, the rights to the property do not revert back to the heirs."

"What can you guarantee?" Molly asked the counsel. "To a ninety-five percent certainty?"

"No," the counsel said. "Nothing is that certain in the law."

Molly was delighted. She would retire with the fee she earned when she won this case. She got up to go and said, "Fuck you all, I'll see you in court."

Bantz and Deere were so terrified they could not speak. Bantz wished with all his heart that Eli Marrion were still alive.

It was Melo Stuart who rose and restrained Molly with an affectionate and imploring hug. "Hey," he said, "we're just negotiating. Be civilized."

He led Molly back to her chair, noticing there were tears in her eyes. "We can make a deal, I'll give up some points in the package."

Molly said quietly to Bantz, "Do you want to risk losing everything? Can your counsel guarantee that you will win? Of course he can't. Are you a fucking businessman or some degenerate gambler? To save a fucking lousy twenty to forty mil, you want to risk losing a billion?"

They cut the deal. Ernest's estate got four million up front and 8 percent of the gross on the picture about to be released. He would get two million and 10 percent of adjusted gross on any other sequels. Ernest's three ex-wives and his children would be rich.

Molly's parting shot was, "If you think I was tough, wait until Cross De Lena hears how you screwed him."

Molly savored her victory. She remembered how one night she had taken Ernest home from a party. She was pretty drunk and extremely lonely and Ernest was witty and intelligent and she thought it might be fun to spend a night with him. Then when they arrived at her home, sobered up by the drive, and she took him to her bedroom, she had looked around despairingly. Ernest was such a shrimp and so obviously sexually shy and he was really a homely man. At that point he was tongue-tied.

But Molly was too fair a person to dismiss him at such a critical time. So she got drunk again and they went to bed. And really, in the dark, it hadn't been too bad. Ernest enjoyed it so much that she was flattered and brought him breakfast in bed.

He gave her a sly grin. "Thank you," he said. "And thank you again." And she perceived that he understood everything she had felt the previous night and was thanking her not only for bringing him breakfast but also as his sexual benefactress. She had always been regretful that she had not been a better actress, but what the hell, she was a lawyer. And now she had performed for Ernest Vail an act of requited love.



Dottore David Redfellow received Don Clericuzio's summons while attending an important meeting in Rome. He was advising the prime minister of Italy on a new banking regulation that would impose severe penal sentences on corrupt bank officials, and naturally he was advising against it. He immediately wound up his arguments and flew to America.

In the twenty-five years of his exile in Italy, David Redfellow had prospered and changed beyond his wildest dreams. At the beginning, Don Clericuzio helped him buy a small bank in Rome. With the fortune he had made in the drug trade and deposited in Swiss banks, he bought more banks and television stations. But it was Don Clericuzio's friends in Italy who helped guide him and build his empire, helped him to acquire the magazines, the newspapers, the TV stations, in addition to his string of banks.

But David Redfellow was pleased also by what he had done on his own. A complete transformation of character. He acquired Italian citizenship, an Italian wife, Italian children, and the standard Italian mistress as well as an honorary doctorate (cost, two million) from an Italian university. He wore Armani suits, spent an hour every week at his barber, acquired a circle of all-male cronies at his coffee bar (which he bought), and entered politics as advisor to the cabinet and the prime minister. Still, once a year he made his pilgrimage to Quogue to fulfill any wishes of his mentor, Don Clericuzio. So this special summons filled him with alarm.

Dinner was waiting for him at the Quogue mansion when he arrived, and Rose Marie had outdone herself because Redfellow was always rapturous about the restaurants of Rome. Assembled to honor him was the entire Clericuzio clan: the Don himself; his sons, Giorgio, Petie, and Vincent; his grandson, Dante; and Pippi and Cross De Lena.

It was a hero's welcome. David Redfellow, the college-dropout drug king, the louche dresser with an earring in his ear, the hyena riding the kills of sex, had transformed himself into a pillar of society. They were proud of him. Even more, Don Clericuzio felt he was in Redfellow's debt. For it was Redfellow who had taught him a great lesson in morality.

In his early days Don Clericuzio had suffered a strange sentimentality. He had believed that the forces of law could not be generally corrupted in the matter of drugs.

David Redfellow was a twenty-year-old college student in 1960 when he first started dealing drugs, not for profit but simply so he and his friends could have a steady cheap supply. An amateur endeavor, just cocaine and marijuana. In a year it had grown so big he and his classmate partners owned a small plane that brought goods over the Mexican and South American borders. Quite naturally they soon ran afoul of the law, and that was where David first showed his genius. The six-man partnership was earning vast amounts of money, and David Redfellow laid on such massive bribes that he soon had on his payroll a roster of sheriffs, district attorneys, judges, and hundreds of police along the Eastern seaboard.

He always claimed it was quite simple. You learned the official's yearly salary and offered him five times that amount.

But then the cartel of Colombians appeared on the scene, wilder than the wildest of the Old West movie Indians, not just taking scalps but whole heads. Four of Redfellow's partners were killed, and Redfellow made contact with the Clericuzio Family and asked for protection, offering 50 percent of his profits.

Petie Clericuzio and a crew of soldiers from the Bronx Enclave became his bodyguards, and this arrangement lasted until the Don exiled Redfellow to Italy in 1965. The drug business had become too dangerous.

Now, gathered together over dinner, they congratulated the Don on the wisdom of his decision many years before. Dante and Cross heard the story of Redfellow for the first time. Redfellow was a good storyteller and he praised Petie to the skies. "What a fighter," he said. "If it wasn't for him I would never have lived to go to Sicily." He turned to Dante and Cross and said to them, "It was the day you both were christened. I remember you both never flinched when they almost drowned you in Holy Water. I never dreamed that some-day we would be doing business together, as grown men."

Don Clericuzio said drily, "You will not be doing business with them, you will do business only with me and Giorgio. If you need help you can call on Pippi De Lena. I have decided to go on with the business I spoke to you about. Giorgio will tell you why."

Giorgio told David the latest developments, that Eli Marrion was dead and Bobby Bantz had taken over the Studio, that he had taken away all the points Cross owned in *Messalina,* and returned his money with interest.

Redfellow enjoyed that story. "He is a very clever man. He knows you will not go to court so he takes away your money. That's good business."

Dante was drinking a cup of coffee, and he eyed Redfellow with distaste. Rose Marie, who was sitting beside him, put her hand on his arm.

"You think that's funny?" Dante said to Redfellow.

Redfellow studied Dante for a moment. He made his face very serious. "Only because I know that in this instance it is a mistake to be so clever."

The Don observed this exchange and it seemed to amuse him. In any case he was frivolous, a rare occurrence, which his sons always recognized and enjoyed.

"So Grandson," he said to Dante, "how would you solve this problem?"

"Send him swimming to the bottom of the ocean," Dante said, and the Don smiled at him.

"And you, Croccifixio? How would you solve this situation?" the Don asked.

"I'd just accept it," Cross said. "I'd learn from it. I just got out-foxed because I didn't believe they'd have the balls."

"Petie and Vincent?" the Don asked.

But they refused to answer. They knew the game he was playing.

"You can't just ignore it," the Don said to Cross. "You will be known for a fool and men all over the world will refuse you any re-spect."

Cross was taking the Don seriously. "Eli Marrion's house still holds his paintings and they're worth about twenty or thirty million. We could hijack them and hold them for ransom."

"No," the Don said. "That would expose you, reveal your power, and no matter how delicately handled, could lead to danger. It is too complicated. David, what would you do?"

David puffed on his cigar, thoughtfully. He said, "Buy the Studio. Do a civilized businesslike thing. With our banks and communica-tions companies, buy LoddStone."

Cross was incredulous. "LoddStone is the oldest and richest film studio in the world. Even if you could put up the ten billion, they wouldn't sell it to you. That's simply not possible."

Petie said in his joker's voice, "David my old buddy, you can get your mitts on ten billion? The man whose life I saved? The man who said he could never repay me?"

Redfellow waved him away. "You don't understand how big money works. It's like whipped cream, you get a small amount and whip it up into a big froth with bonds, loans, stock shares. Money is not the problem."

Cross said, "The problem is how to get Bantz out of the way. He controls the Studio and whatever his faults, he is loyal to Marrion's wishes. He would never agree to selling the Studio."

"I'll go out there and give him a kiss," Petie said.

Now the Don made his decision. He said to Redfellow, "Carry out your plan. Get it done. But with all caution. Pippi and Croccifixio will be at your command."

"One more thing," Giorgio said to Redfellow. "Bobby Bantz, by the terms of Eli Marrion's will, has total command over the Studio for the next five years. But Marrion's son and daughter have more stock in the company than Bantz. Bantz can't get fired but if the Studio is sold, the new owners will have to pay him off. So that's the problem you have to solve."

David Redfellow smiled and puffed on his cigar. "Just like the old days. Don Clericuzio, the only help I need is yours. Some of those banks in Italy may be reluctant to gamble on such a venture. Remember, we will have to pay a big premium over the actual worth of the Studio."

"Don't worry," the Don said. "I have a lot of money in those banks."

Pippi DeLena had watched all this with a wary eye. What disturbed him was the openness of this meeting. By procedure only the Don, Giorgio, and David Redfellow should have been present. Pippi and Cross could have been given orders separately to help Redfellow. Why had they been let in on these secrets? Even more important, why were Dante, Petie, and Vincent brought into the circle? All this was not like the Don Clericuzio he knew, who always kept his plans as secret as possible.

Vincent and Rose Marie were helping the Don up the stairs to go to bed. He had stubbornly refused to have a lift chair installed on the railings.

As soon as they were out of sight, Dante turned to Giorgio and said furiously, "And who gets the Studio when we own it? Cross?"

David Redfellow interrupted coolly. "I will own the Studio. I will run it. Your grandfather will have a financial interest. This will be documented."

Giorgio agreed.

Cross said laughing, "Dante, neither one of us can run a movie studio. We're not ruthless enough."

Pippi studied all of them. He was good at scenting danger. That's why he had lived so long. But this he couldn't figure out. Maybe the Don was just getting old.

Petie drove Redfellow back to Kennedy Airport where his private jet waited. Cross and Pippi had used a chartered jet from Vegas. Don Clericuzio absolutely forbade the owning of a jet by the Xanadu or any of his enterprises.

Cross drove their rented car to the airport. During the drive, Pippi said to Cross, "I'm going to spend some time in New York City. I'll just keep the car when we get to the airport."

Cross saw that his father was worried. "I didn't do well in there," he said.

"You were OK," Pippi said. "But the Don was right. You can't let anybody screw you twice."

When they arrived at Kennedy, Cross got out and Pippi slid across the seat to get behind the wheel. Through the open window, they shook hands. In that moment Pippi looked up at his son's handsome face and felt an enormous wave of affection. He tried to smile as he slapped Cross gently on the cheek and said, "Be careful."

"Of what?" Cross asked, his dark eyes searching his father's.

"Everything," Pippi said. Then, startling Cross, he said, "Maybe I should have let you go with your mother but I was selfish. I needed you around."

Cross watched his father drive away and for the first time he realized how much his father worried about him, how much his father loved him.

# CHAPTER 15

MUCH TO HIS OWN DISMAY, Pippi De Lena decided to get married, not for love but for companionship. True, he had Cross, he had the cronies at the Xanadu Hotel, he had the Clericuzio Family and a vast network or relatives. True, he had three mistresses and he ate with good and sincere appetite; he enjoyed his golf and was down to a ten handicap, and he still loved to dance. But as the Don would say, he could go dancing to his coffin.

So in his late fifties, robust in health, sanguine in temperament, rich, semiretired, he longed for a settled home life and perhaps a new batch of kids. Why not? The idea appealed to him more and more. Surprisingly, he yearned to be a father again. It would be fun to raise a daughter, he had loved Claudia as a child, though they no longer spoke. She had been so cunning and so forthright at the same time, and she had made her way in the world as a successful screen-play writer. And who knows, maybe someday they would make up. In some ways she was as stubborn as he was, so he understood her and he admired the way she stood up for what she believed in.

Cross had lost the gamble he had taken in the movie business, but one way or another his future was assured. He still had the Xanadu and the Don would help him recover from the risk he had taken with his new venture. He was a good kid, but he was young and the young must take risks. That's what life was all about.

After dropping off Cross at the airport, Pippi drove to New York City to spend a few days with his East Coast mistress. She was a good-looking brunette, a legal secretary with a sharp New York wit, and a great dancer. True, she had a tongue that lashed out, she loved to spend money, she would be an expensive wife. But she was too old, over forty-five. And she was too independent, a great quality for a mistress but not for the kind of marriage that Pippi would demand.

It was a pleasurable weekend with her, though she spent half the Sunday reading the *Times*. They ate in the finest restaurants, went dancing in the nightclubs, and had great sex in her apartment. But Pippi needed something more placid.

Pippi flew to Chicago. His mistress there was the sexual equivalent of that brawling city. She drank a little too much, she partied too exuberantly, she was happy-go-lucky and a lot of fun. But she was a little lazy, a little too messy, Pippi liked a clean home. Again, she was too old to start a family, at least forty, she said. But what the hell. Was he up to running around with a really young broad? After two days in Chicago, Pippi crossed her off the list.

With both, he would have a problem settling them in Vegas. They were big-city women, and Vegas, Pippi knew in his heart, was really a hick cow town where casinos took the place of cattle. And there was no way that Pippi would live in any place but Vegas, for in Vegas nighttime did not exist. Electric neon banished all ghosts, the city shone like a rosy diamond in the desert at night, and after dawn the hot sun burned away all the wraiths that had escaped the neon.

His best shot was his mistress in Los Angeles, and Pippi was pleased that he had geographically positioned them so neatly. There could be no accidental confrontations, no mental struggles in choosing between them. They served a certain purpose and they could not interfere with any temporary love affairs. Indeed, looking back, he was pleased at how he had conducted his life. Daring but prudent, brave but not foolhardy, loyal to the Family and rewarded by them. His only mistake had been in marrying a woman like Nalene, and even there, what woman could have given him more happiness for eleven years. And what man could boast of having made only one mistake in his lifetime? What was it the Don always said, It was OK to make mistakes in life as long as it was not a fatal mistake.

He decided to go directly to L.A. and not stop in Vegas. He called to notify Michelle that he was on his way and refused her offer to pick him up at the airport. "Just be ready for me when I get there," he told her. "I've been missing you. And I've got something important to tell you."

Michelle was young enough, thirty-two, and she was more tender, more giving, more easy on the nerves, maybe because she had been born and raised in California. She was also good in bed, not that the others were not, for this was a primary qualification for Pippi. But she had no sharp edges, she wouldn't be trouble. She was a little kooky, she believed in New Age crap called channeling and being able to talk to spirits, and talked about all the past lives she had lived, but she could also be fun. Like many California beauties, she had dreamed of being an actress, but that had been knocked out of her head. She was completely wrapped up in yoga and channeling now, in physical health, running and going to the gym. And besides, she always complimented Pippi on his karma. For of course none of these women knew his true vocation. He was simply an administrative officer of the hotel association in Vegas.

Yes, with Michelle, he could stay in Vegas, they could keep an apartment in L.A. and when they got bored they could make the forty-minute flight to L.A. for a couple of weeks. And maybe to keep her busy, he would buy her a gift shop in the Hotel Xanadu. It could really work out. But what if she said no?

Something struck his memory: Nalene reading *Goldilocks and the Three Bears* when the children were small. He was just like Goldilocks. The New York woman was too hard, the Chicago woman was too soft, and the L.A. woman was just right. The thought gave him pleasure. Of course, in real life nothing was "just right."

When he deplaned in L.A., he breathed in the balmy air of California, not even noticing the smog. He rented a car and drove first to Rodeo Drive, he loved to bring his women little gifts as a surprise and enjoyed walking down the street of fancy shops that held the luxuries of the world. He bought a gaudy wristwatch in the Gucci store; a purse in Fendi's, though he thought it ugly; a Hermès scarf; and some perfume in a bottle that looked like an expensive sculpture. When he bought a box of expensive lingerie, he was in such good spirits that he kidded the saleswoman, a young blonde, that it was for himself. The girl gave him one look and said, "Right . . ."

Back in the car, three thousand dollars poorer, he headed for Santa Monica, the goodies in the passenger seat, gifts crammed into a gaily colored Gucci shopping bag. In Brentwood, he stopped in the Brentwood Mart, a favorite place. He loved the food stores that boxed an open square studded with picnic tables where you could have a cold drink and eat. The food on the plane had been terrible, and he was hungry. Michelle never kept food in the refrigerator because she was always dieting.

In one store he bought two roast chickens, a dozen barbecued spareribs, and four hot dogs with all the trimmings. In another shop, he bought fresh baked white and rye bread. At an open stand he bought a huge glass of Coke and sat down at one of the picnic tables for a final moment of solitude. He ate two of the hot dogs, half of one of the roast chickens, and some French fries. He had never tasted anything so good. He sat in the golden light of the late afternoon sun in California, the sweet balmy air washed his face clean. He hated to leave but Michelle was waiting. She would be bathed and scented and a little tipsy and she would take him to bed immediately before he could even brush his teeth. He would propose to her before they started.

The shopping bag holding the food was decorated with type telling some fable about food, an intellectual shopping bag as befitted the intellectual clientele of the Mart. When he put it into the car, he read only the beginning line, "Fruit is the oldest product of human consumption. In the Garden of Eden . . ." Jesus, Pippi thought.

He drove to Santa Monica and stopped in front of Michelle's condo, which was in a two-story-high series of Spanish-looking bungalows. When he got out of the car he carried the two bags automatically in his left hand, leaving his right hand free. Out of habit, he surveyed the street up and down. It was lovely, no cars parked, the Spanish styles provided commodious driveways and a mildly religious benignity. The runners along the curbs were hidden by flowers and grass, the heavy-branched trees made a canopy against the descending sun.

Pippi now had to walk down a long alleyway whose wooden, green-painted fences were draped with roses. Michelle's apartment was in the back, a relic of the old Santa Monica, which was still bucolic. The buildings themselves were of seemingly old wood, and each separated swimming pool was adorned by white benches.

Outside the alleyway, far down the other end, Pippi heard the growling motor of a stationary vehicle. It alerted him, he was always alert. At the same moment he caught sight of a man rising from one of the benches. He was so surprised that he said, "What the fuck are you doing here?"

The man's hand did not come out to greet him and in that instant everything was clear to Pippi. He knew what was going to happen. His brain processed so much information that he could not react. He saw the gun appear, so small and inoffensive, saw the tension on the killer's face. Understood for the first time the look on the faces of men he had put to death, their supreme astonishment that life was at an end. And he understood that finally he would have to pay the price for living his life. He even thought briefly that the killer had planned badly, that this was not how he would have done it.

He tried his best, knowing there was no mercy. He dropped the shopping bags and lunged forward, at the same time reaching for his gun. The man came forward to meet him, and Pippi in exultation reached for him. Six bullets carried his body into the air and flung it into a pillow of flowers at the foot of the green fence. He smelled their fragrance. He looked up at the man standing over him and said, "You fucking Santadio." Then the final bullet crashed into his skull. Pippi De Lena was no more.

# CHAPTER 16

**E**ARLY ON THE DAY Pippi De Lena was to die, Cross picked up Athena at her Malibu home and they drove to San Diego to visit Athena's daughter, Bethany.

Bethany had been prepared by the nurses, she was dressed to go out. Cross could see she was a blurry reflection of her mother, and tall for her age. There was still the blankness in her face and eyes, and her body was too slack. Her features did not seem to have real definition, as if partially dissolved, like a bar of used soap. She still wore the red plastic apron that she used to protect her clothes when she was painting. She had been painting on the wall since early that morning. She didn't acknowledge seeing them, and she received her mother's hug and kisses with a shrinking away of her body and face.

Athena disregarded this and hugged her even harder.

The day was to be a picnic at a wooded lake nearby. Athena had packed a lunch basket.

On the short drive, Bethany sat between them, with Athena driving. Athena frequently brushed back Bethany's hair and caressed her cheek while Bethany stared straight ahead.

Cross thought of how when the day was done he and Athena would be back in Malibu making love. He was imagining her naked body on the bed and him standing over her.

Suddenly Bethany spoke, and it was to him. She had never acknowledged him before. She stared at him with her flat green eyes and said, "Who are you?"

Athena answered, and her voice was perfect, as if it was the most natural thing in the world for Bethany to ask. She said, "His name is

Cross and he's my very best friend." Bethany seemed not to hear and retired into her world again.

Athena parked the car a few yards from a dazzling lake nestled in the forest, a tiny blue gem in a vast cloth of green. Cross took the basket of food, and Athena unpacked it onto a red cloth she spread over the grass. She also put out crisp green napkins and forks and spoons. The cloth was embroidered with musical instruments that caught Bethany's attention. Then Athena spread out a pile of different sandwiches, glass bowls of potato salad, and sliced fruits. Then a plate of sweet cakes oozing cream. And a platter of fried chicken. She had prepared everything with the care of a catering professional because Bethany loved food.

Cross went back to the car and took a case of soda from the trunk. There were glasses in the basket and he poured soda for them. Athena offered her glass to Bethany, but Bethany struck her hand aside. She was watching Cross.

Cross stared into her eyes. Her face was so rigid it could have been a mask instead of flesh, but her eyes were now alert. It was as if she was trapped in some secret cave, that she was being smothered but could not call for help, that her flesh was blistered and she could not bear to be touched.

They ate, and Athena took on the role of the insensitive chatterbox, trying to make Bethany laugh. Cross marveled at how skillful she was, affectedly irritating and boring, as if the autistic behavior of her child was perfectly natural, treating Bethany as a fellow gossip though the girl never answered. It was an inspired monologue she created to ease her own pain.

Finally it was time for dessert. Athena unwrapped one of the creamy cakes and offered it to Bethany, who refused it. She offered one to Cross and he shook his head. He was getting very nervous because, though Bethany had consumed an enormous amount of food, it was obvious she was very angry with her mother. He knew that Athena sensed it, too.

Athena ate the pastry and exclaimed enthusiastically about how delicious it was. She unwrapped another two and set them before Bethany. The girl usually loved sweets. Bethany took them off the tablecloth and put them on the grass. In a few minutes they were covered with insects. Then Bethany picked up the two cakes and shoved one into her mouth. She handed the other to Cross. Without a moment's hesitation, Cross put the pastry into his mouth. There was a tickling sensation all across his palate and on the sides of his gums. He quickly gulped some soda to wash it down. Bethany looked at Athena.

Athena had the studied frown of an actress planning to do a difficult scene. Then she laughed, a wonderfully infectious laugh, and clapped her hands. "I told you it was delicious," she said. She unwrapped another pastry, but Bethany refused and so did Cross. Athena threw the pastry onto the grass and then took her napkin and wiped Bethany's mouth and then did the same to Cross. She was enjoying herself, it seemed.

On the drive back to the hospital, she spoke to Cross with some of the same inflections she used with Bethany. As if he, too, were autistic. Bethany watched her carefully and then turned to stare at Cross.

When they dropped the child off at the hospital, Bethany took Cross by the hand for a moment. "You're beautiful," she said, but when Cross tried to kiss her good-bye, she turned her head away. Then she ran.


Driving back to Malibu, Athena said excitedly, "She responded to you, that's a very good sign."

"Because I'm beautiful," Cross said dryly.

"No," Athena said, "because you can eat bugs. I'm at least as beautiful as you are and she hates me . . ." She was smiling joyfully, and as always her beauty made Cross dizzy and alarmed him.

"She thinks you're like her," Athena said. "She thinks you're autistic."

Cross laughed, he enjoyed the idea. "She may be right," he said. "Maybe you should put me in the hospital with her."

"No," Athena said, smiling. "Then I couldn't have your body whenever I wanted it. Besides, I'm going to take her out after I finish *Messalina*."

When they arrived at her Malibu house, Cross went in with her. They had planned for him to spend the night. By this time he had learned to read Athena: The more vivacious she acted, the more disturbed she was.

"If you're upset, I can go back to Vegas," he said.

Now she looked sad. Cross wondered how he loved her most, when she was naturally exuberant, when she was stern and serious, or when she was melancholy. Her face changed so magically in its beauty that he always found his feelings matching hers.

She said to him fondly, "You've had a terrible day and you shall have your reward." There was a mocking tone to her voice, but he understood it was a mockery of her own beauty, she knew her magic was false.

"I didn't have a terrible day," Cross said. And it was true. The joy he felt that day, with the three of them alone by the lake in the vast forest, reminded him of his childhood.

"You love ants on your pastry . . ." Athena said sadly.

"They weren't bad," Cross said. "Can Bethany get better?"

"I don't know but I'll keep searching until I find out," Athena said. "I have a long weekend coming up when they won't need to shoot *Messalina.* I'm going to fly to France with Bethany. There's a great doctor in Paris and I'm going to take her for another evaluation."

"What if he says there's no hope?" Cross said.

"Maybe I won't believe him. It doesn't matter," Athena said. "I love her. I'll take care of her."

"Forever and ever?" Cross asked.

"Yes," Athena said. Then she clapped her hands together, her green eyes shining. "Meanwhile, let's have some fun. Let's take care of ourselves. We'll go upstairs and shower and jump into bed. We'll make mad passionate love for hours. Then I'll cook us a midnight supper."

For Cross, he was a child again waking up with a day of pleasure before him, the breakfast his mother prepared, the playing of games with his friends, the hunting trips with his father, then supper with his family, Claudia, Nalene, and Pippi. The card games afterward. It was that innocent a feeling. Before him was making love to Athena in the twilight, watching the sun disappear over the Pacific from the balcony, the sky painted with marvelous reds and pinks, the touch of her warm flesh and silky skin. Her beautiful face and lips to kiss. He smiled and led her up the stairs.

The phone in the bedroom rang, and Athena ran up ahead of Cross to answer it. She covered the mouthpiece and in a startled voice said, "It's for you. A man named Giorgio." He had never received a phone call at her house before.

This could only be trouble, Cross thought, and so he did something he never thought he was capable of doing. He shook his head.

Athena said into the phone, "He's not here. . . . Yes, I'll tell him to call you when he comes." She hung up the phone and asked, "Who's Giorgio?"

"Just a relative," Cross said. He was stunned by what he had done, and why: because he could not give up a night with Athena. That was a grievous crime. And then he wondered how Giorgio knew he would be here and what Giorgio wanted. It must be something important, he thought, but still it could wait until morning. More than anything else he was desperate for the hours of making love to Athena.

It was the moment they'd been waiting for all day, all week; they were stripping off their clothes before showering together but he couldn't resist embracing her, their bodies still sweaty from the picnic. Then she took his hand and led him under the spraying water.

They dried each other with the large orange towels and, wrapped in them, stood on the balcony to watch the sun slide gradually behind the horizon. Then they went inside to lay on the bed.

When Cross made love to her, it seemed that all the cells of his brain and body flew out and he was left in some feverish dream; he was a ghost whose wisps were filled with ecstasy, a ghost who entered her flesh. He lost all his caution, all his reason, he didn't even study her face to see if she was acting, if she truly loved him. It seemed to go on forever, until they fell asleep in each other's arms. When they woke they were still entwined, lit by a moon whose light seemed brighter than the sun's. Athena kissed him and said, "Did you really like Bethany?"

"Yes," Cross said. "She's part of you."

"Do you think she can get better?" Athena asked. "Do you think I can help her get better?"

At that moment Cross felt as though he would give up his life to make the girl well. He felt the urge to sacrifice for the woman he loved, which many men feel but which until that time had been completely alien to him.

"We can both try to help," Cross said.

"No," Athena said, "I have to do it by myself."

They fell asleep again, and when the phone rang the air was misty with the newly born dawn. Athena picked up the phone, listened, and then said to Cross, "It's the guard at the gate. He says four men in a car want to come and see you."

Cross felt a shock of fear. He took the phone and said to the guard, "Put one of them on the phone."

The voice he heard was Vincent's. "Cross, Petie is with me. We got some really bad news."

"OK, put the guard on," Cross said, and then, to the guard, "They can come in."

He had completely forgotten about Giorgio's call. That's what love does, he thought contemptuously. I won't live a year if I keep this up.

He slipped on his clothes quickly and ran downstairs. The car was just pulling up to the front of the house, the sun, still half hidden, threw its light from over the horizon.

Vincent and Petie were getting out of the back of a long limousine. Cross could see the driver and another man in front. Petie and Vincent walked the long garden path to the door and Cross opened it for them.

Suddenly Athena was standing beside him, clad in slacks and a pullover, nothing beneath. Petie and Vincent were staring at her. She had never looked more beautiful.

Athena led them all into the kitchen and started making coffee, and Cross introduced them as his cousins.

"How did you guys get here?" Cross asked. "Last night you were in New York."

"Giorgio chartered us a plane," Petie said.

Athena was studying them as she made the coffee. Neither of them showed any emotion. They looked like brothers, both were big men, but Vincent was pale as granite, while Petie's leaner face was tanned red with weather or drink.

"So what's the bad news?" Cross said. He expected to hear that the Don had died, that Rose Marie had really gone crazy, or that Dante had done something so terrible that the Family was in crisis.

Vincent said with his usual curtness, "We have to talk to you alone."

Athena poured them coffee. "I tell you all my bad news," she said to Cross. "I should hear yours."

"I'll just leave with them," Cross said.

"Don't you be so fucking condescending," Athena said. "Don't you dare leave."

At this Vincent and Petie reacted. Vincent's granite face flushed with embarrassment, Petie gave Athena a speculative grin, as if she was someone to be watched. Cross, seeing this, laughed and said, "OK, let's hear it."

Petie tried to soften the blow. "Something happened to your father," he said.

Vincent broke in savagely, "Pippi got shot by some punk eggplant mugger. He's dead. So is the mugger, a cop named Losey shot him as he was running away. They need you in L.A. to identify the body and do the paperwork. The old man wants him buried in Quogue."

Cross lost his breath. He wavered for a moment, trembling in some dark wind, then he felt Athena holding his arm with both her hands.

"When?" Cross asked.

"About eight last night," Petie said. "Giorgio called for you."

Cross thought, While I was making love, my father was lying in the morgue. He felt an extraordinary contempt for his moment of weakness, an overwhelming shame. "I have to go," he said to Athena.

She looked at his stricken face. She had never seen him so.

"I'm sorry," she said. "Call me."

· · ·

In the backseat of the limousine, Cross heard the other two men offering condolences. He recognized them as soldiers from the Bronx Enclave. As they moved through the Malibu Colony gate and then onto the Pacific Coast Highway, Cross detected a sluggishness of movement. The car they were riding in was armored.

Five days later the funeral of Pippi De Lena was held in Quogue. The Don's estate held its own private cemetery as the mansion held its own private chapel, and Pippi was buried in the grave next to Silvio, to show the Don's respect.

Only the Clericuzio clan and the most valued soldiers of the Bronx Enclave attended. Lia Vazzi came from the Hunting Lodge in the Sierras at the request of Cross. Rose Marie was not present. On hearing of Pippi's death, she had one of her fits and was taken to the psychiatric clinic.

But Claudia De Lena was there. She flew in to comfort Cross and to say good-bye to her father. What she had not been able to do when Pippi was alive, she felt she must do after his death. She wanted to claim a part of him for herself, to show the Clericuzio that he was as much her father as he was part of their Family.

The lawn in front of the Clericuzio mansion was decorated with a huge floral wreath the size of a billboard, and there were buffet tables and waiters and a bartender at a makeshift table to serve the guests. It was strictly a day of mourning, and no Family business was discussed.

Claudia cried bitter tears for all the years she'd been forced to live without her father, but Cross received condolences with a quiet dignity and showed no signs of grief.

The next night he was on the balcony of his suite in the Xanadu Hotel watching the riot of colors on the neoned Strip. Even this far up he could hear the sounds of music, the buzz of gamblers crowding the Strip looking for a lucky casino. But it was quiet enough for him to analyze what had happened in the last month. And to reflect on the death of his father.

Cross did not believe for a moment that Pippi De Lena had been shot down by a punk mugger. It was impossible for a Qualified Man to meet such a fate.

He reviewed all the facts he had been told. His father had been shot by a black mugger named Hugh Marlowe. The mugger was twenty-three years old, with a record as a drug dealer. Marlowe had been killed while fleeing the scene by Detective Jim Losey, who had been trailing Marlowe in a drug case. Marlowe had a gun in his hand and pointed it at Losey who had therefore shot him down, a clean shot through the bridge of his nose. When Losey investigated, he discovered Pippi De Lena, and immediately called Dante Clericuzio. Before he notified even the police. Why would he do so even if he was on the Family payroll? A great irony—Pippi De Lena, the ultimate Qualified Man, the Clericuzio Number One Hammer for over thirty years, murdered by a raggedy drug-dealing mugger.

But then why had the Don sent Vincent and Petie to transport him with an armored car and guarded him until the funeral? Why had the Don taken such elaborate precautions? During the funeral he had asked the Don. But the Don said only that it was wise to be prepared until all the facts were known. That he had made a full investigation and it seemed all the facts were true. A petty thief had made a mistake and a foolish tragedy had ensued, but then, the Don said, most tragedies were foolish.

There was no doubting the Don's grief. He had always treated Pippi as one of his sons, had indeed given him some preference, and had said to Cross, "You shall have your father's place in the Family."

But now Cross on his balcony overlooking Vegas pondered the central issue. The Don never believed in coincidence and yet here was a case bursting with coincidence. Detective Jim Losey was on the Family payroll and out of the thousands of detectives and policemen in Los Angeles, it was he who stumbled on the killing. What were the odds on that? But put that aside. Even more important, Don Domenico Clericuzio well knew it was impossible for a street mugger to get that close to Pippi De Lena. And what mugger fired six shots before fleeing? Never would the Don believe such a case.

So the question came. Had the Clericuzio decided that their greatest soldier was a danger to them? For what reason? Could they disregard his loyalty and devotion as well as their own affection for him? No, they were innocent. And the strongest evidence in their favor was that Cross himself was still alive. The Don would never allow that if they had killed Pippi. But Cross knew that he himself must be in danger.

Cross thought about his father. He had truly loved him, and Pippi was hurt that Claudia had refused to speak to him while he was alive. Yet she went to the funeral. Why? Could it be that she had finally remembered how good he was to both of them before their family fell apart?

He thought of that terrible day when he had chosen to go with his father because he realized what his father really was, knew that he could really kill Nalene if she took both children. But he had stepped up and taken his father's hand, not because of love but because of the fear in Claudia's eyes.

Cross had always thought his father was protection against the world they lived in, always thought his father invulnerable. A giver of death, not a receiver. Now he himself would have to guard against his enemies, even perhaps the Clericuzio. After all, he was rich, he owned half a billion worth of the Xanadu, his life was now worth taking.

And that made him think of the life he was now leading. To what purpose? To grow old like his father, taking all risks and then still to be killed? True, Pippi had enjoyed his life, the power, the money, but now to Cross it seemed to have been an empty life. His father had never known the happiness of loving a woman like Athena.

He was only twenty-six years old; he could make a new life. He thought of Athena and that he would see her tomorrow working for the first time, observe her make-believe life and see all the masks she could wear. How Pippi would have loved her, he loved all beautiful women. But then he thought of the wife of Virginio Ballazzo. Pippi had been fond of her, eaten at her table, hugged her, danced with her, played boccie with her husband, then planned the killing of them both.

He sighed and rose to go back into his suite. Dawn was breaking, and its light misted the neon that hung like a great theater curtain over the Strip. He could look down and see the flags of all the great casino hotels, the Sands, Caesars, the Flamingo, the Desert Inn, and the shooting volcano of the Mirage. The Xanadu was greater than them all. He watched the flags flying over the Xanadu Villas. What a dream he had lived in, and now it was dissolving, Gronevelt dead and his father murdered.

Back in his room he picked up the phone and called Lia Vazzi to come up and have breakfast with him. They had traveled from the funeral in Quogue to Vegas together. Then he called for breakfast for both of them. He remembered that Lia was fond of pancakes, an exotic dish to him still after all his years in America. The security guard arrived with Vazzi the same time as breakfast did. They ate in the kitchen of the suite.

"So what do you think?" Cross asked Lia.

"I think we should kill this detective Losey," Lia said. "I told you that a long time ago."

"So you don't believe his story?" Cross asked.

Lia was cutting his pancakes into strips. "It's a disgrace, that story," he said. "There is no way a Qualified Man like your father would let a rascal get that close to him."

"The Don thinks it's true," Cross said. "He investigated."

Lia reached for one of the Havana cigars and the glass of brandy Cross had set out for him. "I would never contradict Don Clericuzio," he said. "But let me kill Losey just to make sure."

"And what if the Clericuzio were behind him?" Cross asked.

"The Don is a man of honor," Lia said. "From the old days. If he killed Pippi, he would have killed you. He knows you. He understands you will avenge your father and he is a prudent man."

"But still," Cross said, "who would you choose to fight for? Me or the Clericuzio?"

"I don't have a choice," Lia said. "I was too close to your father and I'm too close to you. They won't let me live if you go down."

Cross for the first time had brandy with Lia for breakfast. "Maybe it's just one of those foolish things," he said.

"No," Lia said. "It's Losey."

"But he has no reason," Cross said. "Still, we'll have to find out. Now I want you to form a crew of six men, those most loyal to you, none from the Bronx Enclave. Have them ready and wait for my orders."

Lia was unusually sober. "Forgive me," he said. "I have never questioned your orders. But on this I beg you to consult with me on the overall plan."

"Good," Cross said. "Next weekend I plan to fly to France for two days. Meanwhile find out all you can about Losey."

Lia smiled at Cross. "You're going with your fiancée?"

Cross was amused by his politeness. "Yes, and with her daughter."

"The one with the quarter of her brain missing?" Lia asked. He did not mean to be offensive. It was an idiom in Italian that also included brilliant people who were forgetful.

"Yes," Cross said. "There is a doctor there who may help her."

"Bravo," Lia said. "I wish you all the best. This woman, does she know about Family matters?"

"God forbid," Cross said, and they both laughed. And Cross was wondering how Lia knew so much about his private life.

# CHAPTER 17

FOR THE FIRST TIME Cross was going to watch Athena work on a movie set, to see her act out false emotions, to be someone other than herself.

He met Claudia in her office at the LoddStone lot, they would watch Athena together. There were two other women in the office, and Claudia introduced them. "This is my brother Cross and this is the director, Dita Tommey. And Falene Fante, who is working today in the picture."

Tommey gave him a searching look, thinking he was handsome enough to be in the business except that he showed no fire, no passion, he would be stone cold dead on the screen. She lost interest. "I'm just leaving," she said as she shook his hand. "I'm very sorry about your father. By the way, you're welcome on my set, Claudia and Athena vouch for you even though you're one of the producers."

Cross became aware of the other woman. She was sort of dark chocolate with an outrageously insolent face and a terrific body, which her clothes flaunted. Falene was far less formal than Tommey.

"I didn't know Claudia had such a handsome brother—and rich, too, from what I hear. If you ever need somebody to keep you company at dinner, give me a call," Falene said.

"I will," Cross said. He was not surprised by the invitation. Plenty of the showgirls and dancers at the Xanadu had been just as direct. This was a girl who was naturally flirtatious, aware of her beauty, and not about to let a man she liked the looks of escape because of social rules.

Claudia said, "We were just giving Falene a little more to do in the film. Dita thinks she's talented and so do I."

Falene gave Cross a big grin. "Yeah, now I shake my ass ten times instead of six. And I get to say to Messalina, 'All the women of Rome love you and hope for your victory.' " She paused for a minute and said, "I hear you're one of the producers. Maybe you can get them to let me shake my ass twenty times."

Cross sensed something in her, something she was trying to hide, despite her vivaciousness.

"I'm just one of the money men," Cross said. "Everybody has to shake their ass at some time or another." He smiled and said with charming simplicity, "Anyway, I wish you luck."

Falene leaned over and kissed him on the cheek. He could smell her perfume, which was heavy and erotic, and then he felt the grateful hug for his goodwill. Then she leaned back. "I have to tell you and Claudia something but in secret. I don't want to get into trouble, especially now."

Claudia, sitting at her computer, frowned and did not answer. Cross took a step away from Falene. He did not like surprises.

Falene noticed these responses. Her voice faltered a little. "I'm sorry about your father," she said. "But there's something you should hear about. Marlowe, the guy who supposedly mugged him, was a kid I grew up with and I knew him really well. Supposedly that detective Jim Losey shot Marlowe who supposedly shot your father. But I know Marlowe never had a gun. He was scared shitless of guns. Marlowe did small-time drugs and played the clarinet. And he was such a sweet coward. Jim Losey and his partner, Phil Sharkey, used to pick him up sometimes and ride him around so that he could spot dealers for them. Marlowe was so scared of jail, he was a police informant. All of a sudden he's a mugger and a murderer. I know Marlowe, he wouldn't harm a soul."

Claudia was silent. Falene waved to her and went out the door, then came back. "Remember," she said, "it's a secret between us."

"It's all gone and forgotten," Cross said with his most reassuring smile. "And your story won't change anything."

"I just had to get it off my chest," Falene said. "Marlowe was such a good kid." She left.

"What do you think?" Claudia said to Cross. "What the hell could that be about?"

Cross shrugged. "Druggies are always full of surprises. He needed dope money and he does a stickup and he gets unlucky."

"I guess," Claudia said. "And Falene is so good-hearted she'll believe anything. But it is an irony, our father dying like that."

Cross looked at her stone-faced. "Everybody gets unlucky once."

He spent the rest of the afternoon watching scenes being shot. One scene showed the hero, unarmed, defeating three armed men. This offended him, it was ridiculous. A hero should never be put in such a hopeless position. All it proved was that he was too dumb to be a hero. Then he watched Athena do a love scene and a quarrel scene. He was a little disappointed, she seemed to do little acting, the other actors seemed to outshine her. Cross was too inexperienced to know that what Athena was doing would register much more forcefully on film, that the camera would work its magic for her.

And he did not discover the real Athena. The acting she did was only for a few short snippets of time, and then there were long intervals in between. You could not see any of the electricity that would flash across the screen. Athena even seemed less beautiful when she was acting before the camera.

He said nothing of this when he spent the night with her that night in Malibu. After they had made love and she was cooking their midnight supper, she said, "I wasn't very good today, was I?" She gave him her catlike grin, which always sent a shock of pleasure through him. "I didn't want to show you my best moves," she said. "I knew you'd be standing there trying to figure me out."

He laughed. Always he was delighted by her perception of his character. "No, you weren't much," he said. "Would you like me to fly with you to Paris Friday?"

Athena was surprised. He knew she was surprised by her eyes. Her face never changed, she was in control. She thought it over. "That could be a big help," she said. "And we could see Paris together."

"And we'll be back Monday," Cross asked.

"Yes," Athena said. "I have to shoot Tuesday morning. We have only a few weeks to go on the picture."

"And then?" Cross asked.

"Then I'll retire and take care of my daughter," Athena said. "Besides, I don't want to keep her a secret much longer."

"The doctor in Paris is the final word?" Cross asked.

"Nobody's the final word," Athena said. "Not on this stuff. But he's close."

On Friday evening they flew to Paris on a specially chartered plane. Athena was disguised in a wig, and her makeup veiled her beauty in such a way as to make her even look homely. She wore loosely fitting clothing that hid her figure entirely and in some ways made her look matronly. Cross was amazed. She even walked differently.

On the plane Bethany was fascinated to find herself looking down on the earth. She roamed the plane looking out all the different windows. She seemed a little startled, her usually blank expression became almost normal.

They went from the plane to a small hotel off Georges-Mandel Avenue. They had a suite with two separate bedrooms, one for Cross and one for Athena and Bethany, the sitting room between them. It was ten in the morning; Athena removed her wig and makeup and changed her clothes. She could not bear to be homely in Paris.

At noon the three of them were in the doctor's office, a small chateau set on its own grounds and enclosed by an iron fence. There was a guard at the gate, and after checking their names he let them in.

They were met at the door by a maid who led them into a huge sitting room, which was densely furnished. There the doctor awaited them.

Dr. Ocell Gerard was a huge, heavy man, carefully dressed in a beautifully cut suit of brown pin stripes, a white shirt, and a dark brown silk tie to match. He had a round face, which should have had a beard to hide his heavy jowls. His thick lips were a dusky red. He introduced himself to Athena and Cross but ignored the child. Both Athena and Cross felt an immediate aversion to the man. He did not look like a doctor suitable to the sensitive profession he practiced.

There was a table set for tea and pastries. A maid attended to them. They were joined by two nurses, young women clad in strict professional attire, white caps and ivory-colored blouses and skirts. The two nurses watched Bethany intensely all during the meal.

Dr. Gerard addressed Athena. "Madame, I would like to thank you for your very generous contribution to our Medical Institute for Autistic Children. I have observed your request for complete confidentiality, which is why I'm conducting this examination here in my own private center. Now tell me exactly what you expect of me." His voice was a mellow bass, it was magnetic. It attracted Bethany's attention, and she stared at him, but he ignored her.

Athena was nervous, she really didn't like the man. "I want you to evaluate. I want her to have some sort of normal life if possible and I will give up everything to achieve that. I want you to accept her into your Institute, I am willing to live in France and help in her schooling."

She said this with enchanting sadness and hope, with such an air of self-abnegation, that the two nurses gazed at her almost adoringly. Cross was aware she was using all her acting skills to convince the doctor to take Bethany into the Institute. He saw her reach her arm out to clasp Bethany's hand with a caressing gesture.

Only Dr. Gerard seemed unimpressed. He did not look at Bethany. He addressed himself directly to Athena. "Do not deceive yourself," he said. "All your love will not help this child. I have examined her records and there is no doubt she is genuinely autistic. She cannot return your love. She does not live in our world. She does not even live in the world of animals. She lives on a different star, absolutely alone."

He continued, "You are not at fault. Nor, I believe, is the father. This is one of those mysterious complexities of the human condition. Here is what I can do. I will examine and test her more thoroughly. Then I will tell you what we at the Institute can and cannot do. If I cannot help, you must take her home. If we can, you will leave her with me in France for five years."

He spoke to one of the nurses in French, and the woman left and returned with a huge book containing photographs of famous paintings. She gave the book to Bethany, but it was too big to fit on her lap. For the first time Dr. Gerard spoke to her. He spoke to her in French. She immediately put the textbook on the table and began to turn the pages. Soon she was lost in studying the pictures.

The doctor seemed ill at ease. "I don't mean to be offensive," he said. "But this is in the best interest of your child. I know Mr. De Lena is not your husband, but is it possible he is the father of your child? If so, I would want to test him."

Athena said, "I did not know him when my daughter was born."

"*Bon,*" the doctor said. He shrugged. "Such things are always possible."

Cross laughed. "Maybe the doctor sees some symptoms in me."

The doctor's thick red lips pursed as he nodded and smiled amiably. "You do have certain symptoms. So do we all. Who knows? A centimeter either way, all of us could be autistic. Now I must make a thorough examination of the child and run some tests. It will take at the very least four hours. Why don't the two of you take a stroll through our lovely Paris. Mr. De Lena, your first time?"

"Yes," Cross said.

Athena said, "I want to remain with my daughter."

"As you wish, madame," he said and then spoke to Cross. "Enjoy your stroll. I detest Paris myself. If a city could be autistic, it would be Paris."

A taxi was called, and Cross went back to the hotel room. He had no desire to see Paris without Athena and he needed rest. Besides, he had come to Paris to clear his head, to think things out.

He pondered what Falene had told him. He remembered that Losey had come to Malibu alone, detectives usually worked in pairs. Before leaving Paris he had asked Vazzi to look into it.

At four, Cross was back in the doctor's sitting room. They were waiting for him. Bethany was poring over the book of paintings, Athena was pale, the only physical sign that Cross knew could not be acting. Bethany was also gobbling a plate of pastries, and the doctor took it away from her, saying something in French. Bethany did not protest. A nurse came then to take her to the playroom.

"Forgive me," the doctor said to Cross. "But I must ask you some questions."

"Whatever you like," Cross said.

The doctor rose from his chair and strode about the room. "I will tell you what I have told madame," the doctor said. "There are no miracles in these cases, absolutely none. With long training there could be enormous improvement, in some cases, not many. And with Mademoiselle, there are certain limits. She must stay in my institution in Nice for five years at least. We have teachers there who can explore every possibility. In that time we will know whether it is possible for her to live a nearly normal life. Or whether she must be institutionalized forever."

Here Athena began to weep. She held a small blue silk handkerchief to her eyes and Cross could smell its perfume.

The doctor looked at her impassively. "Madame has agreed. She will join the Institute as a teacher. . . . So."

He sat directly across from Cross. "There are some very good signs. She has genuine talent as a painter. Certain senses alert, not withdrawn. She was interested when I spoke French, a language she cannot understand but intuits. That is a very good sign. Another good sign: The child showed some signs of missing you this afternoon, she has some feeling for another human being and that may be extended. It is highly unusual, but can be explained in not so mysterious a way. When I explored this with her she said you were beautiful. Now, you must not be offended, Mr. De Lena. I ask this question only for medical reasons to help the child, not accuse you. Have you sexually stimulated the girl in any way, perhaps unintentionally?"

Cross was so startled he burst out laughing. "I didn't know she responded to me. And I never gave her anything to respond to."

Athena's cheeks were red with anger. "This is ridiculous," she said. "He was never alone with her."

The doctor persisted. "Have you at any time given her physical caresses? I don't mean clasping her hand, patting her hair, or even kissing her cheek. The girl is nubile, she would respond simply out of physicality. You would not be the first man tempted by such innocence."

"Maybe she knows about my relationship with her mother," Cross said.

"She doesn't care about her mother," the doctor said. "Forgive me, madame, that is one of the things you must accept—nor her mother's beauty or her fame. They literally do not exist for her. It is you who she extends herself to. Think. Perhaps an innocent tenderness, something inadvertent."

Cross looked at him coolly. "If I did it I would tell you. If that would help her."

"Do you feel tenderness for this girl?" the doctor asked.

Cross considered for a moment. "Yes," he said.

Dr. Gerard leaned back and clasped his hands. "I believe you," he said. "And that gives me great hope. If she can respond to you, she may be helped to respond to others. She may tolerate her mother someday and that will be enough for you, am I right, madame?"

"Oh, Cross," Athena said. "I hope you're not angry."

"It's OK, really," Cross said.

Dr. Gerard looked at him carefully. "You are not offended?" he said. "Most men would be extremely upset. One patient's father actually struck me. But you are not angry. Tell me why."

He could not explain to this man, or even to Athena, how the sight of Bethany in her hugging machine affected him. How it reminded him of Tiffany and all the showgirls he had made love to who had left him feeling empty. How his relationships with all the Clericuzio and even with his father left him with feelings of isolation and despair. And finally how all the victims he had left behind seemed the victims of some ghostly world that became real only in his dreams.

Cross looked the doctor directly in the eye. "Maybe because I'm autistic too," he said. "Or maybe because I have worse crimes to hide."

The doctor leaned back and said in a satisfied voice, "Ah." He paused and smiled for the first time. "Would you like to come in for some tests?" They both laughed.

"Now, madame," Dr. Gerard said. "I understand you catch a plane back to America tomorrow morning. Why not leave your daughter with me now. My nurses are very good, and I can assure you the girl will not miss you."

"But I'll miss her," Athena said. "Could I keep her tonight and bring her back tomorrow morning? We have a chartered plane so I can leave when I like."

"Certainly," the doctor said. "Bring her here in the morning. I will have my nurses escort her down to Nice. You have the phone number of the Institute and you can call me as often as you like."

They got up to go. Athena impetuously kissed the doctor on the cheek. The doctor flushed, he was not insensible to her beauty and fame, despite his ogreish appearance.

Athena, Bethany, and Cross spent the rest of the day strolling the streets of Paris. Athena bought new clothes for Bethany, a full wardrobe. She bought painting supplies and a huge suitcase to hold all the new things. They sent everything to the hotel.

They had dinner in a restaurant on the Champs Elysées. Bethany ate greedily, especially the pastries. She had not spoken a word all day or responded to any of Athena's gestures of affection.

Cross had never seen such a show of love as that Athena showed Bethany. Except when as a child he saw his own mother, Nalene, brushing Claudia's hair.

During dinner Athena held Bethany's hand, brushed the crumbs off her face, and explained that she would return to France in a month to stay with her at the school for the next five years.

Bethany paid no attention.

Athena was enthusiastic when she told Bethany how they could learn French together, go to museums together and see all the great paintings, and how Bethany could spend as much time as she wanted on her own paintings. She described how they would travel all over Europe, to Spain, to Italy, to Germany.

Then Bethany spoke the first words of the day. "I want my machine."

As always Cross was stricken by a sense of holiness. The beautiful girl was like a copy of a great portrait painting but without the soul of the artist, as if her body had been left empty for God.

It was after dark when they walked back to their hotel. Bethany was between them, and they swung her hands so that she lifted up in the air, and for once she allowed it, in fact seemed to delight in it so much that they continued past the hotel.

It was at this moment that Cross had the precise feeling of happiness he had had at the picnic. And it consisted of nothing more than the three of them linked together, holding hands. He was filled with wonder and horror at his sentimentality.

Finally they returned to the hotel. After Athena had helped Bethany to bed, she came into the sitting room of the suite, where Cross was waiting for her. They sat side by side on the lavender sofa holding hands.

"Lovers in Paris," Athena said, smiling at him. "And we never got to sleep together in a French bed."

"Are you worried about leaving Bethany here?" Cross asked.

"No," Athena said. "She won't miss us."

"Five years," Cross said, "is a long time. And you're willing to give up five years and your profession?"

Athena got up from the sofa and walked up and down the room. She spoke passionately. "I glory in being able to do without acting. When I was a kid I dreamed of being a great heroine, Marie Antoinette going to the guillotine, Joan of Arc burning at the stake, Marie Curie saving mankind from some great disease. And of course, also giving up everything for the love of a great man, most ridiculous of all. I dreamed of living a heroic life and knew I'd surely go to Heaven. That I would be pure in mind and body. I detested the idea of doing anything that would compromise me, especially for money. I was determined that under no circumstance would I ever harm another human being. Everyone would love me, including myself. I knew I was smart, everyone told me I was beautiful, and I proved to be not only competent but talented.

"So what did I do? I fell in love with Boz Skannet. I slept with men not out of desire but to further my career. I gave life to a human being who may never love me or anyone. Then I very cleverly maneuver or request the murder of my husband. Not so subtly I ask who will murder this husband of mine who is such a threat to me now." She pressed his hand. "And for this I thank you."

Cross said to reassure her, "You didn't do any of those things. It was just your destiny, as we say in my family. As for Skannet, he was a stone in your shoe, another family saying, so why shouldn't you get rid of him?"

Athena kissed him briefly on the lips. "Now I have," she said. "My knight errant. The only trouble is you don't stop at killing dragons."

"After five years, if the doctor says she can't improve, then what?" Cross asked.

"I don't care what anyone says," Athena said. "There's always hope. I'll be with her the rest of my life."

"And you won't miss your work?" he asked.

"Of course I'll miss it, and I'll miss you," Athena said. "But finally I'll do what I believe is right, not just be a heroine in a movie." Her voice was amused. Then she said with a flat tone, "I want her to love me, that's all I want."

They kissed each other good night and went into their separate bedrooms.


The next morning they took Bethany to the doctor's office. Athena had a difficult time saying good-bye to her daughter. She hugged the girl and wept, but Bethany would have none of it. She pushed her mother away and got ready to repulse Cross, but he did not move to embrace her.

Cross was momentarily angry with Athena for being so helpless with her daughter. The doctor, observing this, said to Athena, "When you return, you will need a great deal of training to cope with this child."

"I'll be back as quickly as I can," Athena said.

"You needn't hurry," the doctor said. "She lives in a world where time does not exist."


On the plane back to L.A., Cross and Athena agreed that he would go on to Vegas and not accompany Athena to Malibu. There had only been one terrible moment on the whole trip. For a full half hour Athena had doubled over in her grief, wordlessly crying. Then she became calm.

When they parted Athena said to Cross, "I'm sorry we never got to make love in Paris." But he understood she was being kind. That at this particular time, she was repulsed by the thought of them making love. That like her daughter, she was now separated from the world.

Cross was met at the airport by a big limo driven by a soldier from the Hunting Lodge. Lia Vazzi was in the back. Lia closed the glass partition so that the driver couldn't hear their conversation.

"Detective Losey was up to see me again," he said. "The next time he comes will be his last."

"Be patient," Cross said.

"I know the signs, trust me on this," Lia said. "Something else. A crew from the Bronx Enclave has moved into place in Los Angeles, I don't know by whose orders. I would say you need bodyguards."

"Not yet," Cross said. "You have your six-man crew together?"

"Yes," Lia said. "But they are men who will not act directly against the Clericuzio."

When they got to the Xanadu, Cross found a memo from Andrew Pollard, a complete file on Jim Losey, that made for interesting reading. And a piece of information that could be acted on immediately.

Cross drew a hundred grand from the casino cage, all in C notes. He told Lia they were going to L.A. Lia would be his driver and he wanted no one else with them. He showed him Pollard's memo. They flew to L.A. the next day and rented a car to drive to Santa Monica.

Phil Sharkey was mowing the lawn in front of his house. Cross got out of the car with Lia and identified himself as a friend of Pollard's who was in need of information. Lia carefully studied Sharkey's face. Then he went back to the car.

Phil Sharkey was not as impressive-looking as Jim Losey, but he looked tough enough. He also looked as if his years of police work had burned out his confidence in his fellow human beings. He had that alert suspiciousness, that seriousness of manner, that the best cops have. But he was obviously not a happy man.

Sharkey ushered Cross into his house, which was really a bungalow, the insides dreary and worn; it had the forlorn look of a womanless and childless dwelling. The first thing Sharkey did was call Pollard and confirm the identity of his visitor. Then without offering any courtesy, a seat, or a drink, he said to Cross, "Go ahead, ask."

Cross opened his briefcase and took out a packet of hundreds. "There's ten grand," he said. "That's just for letting me talk. But it will take a little time. How about a beer and a place to sit?"

Sharkey's face broke into a grin. It was curiously affable, the good cop in the partnership, Cross thought.

Sharkey shoved the money casually into his trouser pocket. "I like you," Sharkey said. "You're smart. You know it's money that talks, not bullshit."

They sat at a little round table on the back porch of the bungalow, which overlooked Ocean Avenue to the sandy beach and water beyond, as they drank their beers out of the bottle. Sharkey patted his pocket to make sure the money was still there.

Cross said, "If I hear the right answers, there's another twenty grand for you right after. Then, if you keep your mouth shut about me being here, I'll come around to see you in two months with another fifty grand."

Sharkey gave his grin, but now there was a hint of mischief in it. "In two months you won't care who I tell, is that it?"

"Yes," Cross said.

Sharkey was serious now. "I'm not telling you anything that gets anybody indicted."

"Hey, then you don't know who I really am," Cross said. "Maybe you better call Pollard again."

Sharkey said curtly, "I know who you are. Jim Losey told me I should always treat you right. All the way." And then he put on his sympathetic listening style that was part of his profession.

Cross said, "You and Jim Losey were partners for the last ten years and you were both making good money on the side. And then you retired. I'd like to know why."

"So, it's Jim you're after," Sharkey said. "That's very dangerous. He was the bravest and the smartest cop I ever knew."

"How about honest?" Cross asked.

"We were cops, and in Los Angeles," Sharkey said. "Do you know what the fuck that means? If we do our real job and kick the shit out of the spics and blacks, we could get indicted and lose our jobs. The only ones we could arrest without getting into trouble were the white schmucks who had money. Look, I got no prejudice, but why should I throw white guys in jail when I can't throw the other kind in jail? That's not right."

"But I understand Jim got a chest full of medals," Cross said. "You got some too."

Sharkey gave him a dismissive shrug. "You can't help being a hero cop in this town if you have just a little bit of balls. A lot of those guys didn't know they could do business if they talked nice. And some of them were out-and-out killers. So we had to defend ourselves and we got some medals. Believe me, we never looked for a fight."

Cross was doubting everything Sharkey was saying. Jim Losey was a natural-born strong-arm guy despite his fancy clothes.

"Were you two partners in everything?" Cross asked. "Did you know everything that was going on."

Sharkey laughed. "Jim Losey? He was the boss always. Sometimes I didn't even know exactly what we were doing. I didn't even know how much we were getting paid. Jim handled all that and he gave me what he said was my fair share." He paused a moment. "He had his own rules."

"So how did you make money?" Cross asked.

"We were on the pad for some of the big gambling syndicates," Sharkey said. "Sometimes a payoff for the drug guys. There was a time when Jim Losey wouldn't take drug money but then every cop in the world started taking it, so we did."

"Did you and Losey ever use a black kid named Marlowe to finger big shot drug dealers?" Cross asked.

"Sure," Sharkey said. "Marlowe. A nice kid scared of his own shadow. We used him all the time."

Cross said, "So when you heard Losey shot him running away from a mug-murder, you were surprised?" Cross asked.

"Hell, no," Sharkey said. "Druggies graduate. But they are so fucked up, they always botch it. And Jim, in that situation, never gives the warning we're taught to give. He just shoots."

"But wasn't it a strange coincidence," Cross said, "their paths crossing like that?"

For the first time Sharkey's face seemed to lose its toughness, grow sad. "It's fishy," he said. "The whole thing is fishy. But now I guess I have to give you something. Jim Losey was brave, women loved him and men held him in high regard. I was his partner and I felt the same way. But the truth is he was always a fishy guy."

"So it could have been some sort of setup," Cross said.

"No, no," Sharkey said. "You have to understand. The job makes you take graft. But it doesn't make you a hit man. Jim Losey would never do that. I'll never believe that."

"So why did you take your retirement after that?" Cross asked.

"It was just that Jim was getting me nervous," Sharkey said.

"I met Losey out at Malibu not long ago," Cross said. "He was alone. Does he often operate without you?"

Now Sharkey gave his grin again. "Sometimes," he said. "That particular time he went to take a shot at the actress. You'd be surprised how often he made a score with big stars in that business. Sometimes he had lunches with people and he didn't want me around."

"One other thing," Cross said. "Was Jim Losey a racist? Did he hate blacks?"

Sharkey gave him a look of amused astonishment. "Of course he did. You're one of those bullshit liberals, right? You think that's terrible? Just go out and put a year in on the job. You'll vote to put them all in the zoo."

"I have another question," Cross said. "You ever see him with a short guy wearing a funny hat?"

"An Italian guy," Sharkey said. "We had lunch and then Jim told me to get lost. Spooky guy."

Cross reached into his briefcase and took out another two packets of money. "Here's twenty grand," he said. "And remember, you keep your mouth shut and you get another fifty grand. OK?"

"I know who you are," Sharkey said.

"Sure you do," Cross said. "I instructed Pollard to tell you who I am."

"I know who you really are," Sharkey said with his infectious grin. "That's why I don't take your whole briefcase right now. And why I'll keep quiet for two months. Between you and Losey, I don't know who'll kill me faster."


Cross De Lena realized he had enormous problems. He knew Jim Losey was on the Clericuzio Family "pad." That he received fifty thousand a year as a salary, and bonuses for special jobs, but none of these had included murder. It was enough for Cross to make a final judgment. Dante and Losey had killed his father. It was an easy judgment for him to make, he was not bound by the legal laws of evidence. And his whole training with the Clericuzio helped him make the verdict of guilty. He knew his father's competence and character. No mugger could get close to him. He also knew Dante's character and competence and Dante's dislike for his father.

The big question was this: Had Dante acted on his own or had the Don commanded the killing? But the Clericuzio had no reason; his father had been loyal for over forty years and an important factor in the Family ascension. He had been the great general in the war against the Santadio. And Cross wondered, not for the first time, why no one had ever told him the details of that war, not his father, not Gronevelt, not Giorgio or Petie or Vincent.

The more he thought about it, the more Cross was sure of one thing: The Don had no hand in the killing of his father. Don Domenico was a very conservative man of business. He rewarded loyal service, he did not punish it. He was extremely fair-minded, to the point of cruelty. But the clinching argument was this: He would never have let Cross live if he had killed Pippi. That was the proof of the Don's innocence.

Don Domenico believed in God, he sometimes believed in Fate, but he did not believe in coincidence. The coincidence of Jim Losey being the cop who shot the mugger who shot Pippi would be absolutely rejected by the Don. He had surely made his own investigation and discovered Dante's connection with Losey. And he would not only know Dante's guilt but his motive.

And what about Rose Marie, Dante's mother? What did she know? When she had heard of Pippi's death, she had had her most serious fit, screaming unintelligibly, weeping incessantly, so that the Don had sent her to the East Hampton psychiatric clinic he had funded many years ago. She would be there for at least a month.

Visitors to Rose Marie in the clinic had always been forbidden by the Don, except for Dante, Giorgio, Vincent, and Petie. But Cross often sent flowers and baskets of fruit. So what the hell was Rose Marie so upset about? Did she know about Dante's guilt, understand his motive? At that moment Cross thought about the Don saying that Dante would be his heir. That was ominous. Cross decided he would visit Rose Marie at the clinic, despite the Don's interdiction. He would go with flowers, and fruit, and chocolates and cheeses, with true affection, but with the purpose of tricking her into betraying her son.

Two days later, Cross entered the lobby of the psychiatric clinic in East Hampton. There were two guards at the door, and one escorted him to the reception desk.

The woman at the reception desk was middle-aged and well dressed. When he stated his business, she gave him a charming smile and said he would have to wait a half hour because Rose Marie was undergoing a minor medical procedure. She would notify him when it was done.

Cross sat down in the waiting room of the reception area, just off the lobby, where there were tables and soft armchairs. He picked up a copy of a Hollywood magazine. Reading it, he came across an article on Jim Losey, the detective hero of Los Angeles. The article detailed his heroic achievements, capped by his killing the mugger-murderer Marlowe. Cross was amused by two things. That his father was referred to as the owner of a financial service agency and a typical helpless victim of a brutal criminal. And by the tag line of the article, which asserted that if there were more cops like Jim Losey, street crime would be under control.

A nurse tapped him on the shoulder. She was an impressively strong-looking woman, but she said with a pleasant smile, "I'll bring you up."

Cross picked up the box of chocolates and the flowers he had brought and followed her up a short flight of stairs and then down a long corridor spaced by doors. At the last door the nurse used a master key and opened it. She motioned Cross inside and closed the door after him.

Rose Marie, clad in a gray robe, her hair neatly braided, was watching a small TV. When she saw Cross she jumped up from the couch and flew into his arms. She was weeping. Cross kissed her cheek and gave her the chocolates and flowers.

"Oh, you came to see me," she said. "I thought you hated me for what I did to your father."

"You didn't do anything to my father," Cross said, and led her back to the couch. Then he turned off the TV. He kneeled beside the couch. "I was worried about you."

She reached out and stroked his hair. "You were always so beautiful," she said. "I hated that you were your father's son. I was glad to see him dead. But I always knew terrible things would happen. I filled the air and the earth with poison for him. Now you think my father will let this pass?"

"The Don is a just man," Cross said. "He will never blame you."

"He has fooled you as he has tricked everyone else," Rose Marie said. "Never trust him. He betrayed his own daughter, he betrayed his grandson and he betrayed his nephew Pippi. . . . And now he will betray you."

Her voice had risen to a loud pitch and Cross was afraid she would go into one of her fits.

"Quiet down, Aunt Roe," Cross said. "Just tell me what upset you so that you had to come back here." He stared into her eyes and thought how pretty she must have been as a young girl, the innocence still in her eyes.

Rose Marie whispered, "Make them tell you about the Santadio War, then you will understand everything." She looked past Cross and then covered her head with her hands. Cross turned. The door opened. Vincent and Petie were standing there silently. Rose Marie jumped off the couch and ran into the bedroom and slammed the door shut.

Vincent's granite face showed pity and despair. "Jesus Christ," he said. He went to the bedroom door and knocked, then said through it, "Roe, open the door. We're your brothers. We won't hurt you . . ."

Cross said, "What a coincidence to meet you here. I was visiting Rose Marie too."

Vincent never had any time for bullshit. "We're not here to visit. The Don wants to see you in Quogue."

Cross appraised the situation. Obviously the receptionist had called somebody in Quogue. Obviously, it was a planned procedure. And just as obviously, the Don did not want him talking to Rose Marie. That Petie and Vincent had been sent meant that it was not a hit, they would not be so carelessly exposed.

This was confirmed when Vincent said, "Cross, I'll go with you in your car. Petie can go in his." A hit in the Clericuzio Family would never be one on one.

Cross said, "We can't leave Rose Marie like this."

"Sure we can," Petie said. "The nurse will just shoot her up."


Cross tried to make conversation while he drove. "Vincent, you guys sure got here fast."

"Petie drove," Vincent said. "He's a fucking maniac." He paused for a moment and then said in a worried voice, "Cross, you know the rules, how come you visit Rose Marie?"

"Hey," Cross said, "Rose Marie was one of my favorite aunts while I was growing up."

"The Don doesn't like it," Vincent said. "He's very pissed off. He says it's not like Cross. He knows."

"I'll straighten it out," Cross said. "But I was really worried about your sister. How's she doing?"

Vincent sighed. "This time it may be for keeps. You know she was sweet on your old man when she was a kid. Who could figure Pippi being killed would throw her so much?"

Cross caught the false note in Vincent's voice. He knew something. But Cross only said, "My father was always fond of Rose Marie."

"In the past years she wasn't so fond of him," Vincent said. "Especially when she got into one of her fits. You should hear the things she said about him then."

Cross said casually, "You were in the Santadio War. How come you guys never talk about it to me?"

"Because we never talk about operations," Vincent said. "My father taught us it served no purpose. You just go on. There's plenty of trouble in the present to worry about."

"My father was a big hero though, right?" Cross said.

Vincent smiled for just a moment, his stone face almost softened. "Your father was a genius," Vincent said. "He could plan an operation like Napoleon. Nothing ever went wrong when he planned it. Maybe once or twice because of bad luck."

"So he planned the war against the Santadio," Cross said.

"Ask the Don these questions," Vincent said. "Now talk about something else."

"OK," Cross said. "Am I going to be knocked off like my father?"

The usually cold and stone-faced Vincent reacted violently. He grabbed the steering wheel and forced Cross to park on the side of the highway. His voice choked with emotion when he said, "Are you crazy? Do you think the Clericuzio Family would do such a thing? Your father had Clericuzio blood. He was our best soldier, he saved us. The Don loved him as much as any of his sons. Jesus Christ, why do you ask something like that?"

Cross said meekly, "I just got scared, you guys popping up."

"Get back on the road," Vincent said disgustedly. "Your father and me and Giorgio and Petie fought together during really rough times. There is no way we could go against each other. Pippi just got unlucky, a crazy jigaboo mugger."

They rode the rest of the way in silence.

At the mansion in Quogue, there were the usual two guards at the gate and one man sitting on the porch. There did not seem to be any unusual activity.

Don Clericuzio, Giorgio, and Petie were awaiting them in the den of the mansion. On the bar was a box of Havana cigars and a mug filled with twisted black Italian cheroots.

Don Clericuzio sat in one of the huge brown leather armchairs. Cross went to greet him and was surprised when the Don pushed himself up to stand, with an agility that belied his age, and embraced him. After which he motioned Cross to the huge coffee table on which various dishes of cheeses and dried meats were spread.

Cross sensed that the Don was not yet ready to speak. He made himself a sandwich of mozzarella cheese and prosciutto. The prosciutto was thin slabs of dark red meat fringed with very tender white fat. The mozzarella was a white ball so fresh it was still sweating milk. It was tied off on top with a thick salty knob like the knot in a rope. The closest that the Don had ever come to boasting was that he never ate a mozzarella that was more than thirty minutes old.

Vincent and Petie were also helping themselves to food, while Giorgio served as bartender, bringing wine to the Don and soft drinks to the others. The Don only ate the dripping mozzarella, letting it melt inside his mouth. Petie gave him one of the twisted cheroots and lit it for him. What a wonderful stomach the old man had, thought Cross.

Don Clericuzio said abruptly, "Croccifixio, whatever you seek now from Rose Marie, I will tell you. And you suspect something amiss about your father's death. You are wrong. I have had inquiries made, the story is true as it stands. Pippi was unlucky. He was the most prudent of men in his profession but such ludicrous accidents happen. Let me set your mind at rest. Your father was my nephew and a Clericuzio, and one of my dearest friends."

"Tell me about the war with the Santadio," Cross said.

# BOOK VII

## The Santadio War

# CHAPTER 18

"IT IS DANGEROUS to be reasonable with stupid people," Don Clericuzio said, as he sipped from his wine glass. He put his cheroot aside. "Pay strict attention. It's a long story and everything was not what it seemed to be. It was almost thirty years ago . . ." He motioned to his three sons and said, "If I forget something important, help me." His three sons smiled at the idea that he would forget something important.

The light in the den was a soft golden haze tinged with cigar smoke, and even the smell of the food was so sharply aromatic that it seemed to affect the light.

"I became convinced of that after the Santadio . . ." He paused a moment to sip his wine. "There was a time when the Santadio were our equal in power. But the Santadio made too many enemies, they drew too much attention from the authorities and they had no sense of justice. They created a world without any values and a world without any sense of justice cannot continue to exist.

"I proposed many arrangements with the Santadio, I made concessions, I wanted to live in a world of peace. But because they were strong, they had a sense of power that violent people have. They believe that power is all. And so it came to war between us."

Giorgio interrupted. "Why does Cross have to know this story? How can it benefit him or benefit us?"

Vincent looked away from Cross, Petie stared at him, his head tilted back, appraising. None of the three sons wanted the Don to tell the story.

"Because we owe it to Pippi and Croccifixio," said the Don. And then he spoke directly to Cross. "Make of this story what you will but I and my sons are innocent of the crime you suspect. Pippi was a son to me, you are to me as a grandchild. All of Clericuzio blood."

Giorgio said again, "This can do all of us no good."

Don Clericuzio waved his arm impatiently, then said to his sons, "It's true, what I've said so far?"

They nodded and Petie said, "We should have wiped them out from the beginning."

The Don shrugged and said to Cross, "My sons were young, your father was young, none of them yet thirty. I didn't want to waste their lives in a great war. Don Santadio, God have mercy on his soul, had six sons but he thought of them more as soldiers than as sons. Jimmy Santadio was the oldest and he worked with our old friend Gronevelt, God have mercy on him as well. The Santadio then had half the Hotel. Jimmy was the best of the lot, the only one who saw that peace was the best solution for all of us. But the old man and his other sons were hot for blood.

"Now it was not to my interest for the war to be bloody. I wanted time to use reason, to convince them of the good sense of my proposals. I would give them all of the drugs, and they would give me all of the gambling. I wanted their half of the Xanadu and in return they would control all drugs in America, a dirty business that required a violent and firm hand. A very sensible proposal. There was far more money in drugs and it was a business that did not involve long-term strategy. A dirty business with a lot of operational work. All this added to the Santadio strength. I wanted the Clericuzio to control all of gambling, not as risky as drugs, not as profitable, but, managed cleverly, more valuable in the long term. And this added to the Clericuzio strength. I always aimed to finally be a member of society, and gambling could become a legal gold mine with none of the everyday risk and dirty work. In this, time has proved me justified.

"Unfortunately, the Santadio wanted everything. Everything. Think of it then, nephew, it was a very dangerous time for us all. By then the FBI knew we Families existed and cooperated with each other. The government, with its resources and technology, brought many Families down. The wall of *omertà* was cracking.

"Young men, born in America, were cooperating with the authorities to save their own skins. Luckily, I established the Bronx Enclave, and brought new people from Sicily to be my soldiers.

"The only thing I have never been able to understand is how women can cause so much trouble. My daughter, Rose Marie, was eighteen years old at this time. How did she become besotted over Jimmy Santadio? She said they were like Romeo and Juliet. Who were Romeo and Juliet? Who in Christ's name were those people? Certainly not Italians. When I was told of this, I reconciled myself. I reopened negotiations with the Santadio Family, I lowered my demands so that the two Families could exist together. In their stupidity, they read this as a sign of weakness. And so began the whole tragedy that has lasted all these years."

Here the Don broke off. Giorgio helped himself to a glass of wine, a slice of bread, and a chunk of the milky cheese. Then he stood behind the Don.

"Why today?" Giorgio asked.

"Because my great nephew here is worried about how his father died and we must dispel any suspicions he may have of us," the Don said.

"I have no suspicions of you, Don Domenico," Cross said.

"Everyone has suspicions of everything," the Don said. "That's human nature. But let me continue. Rose Marie was young, she had no knowledge of worldly affairs. She was heartbroken when at first both Families opposed the match. But she had no real idea why. And so she decided to bring everyone together, she believed love would conquer all, she later informed me. She was very loving then. And she was the light of my life. My wife died young, and I never remarried because I could not bear to share Rose Marie with a stranger. I denied her nothing and I had high hopes for her future. But a marriage with the Santadio, I could not bear. I forbade it. I was young then too. I thought my orders would be obeyed by my children. I wanted her to go to college, marry someone from a different world. Giorgio, Vincent, and Petie had to support me in this life, I needed their help. And I had hopes that their children could also escape to a better world. And my youngest son,

Silvio." The Don pointed to the photograph on the mantelpiece of the den.

Cross had never really taken a close look at the photo, he had not known its history. The photo was of a young man of twenty who looked very much like Rose Marie, only more gentle, his eyes grayer and more intelligent. It was a face that showed such a good soul that Cross wondered if it had been retouched.

The air in the windowless room was becoming more pungent with cigar smoke. Giorgio had lit a huge Havana.

Don Clericuzio said, "I doted on Silvio even more than on Rose Marie. He had a better heart than most people. He had been accepted to the university with a scholarship. There was every hope for him. But he was too innocent."

Vincent said, "He had no street smarts. None of us would have gone. Not like he did, without protection."

Giorgio took up the story. "Rose Marie and Jimmy Santadio were shacked up in this Commack Motel. And Rose Marie came up with the idea that if Jimmy and Silvio talked, they could bring the two Families together. She called Silvio and he went to the motel without telling anybody. The three of them discussed strategies. Silvio always called Rose Marie 'Roe.' His last words to her were, 'Everything is going to be okay, Roe. Dad will listen to me.' "

But Silvio was never to speak to his father. Unfortunately, two of the Santadio brothers, Fonsa and Italo, were doing a guardian-like surveillance on their brother Jimmy.

The Santadio with their violent paranoia suspected that Rose Marie was leading their brother Jimmy into a trap. Or at least luring him into a marriage that would lessen their own power in their Family. And Rose Marie was offensive to them with her ferocious courage and determination to marry their brother. She had even defied her own father, the great Don Clericuzio. She would stop at nothing.

Recognizing Silvio, when he left the motel they trapped him on the Robert Moses Causeway and shot him dead. They stripped him of his wallet and watch to make it look like a robbery. It was typical of the Santadio mentality, their act was one of savagery.

Don Clericuzio was not deceived for a moment. But then Jimmy Santadio came to the wake, unguarded and unarmed. He requested a private audience with the Don.

"Don Clericuzio," he said, "my sorrow is nearly equal to yours. I place my life in your hands if you think the Santadio are responsible. I talked to my father and he gave no such order. And he authorizes me to say to you that he will reconsider all your proposals. He gave me permission to marry your daughter."

Rose Marie had come to hold Jimmy's arm. And there was such a pitiful look on her face that for the moment the Don's heart melted. Sorrow and fear gave her a tragic beauty. Her eyes were startling, so dark and bright with tears. And there was a stunned, uncomprehending look on her face.

She turned from the Don and looked at Jimmy Santadio with such love that Don Clericuzio for one of the few times in his life thought of mercy. How could he bring sorrow to such a beautiful daughter?

Rose Marie said to her father, "Jimmy was so horrified that you might think his family had anything to do with it. I know they didn't. Jimmy promised me that his family would come to an agreement."

Don Clericuzio had already convicted the Santadio Family of the murder. He did not require any proof. But mercy was another matter.

"I believe and accept you," the Don said, and indeed he believed in Jimmy's innocence, though that would make no difference. "Rose Marie, you have my permission to marry but not in this house, nor will any of my family be present. And Jimmy, tell your father that we will sit down together and discuss business after the marriage."

"Thank you," Jimmy Santadio said. "I understand. The wedding will be in our Palm Springs house. In one month all my family will be there and all your family will be invited. If they choose not to come then it's their decision."

The Don was offended. "So quickly after this?" He gestured toward the coffin.

And then Rose Marie collapsed into the Don's arms. He could sense her terror. She whispered to him, "I'm pregnant."

"Ah," the Don said. He smiled at Jimmy Santadio.

Rose Marie whispered again. "I'll name him after Silvio. He'll be just like Silvio."

The Don patted her dark hair and kissed her cheek. "Good," he said. "Good. But I still will not attend the wedding."

Now Rose Marie had recovered her courage. She lifted her face to his and kissed him on the cheek. Then she said, "Dad, somebody has to come. Somebody has to give me away."

The Don turned to Pippi who was standing beside him. "Pippi will represent the Family at the wedding. He's a nephew and he loves to dance. Pippi, you will give your cousin away and then you can all dance to the bottom of the ocean."

Pippi bent to kiss Rose Marie's cheek. "I'll be there," he said with false gallantry, "and if Jimmy doesn't show up, we'll run away together."

Rose Marie gratefully raised her eyes and came into his arms.


A month later Pippi De Lena was on the plane from Vegas to Palm Springs to attend the wedding. That month had been spent with Don Clericuzio in the Quogue mansion, and in meetings with Giorgio, Vincent, and Petie.

The Don clearly instructed that Pippi was to be in charge of the operation. That his orders were to be treated as orders from the Don himself, no matter what the orders might be.

Only Vincent dared to question the Don. "What if the Santadio didn't kill Silvio?"

The Don said, "It doesn't matter, but it reeks of their stupidity, which will endanger us in the future. We will only have to fight them at another time. Of course, they are guilty. Ill will itself is murder. If the Santadio are not guilty then we must agree that Fate itself is against us. Which would you rather believe?"


For the first time in his life, Pippi noted that the Don was distraught. He spent long hours in the chapel in the basement of his house. He ate very little, and drank more wine, which was unusual for him.

And he put Silvio's framed photo in his bedroom for a few days. One Sunday he asked the priest saying Mass to hear his confession.

On the last day, the Don had a meeting with Pippi alone.

"Pippi," the Don said, "this is a very tricky operation. There may be a situation when the question comes up if Jimmy Santadio is to be spared. Do not. But no one is to know this is my order. That deed must be on your head. Not on mine, not Giorgio or Vincent or Petie. Are you willing to take the blame?"

"Yes," Pippi said. "You don't want your daughter to hate you or reproach you. Or her brothers."

"A situation may arise where Rose Marie is at risk," the Don said.

"Yes," Pippi said.

The Don sighed. "Do everything to safeguard my children," he said. "You must make the final decisions. But I never gave you the order to kill Jimmy Santadio."

"And if Rose Marie discovers it was . . ." Pippi asked.

The Don looked directly at Pippi De Lena. "She is my child and the sister of Silvio. She will never betray us."


The Santadio mansion in Palm Springs had forty rooms on just three floors, built in the Spanish style to harmonize with the surrounding desert. It was separated from that enormous field of sand by an encircling wall of redstone. The compound within held not only the house but a huge swimming pool, a tennis court, and a boccie alley.

On this wedding day there was a massive barbecue pit, a platform for the orchestra, and a wooden dance floor, laid over the lawn. This floor was surrounded by long banquet tables. Parked by the huge bronzed gates of the compound were three large catering trucks.

Pippi De Lena arrived early Saturday morning with a suitcase filled with wedding clothes. He was given a room on the second floor, the bright golden light of the desert sun pouring in the windows. He started to unpack.

The church ceremony would be held in Palm Springs only a half hour away. The religious rites would begin about noon. Then the guests would return to the house for the celebration.

There was a knock on the door and Jimmy Santadio came in. His face was shiny with happiness and he gave Pippi a vigorous hug. He was not yet dressed in his wedding clothes and looked very handsome in loose white slacks and a gray-and-silver silk shirt. He held Pippi's hands in his to show his affection.

"It's great you came," Jimmy said, "and Roe is thrilled you're giving her away. Now before everything starts, the old man wants to meet you."

Still holding his hand, he led Pippi down to the first floor and down a long corridor to Don Santadio's room. Don Santadio lay in bed clad in blue cotton nightclothes. He was far more decrepit than Don Clericuzio but he had the same sharp eyes, the alert listening manner; his head was round as a ball and bald. He beckoned Pippi close to him and held out his arms so that Pippi could embrace him.

"How just it is that you came," the old man said, his voice was hoarse. "I count on you to help our two Families embrace each other as we two have done. You are the dove of peace we must have. Bless you. Bless you." He sank back on the bed and closed his eyes. "How happy I am this day."

There was a nurse in the room, a stout middle-aged woman. Jimmy introduced her as a cousin. The nurse whispered that they should leave, the old Don was conserving his strength to join the celebration later in the day. For a moment Pippi reconsidered. It was obvious that Don Santadio did not have long to live. Then Jimmy would become the head of his Family. Perhaps things still could be worked out. But Don Clericuzio could never accept the murder of his son, Silvio; there never could be real peace between the two Families. In any case, the Don had given him strict instructions.

Meanwhile two of the Santadio brothers, Fonsa and Italo, were searching Pippi's room for weapons and communications equipment. Pippi's rental car had also been thoroughly checked.

The Santadio had prepared lavishly for the wedding of their prince. Huge woven baskets filled with exotic flowers were scattered all over the compound. There were colorful pavilions stocked with bar-

tenders pouring champagne. There was a jester in a medieval costume doing magic tricks for the children, and music blasted out of
speakers strung along the compound. Each guest was given a lotto
ticket for a prize of twenty thousand dollars that was to be drawn
later. What could be more splendid?

Huge gaily colored tents had been pitched all over the manicured
lawn to protect the guests from the desert heat. Green tents over the
dance floor, red over the orchestra. Blue tents over the tennis court,
which held the wedding gifts. These included a silver Mercedes for
the bride and a small private plane for the groom, from Don Santadio himself.

The church ceremony was simple and short, and the guests returned to the Santadio compound to find the orchestra playing. Food
counters and three separate bars were put in their own tents, one decorated with scenes of hunters pursuing wild boars, another filled
with highball glasses containing fruity tropical drinks.

The wedding couple danced the first dance in lonely splendor.
They danced in the shade of the tent, the red desert sun peeked into
the corners and bronzed their happiness as they ducked their heads
into the patches of sunlight. They were so obviously in love that the
crowd cheered and clapped. Rose Marie had never looked so beautiful, nor Jimmy Santadio so young.

When the band stopped playing, Jimmy plucked Pippi out of the
crowd and presented him to the more than two hundred guests.

He said, "This is Pippi De Lena who gave the bride away, and he
represents the Clericuzio Family. He is my dearest friend. His
friends are my friends. His enemies are my enemies." He raised his
glass and said, "We all drink to him. And he gets the first dance with
the bride."

As Pippi and Rose Marie danced, she whispered to him, "You'll
bring the Families together, won't you Pippi?"

"It's a cinch," Pippi said, and whirled her around.

Pippi was the marvel of the celebration, never had there been a
more convivial wedding guest. He danced every dance, and was
lighter on his feet than any of the younger men. He danced with
Jimmy and then with the other brothers, Fonsa, Italo, Benedict,

Gino, and Louis. He danced with the children and the matrons. He waltzed with the orchestra leader, and sang with the band, rowdy songs in Sicilian dialect. He ate and drank with such abandon that his tux was spotted with tomato sauce and the fruity juice of the cocktails and the wine. He hurled the boccie balls with such élan that the court became the center of the wedding for an hour.

After boccie, Jimmy Santadio drew Pippi aside. "I'm counting on you to make everything work," he said. "Our two Families together, nothing can stop us. Me and you." It was Jimmy Santadio at his charming best.

Pippi mustered every ounce of sincerity for his answer. "We will. We will." And he wondered if Jimmy Santadio was as honest as he seemed. By now he must know that somebody in his Family had committed the murder.

Jimmy seemed to sense this. "I swear to you, Pippi, I had nothing to do with it." He took Pippi's hand in his. "We had nothing to do with Silvio's death. Nothing. I swear on the head of my father."

"I believe you," Pippi said and pressed Jimmy's hands. He had a moment of doubt, but it didn't matter. It was too late.

The red desert sun faded to twilight, and lights came on all over the compound. This was the signal for a formal dinner to be served. And all the brothers, Fonsa, Italo, Gino, Benedict, and Louis, proposed a toast to the bride and groom. To the happiness of the marriage, to the special virtues of Jimmy, to Pippi De Lena, their great new friend.

Old Don Santadio was too ill to leave his bed but sent his heartiest good wishes in which he mentioned the plane he had given his son, at which everybody cheered. Then the bride herself cut a huge slice of the wedding cake and brought it to the old man's bedroom. But he was asleep, so they gave it to his nurse, who promised to feed it to him when he woke up.

Finally, toward midnight, the party broke. Jimmy and Rose Marie retired to their bridal chamber, saying they would leave on their honeymoon to Europe the next morning and they needed their rest. At which the guests hooted derisively and made vulgar remarks. All in high spirits and good humor.

The hundreds of cars left the compound and sped off into the desert. The catering trucks were packed, the personnel pulled down the tents and assembled the tables and chairs, then pulled up the platform and even hastily policed the grounds to be certain there was no garbage. Finally they were through; they would finish it up the next day.

At Pippi's request, a ceremonial meeting had been arranged with the five Santadio brothers, to be held after the guests had left. They would exchange gifts to celebrate the new friendship of the two Families.

At midnight they gathered together in the huge dining room of the Santadio mansion. Pippi had a suitcase full of Rolex watches (genuine, not knockoffs). There was also a large Japanese kimono studded with hand-painted sexual scenes of Oriental lovemaking.

Fonsa shouted out, "Let's bring it up to Jimmy right now."

"Too late," Italo said cheerily. "Jimmy and Rose Marie are on their third round."

And they all laughed.

Outside, the desert moon isolated the compound in an icy white light. Chinese lanterns hanging on compound walls made red circles in the white moonbeams.

A large truck, the word CATERING limned in gold paint on its side, rumbled up to the gates of the Santadio compound.

One of the two guards approached the truck, and the driver told him they had come back to pick up a forgotten generator.

"This late?" the guard said.

As he spoke the driver's helper got out of the truck and moved toward the other guard. Both guards were sluggish with the food and drink from the wedding.

In one synchronized movement two things happened: The driver reached down between his legs and showed a gun with a silencer, then fired three times directly into the first guard's face. The driver's helper grabbed the other guard in a stranglehold and with a large, sharp knife in one swift motion cut his throat.

They were dead on the ground. The soft hum of a motor sounded as the large metal platform on the rear of the truck quickly descended and twenty soldiers of the Clericuzio sprang out. Stocking masked, dressed in black, armed with silenced guns, led by Giorgio, Petie, and Vincent, they spilled all over the compound. A special crew cut through the telephone lines. Another crew spread out to command the compound. Ten of the masked men with Giorgio, Petie, and Vincent crashed into the dining room.

The Santadio brothers held their wine glasses to toast Pippi, he stepped away from them. No words were spoken. The invaders opened fire and the five Santadio brothers were torn apart by a hail of bullets. One of the masked men, Petie, stood over them and gave all five the coup de grace, a bullet under the chin. The floor glittered with broken glass.

Another masked man, Giorgio, handed Pippi a mask and black trousers and sweater. Pippi quickly changed and threw his discarded clothes into a bag held by another masked invader.

Pippi, still unarmed, led Giorgio, Petie, and Vincent down the long corridor to the bedroom of Don Santadio. He pushed open the door.

Don Santadio had finally woken and was eating the bridal cake. He took one look at the four men, made the sign of the cross, and put a pillow over his face. The dish holding the cake slipped to the floor.

The nurse was reading in the corner of the room. Petie was on her like a great cat, gagging her and then tying her to the chair with thin nylon rope.

It was Giorgio who advanced to the bed. He reached out gently and pulled the pillow from Don Santadio's head. He hesitated a moment and then fired two shots, the first in the eye, the second, lifting up the round bald head, upward from under the chin.

They regrouped. Vincent finally armed Pippi, he handed over a long silver rope.

Pippi led them from the room down the long corridor and then up to the third floor, which held the bridal chamber. The corridor was littered with flowers and baskets of fruit.

Pippi pushed against the bridal chamber door. It was locked. Petie took off one of his gloves and produced a pick. With this he easily opened the door and pushed it back.

Rose Marie and Jimmy were sprawled on the bed. They had just finished making love, and their bodies were almost liquid with released sensuality. Rose Marie's see-through negligee was bunched above her waist, and the straps had slipped down, exposing her breasts. Her right hand was on Jimmy's hair, the left on his stomach. Jimmy was completely naked, but he sprang up as soon as he saw the men and pulled a bedsheet to use as a robe. He understood everything. "Not here, outside," he said, and advanced toward them.

Rose Marie, for a fraction of a second, was still uncomprehending. As Jimmy moved toward the door, she clutched at him but he evaded her. He went through the door surrounded by the masked Giorgio, Petie, and Vincent. And then Rose Marie said, "Pippi, Pippi, please don't." It was only when the three men turned to look at her that she realized that they were her brothers. "Giorgio, Petie, Vincent. Don't. Don't."

This was the most difficult moment for Pippi. If Rose Marie talked, the Clericuzio Family was doomed. His duty was to kill her. The Don had not specifically instructed him on this; how could he condone the killing of his daughter? Would her brothers obey him? And how did she know it was them? He made the decision. He closed the door behind him and was out in the corridor with Jimmy and Rose Marie's three brothers.

Here the Don had been explicit. Jimmy Santadio was to be strangled. It was perhaps the mark of mercy that there should be no penetrations of his body for his loved ones to weep over. It was perhaps from some tradition of not shedding a loved one's blood while consecrating him to death.

Suddenly Jimmy Santadio let the bedsheet drop, and his hands reached out and ripped Pippi's mask from his face. Giorgio grabbed one of his arms, Pippi the other. Vincent dropped to the floor and grabbed Jimmy's legs. Now Pippi had his rope around Jimmy's neck and bent him to the floor. Jimmy had a twisted smile on his lips, curiously pitying as he stared into Pippi's face: that this act would be avenged by Fate or some mysterious God.

Pippi pulled the cord tight, Petie reached to help with the pressure, and they all sank to the floor of the corridor, where the white bedsheet received Jimmy Santadio's body like a shroud. Inside the bridal chamber, Rose Marie began to scream . . .

The Don had finished speaking. He lit up another cheroot and sipped his wine.

Giorgio said, "Pippi planned the whole thing. We got away clean and the Santadio were wiped out. It was brilliant."

Vincent said, "It solved everything. We haven't had any trouble since."

Don Clericuzio sighed. "It was my decision and it was wrong. But how were we to know Rose Marie would go mad? We were in crisis and this was our only opportunity to strike a decisive blow. You must remember that at that time, I was not yet sixty, I thought too much of my power and intelligence. I thought then certainly it would be a tragedy for my daughter but widows do not grieve forever. And they had killed my son Silvio. How could I forgive that, daughter or no daughter? But I learned. You cannot come to a reasonable solution with stupid people. I should have wiped them out at the very beginning. Before the lovers met. I would have saved my son and daughter." He paused for a moment.

"So, you see, Dante is Jimmy Santadio's son. And you, Cross, shared a baby carriage with him when you were infants, your first summer in this house. All those years I have tried to make up to Dante for the loss of his father. I tried to help my daughter recover from her grief. Dante was brought up as a Clericuzio and he will, with my sons, be my heir."

Cross tried to understand what was happening. His whole body quivered with revulsion toward the Clericuzio and the world they lived in. He thought of his father, Pippi, playing the role of Satan, seducing the Santadio to their death. How could such a man be his father? He thought then of his beloved aunt, Rose Marie, living all those years with her heart and her mind broken, knowing that her husband had been murdered by her father and her brothers. That her own family had betrayed her. He even thought of Dante with some pity, now Dante's guilt was established. And then he wondered about the Don. Surely he did not believe the story of Pippi's mugging. Why did he seem to accept it, a man who had never believed in coincidence. What was the message here?

Cross could never read Giorgio. Did he believe in the mugging killing? It was obvious that Vincent and Petie believed it. But now he understood the special bond between his father and the Don and his three sons. They had been soldiers together in the massacre of the Santadio. And his father had spared Rose Marie.

Cross said, "And Rose Marie never talked?"

"No," the Don said, sardonically. "She did even better. She became crazy." There was just a hint of pride in his voice. "I sent her to Sicily and brought her back in time for Dante to be born on American soil. Who knows, someday he might be president of the United States. I had dreams for the little boy but the combination of Clericuzio and Santadio blood was too much for him.

"And you know the most terrible thing?" the Don said. "Your father, Pippi, made a mistake. He should never have spared Rose Marie, though I loved him for it." He sighed. He took a sip of wine and, looking Cross full in the face, he said, "Be aware. The world is what it is. And you are what you are."

On the flight back to Vegas, Cross pondered the riddle. Why had the Don finally told him the story of the Santadio War? To prevent him from visiting Rose Marie and hearing a different version? Or was he warning him off, telling him not to avenge his father's murder because Dante was involved. The Don was a mystery. But of one thing Cross was sure. If it was Dante who killed his father, then Dante must kill him. And surely Don Domenico Clericuzio knew that, too.

# CHAPTER 19

**D**ANTE CLERICUZIO did not have to hear this story. His mother, Rose Marie, had whispered it into his tiny ear from the time he was two years old: whenever she had one of her fits, whenever she felt her grief for the lost love of her husband and her brother Silvio, whenever her terror of Pippi and her brothers overcame her.

It was only when Rose Marie had her worst fits that she accused her father, Don Clericuzio, of the death of her husband. The Don always denied giving the order, as he denied that his sons and Pippi had carried out the massacre. But after she accused him two times, he packed her off to the clinic for a month. After that, she only ranted and raved, and never accused him directly again.

But Dante remembered her whisperings always. As a child he loved his grandfather and believed in his innocence. But he schemed against his three uncles though they always treated him tenderly. Especially, he dreamed of vengeance on Pippi, and though these were fantasies, he thought them for his mother's sake.

When Rose Marie was normal she took care of the widower Don Clericuzio with the utmost affection. To her three brothers she showed sisterly concern. With Pippi, she was distant. And because in those times she had such a sweet visage, it was difficult for her to express malice convincingly. The structure of the bones in her face, the curve of her mouth, and the gentle eyes of liquid brown denied her hate. To her child Dante she showed her overwhelming need to love, which she could no longer feel for any man. She showered him with gifts out of that affection, as did his grandfather and his uncles out of something less pure, a love muddied with guilt. When Rose Marie was normal, she never told Dante the story.

But in her fits she was foul-mouthed, full of curses, even her face could turn into an ugly mask of fury. Dante was always bewildered. When he was seven years old, a doubt entered his mind. "How did you know it was Pippi and my uncles?" he asked her.

Rose Marie cackled with glee. She seemed to Dante a witch out of his fairy-tale books. She told him, "They think they are so clever, that they plan for everything with their masks and special clothes and hats. Do you want to know what they forgot? Pippi was still wearing his dancing shoes. Patent leather and black string bows. And your uncles always grouped themselves together in a particular way. Giorgio always to the front, Vincent a little behind, and Petie always to the right. And the way they looked at Pippi to see if he would give the order to kill me. Because I had recognized them. The way they wavered, almost shrank back. But they would have killed me, they would have. My own brothers." She would then burst into such great weeping that Dante would be terrified.

Even as a small child of seven, he would try to comfort her. "Uncle Petie would never hurt you," he said. "And Grandpa would have killed them all if they did." He wasn't certain of his Uncle Giorgio or even Uncle Vinnie. But in his child's heart, it was Pippi he could never forgive.

By the time Dante was ten years old, he had learned to watch for his mother's fits, and so when she beckoned him to her to tell the Santadio story again, he would quickly take her away into the safety of her bedroom so his grandfather and his uncles would not hear.

By the time Dante grew into manhood, he was too clever to be fooled by all the disguises of the Clericuzio Family. He was of so humorously malicious a nature that he showed his grandfather and his uncles that he knew the truth. And he could perceive that his uncles were not that fond of him. Dante had been designated to join the legal social world, to perhaps take Giorgio's place and learn the financial complexities, but he showed no interest. He had even taunted his uncles that he had no interest in the sissy side of the Family. Giorgio listened to this with a coolness that for a moment frightened the sixteen-year-old Dante.

Uncle Giorgio said, "OK, you won't." There was sadness in his voice and some anger, too.

When Dante quit high school in his senior year, he was sent to work in Petie's construction company in the Bronx Enclave. Dante was a hard worker and developed huge muscles from the hard, grueling work on the building sites. Petie put him on crews of soldiers from the Bronx Enclave. When Dante was old enough, the Don decreed the boy would be a soldier under Petie.

The Don had come to his decision only after reports from Giorgio on Dante's character, and some acts committed by Dante. The young boy was accused of rape by a pretty high school classmate and of assault with a small knife by another fellow student, a boy his own age. Dante had begged his uncles not to let his grandfather know and they had promised him, but of course they had reported to the Don immediately. These charges were settled by large sums of money before Dante could be prosecuted.

And it was during his teenage years that his jealousy of Cross De Lena increased. Cross had grown into a tall, extraordinarily handsome youth with a mature courtesy. All the women in the Clericuzio clan adored him, fussed over him. His female cousins flirted with him, something they never did with the Don's grandson. Dante, wearing his Renaissance hats, with his sly humor and his short and hugely muscular body, was frightening to these young girls. Dante was too clever not to observe all this.

When Dante was taken to the Hunting Lodge in the Sierras, he enjoyed trapping more than shooting. When he fell in love with one of the female cousins, as was perfectly natural in the close-knit Clericuzio clan, he was too direct in his advances. And he was too familiar with the daughters of the Clericuzio soldiers who lived in the Bronx Enclave. Finally Giorgio, who had the role of an instructive, punitive parent, enrolled him with the owner of a New York City high-class bordello to quiet him down.

But Dante's enormous curiosity, his cunning cleverness, made him the only one of his generation of the Clericuzio who really knew what the Family did. So it was finally decided he would be given operational training.

As time went on, Dante felt a growing separation from his Family. The Don was as fond of him as ever and made clear to him that he was an heir to the Empire, but he no longer shared his thoughts with his grandson, no longer gave him his insights, his secret little pearls of wisdom. And the Don did not support Dante's suggestions and ideas on strategy.

His uncles, Giorgio, Vincent, and Petie, were not as warm in their affection as when he was a child. Petie, it was true, seemed more of a friend, but then he had been trained by Petie.

Dante was clever enough to think that maybe the fault was his, because he had betrayed his knowledge of the massacre of the Santadio and his father. He even asked questions of Petie about Jimmy Santadio, and his uncle told him how much they had respected his father and how sad they had been about his death. It was never said openly, never admitted, but Don Clericuzio and his sons understood that Dante knew the true story, that Rose Marie, in her fits, had disclosed the secret. They wanted to make amends, they treated him as a child prince.

But what most formed Dante's character was his pity and love for his mother. In her fits she inflamed in him a hatred for Pippi DeLena; she exonerated her father and brothers.

All these things helped Don Clericuzio make his final decision, for the Don could read his grandson's mind as easily as he could read his prayer book. The Don judged that Dante could never take part in the final retreat to the cloak of society. His Santadio and (the Don was a fair man) Clericuzio blood was too ferocious a mixture. Therefore Dante would join the society of Vincent and Petie, of Giorgio and Pippi De Lena. They would all fight the final battle together.

And Dante proved to be a good soldier, though an irrepressible one. He had an independence that made him flout the Family rules, and indeed he sometimes did not comply with specific orders. His ferocity was useful when a confused *Bruglione* or an undisciplined soldier stepped over the Family line and had to be dispatched to a less complex world. Dante was not subject to control except by the Don himself, and mysteriously the Don refused to chastise him personally.

Dante feared for his mother's future. That future depended on the Don, and as her fits occurred more often, Dante could see the Don becoming more impatient. Especially when Rose Marie would make a grand exit by drawing a circle with her foot and then spitting in the middle while screaming she would never enter the house again. That was when the Don would ship her off to the clinic again for a few days.

So Dante would coax her out of her fits, restore her to her natural sweetness and affection. But there was always the dread that finally he could not protect her. Unless he became as powerful as the Don himself.

The only person in the world Dante feared was the old Don. It was a feeling that came from his experiences with his grandfather as a child. And it sprang, too, from his sense that the sons feared Don Clericuzio as much as they loved him. Which was amazing to Dante. The Don was in his eighties, he no longer had physical strength, he rarely left his mansion, and his height was diminished. Why fear him?

True, he ate well, he made an imposing appearance, the only physical disarray time had done was to soften his teeth so that his diet was reduced to pasta, grated cheese, stewed vegetables, and soups. Meats were simmered to shreds in tomato sauces.

But the old Don had to die soon, so there would be shifts of power. What if Pippi became Giorgio's right-hand man? What if Pippi seized power by sheer force? And if that happened, Cross would ascend, especially since he had acquired so much wealth with his share of the Xanadu.

So there were practical reasons, Dante assured himself, not his hatred of Pippi, who dared to criticize him to his own Family.

Dante had made his original contact with Jim Losey when Giorgio decided that Dante should have some points of power and designated him to deliver Losey's salary from the Family.

Of course precautions had been taken to protect Dante if Losey should ever turn traitor. Contracts were signed that showed Losey to be working for a Family-controlled security corporation as a consultant. The contract specified confidentiality and that Losey be paid in cash. But in the security corporation's tax filings, the money was reported as expenses, with Losey using a corporation dummy as recipient.

Dante had made special payments to Losey over several years before he initiated a more intimate relationship. He was not intimidated by Losey's reputation, he sized him up as a man who was at a juncture where he was thinking of accumulating a very large nest egg for his old age. Losey had a hand in everything. He was protecting drug dealers, taking Clericuzio money to protect gambling, was even dabbling in strong-arming certain high-powered retail merchants into paying extra protection fees.

Dante exerted all his charm to make a good impression on Losey; both his sly and vicious sense of humor and his disregard for accepted moral principles appealed to Losey. Dante reacted particularly well to Losey's bitter tales of his war against the blacks who were destroying Western civilization. Dante himself had no racial prejudices. Blacks had no influence on his life, and if they did they would be mercilessly removed.

Dante and Losey had a powerful common urge. They were both dandies interested in their looks, and they both had a similar sexual drive for the domination of women. Not so much erotic but as an expression of power. They took to spending time together when Dante was in the West. They went to dinner together and cruised the nightclubs. Dante never dared to bring him to Vegas and the Xanadu, and it was not to his purpose.

Dante loved to tell Losey of how he was first the abject extravagant courter of women, and the women were imperious in the power of their beauty. And then how he enjoyed the imperiousness by maneuvering them into a position where they could not escape the unwilling giving of sex. Losey, a little contemptuous of Dante's trick, would tell how he would break women down from the very beginning with his extraordinary macho presence, and then humiliate them.

Both of them declared that they would never force a woman to have sex who did not respond to their courtship. They both agreed that Athena Aquitane would be a grand prize if she ever gave them an opening. When they roved around the L.A. clubs together and picked up women, they would compare notes and laugh at those vain women who thought they could go to the utmost limit and then refuse the final act. Sometimes the protests would be too vehement, and then Losey would show his shield and tell the women he would bust them for prostitution. Since many of them were soft hookers, the threat worked.

They spent evenings of camaraderie, orchestrated by Dante. Losey, when not telling the "nigger" stories, tried to define the varieties of hookers.

There were first the out-and-out prostitutes who held one hand out for money and grabbed your cock with the other. Then there was the soft hooker who was attracted to you and gave you a friendly screw and then, before you left in the morning, asked you for a check to help pay the rent.

Then there was the soft hooker who loved you but loved others too and established a long-term relationship studded with gifts of jewelry for every holiday, including Labor Day. Then there were the freelance nine-to-five secretaries, airline stewardesses, shop clerks in fancy boutiques, who invited you up to their apartment for coffee after an expensive dinner and then tried to throw you out on your ass to freeze in the street without even a hand job. These were their favorites. Sex with them was exciting, fraught with drama, tears, and subdued cries for forbearance and patience, which produced a sex that was better than love.

One night after they had dinner at Le Chinois, a restaurant in Venice, Dante suggested they take a stroll along the boardwalk. They sat on a bench and watched the human traffic go by, beautiful young girls on Rollerblades, pimps of all colors pursuing them and shouting endearments, the soft hookers selling T-shirts decorated with sayings incomprehensible to the two men. Hare Krishnas with begging bowls, bearded groups of singers with guitars, family groups with cameras, and reflecting them, the black ocean of the Pacific, on whose sandy beaches isolated twosomes crouched under blankets they believed disguised their fornication.

"I could lock up everybody here for probable cause," Losey said, laughing. "What a fucking zoo."

"Even those pretty young kids on skates?" Dante asked.

"I'd just bust them for carrying pussies as a dangerous weapon," Losey said.

"Not many eggplants here," Dante said.

Losey stretched out on the beach, and when he spoke it was with a fair imitation of a Southern accent.

"I think I've been too hard on my black brethren," he said. "It's like the liberals always say, it all springs from their having been slaves."

Dante waited for the punch line.

Losey linked his hands behind his head and pulled back his jacket to let his gun holster show to scare off any reckless punks. Nobody paid attention, they had spotted him for a cop by his first step on the boardwalk.

"Slavery," Jim Losey said. "Demoralizing. It was too easy a life for them so it made them too dependent. Freedom was too hard. On the plantations they were taken care of, three meals a day, free rent, they were clothed and they were given good medical attention because they were valuable property. They weren't even responsible for their children. Imagine. The plantation owners fucked their daughters and gave those children jobs for the rest of their lives. Sure they worked but they were always singing, so how hard could they be working? I'll bet five white guys could do the work of a hundred niggers."

Dante was tickled. Was Losey serious? It didn't matter, he was expressing an emotional view not a rational one.

They were enjoying themselves, it was a balmy night, the world they observed gave them a comfortable feeling of security. These people were never a danger to them.

Then Dante said, "I've got a really important proposition to put to you. Do you want the rewards first or the risks first?"

Losey smiled at him. "Rewards first, always."

Dante said, "Two hundred grand cash up front. A year later, a job as head of security at the Xanadu Hotel. With a salary five times what you get now. Expense account. Big car, room, board, and all the pussy you can eat. You get to do all the background checks on the hotel showgirls. Plus bonuses like you make now. And you don't have the risk of being the primary shooter."

"Sounds too good," Losey said. "But somebody has to get shot. That's the risk, right?"

"For me," Dante said. "I'm the shooter."

"Why not me?" Losey asked. "I have the badge to make it legal."

"Because you wouldn't live six months after it," Dante said.

"And what do I do?" Losey asked. "Tickle your ass with a feather?"

Dante explained the whole operation. Losey whistled to express his admiration for the daring of the idea.

"Why Pippi De Lena?" Losey asked.

"Because he's about to turn traitor," Dante said.

Losey was still looking doubtful. It would be the first time he committed the crime of cold-blooded murder. Dante decided to give it something extra.

"You remember that Boz Skannet suicide?" he said. "Cross made that hit, not personally, but with a guy named Lia Vazzi."

"What does he look like?" Losey asked. When Dante had described Vazzi he realized it was the man accompanying Skannet when he had stopped him in the hotel lobby. "Where can I find this Vazzi guy?"

For a long moment Dante considered. He was doing something that broke the only really holy law of the Family. Of the Don. But it might get Cross out of the way, and Cross would be someone to fear after Pippi's death.

"I'll never tell anybody where it came from," Losey said.

Dante for a moment reconsidered, then he said, "Vazzi lives in a hunting lodge my family owns up in the Sierras. But don't do anything until we finish with Pippi."

"Sure," Losey said. He would do what he liked. "And I get my two hundred grand right up front, right?"

"Right," Dante said.

"Sounds good," Losey said. "One thing. If the Clericuzio come after me, I'll sell you down the river."

"Don't worry," Dante said amiably. "If I hear that, I'll kill you first. Now we just have to work out the details."

It all went as they planned.

When Dante fired the six shots into Pippi De Lena's body and when Pippi whispered, calling him a "fucking Santadio," Dante felt an exultation he had never felt before.

# CHAPTER 20

LIA VAZZI, for the first time, deliberately disobeyed the order of his boss, Cross De Lena.

It was unavoidable. Detective Jim Losey had made another visit to the Hunting Lodge and had again asked questions about Skannet's death. Lia denied all knowledge of Skannet and claimed he had just happened to be in the hotel lobby at that particular time. Losey patted him on the shoulder, then lightly slapped him across the face. "OK, you little guinea prick," he said, "I'll get you soon."

In his mind Lia signed a death warrant for Losey. No matter what else happened, and he knew his future was in peril, he would make sure of Losey's fate. But he had to be very careful. The Clericuzio Family had strict rules. You never harmed a police officer.

Lia remembered driving Cross to the meeting with Phil Sharkey, Losey's retired partner. He had never believed that Sharkey would remain quiet on the promise of a future fifty grand. Now he was sure that Sharkey had informed Losey of that meeting and probably had seen Vazzi waiting in the car. If this was true, there would be a great danger to Cross and himself. In essence he distrusted the judgment of Cross, police officers stuck together like Mafioso. They had their own kind of *omertà*.

Lia recruited two of his soldiers to drive him down from the Hunting Lodge to Santa Monica, the home of Phil Sharkey. He was confident that just by talking to Sharkey he would know if the man had informed Losey of the visit by Cross.

The outside of Sharkey's house was deserted, the lawn empty except for an abandoned mower. But the garage door was open, a car in it, and Lia walked up the cement path to the door and rang the bell. There was no answer. He kept ringing. He tested the knob, the door was not locked, now there was a choice to be made. Did he go in or leave immediately? He wiped his prints off the knob and bell with the tail of his tie. Then he went through the door into the small hallway and called Sharkey's name in a shout. There was no answer.

Lia moved through the house; the two bedrooms were bare, he looked into the closets and under the beds. He went through the living room, looking under the sofa and through the cushions. Then he went into the kitchen and to the patio table where there was a container of milk and a paper plate that held a partially eaten cheese sandwich, white bread with dehydrated yellow mayo on the edges.

There was a slatted brown door in the kitchen, and Lia opened it to reveal a shallow basement only two wooden steps down, sort of a dropped room with no windows.

Lia Vazzi descended the two steps and looked behind a mound of used bicycles. He opened a closet with huge doors. In it was a policeman's uniform hanging all by itself, on the floor was a pair of thick black shoes, and resting on the shoes was a braided street policeman's cap. That was all.

Lia went to the one trunk on the floor and pulled up the lid. It was surprisingly light. The interior was filled to the top with neatly folded gray blankets.

Lia went back up the stairs and stood on the patio staring at the ocean. Burying a body in the sand was foolhardy, so he dismissed the idea. Maybe somebody had come by and picked Sharkey up. But for an assassin there would be a risk of being seen. Also, Sharkey would be a dangerous man to kill. So, Lia reasoned, if the man was dead he had to be in this house. Immediately he went back down to the basement and threw all the wool blankets out of the trunk. And sure enough, there at the bottom was first the large head, and then the lean body. There was a hole in Sharkey's right eye and over it a thin cake of blood like a red coin. The facial skin, waxy with long death, was pockmarked with black dots. Lia, as a Qualified Man, knew exactly what that meant. Someone trusted had been allowed to come very close to shoot point blank into the eye; those dots were powder marks.

Carefully, Lia folded the blankets, put them back over the body, and then exited the house. He had not left any fingerprints but was aware that fragments of the blankets must have adhered to his clothing. He would have to destroy the clothes thoroughly. His shoes, too. He had his soldiers drive him to the airport, and while he was waiting for a plane to take him to Vegas, he bought a change of clothing including new shoes in one of the stores in the airport mall. Then he bought a carry-on bag and put his old clothes into it.

In Vegas he checked into the Xanadu and left a message for Cross. Then he showered thoroughly and dressed again in his new clothes. He waited for Cross to call.

When the call came, he told Cross he would be up to see him. He brought the bag of his old clothing, and the first thing he said to Cross was "You just saved yourself fifty grand."

Cross looked at him and smiled. Lia, usually a natty dresser, had bought a flowery shirt, blue canvas pants, and a light jacket, also blue. He looked like a low-caste casino hustler.

Lia told him about Sharkey. He attempted to make excuses for his actions, but Cross dismissed them. "You're in this with me, you have to protect yourself. But what the hell does this mean?"

"Simple," Lia said. "Sharkey was the only one who could tie Losey with Dante. Otherwise it's just your say-so. Dante made Losey kill his partner."

Cross said, "How the hell could Sharkey be that dumb?"

Lia shrugged. "He figured he could get money from Losey and then get the fifty from you anyway. He knew that Losey must be playing for big stakes because of the money you gave him. After all, he was a detective for twenty years, he could figure these things out. And he never dreamed Losey would kill him, his old partner. He didn't figure on Dante."

"They were extreme," Cross said.

"In this situation you cannot allow an extra player," Lia said. "I must say I'm surprised that Dante could see that particular danger. He must have convinced Losey, who really would not want to kill an old partner. We all have our sentimentalities."

"So now Dante is controlling Losey," Cross said. "I thought Losey was tougher than that."

"You're talking about two different classes of animal," Lia said. "Losey is formidable, Dante is crazy."

"So Dante knows I know about him," Cross said.

"Which means I have to act very quickly," Lia said.

Cross nodded. "It will have to be a Communion," he said. "They will have to disappear."

Lia laughed. "Do you think that will deceive Don Clericuzio?" he said.

"If we plan it right, nobody can blame us," Cross said.

Lia spent the next three days with Cross going over plans. During that time he burned his old clothes in the hotel incinerator with his own hands. Cross exercised by shooting a lone eighteen holes of golf, with Lia accompanying him to drive the golf cart. Lia could not understand the popularity of golf in all the Families. To him it was a quaint aberration.

On the night of the third day they sat on the balcony of the penthouse. Cross had laid out the brandy and Havana cigars. They watched the crowds on the Strip below.

"No matter how clever they are, my death so soon after my father's would compromise Dante with the Don," Cross said. "I think we can wait."

Lia puffed on his cigar. "Not too long. Now they know you spoke with Sharkey."

"We have to get them both at the same time," Cross said. "Remember, it will have to be a Communion. Their bodies must not be found."

Lia said, "You're putting last things first. And first we have to be sure we can kill them."

Cross sighed. "It's going to be very difficult. Losey is a dangerous man and careful. Dante can fight. We have to isolate them in one place. Can it be done in Los Angeles?"

"No," Lia said. "That is Losey's territory. He is too formidable there. We will have to do it in Vegas."

"And break rules," Cross said.

"If it's a Communion then nobody will know where they were killed," Lia said. "And we are already breaking the rule by killing a police officer."

"I think I know how to get them to Vegas at the same time," Cross said. He explained the scheme to Lia.

"We will have to use more bait," Lia told Cross. "We have to make sure Losey and Dante come when we want them here."

Cross drank another brandy. "OK, here's some more bait." He told Lia, and Lia nodded in agreement. "Their disappearance will be our salvation," Cross said. "And it will deceive everyone."

"Except Don Clericuzio," Lia said. "He is the only one to fear."

# BOOK VIII

# Communion

# CHAPTER 21

**V**ERY LUCKILY Steve Stallings did not die until his final close-up scene in *Messalina* was shot. It could have cost millions of dollars in reshooting.

The last scene to be shot was a battle scene that actually took place in the middle of the film. A desert town had been erected fifty miles from Vegas to denote the base of the Persian army that was to be destroyed by the Emperor Claudius (Steve Stallings) accompanied by his wife, Messalina (Athena).

At the end of the day, Steve Stallings retired to his hotel suite in the small town. He had his cocaine and his booze and two female companions for the night, and he was going to kick everybody's ass, he was pissed off. For one thing, his part in the picture had been cut to a character part, not a star. He realized he was shifting into a secondary career, an inevitable fate for aging stars. Another thing, Athena had been distant from him all during the shoot, he had hoped for more. Also—and this was, he himself felt, a little childish—at the wrap party and showing of the rough cut, he was not getting star treatment; he had not been given one of the Xanadu Hotel's famous Villas.

After his long years in the movie business, Steve Stallings knew how the power structure worked. When he was a Bankable Star, he could override everyone. Theoretically, the studio chief was boss, he gave the green light for a picture. A powerful producer who brought a "property" to the studio was also the boss, he got the elements together—i.e., stars, director, screenplay—supervised the development of the script, and raised independent money from people who were given a credit as associate producers but had no power. For that period he was the boss.

But once the picture started shooting, it was the director who was the boss. Providing he was an A director or the even more powerful Bankable Director (that is, one who would assure an audience in the film's opening weeks and attract Bankable Stars to appear in the movie).

The director had complete charge over the picture. Everything had to go through him. The costumes, music, sets, how the actors played their parts. Also, the Directors Guild was the most powerful union in the movie business. No name director would accept the job of replacing another director.

But all these people, powerful as they were, had to bow to the Bankable Star. A director who had two Bankable Stars in the same movie was like a man riding two wild horses. His balls could be scattered to the four winds.

Steve Stallings had been such a star and knew he no longer was.

The day's shoot had been physically taxing and Steve Stallings needed relaxation. He showered, ate a big steak, and when the two girls came up, local talent and not bad looking at all, he fed them cocaine and champagne. For once he relaxed his prudence, after all his career was entering its twilight years, and he didn't really have to be careful anymore. He went heavy on the coke.

The two girls were wearing T-shirts emblazoned with STEVE STALLINGS ASS KISSERS, in tribute to his buttocks, admired by fans all over the world, male and female. They were properly awestricken, and it was only after the cocaine that they peeled off their T-shirts and bundled in with him. This cheered him up somewhat. He took another snort of cocaine. The girls were caressing him, stripping off his shorts and shirt. Stallings daydreamed as they fiddled, their fiddling putting him at ease.

Tomorrow at the wrap party, he would see all his conquests. He had screwed Athena Aquitane, he had screwed Claudia who had written the movie, he had even screwed Dita Tommey long ago, when she wasn't yet fully convinced of her true sexual orientation. He had screwed Bobby Bantz's wife and, though she no longer counted because she was dead, Skippy Deere's wife. It always gave him a feeling of virtuous fulfillment when at a dinner party he looked around and tallied up all the women who were now sitting so placidly with their husbands and lovers. He was an intimate of them all.

There was a distraction. One of the girls was sticking a finger up his ass and that always annoyed him. He had hemorrhoids. He rose from the bed to snort some more cocaine and take a full swig of champagne, but the wine upset his stomach. He felt nauseous and then disoriented. He didn't quite know where he was.

Suddenly, he was aware of a great fatigue: his legs sagged, the glass fell from his hand. He was bewildered. Very far away he heard one of the girls scream and he was furious with her for screaming, and then the very last thing he felt was a lightning bolt exploding in his head.

W hat happened next could only have happened with a combination of stupidity and malice. One girl had screamed because Steve Stallings had toppled over her onto the bed and had lain there, mouth open and eyes staring, so obviously dead that both girls panicked and just kept screaming. The screaming attracted the hotel personnel and a number of people who were gambling in the tiny hotel casino, which held only slots, a dice table, and a large, round poker setup. These people followed the screaming and came upstairs.

There were, outside Stalling's hotel room, with its now-open door, several people staring at his naked body sprawled out on the bed. In what seemed just a few minutes, an additional crowd gathered from the town, hundreds of them. They crowded into the room to touch his body.

At first there were just reverent touches for the man who had made women all over the world fall in love with him. Then some women kissed him, other women touched his testicles, his penis, one women took out a pair of scissors from her purse and cut off a great thatch of glossy black hair to expose the underlying fuzz of gray on his skull.

The malice came in because Skippy Deere had been one of the first to arrive and had failed to call the police immediately. He watched the first wave of women approach Steve Stallings's body. He had a clear view. Stallings's mouth was open as if he had been caught in the act of singing and there was a look of astonishment on his face.

The first woman who reached him—Deere saw her clearly—gently closed his eyes and pushed his mouth shut before she softly kissed him on the forehead. But she was pushed aside by the next wave who were not so restrained. And Deere felt the malice within him, the horns Stallings had given him years ago seemed to tingle, and he let the invasion continue. Stallings often boasted that no women could resist him and he was certainly on the mark. Even dead, women were caressing his body.

Only when a piece of Stallings's ear vanished and he had been turned sideways to show his famous buttocks, his whole body deathly pale, did Deere finally call the police and take command of the situation and solve all the problems. That was what producers did. That was their forte.

Skippy Deere made all the arrangements for the body to be autopsied immediately and then shipped to Los Angeles, where the funeral would be held three days later.

The autopsy showed that Stallings had died of a cerebral aneurysm which, when it exploded, sent all his blood rushing through his head.

Deere hunted down the two young girls who had been with him and promised them they would not be prosecuted for cocaine use and that they would be signed for small parts in a new movie he was producing. He would pay them a thousand a week for two years. However, there was a moral turpitude clause that would end the contract if they talked to anyone about Stallings's death.

Then he took the time to call Bobby Bantz in L.A. and explain what he had done. He also called Dita Tommey to give her the news and have her tell all the *Messalina* personnel, above the line and below the line, to be sure to attend the showing in Vegas and the wrap party. Then, shaken more than he would admit, he took two Halcions and went to sleep.

# CHAPTER 22

THE DEATH OF Steve Stallings did not affect the showing and wrap party in Vegas. That was Skippy Deere's expertise. And the emotional structure of movie making. It was true that Stallings had been a star, but he had ceased to be a Bankable Star. It was true that he had made love to many women in their bodies, and millions more in their minds, but his love had never been more than reciprocal pleasure. Even the women in the picture, Athena, Claudia, Dita Tommey, and the three other featured female stars, were less grieved than would be imagined by romantics. Everyone agreed that Steve Stallings would want the show to go on, nothing would distress him more than to have the wrap party and screening canceled because of his death.

In the film industry you said good-bye to most of your lovers at the end of a picture as politely as you did in the old days to your dancing partner at a ball.

Skippy Deere claimed it was his idea to hold the wrap party at the Xanadu Hotel and to show a very rough cut of the picture that same night. He knew that Athena would be leaving the country in the next few days and wanted to make sure that Athena did not have to reshoot any scenes.

But, in reality, it was Cross who proposed the idea of a wrap party and showing of the film at the Xanadu Hotel. He asked it as a favor.

"It will be great publicity for the Xanadu," Cross told Deere. "And here's what I'll do for you. I'll comp everybody on the picture and anybody you invite for one night—room, food, beverage. I'll give you and Bantz a Villa. I'll give Athena a Villa. I'll provide security so nobody gets to see the rough cut—like the press—that you don't want to. You've been screaming for years you wanted a Villa."

Deere pondered this. "Just for publicity?"

Cross grinned at him. "Also you get hundreds of people loaded with big cash. The casino will get a good part of it."

"Bantz doesn't gamble," Deere said. "I do. You'll get my money."

"I'll give you fifty grand in credit," Cross said. "If you lose we won't press for payment."

That convinced Deere. "OK," he said. "But it has to be my idea or I can't sell it to the Studio."

"Certainly," Cross said. "But Skippy, you and I have done a lot of things together. And I've always come out on the short end. This time it's different. This time you have to come through." He smiled at Deere. "This time you can't disappoint me."

For one of the few times in his life Deere felt a thrill of apprehension and did not quite know why. Cross was not making a threat. He seemed genial, he seemed to be just stating a fact.

"Don't worry," Skippy Deere said, "We finish shooting in three weeks. Make your plans for then."

Then Cross had to make sure that Athena would agree to come to the wrap party and showing of the rough cut. "I really need it for the Hotel and a chance to see you again," he said to her.

She agreed. Now Cross had to make sure that Dante and Losey would come to the party.

He invited Dante to come to Vegas to talk about LoddStone's and Losey's plan to make a picture based on Losey's adventures in the police department. Everybody knew that Losey and Dante were now good buddies.

"I want you to put in a word for me with Jim Losey," Cross told Dante. "I want to be a coproducer on his film and I'm willing to invest half the budget."

Dante was amused by this. "You're really serious about this movie business," he said, "Why?"

"Big money," Cross said. "And broads."

Dante laughed. "You've got big money and broads already," he said.

"Class. Big money and class broads," Cross said.

"How come you don't invite me to this party?" Dante asked. "And how come I never get a Villa?"

"Put the word in for me with Losey," Cross said, "and you'll get both. Bring Losey along. Plus if you're looking for a date I can fix you up with Tiffany. You've seen her show."

To Dante, Tiffany was the ultimate personification of pure lust, her breasts so full, her smooth, elongated face with its thick lips and wide mouth, her height and long, shapely legs. For the first time Dante was enthusiastic. "No shit," he said. "She's twice as big as me. Imagine? You've got a deal."

It was a little too obvious, but Cross was counting on the fact that the interdiction on violence in Vegas by all the Families would make Dante confident.

Then Cross added casually, "Even Athena is coming. And she's the main reason I want to stay in the movie business."


Bobby Bantz, Melo Stuart, and Claudia flew to Vegas on the Studio jet. Athena and the rest of the cast arrived from the shoot in their personal trailers, as did Dita Tommey. Senator Wavven would represent the state of Nevada, as would Nevada's governor, who had been handpicked for the job by Wavven himself.

Dante and Losey would have two apartments in one of the Villas. Lia Vazzi and his men would occupy the other four apartments.

Senator Wavven and the governor and their entourages would occupy another Villa. Cross had arranged a private dinner for them with selected showgirls. He hoped that their presence would help take the heat off any investigation of what was to happen. That they would use their political influence to smother any publicity and legal pursuit.

Cross was breaking all the rules. Athena had a Villa, but Claudia, Dita Tommey, and Molly Flanders also had apartments in that Villa. The remaining two apartments held a four-man crew of Lia Vazzi's men, to guard Athena.

A fourth Villa was assigned to Bantz and Skippy Deere and their entourages. The remaining three Villas were occupied by twenty of Lia's men, who would replace the usual security guards. However, none of the Vazzi crews were to be involved in the real action, they did not know Cross's true purpose. Lia and Cross were to be the only executioners.

Cross shut down the Villas' Pearl Casino for the two days. Most of the Hollywood personnel, no matter how successful, could not afford to play the casino's stakes. Those superrich guests who had already booked were informed that the Villas were undergoing repairs and renovations and could not accommodate them.

In their plan Cross and Lia Vazzi had determined that Cross would kill Dante and that Lia would kill Losey. If the Don decided on their guilt and determined that Lia had actually done the job on Dante, he might wipe out Lia's whole family. If the Don found the truth, he would not extend his vengeance to Claudia. She, after all, had Clericuzio blood.

Also, Lia had a personal vendetta against Jim Losey, he hated all representatives of government, and why not mix a little personal pleasure in with such a dangerous business.

The real problem was how to isolate the two men and make the bodies disappear. It had always been the rule of all the Families all over America that no execution could be carried out in Vegas, in order to preserve the public acceptance of gambling. The Don was a strong enforcer of that rule.

Cross hoped Dante and Losey would not suspect a trap. They did not know that Lia had discovered Sharkey's body and therefore knew of their intentions. The other problem was how to prepare for Dante's strike against Cross. And then Lia established a spy in Dante's camp.


Molly Flanders flew in early on the day of the party, she and Cross had business. She brought with her a justice of the Supreme Court of California and a monsignor of the Catholic Diocese of Los Angeles. They would serve as witnesses when Cross signed the will she had also prepared and brought. Cross knew that his chances of remaining alive were small, and he had carefully considered where his half of the Xanadu Hotel should go. His interest was worth $500 million, and that was nothing to be sneezed at.

The will left Lia's wife and children a comfortable pension for life. The rest he divided between Claudia and Athena, with Athena's portion held in trust for her daughter, Bethany. It struck him that there was no one else in the world he cared enough about to leave his money to.

When Molly, the judge, and the monsignor arrived in the penthouse suite, the judge congratulated him on his good sense for making a will at so young an age. The monsignor calmly surveyed the luxury of the suite as if to weigh the wages of sin.

They were both good friends of Molly's, who had done pro bono work for them. She had called in her markers at the special request of Cross. He wanted witnesses who could not be corrupted or intimidated by the Clericuzio.

Cross gave them drinks, and the signing of the will was completed. The two men left; though they had been invited, they did not want their reputations sullied by attending a movie wrap party in the gambling hell of Las Vegas. They were, after all, not elected officials of the state.

Cross and Molly were alone in the suite. Molly gave him the original of the will. Cross said, "You have a copy for yourself, right?"

"Of course," Molly said. "I must say I was surprised when you gave me your instructions. I had no idea you and Athena were so close. And besides she's pretty rich in her own right."

"She may need more money than she has," Cross said.

"Her daughter?" Molly said. "I know about her. I'm Athena's personal attorney. You're right, Bethany may need that money. I had you figured differently."

"You did?" Cross said. "How so?"

Molly said quietly, "I had the idea that you took care of Boz Skannet. I had you figured as a Mafia guy with no mercy. I remember about that poor kid I got off from a murder rap. And that you mentioned him. And that he was killed supposedly in some drug deal."

"And now you see how wrong you were," Cross said, smiling at her.

Molly looked at him coldly. "And I was very surprised when you let Bobby Bantz screw you out of your profit share in *Messalina*."

"That was small potatoes," Cross said. He thought of the Don and David Redfellow.

"Athena is going to France the day after tomorrow," Molly said. "For quite a while. Are you going with her?"

"No," Cross said. "I have too many things here."

"OK," Molly said. "I'll see you at the movie screening and the wrap party. Maybe the rough cut of the film will give you an idea of the fortune Bantz gypped you out of."

"It doesn't matter," Cross said.

"You know, Dita put in a card at the beginning of the rough cut. Dedicated to Steve Stallings. Bantz will be really pissed off at that."

"Why?" Cross asked.

"Because Steve screwed all the women Bantz couldn't," Molly said. "What shits men are," she added. Then she left.

Cross went to sit on his balcony. The Vegas street below him was crowded, people sifting into the hotel casinos that lined the strip on either side. The neon marquees flashed their signs: Caesars, the Sands, the Mirage, the Aladdin, the Desert Inn, the Stardust—purples, reds, and greens, a mixed rainbow to which there was no end until you lifted your eyes to the desert and mountains that lay beyond. The blazing afternoon sun could not subdue them.

The *Messalina* people would not begin to arrive until three, and then he would see Athena for the last time if things went wrong. He picked up the balcony phone and called the Villa where he had housed Lia Vazzi and told him to come up to the penthouse suite so that they could go over their plans one more time.

*Messalina* wrapped at noon. Dita Tommey had wanted the last shot of the rising sun illuminating a terrible slaughter of the Roman battlefield. Athena and Steve Stallings looking down. She shot a double for Stallings and used a shadow over his face for disguise. It was nearly three in the afternoon before the camera truck, the huge mobile trailers that served as homes on the set, the mobile catering kitchens, the wardrobe trailers and vehicles carrying weapons of the time before Christ, rolled into Vegas. Many others came as well, because Cross had treated this occasion in the Old Vegas style.

He had comped everyone who worked on *Messalina*, above the line and below the line, with room, food, and beverage. LoddStone Studios had supplied the list of over three hundred names. Certainly it was generous, certainly it created goodwill. But these three hundred people would leave a substantial part of their wages in the casino drop. This he had learned from Gronevelt. "When people feel good, when they want to celebrate, they gamble."

The rough cut of the movie *Messalina* would be played at ten P.M., but without music and special effects. After the screening would come the wrap party. The huge Xanadu ballroom where the party for Big Tim had been held was cut into two parts. One to show the film, the other, larger part for the buffet and orchestra.

By four in the afternoon, everybody was in the Hotel and the Villas. It was not to be missed by anyone: everything free in the convergence of two glamorous worlds, Hollywood and Las Vegas.

The press was infuriated by the tight security. Access was barred to the Villas and the ballroom. It was not even possible to photograph the players in this glamorous event. Not the stars of the film, the director, the senator and the governor, the producer and the head of the Studio. They could not even get into the screening of the rough cut of the film. They prowled around the casino and offered huge bribes to the gamblers below the line for their IDs to get into the ballroom. Some were successful.

Four crew members, two cynical stuntmen, and two women from the catering team sold their IDs to reporters for a thousand dollars apiece.

Dante Clericuzio and Jim Losey were enjoying the luxury of their Villa. Losey shook his head in wonderment. "A burglar could live for a year on just the gold from the bathroom," he said aloud.

"No, he couldn't," Dante said. "He'd be dead in six months."

They were sitting in the living room of Dante's apartment. They hadn't called room service because the huge kitchen refrigerator was stuffed with trays of sandwiches and caviar canapés, bottles of imported beer and the finest wines.

"So we're all set," Losey said.

"Yep," Dante said, "and when we're done, I'll ask my grandfather for the Hotel. Then we'll be set for life."

"The important thing is that we get him here alone," Losey said.

"I'll do that, don't worry," Dante said. "Worse comes to worst, we'll drive him out to the desert."

"How do you get him here in this Villa?" Losey said. "That's the important thing."

"I'll tell him Giorgio flew in secretly and wants to see him," Dante said. "Then I do the job and you clean up after me. You know crime scenes, what they'll look for."

He said musingly, "The best way is to drop him into the desert. They may never find him." He paused for a moment. "You know Cross ducked Giorgio the night Pippi died. He won't dare do it again."

"But what if he does?" Losey asked. "I'll be waiting here all night jerking off."

"Athena's Villa is next door," Dante said. "You just tap on it and get lucky."

"Too much heat," Losey said.

Dante said with a grin. "We can take her out into the desert with Cross."

"You're crazy," Losey said. And he realized this was true.

"Why not?" Dante said. "Why not have some fun? The desert is big enough to dump two bodies."

Losey thought of Athena's body, her lovely face, her voice, her regal air. Oh, he and Dante would have fun. He was already a murderer, he might as well be a rapist. Marlowe, Pippi De Lena, and his old partner, Phil Sharkey. He was a three-time murderer and too shy to commit rape. He was turning into one of those morons he had arrested all his life. And for a woman who sold her body to the whole world. But this little prick before him with the funny hat was really a piece of work.

"I'll give it a shot," Losey said. "I'll invite her in for a drink and if she comes, she's asking for it."

Dante was amused by Losey's rationalization. "Everybody asks for it," he said. "We ask for it."

They went over the details, and then Dante went back to his apartment. He ran a bath; he wanted to use the expensive scents in the Villa. As he lay in the hot, perfumey water, his black, horselike Clericuzio hair soaped into a white, heavy topknot, he thought about what his fate would be. After he and Losey dumped the body of Cross into the desert, miles from Vegas, the toughest part of the operation would begin. He would have to convince his grandfather that he was innocent. If worse came to worst, he could confess to Pippi's death also, and his grandfather would forgive him. The Don had always showed him a special love.

Also, now, Dante was the Family Hammer. He would apply for appointment as *Bruglione* of the West and the overlordship of the Xanadu Hotel. Giorgio would oppose him, but Vincent and Petie would be neutral. They were content to live on their legal enterprises. And the old man could not live forever, Giorgio was a white-collar guy. There would come a time when the warmaker would become the emperor. He would not retreat into society. He would lead the Family back to its glory. He would never give up the power over life and death.

Dante left the bath and showered to get all the soap out of his ropy hair. He anointed his body with the colognes from their fancy bottles, sculpted his hair from delicate tubes of aromatic gels, reading the directions carefully. Then he went to the suitcase that held his Renaissance hats and chose one encrusted with precious jewels that had the shape of a custard. Its threads were gold and purple. Lying there it looked ridiculous, but when he put it on his head, Dante was enchanted. It made him look like a prince. Especially the row of studded green gems sewed along the front. This was how Athena would see him tonight, or failing that, Tiffany. But the two could wait if necessary.

As he finished dressing, Dante thought of what his life would come to be. He would live in a Villa, as luxurious as any palace. He would have an inexhaustible supply of beautiful women, a self-supporting harem dancing and singing in the Xanadu Hotel showroom. He could eat in six different restaurants with six different national cuisines. He could order the death of an enemy, reward a friend. He would be as close to being a Roman emperor as modern times allowed. Only Cross stood in the way.

Jim Losey, finally alone in his apartment, was contemplating the course his life had taken. He had been, for the first half of his career, a great cop, a true knight defending his society. He'd had an intense hatred for all criminals, especially blacks. And then gradually he had changed. He resented the charges in the media that cops were brutal. The very society he was defending from scum was attacking him. His superiors, with their gold-braided uniforms, sided with the politicians who talked shit to the people. All that bullshit about how you couldn't hate blacks. What was so bad about that? They committed most of the crimes. And wasn't he a free American who could hate whoever he wanted to hate? They were the cockroaches who would eat away all civilization. They didn't want to work, they didn't want to study, burning the midnight oil was a joke to them unless it meant shooting basketball under the light of the moon. They mugged unarmed citizens, they turned their women into whores, and they had an intolerable disrespect for the law and its enforcers. It was his job to protect the rich from the malice of the poor. And his own desire was to become rich. He wanted the clothing, the cars, the food, the drink, and above all, the women the rich could afford. And surely that was American.

It had started with bribes to protect the gambling, then some frame-ups of drug dealers to make them pay protection. He had been proud of his "hero cop" status, the recognition he received for the courage he had shown, but there was no monetary reward. He was still buying cheap clothes, he still had to be very careful with his money to make his paycheck stretch out. And he, who guarded the rich against the poor, received no reward, indeed was one of the poor. But the final straw was that in public esteem he was lower than the criminal. Some of his friends, law enforcers, had been prosecuted and sent to jail for doing their duty. Or fired from their jobs. Rapists, burglars, lethal muggers, armed robbers in broad daylight, had more rights than cops.

Over the years, Losey sold himself his story in his head. The press and TV reviled law enforcers. The fucking Miranda rights, the fucking ACLU; let those fucking lawyers do patrol for six months, they'd grow a lynching tree.

After all, he used the tricks, the beatings, and the threats to get some scumbag to confess his crime and to put him away from society. But Losey could not sell himself completely, he was too good a cop. He could not sell himself on having become a murderer.

Forget all that; he would be rich. He would fling his badge and his bravery citations into the face of the government and the public. He would be security chief for the Xanadu Hotel at ten times the salary, and from this Paradise in the desert, he would watch with pleasure as Los Angeles crumbled under the assault of criminals he would no longer fight. Tonight he would see the movie *Messalina* and go to the wrap party. And maybe get a shot at Athena. Here his mind cringed, even as he felt his body ache with the thought of exercising such sexual power. At the party, he'd pitch a feature film to Skippy based on his career, the greatest hero cop in the LAPD. Dante had told him that Cross wanted to invest, which was really funny. Why kill off a guy who would invest in his movie? That was simple. Because he knew Dante would kill him if he backed out. And Losey, tough as he was, knew he could not kill Dante. He knew the Clericuzio too well.

For a flash he thought of Marlowe, a good nigger, really sweet, always so cheerful and cooperative. He had always liked Marlowe, and his murder was the one thing he felt sorry about.

Jim Losey still had hours to wait before the screening and the party. He could go gamble in the main casino, but gambling was a mug's game. He decided against it. He had a big night ahead. First the movie and the party, then at three in the morning he would have to help Dante kill Cross De Lena and bury him in the desert.

Bobby Bantz invited the above-the-line principals of *Messalina* to his Villa for celebratory drinks at five that evening: Athena, Dita Tommey, Skippy Deere, and as a courtesy, Cross De Lena. Only

Cross declined, claiming pressure of duties at the Hotel on this special night.

Bantz had brought his latest "conquest," a seemingly fresh young girl named Johanna, discovered by a talent scout in a small town in Oregon. She was signed to a five-hundred-dollar-a-week contract for two years. Beautiful but completely untalented, she gave off such a virginal air that the innocence was a separate attraction. And yet with a shrewdness beyond her years, she had refused to sleep with Bobby Bantz until he promised to bring her to Vegas for the showing of *Messalina*.

Skippy Deere, with an adjoining apartment in Bantz's Villa, chose to be a squatter in Bantz's place, and so prevented Bantz from getting in a quick screw with Johanna, which made Bantz irritable. Skippy was pitching an idea for a feature film that he really was crazy about. Being crazy for a property was a legitimate part of a producer's job.

Deere was telling Bantz about Jim Losey, the greatest hero cop in the LAPD, a big, handsome son of a bitch, who might even be able to play the title role himself, since it would be a story about his life. One of those great "true" life stories where you could invent anything bizarre.

Deere and Bantz both knew that Losey playing himself was a fantasy, invented to con Losey so that he would sell his story cheap, and also for public hype.

Skippy Deere outlined the story with great enthusiasm. Nobody could sell a nonexistent property better. In a moment of pure exhilaration, he picked up the phone and, before Bantz could protest, invited the detective to the five P.M. cocktail party. Losey asked if he could bring a friend, and Deere assured him he could, assuming it was a girlfriend. Skippy Deere, as a producer of films, liked to mix different worlds together. You never knew what miracle might emerge.

Cross De Lena and Lia Vazzi were in the Xanadu penthouse suite reviewing the details of what they would do that night.

"I have all the men in place," Lia said. "I control the Villa compound. None of them know what you and I will do, they will have no part in that. But I have word that Dante has a crew from the Enclave digging your grave in the desert. We have to be careful tonight."

"After tonight is what I worry about," Cross said. "Then we have Don Clericuzio to deal with. Do you think he'll buy the story?"

"Not really," Lia said. "But that is our only hope."

Cross shrugged. "I have no choice. Dante killed my father and so now he has to kill me." He paused for a moment and then said, "I hope the Don was not on his side from the beginning. Then we have no chance."

Lia said cautiously, "We could abort everything and lay our troubles in front of the Don. Let him decide and act."

"No," Cross said. "He can't decide against his grandson."

"You're right, of course," Lia said. "But still, the Don has gone a little soft. He let those Hollywood people cheat you, and that in his youth he would never have allowed. Not the money, the disrespect."

Cross poured more brandy into Lia's glass and lit his cigar. He did not tell him about David Redfellow. "How do you like your room?" he said jokingly.

Lia puffed on his cigar. "What nonsense. So beautiful. To what purpose? Why does anyone have to live like that? It is too much. It takes away your strength. It arouses envy. It's not clever to insult the poor like that. Why then would they not want to kill you? My father was a rich man in Sicily but never did he live in luxury."

"You don't understand America, Lia," Cross said. "Every poor man who sees the inside of that Villa rejoices. Because he knows in his heart someday he will live in just such a place."

At that moment the private phone in the penthouse rang. Cross picked it up. His heart gave a little jump. It was Athena.

"Can we meet before the movie shows?" she asked.

"Only if you come to my suite," Cross said. "I really can't leave here."

"How gallant," Athena said coolly. "Then we can meet after the wrap party, I'll leave early and you can come to my Villa."

"I really can't," Cross said.

"I'm leaving in the morning for L.A.," Athena said. "Then the day after, I fly to France. We won't meet in private until you come there . . . if you come."

Cross looked at Lia, who shook his head and frowned. So Cross said to Athena, "Can you come to me here, now? Please?"

He waited for a long time before she said, "Yes, give me an hour."

"I'll send a car and security for you," Cross said. "They'll be waiting outside your Villa." He hung up the phone and said to Lia, "We have to watch out for her. Dante is crazy enough to do anything."

The cocktail party in Bantz's Villa was graced by beauty.

Melo Stuart brought a young actress with a great stage reputation that he and Skippy Deere planned to cast as the female lead in the Jim Losey Story. She had a strong Egyptian beauty, bold features, an imperious manner. Bantz had his new find, Johanna, last name not decided, the innocent virgin. Athena, who had never looked so radiant, was surrounded by her friends: Claudia, Dita Tommey, and Molly Flanders. Athena was unusually quiet, but still Johanna and the stage actress, Liza Wrongate, looked at her almost in awe and envy. Both came to Athena, the Queen they hoped to replace.

Claudia asked Bobby Bantz, "Didn't you invite my brother?"

"Sure," Bantz said. "He was too busy."

"Thanks for giving Ernest's family his points," Claudia said, grinning.

"Molly robbed me," Bantz said. He had always liked Claudia, maybe because Marrion had liked her, so he didn't mind her kidding. "She held a cannon to my head."

"But you could have made it tough," Claudia said. "Marrion would approve."

Bantz stared at her blankly. He felt suddenly tearful. Never would he be the man Marrion had been. And he missed him.

Meanwhile Skippy Deere had cornered Johanna and was telling her about his new film, which had a great cameo of an innocent young girl grossly raped and killed by a drug dealer. "You look perfect for the part. You don't have much experience but if I can get it past Bobby, you can come and test." He paused for a moment and then said in a warm, confidential manner, "I think you should change your name. Johanna is too square for your career." Implying the stardom that lay ahead.

He noted how her face flushed; really it was touching how young girls believed in their beauty, desired to be stars, as passionately as Renaissance girls wanted to be saints. When Ernest Vail's cynical smile appeared before him, Deere thought: Laugh as much as you like, still it was a spiritual desire. In both instances it would lead more often to martyrdom than glory, but that was part of the deal.

Johanna went off predictably to talk to Bantz. Deere joined Melo Stuart and his new girlfriend, Liza. Though she was talented on stage, Skippy had doubts about her future on the movie screen. The camera was too cruel for her kind of beauty. And her intelligence would make her unfit for many roles. But Melo had insisted she be the female lead in the Losey picture, and there were times when Melo could not be denied. And the female lead was just a bullshit, carry-the-water-bag part.

Deere kissed Liza on both cheeks. "I saw you in New York," he said. "Marvelous performance." He paused for a moment and said, "I'll hope you take the part in my new movie. Melo thinks it will be your breakthrough on film."

Liza gave him a cold smile. "I have to see the script," she said. Deere felt that flash of resentment he always felt. She was getting the break of her life and she wanted to see a fucking script. He could see Melo smiling with amusement.

"Of course," Deere said. "But believe me I would not send you a script that was not worthy of your talent."

Melo, never as ardent a lover as he was a businessman, said, "Liza, we can guarantee you the leading female role in an A feature. The script is not a sacred text as in the theater. It can be changed to please you."

Liza gave him a slightly warmer smile. She said, "You believe that crap too? Stage plays are rewritten. What do you think we do when we try them out of town?"

Before they could answer, Jim Losey and Dante Clericuzio entered the apartment. Deere rushed over to greet them and introduce them to the others at the party.

Losey and Dante were an almost comical pair. Losey, tall, handsome, impeccably tailored—full shirt and tie, despite the intense July heat of Vegas. And Dante beside him, his hugely muscled body bulging out of a T-shirt, his brightly jeweled Renaissance cap crowning his black ropy hair, and so short. All the others in the room, experts in make-believe worlds, knew these two were not make-believe, despite their weirdness. Their faces were too blank and cold. That could not be duplicated with shadows.

Losey immediately addressed Athena and told her how he looked forward to seeing her in *Messalina*. He abandoned his intimidating style and was almost fawning. Women had always found him charming, could Athena be an exception?

Dante helped himself to a drink and sat on the sofa. No one came near him except Claudia. They had not seen each other more than three times over the years, all they had in common were childhood memories. Claudia kissed him on the cheek. When they were children he had tormented her, but she always remembered him with a certain fondness.

Dante reached up to give her a hug. "*Cugina,* you look beautiful. If you looked like that when we were kids I would never have beaten you up so much."

Claudia plucked his Renaissance hat from his head. "Cross told me about your hats. They make you look cute." She put the hat on her head. "Even the Pope doesn't have a hat this cute."

"And he has a lot of hats," Dante said. "Now who would have thought you'd become such a big wheel in the movie business."

"What do you do these days?" Claudia asked.

"I run a meat company," Dante said. "We supply the hotels." He smiled, then asked, "Listen, could you introduce me to your beautiful star?"

Claudia brought him over to Athena, who was still cornered by Jim Losey putting on his charm. Athena smiled at Dante's Renaissance hat. Dante made himself look disarmingly comical.

Losey continued on with his flattery. "I know your movie will be great," he told her. "After the wrap party maybe you'll let me be your bodyguard back to the Villa, then we can have a drink together." He was playing the good cop role.

Athena was at her best refusing an advance. She smiled at him sweetly. "I'd love to," she said. "But I'm only going to stay a half hour at the party and I wouldn't want you to miss it. I have to catch an early plane tomorrow, then I fly to France. I simply have too many things to do."

Dante was admiring her. He could see she loathed Losey and that she was afraid of him. But she had made Losey think he could somehow have a shot at her.

"I can fly with you to L.A.," Losey said. "What time is your flight?"

"You are nice," Athena said. "But it's a small private charter and all the seats are full."

When she was safely back in her Villa, she called Cross and told him that she was on her way over.

The first thing Athena was aware of was the security. There were guards on the elevator to the penthouse suite of the Xanadu Hotel. There was a special key to unlock the elevator. The elevator itself had security cameras in the ceiling, and its doors opened up into an anteroom that held five men. One was at the elevator door to greet her. Another man was at the lone desk that held a bank of TV screens, and there were two other men playing cards in the corner of the room. Another was seated at the sofa reading *Sports Illustrated.*

They all looked at her with a special appraising, slightly astonished look she had encountered many times, acknowledging that her beauty was of a special variety. But it had long since failed to rouse her vanity; now it only made her aware of some danger.

The man at the desk pushed a button that opened the door to Cross's suite, and she went in, the door swinging shut behind her.

She was in the office part of the suite. Cross met her and led her into the living quarters. He kissed her briefly on the lips and then led her into the bedroom. Without saying a word, they both undressed and held each other naked. For Cross it was such a relief to hold her flesh, to look into her radiant face, that he sighed. "I'd rather just look at you than do anything else in the world."

In reply, she caressed him, made him kiss her, drew him down on the bed. She felt that this was a man who truly loved her, would do anything she commanded, and in return she would give him his every wish. For the first time in a very long time, she responded both physically and mentally. She truly loved him and loved making love to him. Yet she always knew he was dangerous, even to her, in some way.

After an hour they dressed and went out onto the balcony.

Las Vegas was showered in neon lights, the late sun baked the streets and gaudy hotels in a great band of gold. Beyond was the desert and the mountains. Here in time, they were isolated; the green flags of the villas hung limply in the air.

Athena held his hand tightly. "Will I see you at the movie and the wrap party?" she asked.

"I'm sorry, I can't," Cross said. "But I'll see you in France."

"I've noticed it's very hard to get to see you," Athena said. "The locked elevator and all those guards."

Cross said, "It's just for the next few days, too many strange people in town."

"I met your cousin, Dante," Athena said. "That detective seems to be a buddy of his. They make a charming pair. Losey was very interested in my welfare, and my schedule. Dante offered his help too. They were so worried about my getting to L.A. safely."

Cross pressed her hand. "You will," he said.

"Claudia said you and Dante are cousins," Athena said. "Why does he wear those funny hats?"

"Dante is a nice guy," Cross said.

"But Claudia told me the two of you were enemies since you were kids," Athena said.

"Sure," Cross said amiably, "but that doesn't make him a bad person."

They were silent, the streets below were clogged with vehicles and walking people migrating to different hotels for dinner and gambling. Dreaming of pleasure fraught with risk.

"So this is the last time we will see each other," Athena said and pressed his hand as if to nullify what she said.

"I said I'll meet you in France," Cross said.

"When?" Athena asked.

"I don't know," Cross said. "If I don't come, you'll know I'm dead."

"Things are that serious?" Athena said.

"Yes," Cross said.

"And you can't tell me anything about it?" Athena asked.

Cross didn't answer for a moment. "You'll be safe," he said. "And I think I'll be safe. I can't tell you any more than that."

"I'll wait," Athena said. She kissed him and then walked out of the bedroom and out of the suite. Cross watched and then went out to the balcony to see her emerge from the Hotel and onto the colonnade. He saw the car with his security guards drive her to her Villa. Then he picked up the phone and called Lia Vazzi. He told Vazzi to tighten security around Athena even more.


By ten P.M. the theater section of the ballroom of the Xanadu Hotel was full. The audience was gathered waiting for the first rough cut showing of *Messalina*. There was a premiere seating section that consisted of soft armchairs with a telephone console in the middle. There was one empty seat with a wreath of flowers bearing Steve Stalling's name. The other seats held Claudia, Dita Tommey, and Bobby Bantz and his companion, Johanna. Melo Stuart and Liza. Skippy Deere immediately took possession of the phone.

Athena was the last to arrive and was cheered by the crew and stunt men below the line. The above-the-line people, the supporting cast, and all the people seated in the armchairs applauded and kissed her on the cheek as she made her way to the center armchair. Then Skippy Deere picked up the phone and told the projectionist to begin.

Against the black background the line "Dedicated to Steve Stallings" appeared, and the audience applauded in a muted, respectful fashion. The insertion had been opposed by Bobby Bantz and Skippy Deere, but Dita Tommey vetoed them, God only knew why, Bantz said. But what the hell, it was only a rough cut, and besides, the sentimentality would create some press.

Then the picture came on the screen . . .

Athena was mesmerizing, she had even more sexuality on screen than she had in real life and a wit that was no surprise to anyone who knew her well. Indeed Claudia had written lines specifically to show off this quality in her. No cost had been stinted, and the crucial sex scenes were done in good taste.

There was no question that *Messalina,* after all its troubles, would be a major hit. And that, without final music and special effects. Dita Tommey was ecstatic, she was finally a Bankable Director. Melo Stuart was calculating how much he would ask for Athena's next picture; Bantz, looking not too happy, was worrying about the same thing. Skippy was counting the money he would make; finally he could own his own jet.

Claudia was more thrilled than any of them. Her creation was up on the screen. She had sole credit and it was an original screenplay. Thanks to Molly Flanders, she had *gross* points. Of course, there had been a little rewrite by Ben Sly but not enough for a credit.

Everybody was clustered around Athena and Dita Tommey, congratulating them. But Molly had her eye on one of the stunt men. Stunt men were crazy bastards, but they had hard bodies and were great in bed.

The wreath for Steve Stallings had been brushed to the floor, and people were trampling it. Molly could see that Athena had detached herself from the crowd to pick it up and place it back on the chair. Athena caught Molly's eye and they both shrugged, Athena giving a shy smile as if to say, That's movies.

The crowd moved to the other side of the ballroom. A small band was playing, but everyone rushed the buffet tables. Then the dancing began. Molly went up to the stunt man, who was glowering around; it was at these parties they were most vulnerable. They felt their work was not appreciated, and they resented like hell when the flabby male star was allowed to punch them out on screen when they could kill the faggot bastard in real life. Just like a stunt man, his cock is already hard, Molly thought, as he led her onto the dance floor.

Athena only spent an hour at the party. Receiving everyone's congratulations, she was gracious, and yet she observed herself being gracious and she hated it. She danced with the "best boy" and other members of the crew and then with a stunt man whose aggressiveness made her decide to leave.

The Xanadu Rolls was waiting for her with an armed driver and two security guards. When she got out of the Rolls at her Villa, she was surprised to see Jim Losey coming out of the adjoining Villa. He approached her. "You were great in that movie tonight," he said. "I've never seen a better body on a woman. Especially that ass."

Athena would have been wary except that the driver and both security guards were already out of the car, positioned. It was part of her theatrical training, the blocking out of the stage where actors position themselves. She noted that they placed themselves so that none of the lines of fire would jeopardize any of them. She also noticed that Losey viewed them with a mild contempt.

"That was not my ass," Athena said, "but thank you anyway." She smiled at him.

Suddenly Losey was holding her hand. "You're the greatest-looking woman I ever met," he said. "Why don't you try a real guy instead of those phony actor faggots."

Athena took her hand away. "I'm an actor too, and we're not phonies. Good night."

"Can I come in for a drink?" Losey asked.

"I'm sorry," Athena said, and rang the bell to the Villa. The door was opened by a butler Athena had never seen before.

Losey took a step to go in with her, and then to her surprise, the butler walked outside and quickly pushed her into the Villa. The three security guards formed a barricade between Losey and the door.

Losey looked at them with contempt. "What the fuck is this?" he said.

The butler remained outside the door. "Miss Aquitane's security," he said. "You will have to leave."

Losey took out his police ID. "You see who I am," he said. "I'll kick the shit out of all of you, and then I'll lock you up."

The butler looked at the ID. He said, "You're Los Angeles. No jurisdiction." He pulled out his own ID. "I'm Las Vegas County."

Athena Aquitane had remained just inside the doorway. She was surprised her new butler was a detective, but now she was beginning to understand. "Don't make a big deal out of it," she said, and closed the door against all of them.

Both men put their IDs back into their jackets.

Losey gave each in turn a hard stare. "I'll remember you guys," he said. None of the men reacted.

Losey turned away. He had more important fish to fry. In the next two hours Dante Clericuzio would be bringing Cross De Lena to their Villa.

Dante Clericuzio, Renaissance hat perched on his head, was having a great time at the wrap party. He used fun to prepare himself for serious action. A girl in the catering crew had caught his attention, but she gave him no encouragement because she had focused on one of the stunt men. The stunt man had given Dante threatening looks. Lucky for him, Dante thought, I have business to do tonight. He looked at his watch, maybe good old Jim had managed to snare Athena. Tiffany had never showed, though she had been promised. Dante decided to start a half hour early. He called Cross, using the private number with the operator.

Cross answered.

"I have to see you right away," Dante said. "I'm in the ballroom. Great party."

"So, come up," Cross said.

"No," Dante said. "These are orders. Not on the phone and not in your suite. Come on down."

There was a long pause. Then Cross said, "I'll be down."

Dante stationed himself so that he could observe Cross making his way through the ballroom. There seemed to be no security around him. Dante patted down his hat and thought back to their childhood together. Cross had been the only boy who had made him fearful, and he had fought him often because of that fear. But he loved the way Cross looked, had often been envious. And he envied his cousin's confidence. It was just too bad . . .

Once he killed Pippi, Dante had known he could not let Cross remain alive. Now, after this, he would have to confront the Don. But Dante had never doubted that his grandfather loved him, he had always shown his love. The Don might not like this, but he would never invoke his awful power to punish his beloved grandson.

Cross was standing before him. Now he had to get Cross to the Villa where Losey was waiting. It would be simple. He would shoot Cross, and then they would drive his body out into the desert and bury him. Nothing fancy, as Pippi De Lena had always preached. The car was already parked behind the Villa for transport.

Cross said to him abruptly, "So what is it?" He did not look suspicious or even wary. "Nice new hat," he said and smiled. Dante had always envied that smile, as though the guy knew everything Dante was thinking.

Dante played it very slow, very low-voiced. He took Cross by the arm and led him outside, in front of the huge colored marquee that had cost the Xanadu Hotel ten million dollars. The flashing blue, red, and purple bathed their figures in cold light blanched by the desert moon. Dante whispered to Cross, "Giorgio flew in, he's at my Villa. Top secret. And he wants to see you right away. That's why I couldn't say anything on the phone."

Dante was delighted that Cross looked concerned. "He told me not to tell you anything, but he's pissed off. I think he found out something about your old man."

At this Cross gave Dante a somber look, almost one of displeasure. Then he said, "OK, let's go." And he led Dante through the grounds of the Hotel to the Villa compound.

The four guards at the compound gates recognized Cross and waved them through.

Dante opened the door with a flourish and doffed his Renaissance hat. He said, "After you," and smiled slyly, which gave his face a puckish humor.

Cross walked in.

. . .

Jim Losey was filled with cold rage when he turned away from Athena's guards and walked back to his own Villa. Yet there was a part of his brain that assessed the situation, gave out a warning signal. What were all those guards doing around? But, shit, she was a movie star and that experience with Boz Skannet must have scared the hell out of her.

He used his key to get into the Villa, it seemed to be deserted, everyone was at the party. He had more than an hour to get ready to receive Cross. He went to his suitcase and unlocked it. There was his Glock, gleaming, wiped clean of oil. He opened his other suitcase, which had a secret pocket. In there was the bullet-filled magazine. He put them together, put on a shoulder holster and tucked the gun inside. He was all set. He noted that he was not nervous, he was never nervous in these situations. That was what made him a good cop.

Losey left the bedroom and walked into the kitchen. There were sure a lot of hallways in this Villa. From the refrigerator, he took a bottle of imported beer and a tray of canapés. He crumbled one with his teeth. Caviar. He gave a little sigh of pleasure, he had never tasted anything so delicious. This was the way to live. This was his for the rest of his life, the caviar, the showgirls, maybe some day Athena. He just had to do his job tonight.

Carrying the tray and bottle, he went into the huge living room.

The first thing that startled him was that the floor and the furniture were covered with plastic sheeting, giving the whole room a ghostly white glow. And then, seated in a plastic-covered armchair, was a man smoking a thin cigar and holding a glass of peach brandy. It was Lia Vazzi.

Losey thought, What the fuck is this? He put the tray and bottle on the coffee table and said to Lia, "I've been looking for you."

Lia puffed his cigar, took a sip of brandy. "And now you've found me," he said. He stood up. "Now you can slap me again."

Losey was too experienced a man not to be alert. He was putting things together. He had wondered why the other apartments in the Villa were vacant, it had struck him as strange. He casually unbuttoned his jacket and grinned at Lia. More than a slap this time, he thought. It would be an hour before Dante arrived with Cross, he could work while waiting. Now that he was armed, he had no fear of being one-on-one with Lia.

Suddenly there was a flood of men in the room. They seeped in from the kitchen, the connecting foyer, from the video/TV room. They were all bigger than Jim Losey. Only two of them had drawn guns.

Losey said to them, "You know I'm a cop?"

"We all know that," Lia said in a reassuring voice. He stepped closer to Losey. At the same time, the two men pressed their guns against Losey's back.

Lia flipped his hand inside Losey's jacket and came out holding the Glock. He handed it to one of the men and then gave Losey a quick pat-down.

"Now," Lia said, "you always had so many questions to ask. Here I am. Ask."

Losey still had no real fear. He was just worried that Dante would arrive with Cross. He could not believe that a man like himself, who had had the great good fortune to remain alive in so many dangerous situations, could finally be overcome.

"I know you set that guy Skannet up," Losey said. "And I'll get you for it sooner or later."

"It will have to be sooner," Lia said. "There's no later. Yes, you are right and now you can die happy."

Losey still could not believe that anyone would dare to murder a police officer in cold blood. Sure, drug dealers would exchange bullets, and sure, some crazy nigger would blow you away because you showed a badge, as would fleeing bank robbers, but no mob guy would have the balls to execute a police officer. It would be too much heat.

He reached out to shove Lia away, to achieve a dominance over the situation. But suddenly there was a shocking line of fire slashing through his stomach and his legs trembled. He started to crumble to his knees. Something thick slapped against his head and his ear was on fire and he could not hear. He sank to his knees and the rug felt like an enormous cushion. He looked up. Standing over him was Lia Vazzi, and in his hands was a thin silk rope.

Lia Vazzi had spent two whole days sewing together the two body bags he would have to use. They were of dark brown canvas with a drawstring at the head. Each bag could contain a large body. There was no possible leakage of blood from the bag, and once you drew the string, you could sling it over your shoulder like an army duffel bag. Losey had not noticed the two bags lying on the sofa. Now the men stuffed his body into one, and Lia drew the string tight. He left the bag leaning upright against the sofa. He gave orders to the men that they were to surround the Villa but were not to appear until he summoned them explicitly. They knew what they were to do after that.

Cross and Dante strolled from the compound gates toward Dante's Villa. The night air was oppressive with the cauldron of heat spewed from the day's desert sun. They were both perspiring. Dante noted that Cross was dressed in slacks, open shirt, and buttoned jacket, that he could be armed . . .

The seven Villas, their green flags waving slightly, made a magnificent sight under the desert moon. They looked like edifices from another century with their balconies, their frilled green awnings over the windows, their huge white doors decorated with gold. Dante held Cross by the arm. "Look at that," he said. "Isn't it beautiful? I hear you're fucking that great-looking broad in the movie. Congratulations. When you get tired of her let me know."

"Sure," Cross said amiably. "She sort of likes you and your hat."

Dante took off his hat and said eagerly, "Everybody likes my hats. Did she really say she likes me?"

"She's enchanted by you," Cross said dryly.

"Enchanted," Dante said musingly. "That's really classy." He wondered for a moment if Losey had been able to get Athena into their Villa for a drink. That would be the icing on the cake. He was

tickled that he had distracted Cross, he had noticed the slight irritation in his cousin's voice.

They were at the door of the Villa. There seemed to be no security
guards around. Dante pressed the bell, waited, and then rang again.
When there was no answer, he took out his key and opened the door.
They entered Losey's suite.

Dante was thinking, Maybe Losey was in the sack with Athena.
Which was a hell of a way to run an operation, but he would have
done the same thing.

Dante led Cross into the living room and was astonished to see the
walls and furniture covered with clear plastic sheets. Leaning
against the sofa was a huge brown duffel bag standing upright. On
the sofa was an empty duffel bag of the same kind. All under plastic.
"Jesus Christ, what the hell is this?" Dante said.

He turned to face Cross. Cross was holding a very small gun in his
hand. "To keep the blood off the furniture," Cross said. "I have to tell
you, I never thought your hats were cute and I never believed that a
mugger killed my father."

Dante was thinking, Where the hell is Losey? He called out to
him, meanwhile thinking that such a small-caliber gun could never
stop him.

Cross said, "All your life you were a Santadio."

Dante whirled sideways to give a smaller target and flung himself
on Cross. His strategy worked; the bullet hit him in the shoulder. He
had a fraction of a second of joy, that he would win, and then the bullet exploded, taking away half of his arm. And he realized there was
no hope. Then he really surprised Cross. With his good arm, he
began pulling up the plastic sheeting from the floor. Blood pouring
from his body, his arms filled with plastic sheeting, he tried to stag-
ger away from Cross, then held up the sheets of plastic as a silvery
shield.

Cross stepped forward. Very deliberately he fired through the
plastic, then fired again. The bullets exploded, and Dante's face was
almost covered with tiny bits of plastic turned red. Dante's left thigh
seemed to separate from his body as Cross fired again. Dante fell,
the white rug now held concentric circles of scarlet. Cross knelt be-

side Dante and wrapped his head with plastic and fired again. The Renaissance cap still on his head exploded upward into the air but remained attached. Cross saw that the hat was secured to the head by some sort of clip but now it rested on an open skull. It seemed to float.

Cross stood up and put the gun in the holster in the small of his back. At that moment Lia came into the room. They looked at each other.

"It's done," Lia said. "Wash off in the bathroom and go back to the Hotel. And get rid of your clothes. I'll take the gun and clean up."

"And the rugs and the furniture?" Cross asked.

"I'll take care of everything," Lia said. "Wash up and go to that party."

When Cross left, Lia helped himself to a cigar that was on a marble-topped table and looked for bloodstains while he was at it. There were none. But the sofa and the floor were soaked. Well, that was it.

He wrapped Dante's body in the plastic sheeting and, with the help of two of his men, stuffed it into the empty canvas bag. Then he gathered all the plastic sheeting in the room and stuffed it into the same bag. When he had finished, he drew the strings tight. First, they carried the bag containing Losey into the Villa garage and threw it into the van. They made another trip with Dante's body bag.

The van had been modified by Lia Vazzi. It had double floors with a space between the two. Lia and his men squeezed the two bags into the hollow space and then rejoined the floor strips.

As a Qualified Man, Lia had prepared for everything. In the van were two cans of gasoline. He himself carried them back into the Villa and poured them over the floors and furniture. He set a fuse that would give him five minutes to get away. Then he got into the van and started the long drive to L.A.

Before him and after him were the members of his crew.

It was early morning before he pulled onto the pavement in front of the yacht that was waiting for him. He unloaded the two bags and brought them aboard. The yacht pulled away from shore.

It was nearly noon when, far out at sea, he watched the iron cage holding the two bodies slowly descend into the ocean. They had made their final Communion.

Molly Flanders disappeared with her stunt man, to his room in the Hotel rather than to the Villa, because Molly, despite her affection for the less worldly in power, had a tiny trace of the old Hollywood snobbism, she didn't want it known she was screwing below the line.

The wrap party began to filter out just as dawn appeared, the sun rising ominously clad in red, a thin trail of blue smoke rising to meet it.

Cross had changed his clothes and showered and then had gone to the party. He was seated with Claudia, Bobby Bantz, Skippy Deere, and Dita Tommey celebrating the sure success of *Messalina*. Suddenly there were shouts of alarm from outside. The Hollywood group ran out and Cross followed them.

A thin pillar of fire rose triumphantly over the neon lights of the Vegas Strip. It mushroomed into a great pillow of plum and rosy clouds against the sandy mountains.

"Oh my God," Claudia said, holding Cross tightly by the arm. "It's one of your Villas."

Cross was silent. He watched the green flag over the Villa being consumed by smoke and fire, heard the fire engines screaming down the Strip. Twelve million dollars going up in flames to hide the blood he'd shed. Lia Vazzi was a Qualified Man who spared no expense, courted no risks.

# CHAPTER 23

BECAUSE HE WAS on official leave, Detective Jim Losey's disappearance wasn't noted until five days after the fire at the Xanadu. The vanishing of Dante Clericuzio was, of course, never reported to any authorities.

The investigation led to the police finding Phil Sharkey's body. Suspicion focused on Losey, and it was assumed he had fled to escape interrogation.

L.A. detectives came to interview Cross because Losey was last seen at the Xanadu Hotel. But there was nothing to show any connection between the two men. Cross explained he had only seen him briefly on the night of the party.

But Cross was not worried about the law. He was waiting to hear from Don Clericuzio.

Surely the Clericuzio knew that Dante was missing, surely they knew he had been at the Xanadu when last seen. Why then had they not contacted him for information. Could the whole matter be passed over so easily? Cross did not believe that for a moment.

He continued to run the Hotel day by day, busy with plans to rebuild the burned-out Villa. Lia Vazzi had certainly taken care of the bloodstains.

Claudia came to visit him. She was brimming over with excitement. Cross arranged for dinner to be brought up to his suite so they could talk in private.

"You're not going to believe this," she said to Cross. "Your sister is going to be head of LoddStone Studios."

"Congratulations," Cross said, giving her a brotherly hug. "I always said you were the toughest of the Clericuzio."

"I went to our father's funeral for your sake. I made that clear to everyone," Claudia said with a frown.

Cross laughed. "You certainly did, and you pissed everybody off except the Don himself who said, 'Let her go make pictures and God bless her.' "

Claudia shrugged. "I don't care about them. But let me tell you what happened because it is so strange. When we all left Vegas in Bobby's jet, everything seemed perfect. But when we landed in L.A., all hell broke loose. Detectives arrested Bobby. For guess what?"

"Making lousy movies," Cross teased.

"No, listen, this is weird," Claudia said. "Remember that girl Johanna that Bantz had with him at the wrap party? Do you remember what she looked like? Well, it turns out she was only fifteen years old. They got Bobby on statutory rape and white slavery because he took her across the state border." Claudia's eyes were wide with excitement. "But it was all a setup. Johanna's mother and father were there screaming bloody murder that their poor daughter had been raped by a man forty years older."

"She sure didn't look fifteen," Cross said. "Though she did look like a good hustler."

"It would have made a terrible scandal," Claudia said. "But good old Skippy Deere took charge. He got Bantz off the hook for that moment. He kept him from being arrested and the whole thing getting into the media. So everything seems squared away."

Cross was smiling. Apparently good old David Redfellow had lost none of his skills.

"It's not funny," Claudia said reproachfully. "Poor Bobby was *framed*. The girl swore that Bobby forced her to have sex in Vegas. The father and mother swore they cared nothing for money but wanted to stop all future rapists of young and innocent girls. The whole Studio was in an uproar. Dora and Kevin Marrion were so upset that they talked about selling the Studio. Then Skippy took charge again. He signed the girl to star in a low-budget film, the script to be written by her father. For very good money. Then he got Benny Sly to rewrite the script in one day for a lot of money. Not bad, by the way, Benny is some kind of genius. We're all set. And then the district attorney of Los Angeles insists he's going to prosecute. The DA that LoddStone got elected, the DA who was treated like a king by Eli Marrion. Skippy even offered him a job at the Studio in Business Affairs at a million a year for five years and he turned it down. He insisted Bobby Bantz be fired as head of the Studio. Then he would make a deal. Nobody knows why he was being so hard-nosed."

"An unbribable public official," Cross said with a shrug. "It happens."

He thought of David Redfellow again. Redfellow would violently disagree that there was any such animal. And Cross envisioned how Redfellow had managed everything. Redfellow probably said to the DA, "I'm bribing you to *do* your duty?" And as for the money, Redfellow would have immediately gone to the limit. Twenty, Cross figured. On a ten-billion buy of the Studio, what the hell was twenty million? And with no risk for the DA. He would be acting strictly according to law. It was really elegant.

Claudia was still talking, fast. "Anyway, Bantz had to step down," she said. "And Dora and Kevin were happy to sell the Studio. Plus the deal for five green lights on their own movies, a billion dollars cash in their pockets. And this little Italian guy appears at the Studio, calls a meeting and announces he will be the new owner. And then right out of the blue, he makes me head of the Studio. Skippy was pissed. Now, I'm his boss. Is this crazy?"

Cross just watched her with amusement, then he smiled.

Suddenly, Claudia stood back and looked at her brother. And her eyes were darker, sharper, more intelligent than he had ever seen before. But she had a good-natured smile on her face when she said, "Just like the boys, right, Cross? Now, I'm doing it just like the boys. And I didn't even have to fuck anybody. . . ."

Cross was surprised. "What's the matter, Claudia?" he asked. "I thought you were happy."

Claudia smiled. "I am happy. I'm just not dumb. And because you're my brother, and I love you, I want you to know that I haven't been fooled."

She walked over and sat on the couch next to him. "I lied when I said I went to Daddy's funeral just for you. I went because I wanted to be part of something that he was part of, that you were part of. I went because I couldn't stay away any longer. But I do hate what they stand for, Cross. The Don as well as the others."

"Does that mean you don't want to run the Studio?" Cross asked.

Claudia laughed aloud. "No, I'm willing to admit I'm still a Clericuzio. And I want to make good movies and make a lot of money. Movies are great equalizers, Cross. I can make a good movie about great women. . . . Let's see what can happen when I use the Family talents for good instead of evil." They both laughed.

Then Cross took her in his arms. He kissed her on the cheek. "I think it's great, really great," he said.

And he meant it for himself as well as for her. For if Don Clericuzio had made her head of the Studio, he did not connect Cross with the disappearance of Dante. The whole scheme had worked.

They had finished dinner and had been talking for hours. When Claudia rose to leave, Cross took a purse of black chips from his desk. "Take a shot at the tables on the house," he said.

She gave him a soft slap on the cheek and said, "Only if you're not going to get into that big brother thing again and talk to me like a child. That last time I wanted to deck you."

He hugged her, it felt good to feel her so close. In a moment of weakness, he said, "You know, I left a third of my estate to you in case anything happens. And I'm very rich. So you can always tell the Studio to fuck off if you want to."

Claudia eyes were shining when she said, "Cross, I appreciate you worrying about me, but I can tell the Studio to fuck off anyway, without your estate . . ." Then suddenly she looked worried. "Is anything wrong? Are you sick?"

"No, no," Cross said. "I just wanted you to know."

"Thank God," Claudia said. "Now that I'm in, maybe you can get out. You can break away from the Family. You can be free."

Cross laughed. "I am free," he said. "I'm going away very soon, to live with Athena in France."

. . .

On the afternoon of the tenth day, Giorgio Clericuzio appeared at the Xanadu to see him, and Cross felt a sinking sensation in his stomach that he knew would lead to panic if he did not control it.

Giorgio left his bodyguards outside the suite with Hotel Security. But Cross was under no illusions, his own bodyguards would follow any order Giorgio gave. And he was not reassured by Giorgio's appearance. Giorgio seemed to have lost weight, and his face was very pale. It was the first time that Cross had seen him look as though he was not in complete control.

Cross greeted him effusively. "Giorgio," he said, "this is an unexpected pleasure. Let me call down and get a Villa ready for you."

Giorgio gave him a tired smile and said, "We can't locate Dante." He paused for a moment. "He's gone off the map and the last time he was seen was here at the Xanadu."

"Jesus," Cross said, "that's serious. But you know Dante, he was not always under control."

Now Giorgio didn't bother to smile. "He was with Jim Losey and Losey is gone too."

"They were a funny combo," Cross said. "I wondered about that."

"They were pals," Giorgio said. "The old man didn't like it but Dante was the guy's paymaster."

"I'll help any way I can," Cross said. "I'll check all the Hotel employees. But you know Dante and Losey weren't officially registered. We never do that for anyone in the Villas."

"You can do that when you get back," Giorgio said. "The Don wants to see you personally. He even chartered a plane to bring you back."

Cross paused for a long moment. "I'll pack a bag," he said. "Giorgio, is it serious?"

Giorgio looked him squarely in the face. "I don't know," he said.

On the chartered plane to New York, Giorgio studied a briefcase full of papers. Cross did not impose himself, though this was a bad sign. In any case Giorgio would never give him any information.

The plane was met by three closed cars and six Clericuzio soldiers. Giorgio got into one car and motioned Cross into another. Again a bad sign. Dawn was breaking when the cars rolled through the security gates of the Clericuzio compound in Quogue.

The door of the house was guarded by two men. Other men were scattered around the compound, but there were no women or children to be seen.

Cross said to Giorgio, "Where the hell is everybody, in Disneyland?" But Giorgio refused to acknowledge the joke.

The first thing Cross saw in the Quogue living room was a circle of eight men, and inside that circle two men were talking in a very amiable way. His heart gave a jump. They were Petie and Lia Vazzi. Vincent was watching them and he looked angry.

Petie and Lia seemed to be on the best of terms. But Lia was dressed only in slacks and a shirt, no jacket or tie. Lia usually dressed formally, so this meant he had been searched and disarmed. And indeed he looked like a cheerful mouse surrounded by merry, menacing cats. Lia gave Cross a sad nod of acknowledgment. Petie never glanced his way. But when Giorgio led Cross into the back den, Petie broke off and followed, as did Vincent.

There, Don Clericuzio was waiting for them. Seated in a huge armchair, he was smoking one of his crooked cigars. Vincent went to him and handed him a glass of wine from the bar. Cross was offered nothing. Petie remained at the door, standing. Giorgio sat down on the sofa next to the Don and motioned to Cross to sit with him.

The Don's face, drawn thin with age, had no trace of emotion. Cross kissed him on the cheek. The Don looked at him and his face softened as if with sadness.

"So Croccifixio," the Don said, "it was all cleverly done. But now you must explain your reasons. I am Dante's grandfather, my daughter is his mother. The men here are his uncles. You must answer to all of us."

Cross tried to keep his composure. "I don't understand," he said.

Giorgio said harshly, "Dante. Where is he?"

"Christ, how should I know?" Cross said as if surprised. "He never reported to me. He could be down in Mexico having a good time."

Giorgio said, "You don't understand. Don't fuck around. You are already judged guilty. Where did you dump him?"

At the bar, Vincent turned away as though he could not look into his face. Behind him Cross could hear Petie coming closer to the sofa.

"Where's the proof?" Cross said. "Who says I killed Dante?"

"I do." It was the Don who spoke. "Understand: I have pronounced you guilty. There is no appeal from that judgment. I brought you here to make your plea for mercy, but you must justify the killing of my grandson."

Hearing that voice, the measured tone, Cross knew that everything was over. For him and Lia Vazzi. But Vazzi already knew. It had been in his eyes.

Vincent turned to Cross, his granite face softened. "Tell my father the truth, Cross, it's your only chance."

The Don nodded. He said, "Croccifixio, your father was more than my nephew, of Clericuzio blood, as you are. Your father was my trusted friend. And so I will listen to your reasons."

Cross prepared himself. "Dante killed my father. I judged him guilty as you judged me guilty. And he killed my father out of revenge and ambition. He was a Santadio in his heart."

The Don did not respond. Cross went on. "How could I not avenge my father? How could I forget my father was responsible for my life? And I had too much respect for the Clericuzio, as my father had, to suspect your hand in the killing. Yet, I think you must have known Dante was guilty and did nothing. So how could I come to you to redress the wrong?"

"Your proof," Giorgio said.

"A man like Pippi De Lena could never be surprised," Cross said. "And Jim Losey at the other end is too much of a coincidence. There is not a man in this room who believes in coincidence. All of you know Dante was guilty. And Don, you yourself told me the story of the Santadio. Who knows what Dante planned after he killed me, as he surely knew he must. Next, his uncles." Cross did not dare to mention the Don. "He counted on your affection," he said to the Don.

The Don had laid his cigar aside. He face was inscrutable but held a touch of sadness.

It was Petie who spoke. Petie had been the closest to Dante. "Where did you dump the body?" Petie asked again. And Cross could not answer him, could not get the words out of his mouth.

There was a long silence and then finally the Don raised his head to all of them and spoke. "Funerals are wasted on the young," he said. "What have they done to celebrate them? How have they inspired great respect? The young have no compassion, no gratitude. And my daughter is already crazy, why should we compound her grief and erase hopes for her recovery. She will be told her son has fled and it will take years for her to know the truth."

And now it seemed that everyone in the room relaxed. Petie came forward and sat on the sofa beside Cross. Vincent, behind the bar, raised a glass of brandy to his lips in what could have been a salute.

"But justice or no, you have committed a crime against the Family," the Don said. "There must be a punishment. For you, money, for Lia Vazzi, his life."

Cross said, "Lia had nothing to do with Dante, for Losey, yes. Let me ransom him. I own half the Xanadu. I will transfer half that ownership to you as payment for me and Vazzi."

Don Clericuzio seemed to ponder this. "You are loyal," he said. He turned to Giorgio and then Vincent and Petie. "If you three agree, I will agree." They did not answer.

The Don sighed as if in regret. "You will sign over half your interest but you must move out of our world. Vazzi must return to Sicily with his family, or not, as he pleases. That is as far as I can go. You and Vazzi must never speak together again. And I order my sons, in your presence, never to avenge their nephew's death. You will have a week to arrange your affairs, to sign the necessary papers for Giorgio." Then the Don spoke in a less harsh voice. "Let me assure you that I had no knowledge of Dante's plans. Now, go in peace and remember I always loved your father like a son."

When Cross left the house, Don Clericuzio got out of his chair and said to Vincent, "To bed." Vincent helped him up the stairs, for the Don now had a certain weakness in his legs. His age was finally beginning to ravage his body.

# EPILOGUE

# Nice, France
# Quogue

ON HIS LAST DAY in Vegas, Cross De Lena sat on his penthouse balcony and looked down on the sun-drenched Strip. The great hotels—Caesars Palace, the Flamingo, the Desert Inn, the Mirage, and the Sands—blazed their neon marquees to challenge the sun.

Don Clericuzio had been specific in his banishment: Cross was never to return to Las Vegas. How happy his father, Pippi, had been here, and Gronevelt had built the city into his own Valhalla, but Cross had never really enjoyed their ease. True, he had enjoyed the pleasures of Vegas, but those pleasures always held the cold flavor of steel.

The green flags of the seven Villas dropped in the desert stillness, but one hung from the burned building, a black skeleton, the ghost of Dante. But he would never see all of this again.

He had loved the Xanadu, he had loved his father, Gronevelt, and Claudia. And yet he had in some sense betrayed them. Gronevelt, by failing to be faithful to the Xanadu; his father, by not being true to the Clericuzio; and Claudia, because she believed in his innocence. Now he was free of them. He would begin a new life.

What could he make of his love for Athena? He had been warned of the dangers of romantic love by Gronevelt, by his father, and even by the old Don. That was the fatal flaw of great men who would control their worlds. Then why was he now ignoring their advice? Why was he placing his fate at the mercy of a woman?

Quite simply, the sight of her, the sound of her voice, the way she moved, her happiness and her sorrow, all made him happy. The world became dazzlingly pleasurable when he was with her. Food became delicious, the sun's heat warmed his bones, and he felt that sweet hunger for her flesh that made life holy. And when he slept with her he never feared those nightmares that preceded the dawn.

It was now three weeks since he had last seen Athena, but he had heard her voice just this morning. He had called her in France to tell her he was coming, and he had caught the happiness in her voice because now she knew he was still alive. It was possible she loved him. And now, in less than twenty hours he would see her.

Cross had faith that someday she would truly love him, that she would reward him for his love, that she would never judge him, and that like some angel she would save him from Hell.

Athena Aquitane was perhaps the only woman in France who put on her makeup and clothes to try to destroy her beauty. Not that she tried to look ugly, she was not a masochist, but she had come to regard her physical beauty as too dangerous for her inner world. She hated the power it gave her over other people. She hated the vanity that still spoiled her spirit. It interfered with what she knew would be her life's work.

On the first day of work at the Institute for Autistic Children in Nice, she wanted to look like the children, to walk like them. She was overcome with the sense of identification. That day, she relaxed her facial muscles to their soulless serenity and limped in the weird, lopsided way of some of the children who had motor damage.

Dr. Gerard observed this and said sardonically, "Oh, very good but you're going in the wrong direction." Then he took her hands in his and said gently, "You must not identify with their misfortune. You must fight against it."

Athena felt rebuked and ashamed. Again her actress vanity had misled her. But she felt herself at peace caring for these children. It did not matter to them that her French was imperfect, they did not grasp the meaning of her words anyway.

Even the distressing realities did not discourage her. The children were sometimes destructive, did not recognize the rules of society. They fought each other and their nurses, they smeared their feces on the walls, they urinated where they pleased. Sometimes they were truly frightening in their ferocity, their repulsion of the outside world.

The only time Athena felt helpless was at night in the small apartment she had rented in Nice, when she studied the literature of the Institute. They were reports on the progress of the children and they were frightening. Then she would crawl into bed and weep. Unlike the movies she had lived in, these reports had mostly unhappy endings.

When she received the call from Cross that he was coming to see her, she felt a surge of happiness and hope. He was still alive and he would help her. Then she had some trepidation. She consulted Dr. Gerard.

"What do you think would be best?" she asked.

"He could be of great assistance to Bethany," Dr. Gerard said. "I would very much like to see how she relates to him over a period of time. And it might be very good for you. Mothers must not be martyrs for their children." She thought about his words on her way to pick up Cross at the Nice airport.

At the airport, Cross had to walk from the plane to the low-slung terminal. The air was balmy and sweet, not the scorching sulfurous heat of Vegas. Along the borders of the concrete reception plaza grew masses of luxurious red and purple flowers.

He saw Athena waiting for him on that plaza, and he marveled at her genius in transforming her appearance. She could not completely hide her beauty, but she could disguise it. Gold-framed tinted glasses turned her eyes from brilliant green to gray. The clothes she was wearing made her look thicker and heavier. Her blond hair was tucked under a country-brimmed hat of blue denim that overlapped the side of her face. He felt a thrill of possession that he was the only one who knew how beautiful she really was.

As Cross approached, Athena took off her glasses and put them in the pocket of her blouse. He smiled at her irrepressible vanity.

Less than an hour later they were in the suite of the Negresco Hotel where Napoleon had bedded Josephine. Or so the hotel brochure on the door still claimed. A waiter knocked and brought in a tray with a bottle of wine and a delicate plate of tiny sandwiches. He left it on the balcony table that overlooked the Mediterranean.

At first they were awkward with each other. She held his hand trustingly yet as if she were in command, and the touch of her warm flesh gave him a rush of desire. But he could see she was not quite ready.

The suite was beautifully furnished, more opulent than any of the Xanadu Villas. The bed had a canopy of dark red silk, the matching drapes were studded with golden fleur-de-lis. The tables and chairs had an elegance that could never have existed in the Vegas world.

Athena led Cross out to the balcony, and as she did so Cross blindly kissed her on the cheek. And then she couldn't help herself, she picked up a wet cotton napkin that was wrapped around the wine bottle and scrubbed her face free of all the disfiguring cosmetics. Her face glistened with drops of water, the skin radiant and pink. She put one hand on his shoulder and kissed him gently on the lips.

From the balcony they could view the stone houses of Nice, tinted the faded greens and blues of paint from hundreds of years ago. Below, the citizens of Nice strolled on the Promenade des Anglais, on the stony beach young men and women, almost nude, splashed into the blue-green water while little children dug themselves into the pebbly sand. Farther out, hawkish white yachts, strung with lights, patrolled the horizon.

Cross and Athena had taken their first sip of wine when they heard the faint roar. From the stone seawall, from what looked like the mouth of a cannon but was really the great eastern pipe of the sewers, a great wave of deep brown water gushed into the pristine blue of the sea.

Athena turned her head away. She said to Cross, "How long will you be here?"

"Five years if you let me," he said.

"That's silly," Athena said frowning. "What will you do here?"

Cross said. "I'm rich, maybe I'll buy a small hotel."

"What happened to the Xanadu?" Athena asked.

"I had to sell my interest," he said. He paused for a moment. "We won't have to worry about money."

"I have money," Athena said. "You have to understand. I'm going to stay here for five years and then I'm going to bring her home. I don't care what they say, I will never put her back in an institution, I'll take care of her for the rest of her life. And if anything happens to her, my life will be with children like her. So you see we can never have a life together."

Cross understood her perfectly. He took a long time to consider his answer.

His voice was strong and determined when he said, "Athena, the only thing I'm sure about now is that I love you and Bethany. You have to believe that. It's not going to be easy, I know that, but we'll try our best. You want to help Bethany, not be a martyr. For that we have to take a final jump. I'll do everything I can to help you. Look, we'll be like gamblers in my casino. The odds are stacked against us, but there's always that chance to beat the odds."

Cross saw her weakening so he pressed on. "Let's get married," he said. "Let's have other children and live our lives like normal people. With our children let's try to make right what seems wrong with our world. All families have some misfortune. I know we can overcome it. Will you believe me?"

Finally Athena looked at him directly. "Only if you believe I truly love you," she said.

In the bedroom when they made love, they took each other on faith; Athena believed that Cross would truly help her save Bethany, and Cross, that Athena truly loved him. When finally she turned her body toward him, she murmured, "I love you. I really do."

Cross bowed his head to kiss her. She said it again, "I truly love you," and Cross thought, What man on earth could disbelieve her?

Alone in his bedroom, the Don pulled the cool sheets up to his neck. Death was approaching, and he was too wily not to detect its nearness. But everything had worked out according to his plans. Ah, how easy it is to outwit the young.

During the last five years he had seen Dante as the great danger to his master plan. Dante would resist the folding of the Clericuzio Family into society. And yet, what could he himself, the Don, do?

Order the killing of his daughter's son, his own grandson? Would Giorgio, Vincent, and Petie obey such an order? And if they did, would they think him some kind of monster? Would they then fear him more than they loved him? And Rose Marie, what would remain of her sanity then, for surely she would sense the truth.

But when Pippi De Lena was killed, the die was cast. The Don immediately knew the truth of the matter, investigated Dante's relationship with Losey and made his judgment.

He had sent Vincent and Petie to guard Cross, armored car and all. And then, to forewarn Cross, told him the story of the Santadio War. How painful it was to set the world straight. And when he was gone, who would there be to make these terrible decisions? He decided now, once and for all, the Clericuzio would make its final retreat.

Vinnie and Petie would deal strictly with their restaurants and construction businesses. Giorgio would buy companies on Wall Street. The withdrawal would be complete. Even the Bronx Enclave would not be replenished. The Clericuzio would finally be safe and fight against the new outlaws who were rising all over America. He would not blame himself for past mistakes, the loss of his daughter's happiness and the death of his grandson. And after all, he had set Cross free.

Before he fell asleep, the Don had a vision. He would live forever, the Clericuzio blood would be part of mankind forever. And it was he, himself, alone who had created this lineage, his own virtue.

But, oh, what a wicked world it was that drove a man to sin.

## ABOUT THE AUTHOR

MARIO PUZO was born in New York and, following military service in World War II, attended New York's New School for Social Research. His best-known novel, *The Godfather*, was preceded by two critically acclaimed novels published in the early sixties, *The Fortunate Pilgrim* and *The Dark Arena*; in 1978 he published *Fools Die*, in 1984 *The Sicilian*, and in 1992 *The Fourth K*. Mario Puzo is also the author of nine screenplays, including *Superman* and *Superman II*, as well as the screen adaptations of all *Godfather* movies, for which he received two Academy Awards.

## ABOUT THE TYPE

This book was set in Times Roman, designed by Stanley Morison specifically for *The Times* of London. The typeface was introduced in the newspaper in 1932. Times Roman had its greatest success in the United States as a book and commercial typeface, rather than one used in newspapers.